"I'm a vampire," Cassius says. "Not a dem̶̶̶̶ ̶̶̶ t a creature of pure evil, not a figment of so̶̶̶ ̶̶̶̶̶̶ ̶̶̶̶̶̶ ̶̶̶nagina-
tion. I drink blood, I'm *extremel̶̶̶* ̶̶̶̶̶̶̶̶̶ ̶̶̶̶ ̶̶̶ ̶̶̶t, I'm
effectively immortal. I'm a ̶̶̶̶̶̶̶̶̶̶̶̶̶̶̶̶̶̶̶̶ natural one, and if you're ̶̶̶̶̶̶̶̶̶̶̶̶̶̶̶̶̶̶̶̶̶̶̶̶̶̶̶̶̶̶ ̶̶̶ng
to have to learn h̶̶̶̶̶̶̶̶̶̶̶̶̶̶̶̶̶̶̶̶̶̶̶̶̶̶̶ ̶̶̶se
I'm *far* from the o̶̶̶̶̶̶̶̶̶̶̶̶̶̶̶̶̶

And, just like tha̶̶̶̶̶̶

"Vampires," I say ̶̶̶̶̶̶̶

"Thirty-seven perce̶̶̶̶̶̶̶ ̶̶̶̶pulation. Worldwide."

"Barely a third. How̶̶̶ ̶̶̶ war going?"

His eyes fade to normal. His fangs recede. "It was over
a long time ago," he says. He straightens up from his feral
crouch, seems almost embarrassed. "You lost."

"So the other sixty or so percent is what, livestock?"

"Forty-three are lycanthropes. Nineteen are golems."

"Why am I here?"

"Because one of the ways this world *is* different from
yours is in the sickness you call insanity. Most supernatural creatures are immune to disease, our minds as well as
our bodies. Only human beings are experienced in dealing
with madness, and, well . . ."

"We're hard to come by?" I've already done the math.
"One percent. That's all that's left of us, you bastard? *One
percent*?"

"Less than that," he says quietly. "Your species numbers
under a million. And one of them is slaughtering *my* people."

"Why should I care?"

"Because catching this madman," Cassius replies, "is the
only hope you have of ever seeing your home again."

"*Dying Bites* is wacky, unpredictable, fresh, and amazing. I
would kill to write as well as DD Barant. Seriously."
—Nancy Holder, author of *Pretty Little Devils*

DYING BITES

Book One of the Bloodhound Files

DD Barant

St. Martin's Paperbacks

This is a work of fiction. All of the characters, organizations, and events portrayed in this novel are either products of the author's imagination or are used fictitiously.

DYING BITES

For information address St. Martin's Press, 175 Fifth Avenue, New York, NY 10010.

ISBN: 0-312-94258-3
EAN: 978-0-312-94258-8

Printed in the United States of America

St. Martin's Paperbacks edition / July 2009

St. Martin's Paperbacks are published by St. Martin's Press, 175 Fifth Avenue, New York, NY 10010.

10 9 8 7 6 5 4 3 2 1

ONE

I think about monsters a lot.

Real ones, I mean, not Frankenstein or Dracula or Godzilla. I work for the FBI's Behavioral Analysis Unit, where I use my degree in criminal psychology to help profile offenders; my area of expertise is homicide-fixated nonstandard patterning. It's my job to figure out why the crazy ones do what they do and who they're going to do it to next. This makes me Miss Popular at cocktail parties—until my third tequila, when certain details that really shouldn't be heard on a full stomach somehow become the punch lines to jokes of incredibly bad taste.

I usually don't get invited back.

Which is why I'm home alone, again, nursing a throbbing hangover and trying to get back to sleep. I've got a bad case of the 3:00 A.M. guilts—you know, when you lie in bed awake and replay all those things you didn't do right? Because, as we all know, nothing solves insomnia like a nice warm glass of regret, depression, and self-loathing.

Okay, I don't really hate myself. But I do piss myself off—quite a bit, actually—and sometimes I need a good, stern talking-to about important elements in my life. I think I was criticizing my own taste in clothes when I finally fell asleep.

It's funny. Dreams can be intimately revealing, or incomprehensible. They can be ridiculous or terrifying, deeply significant or inconsequential. I find other people's dreams intriguing, because extracting meaning from the psychological jumble of a healthy mind is similar in many ways to finding coherence in the fractured mindscape of a psychotic.

But no matter what they represent or how scrambled they are, dreams are just that—dreams. They aren't real. But to those whose grasp on reality isn't quite as solid, a dream can be a message from another dimension, a psychic telegram from their own personal God. It can change their entire life.

I guess that makes *me* crazy, too.

The dream starts simply enough. It's not unusual to dream about your work—I know a shoe salesman who kept having nightmares about ogres who came in demanding sandals—so for me, a dream about catching a killer can be pretty mundane. I'm sitting at my desk doing paperwork, when a colleague walks in and tells me I'm wanted in the Director's office. I get up, walk down a hall, and knock on the Director's door. A voice I don't recognize tells me to come in.

On the other side of the door is my bedroom. That's okay, because I'm wearing my nightshirt. There are two men sitting on my bed, quite formally, backs straight and their legs together. The one on the left is my boss; his name is Robert Miller and he's spoken to me maybe three times in my entire career. He looks vaguely annoyed—but then, that's the only expression I've ever seen on his face.

The other man is a stranger. He's dressed much like the Director, in a plain black business suit, but I can tell at a glance there's something very unusual about him. Sharp eyes, hooked nose, dark hair slicked back, bony, angular features. I have the immediate, strong feeling that he's an undertaker from another country—somewhere in Eastern Europe, maybe, or some corner of Mongolia.

"Agent Valchek," says Miller. "You're being reassigned, effective immediately. This is your liaison. He'll get you settled." Miller doesn't introduce the man, and I don't ask.

"You can bring three things with you," the man says. He has no accent, but somehow that just reinforces the idea that he's a foreigner. In fact, I'm sure this is the first time he's ever been to my country. "The three things you feel are most instrumental to you doing your job. Choose carefully."

I'm pretty straightforward. I grab my handgun, my laptop, and the carton of ammunition I keep under my bed. In typical dream fashion, the undertaker is now standing beside a door in my bedroom wall that wasn't there before. The Director has vanished. The undertaker opens the door and motions me to step through, cautioning me to close my eyes for my own safety.

"Of course, yeah," I say. "Thanks."

The first sensation I'm aware of after stepping through the doorway is the cold wooden floor under my bare feet. There's a strange noise behind me, like a recording of an explosion being played backward. I open my eyes.

I'm standing in an office, one very much like the Director's. The blinds are drawn. A green-shaded lamp throws a pool of light on the desk, and leaning against the front of the desk, arms crossed in front of him, is a young man. He's dressed in standard FBI-wear, black business suit and polished Oxfords. He appears to be around eighteen, handsome in an innocent kind of way, and has curly blond hair that makes him look more like a surfer than a Federal agent.

I note three things in quick succession:

One—I'm still in my nightshirt.

Two—I have a loaded gun in my hand.

Three—*I'm not asleep.*

I file number one as embarrassing but not vital, double-check number three and confirm my first impression, and bring point number two to Mr. Surfer's immediate attention by aiming it at his chest.

"Where the hell am I?" I snarl.

"In my office," he says. "My name is David Cassius. We're going to be working together, Jace."

The gun doesn't seem to impress him. It's a Ruger Super Redhawk Alaskan, a short-barreled revolver chambered with .454 ammunition—it packs a bigger wallop than a Magnum .44, and is sometimes even used for big-game hunting. It can take down a grizzly or a bull moose, and it took me every day for six months at the firing range to learn how to handle the recoil. Cassius looks at it like it's a toy.

"I understand your confusion," he says. His voice is strong, deep, confident, not the voice of a young man at all. I have a good ear for accents and I'm trained to identify over a hundred regional differences, but his escapes me.

"Actually," he continues, "you're not supposed to be fully cognizant yet. I don't suppose I can convince you you're still dreaming?"

"Only if you turn into my father and tell me you're disappointed in my grades." I half-expect exactly that to happen, but Cassius only smiles. It's a boyish, engaging smile, and I bet it makes the sorority girls go all weak and giggly. I seriously consider putting a big hole in it.

"No, I didn't think so. All right, let's take this one step at a time. How do you think you got here?"

"Where I come from, the one with the gun asks the questions," I snap. "Where's your partner?" The undertaker is nowhere in sight.

"You probably mean the . . . one who brought you here. He's at another location; I elected to be the one to officially greet you, but I was told you'd be in a more receptive state."

I'm getting it now. "Okay. So someone drugged me at the party, I was scooped from my apartment, and you expected a little more drool and a lot less firepower. Are we up to speed?"

"Getting there." His smile widens, going from gee-aren't-I-cute to something approaching genuine amusement. "Keep going—I want to see where you end up."

"You're a government spook," I say flatly. "The Bureau doesn't play games like this. CIA, NSA, one of the black-ops outfits that doesn't show up in the budget. You drugged me, hauled me out here . . ."

I stop. He waits.

"Oh, crap," I say. "My gun isn't loaded, is it?"

"See for yourself."

I do. All six chambers are full. I snap the cylinder back

into place and look up, more confused than ever—and starting to be scared. Scenarios involving me being turned into a brainwashed assassin start to percolate in my brain. I level the gun at him again and say, "Full explanation. Now." I'm close to convincing myself he'll say *Kumquat*, and I'll turn into a glassy-eyed zombie.

"You haven't been drugged. I am, as you thought, a government operative—NSA, in fact. You've been brought here because we need someone in your field of expertise—the tracking and apprehension of mentally fractured killers."

It's an odd way to put it, but I guess "mentally fractured" is as accurate as "psychotic." "What's the matter with your own specialists?" I ask. "Or do you just need someone disposable?" I have visions of me tracking down some Senator's son who's gone off his meds, only to wind up in a shallow grave myself once I've caught him.

"You're far from disposable," Cassius says mildly. "As a matter of fact, at the moment you possess one of the most valuable minds on the planet. We're hoping you'll use it to help us. Now ask the *important* question."

Which one? I want to scream. *Am I about to die? Have all those years of making myself think like a psychotic finally turned me into one? Why are you so calm with a loaded revolver held by an* extremely *stressed FBI agent pointed at your heart?*

No.

"If I wasn't drugged," I say, "then how *did* I get here?"

"Through that," Cassius says, and glances behind me.

I'm not stupid. I keep the gun on him and move my body to the side, so I can flick my own glance from him to what's behind me. I'd come through some kind of door, so that's what I expect—but what I see instead is a blank white wall, with some kind of arcane designs scrawled on it in reddish brown. The designs are outlined in a rough semicircle around six feet in diameter—

I've never seen anyone move that fast.

It's still a stupid thing to do. It's virtually impossible to take a gun away from the person who's holding it on you as long as the shooter follows one simple rule: don't get too close to your target.

I haven't.

Cassius actually manages to grab the barrel of the Ruger before I pull the trigger. The first bullet takes him in the sternum, and the next three are placed within inches of that. I'm a very good shot.

The sheer kinetic energy throws him backward across the room. He lands on his back on the desk, arms thrown to either side.

"Damn," I whisper. "Just another crazy—"

And then he sits up.

There's no blood on him, but his shirt and jacket have ragged, gaping holes—and all I can see through those holes is pale, unmarked skin. No body armor, no bulletproof vest. No way.

He looks more annoyed than anything. Thinking back on it later, I'm pretty sure that's the real reason I put the next two shots into his face.

I can actually see the impacts this time. His skin dimples like an invisible finger just poked him—once in the cheek, once in the forehead—and then the flattened remains of the slugs fall onto the carpet. I wonder why the force didn't drive him backward like the first time, and then I realize he's braced himself by holding on to the edges of the desk. The desk is large and solid, unlike my present grasp of reality.

The gun is empty, but I've got a carton of ammunition in my other hand. And a laptop tucked under my arm. Right now, they both seem pretty useless.

Cassius gets off the desk. He sighs. "If I was going to hurt you," he says reasonably, "now would be the time, wouldn't it?"

He looks down at the shredded remains of his tie. He sighs again. "Please," he says, and motions to a leather sofa along one wall. "Sit. Or perhaps you'd like to discharge your weapon again?"

My mind is desperately trying to find some explanation

that fits the facts, but it's not doing so good. In fact, the idea that I'm still dreaming is looking better and better. I stride over to the sofa, toss down my gun, put down the laptop and place the ammo on top of it. Then I sit down, cross my arms, try to ignore the fact that the only thing I'm wearing is an oversize T-shirt with a picture of a panda on it, and glare at Cassius. "Okay. Talk."

"I apologize for trying to disarm you. It was rude of me."

"If you're looking for an apology in return, you're not going to get one."

"What a surprise. This isn't your world, Agent Valchek." His tone is suddenly noticeably colder—I think I finally managed to piss him off. "I realize that in your world, magic is something only children believe in. Here, it is real. You were brought through an interdimensional portal by extremely powerful sorcery, and it was not done lightly. We need your help."

I smile, and shake my head. "Okay, now you've gone too far. Some kind of covert spy operation I might have bought, but this? Over the top. So now I'm thinking practical joke, with really *excellent* special effects. New TV show, maybe? Special blanks in my gun, maybe hypnosis—"

And then he *moves* again, in that ultrafast way only animals can, and his face is about a foot away from mine.

"Does this look like special effects?" he says, and grins.

The grin isn't meant to be friendly. He's showing me his teeth.

His incisors are sharp—and as I watch, they get longer. His eyes—a very startling blue—turn bloodred.

I swallow. "Kind of," I say. "But only when I'm on the other side of the screen."

"Welcome to *this* side," he says. "I'm a vampire. Not a demon, not a creature of pure evil, not a figment of some writer's imagination. I drink blood, I'm *extremely* allergic to sunlight, I'm effectively immortal. I'm a supernatural creature, not a natural one, and if you're going to survive here, you're going to have to learn how to deal with beings like me—because I'm *far* from the only one."

And, just like that, I believe him. The human mind always searches for order, no matter how chaotic or insane events become—we want to believe in a pattern, *any* pattern, and when somebody offers you one in the middle of a storm of craziness, you grab it and hang on until something better comes along.

"Vampires," I say calmly. "Lots?"

"Thirty-seven percent of the population. Worldwide."

"Barely a third. How's the war going?"

His eyes fade to normal. His fangs recede. "It was over a long time ago," he says. He straightens up from his feral crouch, seems almost embarrassed. "You lost."

"So the other sixty or so percent is what—livestock?"

"Forty-three are lycanthropes. Nineteen are golems."

"Werewolves and living clay. How's that work? The bloodsuckers and werewolves take turns biting each other while the Jewish statues referee?"

"We aren't monsters, Jace. We drink the blood of animals, not men. We shop in supermarkets, we drive cars. This world isn't so different from your own."

"*Why am I here?*" I shout. Bulletproof vampire or not, I'm about ready to rip the truth out of him with my bare hands.

"Because one of the ways this world *is* different from yours is in the sickness you call insanity. Most supernatural creatures are immune to disease—our minds as well as our bodies. Only human beings are experienced in dealing with madness, and—well . . ."

"We're hard to come by?" I've already done the math. "One percent. That's all that's left of us, you bastard? *One percent?*"

"Less than that," he says quietly. "Your species numbers under a million. And one of them is slaughtering *my* people."

"Why should I care?"

"Because catching this madman," Cassius replies, "is the only hope you have of ever seeing your home again."

Suddenly I don't feel so well. Nauseous, dizzy, one step removed from reality. *Which is exactly right*, I think and a huge wave of relief surges through me. *This can't be real, be-*

cause I feel like I'm about to throw up and I never, ever do the Technicolor yawn. Not when I saw my first floater, not when they hazed me at the Academy, not when we opened that root cellar outside of Augusta. Therefore, this is something simple—a brain tumor, maybe—and not the horrifying predicament the Vampire Surfer just described.

I sigh happily, throw up all over my panda, and pass out.

I wake up in a hospital bed. I put a checkmark in the "Brain Tumor" column and look around for professional corroboration.

No one in the room but me. Vomit-stained panda shirt replaced by standard-issue green hospital gown. No plastic ID band on my wrist, though. Odd.

Also, I'm strapped to the bed. Maybe I should have mentioned that first.

The door opens and a doctor walks in. He looks like a doctor, anyway, white coat over blue scrubs, with a stethoscope slung around his neck and a clipboard in his hands. He's in his thirties, clean shaven, with shaggy brown hair and a face that reminds me a little of a young Harrison Ford.

"Ms. Valchek," he says, smiling at me. "I'm Dr. Adams. Sorry about the restraints—you were convulsing when you were first brought here, and we didn't want you to hurt yourself." He starts undoing buckles.

"Where am I?" I ask, resisting the urge to grab him by the throat. Ask questions, *then* shoot. As soon I find out where my gun is.

"St. Francis Infirmary." He finishes unbuckling the straps and steps back. "How are you feeling?"

I lift my hand and put it to my forehead. "My head hurts. I'm a little queasy. And I think I may have had some kind of hallucinatory episode."

He nods. "The nausea and headache are common in cases of RDT—though there aren't that many case histories to study. Hallucinations are a more severe symptom, though;

they usually only manifest in the later stages of the syndrome."

"So I guess my RDT is pretty bad. What's that stand for—Raging Doom Tumor?"

"Reality Dislocation Trauma. To put things simply, Ms. Valchek, you come from another universe, with a different set of physical laws. Your body doesn't like it. It's trying to reject what it's being told on a very basic level, but there's nowhere to go."

I stare at him. I like to think I'm adaptable, but I kind of had my heart set on the whole brain cancer thing. Rational, tragic, possibly fixable—all I had to do was pick out some fashionable head scarves for my post-operative look. And now?

Now I don't have to worry about any of that. Just vampires, werewolves, and being allergic to existing.

"I know it's a big shock," Dr. Adams says. "But it's not as bad as it sounds. There is a treatment available; it's effective and noninvasive. I was just waiting for you to wake up before administering it."

"Does it involve ruby slippers?" He gives me the blank look I often get when I'm trying to be funny. "Never mind." A sudden and very nasty thought strikes me. "Wait a minute. Does this mean I'm going to be developing a sudden aversion to sunlight and/or silver?"

Now he's the one who looks shocked. "Of course not! Ms. Valchek, we have something here called the Hippocratic oath, and we take that very seriously. Turning a human being against their will is a Federal crime, not to mention *extremely* rare. No, the treatment you're going to receive—"

The door opens and a nurse enters, holding a white mug with steam rising from it. She doesn't seem to have fangs or claws or an excessive amount of body hair, but I study her suspiciously just the same; she's young, Asian, and has blue streaks in her short dark hair. She hands the mug to Adams, giving me a curious glance in return.

"Ah, thank you," he says. I guess in this reality nurses are expected to bring doctors their coffee, or maybe Miss Blue Streaks is just a suck-up.

To my surprise, he hands the mug to me. "And here it is. Drink up, but be careful—it's hot."

I take the mug and sniff it. It doesn't smell that bad, kind of like juniper with a hint of ginger. "What—you're going to cure me with tea?"

"It's an herbal preparation called Urthbone, specifically formulated to reinforce your connection to this world. It'll help ground you, physically and psychically—basically, a spiritual immunosuppressant."

I try a sip. Bitter, of course. But if they were trying to poison me, I'd already be dead. Or undead. Or hairy.

Maybe it's just wishful thinking, but I start feeling better immediately. I take a proper mouthful, ignoring the heat—I like my coffee hot.

"Oh, God," I say.

"What?" He's closer in an instant, looking concerned.

"You *do* have coffee in this world, right?"

He smiles. It's a nice smile, warm, completely unlike Cassius' relaxed smirk. "Yes, we have coffee. I'll get you some as soon as you finish the Urthbone. Before you do, though, there are some side effects you should be aware of."

Of course. I take another swallow anyway—in for a penny, in for a pound. "Go ahead."

"You'll experience an increase in empathy as your life force becomes attuned to this plane of reality. You'll be able to tell what the people near you are feeling—it may even affect your own emotions. If so, let me know and I'll adjust the dosage."

I nod. Compared to seizures and hallucinations, a little sensitivity to the moods of others doesn't seem so bad. My colleagues are always telling me I need to be more sensitive, anyway.

"Where's my handler?" I ask. "Cassius."

"He's a busy man. He'll be by to debrief you eventually, but he thought you needed a little time to acclimatize, first. I have to apologize for how you've been treated, Ms. Valchek—dimensional extractions aren't done very often, but there *are* protocols for a new arrival. You should have been eased into your transition, not yanked fully conscious into the Director's office."

"Call me Jace. And it's fine—I'm used to being thown in the deep end of the pool." I take a long breath and let it out, trying to shift into Active Case mode. In abductions or murders, the first forty-eight hours are always the crucial ones; you have to learn to hit the ground running and go full tilt. I'd gotten through multiple homicide, rape, and pedophile cases—I could get through this.

"If you've got any questions, Jace, I'd be happy to answer them. And please, call me Pete."

"Okay. Pull up a chair—there's one or two tiny details I might need clarified."

He grabs a plastic stool from near the door and sits. "Go ahead."

Where to begin? I think about it and realize just how big a problem this could be. It depends on how knowledgeable he is about not only his own world but also mine. "Let's start with broad strokes, Dr. Pete. My world doesn't have magic, yours does. What kind of magic are we talking about? Witchcraft, voodoo, gypsy curses? Gandalf, Dumbledore, or Aleister Crowley?"

His face does one of those things where the bottom half smiles and the upper half frowns. "Most magic is based upon animist principles—the idea that all things, animate and inanimate, have a spirit inside them. Different cultures interpret this energy in different ways, but the principles remain the same. The terms 'witchcraft' and 'voodoo' are seldom used, but elements of both approaches still exist. The two major forms are Japanese Shintoism and African Shamanism, though there are hundreds of different subdisciplines and offshoots within each. Vampires tend to like the formalism of the Shinto, while werekind lean toward the African."

"How about you?"

"I'm a Shamanist. Guess I like the earthier approach."

"So you're a . . ."

"Lycanthrope, yes."

His brown eyes meet mine. I find it hard to imagine him howling at a full moon—he seems more the milk-and-cookies-before-bedtime type. "Sorry if I seem skeptical. But try to see it from my point of view—where I'm from, this is just flat-out impossible."

"I get it. I can give you more *immediate* proof, of course." He raises an eyebrow—a pretty thick eyebrow, actually.

"Change, you mean? Right here, right now? You can do that?"

"Sure. All lycanthropes assume were form for three days a month, but we can shift whenever we want. There are some disadvantages, though—our mouths aren't properly shaped for speaking, for instance. But we still have hands, so we use sign language."

"Okay, go for it."

"Not until you've finished your tea. I want you grounded before I inflict further psychic trauma." He smiles. "Ask me another question."

"How much do you know about my world?"

"A little. I was given a dossier by the NSA when they assigned me to you, with a cultural overview put together by government shamans. They defined what they call the cusp divergence at sometime in the twelfth century; before that, our worlds were practically identical. Afterward, not so much."

"So vampires and werewolves showed up here in the twelfth century?"

He shakes his head, then brushes a shaggy lock of hair back from his eyes. "No, our kind have been around a lot longer than that—but until then, we'd largely stayed underground. It was something that happened in *your* world that caused the divergence. You developed a technology called firearms."

"We—wait. Are you saying this world doesn't have *guns*?"

"That's correct. We have weapons, of course—just not that particular innovation. Can't say I'm sorry—from the description I read, they sound unreliable and potentially lethal to the user as well as the target."

I'm not about to waste time arguing the merits of sidearms with a doctor. "Okay, so we invented guns and you guys stuck with, what, longbows and swords?"

"Amongst other things. It was around that time that golems started being used for warfare."

"Golems. Details, please."

"A golem is an artificial person, usually man-shaped but sexless. Basic animist magic: shape a humanoid form and charge it with life force. Early versions were made of clay and—despite certain legends—usually charged with the essence of some simple but strong animal. The famous Golem of Prague was powered by the spirit of a bull."

"And they were used as soldiers?"

"Yes, but without much success—they were hard to kill, but moved slowly. It wasn't until the Song Dynasty in China began building large golems—fifteen feet tall or so—and using them as a combination battering ram and mobile catapult that warfare really started to change."

I try to wrap my head around that. "Giants made out of clay."

"Fired pottery, actually, filled with pebbles. The joints were hinged metal. They were incredibly strong—they'd rain boulders of a hundred pounds or more down on the enemy from half a mile away."

I try to imagine what it would have looked like to a fortress under siege: a row of terra-cotta titans standing back and hurling rock after rock, while three or four of them charge at the front gates, a handy redwood tucked under their arms. No wonder these people aren't impressed by guns; while we were still experimenting with fireworks, they'd invented a tank that could follow orders.

"If the Chinese had been able to keep the golem-making process a secret, they might have been able to conquer the world—but it wasn't their discovery to begin with. A sorcerer named Ahasuerus claimed to have perfected the ritual, and disseminated the procedure to most of the civilized world. The shift to golem warfare is what eventually led to the supernatural races coming out of the shadows."

On my world, we'd started with bottle rockets and wound up with nuclear warheads—I'm almost afraid to ask what golems have evolved into. "I take it the current models are substantially different?"

He chuckles. "Very much. The standard, mass-produced golem today is basically a human-shaped plastic bag filled with sand—cheaper than clay, and more flexible. They're used mainly for manual labor or clerical work, though law enforcement and the military utilize them, too. They're animated largely by slaughtered livestock, but not always."

Ritual sacrifice, check. Barnyard-powered robots, check. Rising sense of unreality . . . hmm. Actually, that's subsiding. I take another long sip of tea. "So we studied David and built a better slingshot, while you went the new-and-improved Goliath route. How do vampires and werewolves figure in all this?"

"As mercenaries, in the beginning. Hemovores made excellent assassins, while lycanthropes are natural soldiers—fast, savage, hard to kill. After a few hundred years the supernatural races were taken for granted, if not accepted as equals. It culminated in the treaty of 1388, when a universal armistice was declared between the three races—golems weren't considered people back then. After that, killing a member of another species—for blood, meat, or any other reason—was declared to be murder. Except in times of war, of course."

"Of course. So vampires stuck to animal blood, werewolves crossed long pig off the buffet menu, and human beings put away the stakes and silver. One big happy. Sure."

His smile turns wry. "I'm not trying to sugarcoat the situation, okay? But what happened after that wasn't genocide, it was evolution. Vampires did what they did best—which was get craftier as they get older—and weres did what they did best, which was breed, hunt, and eat. Hemovores insinuated themselves into hierarchies where they could take control from the top—turn a King and his court and you pretty much have yourselves a country—while weres took a slower but just as effective approach."

"Have lots of kids and feed them people?"

He pauses. Though his expression doesn't change, I can *feel* his reaction—a spike of anger that seems completely at odds with his personality. I almost expect the next thing out of his mouth to be a snarl. "No," he says, his voice calm. "They converted."

"What, to vampires?"

"No. Catholicism."

"How did *that* work?"

"It was a better fit than you might think. Werewolves are animals, and animals are creatures of God—that's the theological argument. We don't have a problem with the crucifix—as long as it's not made of silver—and the Catholic Church has always encouraged procreation. It took a few generations, but by the end of the Renaissance even the Pope was a lycanthrope."

"And most of the royals were vampires—so basically, civilization was being run by the nonhumans by that point."

"Not yet. We were still in the minority, and many countries had instituted laws designed to keep us "nonhumans" in check. But hemovores and lycanthropes *aren't* "nonhuman"; we're just a different *kind* of human. One that's better suited to survive certain things . . . like the Black Death."

I see where this is heading. "Got it. Millions died, but not vamps or weres. I'll bet recruitment hit a new high, too— better undead than bubonic, right? And the fact that plague was carried by fleas would have worked out nicely for the fur-enhanced, too."

"Nobody knew that at the time. But yes, it was no doubt a factor."

"Let's skip ahead, okay? I'm guessing that after that, it was pretty much downhill for us nonfanged types. How long did it take? Was it a gradual decline, or something more dramatic?" I try to keep from sounding bitter, but that's never been a skill I really developed.

"World War One. Most people agree that's when things

really changed." He sounds different now, less removed; he isn't discussing history anymore, he's talking about something he has a personal connection to. I suddenly realize that a werewolf's life span is probably a lot longer than a human's.

"The war itself killed millions, but the Spanish Flu pandemic that followed killed even more. Humans accounted for around fifty percent of the global population before the war, and they were firmly in the minority by the end. The last human-only government fell in 1918. Over the next twenty years, their numbers plummeted as many chose a new life as a vampire or lycanthrope."

"The tipping point," I say. "A lot of people saw the writing on the wall, and just gave up."

"That's one way to look at it."

The last of the tea's gone cold in my hand. I slug it back with a grimace, then hand him the mug. "Rats deserting a sinking ship is another."

"Maybe just rats learning how to swim," he offers. "But that doesn't really work, either. The ship is still here, Jace—"

"You know, I think I'll skip that coffee," I say. "I'm tired. Get the light on the way out, will you?"

He doesn't argue. "Sure," he says. "I'll be back after you've gotten some sleep."

I slide down under the covers and turn my back to him. A moment later, I'm alone in the dark.

Really alone.

TWO

Morning. I open my eyes and the last minuscule hope that everything was just a dream evaporates with a tiny, melo-dramatic scream. *Good riddance*, I think. I'd rather deal with reality—no matter how bleak—than have some ridicu-lous, forlorn hope distracting me. Yeah, and I hate kittens and puppies, too.

I'm a little testy before that first hit of caffeine.

I sit up and look around. Same hospital room, same plas-tic chair, same wardrobe. There are two doors but no window. I get up and investigate—the one Dr. Pete came in through is locked and the other's the bathroom. I use the facilities, and note that a toilet is pretty much a toilet, no matter what uni-verse you're in.

They're probably watching me, but I can't spot the cam-eras. I check the wardrobe and find clothes in my size: under-wear, socks, black slacks and a black turtleneck sweater, black leather loafers with rubber soles. I shrug and get dressed; everything fits.

No gun, of course. It's probably disassembled in some NSA lab by now, while a dozen or so techs have geekgasms trying to reverse-engineer it. I hope one of them shoots him-self in the eye.

Around then my head informs me, none too gently, that it requires coffee *immediately*, and probably some more of that Urthbone concoction.

I hear the door unlock. It opens, and Dr. Pete comes in

with a tray—it holds a large mug of coffee, a little wooden pitcher, a small porcelain bowl and a tall glass of something brown and murky.

"I see you're up, good. I brought you the Urthbone cold, today—thought you might like to try it both ways."

"Uh-huh," I say. I grab the glass and chug it back. Cold, it reminds me of herbal iced tea with a side of aspirin. I put the empty glass down on the tray and grab the coffee. "Thanks."

"I see you're a woman with priorities."

I take a healthy swallow. Ah. If whisky is the water of life, coffee is the whisky of Nirvana. "Brain . . . activating," I mutter. "Will to live . . . returning."

"Good to hear. How'd you sleep?"

"Fine." I'm halfway through the mug already. "For a prisoner."

"Sorry, that was beyond my control. But the door is open now—you're not going to be treated like a captive."

"No, just an abductee. Technically, this entire *universe* is my prison."

He shrugs. "Sure. But the same holds true for everyone, doesn't it? Technically, you were a prisoner in your *own* universe."

I glare at him over the rim of the mug and take another swallow. "I have a rule, Doctor—no existential philosophy before the second cup of coffee." I hand him the empty mug.

He takes it and sets it down on the table beside the bed. "I have a rule, too: my patients don't leave until they're fit to do so. So sit down—you don't have to get undressed, but there are a few basic tests I have to perform."

He checks my eyes, my reflexes, my blood pressure, asks me if I had any nightmares or felt dizzy since I woke up. I tell him the truth, which is that I feel fine.

"Okay," he says. "The Urthbone seems to be doing its job." He pulls a sealed plastic bag out of his pocket and gives it to me. "You can mix this on your own—directions are on the outside. Let it steep overnight, make sure you take at least six ounces a day. If you have any recurrence of symptoms, let me know right away."

"Absolutely. I just have a few quick questions, all right?"

"Go ahead."

"It sounds like you're discharging me. Where the hell am I going? What bed will I be sleeping in while my tea steeps? Whose stove will I be boiling water on? And how do I contact you, anyway—pee on the nearest fence post and hope you get the message?"

"My phone number's on the bag. The other questions you'll have to take up with the Director; he's sending someone to pick you up after breakfast." Dr. Pete gives me an encouraging smile. "You'll be fine. The Agency will provide you with a place to live, clothing, all your essential needs. You'll get the same salary any agent does, plus a healthy bonus for your . . . situation."

"Kidnap victims rate a higher pay grade? Well, that makes up for everything."

"Come on. Let's get something to eat."

I follow him out the door. It occurs to me that so far, all I've seen of this world has been two small rooms, and I've only met two—well, three, if you count undertaker guy—people. That's about to change.

I'm not sure what to expect, but all I get is an empty corridor that seems more like part of an office than a hospital. We walk down it and into what looks like a smallish cafeteria. The nurse with the blue-streaked hair sits in one corner, across from a bulky black man in scrubs. Both glance at us, then go back to their meals.

It's completely mundane until we get to the food counter. Eggs, bacon, ham, sausage—a little protein-heavy, but nothing that strange. Then I notice the rows of plastic bottles half-submerged in a tray of melting ice.

I pick one up. Looks like tomato juice. The logo reads: JUICY PIG in brilliant crimson, and below that is a cartoon bat wearing a monocle and saying, "Bloody good!"

"Want that heated up?" the bearded man behind the counter asks.

"No," I say, putting it back. "I'll stick with eggs, thanks."

Once again, there's no windows. I guess in a society full

of vampires, that makes sense, but it just reinforces the fact that I'm here against my will. I'm not that hungry—the ghost of last night's tequila is currently haunting my lower abdomen—but I make myself eat.

Dr. Pete has a ham steak, scrambled eggs, and coffee, and I study him as we eat. I feel kind of strange, almost drugged—the jumpy, nervous feeling in my stomach is slowly being smothered by a completely irrational feeling of ease. Of course, the Urthbone could have almost anything in it—

I abruptly realize that what I'm experiencing is exactly what Dr. Pete warned me about. The sense of relaxed competence is coming from *him*—I'm feeling what he's feeling.

And just as suddenly, I'm not—because the idea that my emotions aren't my own provokes an immediate feeling of anger and revulsion, which apparently trumps the doctor's warm fuzzies. Good to know; I can always count on my natural orneriness to kick in, usually at inappropriate times.

But part of me wants to give in, to go back to that feeling. Dr. Pete, it seems, is one of those people who love their job; he feels at home here, feels confident and strong and valued. I think there was a two-hour period when I felt that way at the Bureau, right between considering myself an incompetent newbie and hitting old-timer burnout. I don't remember it very well.

But Dr. Pete knows that feeling intimately. It strikes me that I'm being played, that the reason the good and sincere doctor was assigned to me was exactly because of how I'd respond. Maybe they even thought I'd be attracted to him—he *is* cute, in a slightly unkempt, puppy-doggish kind of way.

Well, if that's what "they" thought, they're barking up the wrong agent. I don't do romance, in the same way that I don't do heroin, Russian roulette, or nude alligator wrestling. I consider all of the above to be stupid, self-destructive, and demeaning, and these are things up with which I will not put.

I'm a survivor. Everybody knows that in order to survive you have to be adaptable, but nobody tells you that "adapting" means being able to give up the things you care about. Or, sometimes, the people.

Dr. Pete notices me glaring at him accusingly. "Whuh?" he says, his mouth full of eggs. I feel his confusion, coupled with wariness—*Is this woman going to do something crazy?*—and my anger subsides a little. *Great. Welcome to the roller coaster, don't forget to strap in.* And I thought PMS was bad.

"Nothing. Just getting used to the medication, that's all."

He swallows before speaking. "It may be intense at first. Just try to stay conscious of where the emotions are coming from; after a while, you should be able to separate your feelings from those around you."

Sure, I've got plenty of experience doing that. But even though I try to keep a layer of Kevlar between my heart and the rest of the world, the damn thing keeps breaking anyway. . . .

I finish my food and push the plate away. "So what can you tell me about the case?"

"Nothing, I'm afraid. The NSA doesn't give high-level briefings to lowly MDs."

About what I'd expected, but I had to try. "How about Cassius, then? What's my new boss like?"

"Remember what I said about vampires getting craftier as they get older? Well, Cassius is old—*real* old. No one knows how old for sure, but he plays up the Roman angle a lot. There are all kinds of rumors about him, but I think he starts half of those himself."

"For instance?"

"That he's the original model for Michelangelo's statue, for one."

I think about it. "I can see a certain resemblance. How about something a little less like high school gossip?"

"He's also supposed to be the one that personally cut off Stalin's head."

"Stalin was a vampire?"

"Lycanthrope. Silver-edged sword."

"Right. How long's Cassius been Director?"

"Since 1935."

"Guess there's not a lot of room for advancement when everybody's immortal."

"Not everyone is." He took a long sip of his coffee. "Lycanthropes live around three hundred years. We're immune to most diseases, but not all; we don't have the virtual invulnerability that hemovores possess, but we do heal very quickly. We can recover from any wound short of decapitation, except those caused by silver."

"Okay. Are there any weird discrepancies I should be aware of?"

"Like what?"

"Differences between my world's mythology and your world's facts. Like, does garlic still repel vampires, or do I have to stock up on paprika? Is a wooden stake through the heart still effective, or do I have to aim for the spleen?"

"Wood of any kind will penetrate hemovore flesh, and wood through the heart or the brain will usually prove fatal. They find garlic intensely repulsive, so much so that possession of undiluted garlic by anyone other than a police officer is a misdemeanor. The major area of vulnerability for a vampire, ironically enough, is his neck; it doesn't have the same kind of resistance to damage that the rest of his body does. The leading cause of hemovore death is accidental decapitation, usually due to a car wreck."

"How about silver and vampires?"

"A silver blade will cut vampire flesh, but it will heal. Sunlight's a bigger problem, but it's not immediately fatal—it takes direct exposure of a minute or longer to cause critical body-wide collapse and burnout. Emergency rooms deal with minor burns on a daily basis—bad ones can scar, but most fade away within a few weeks."

"Why do you switch back and forth between 'vampire' and 'hemovore' but always stick to 'lycanthrope' instead of 'werewolf'?"

He blushes. "That's, uh, my mistake. 'Vampire' and 'werewolf' are both considered impolite—I guess I was using them because I was trying to make you feel comfortable."

"The *V* word, huh? But 'were' is okay?"

" 'Were' is, 'werewolf' isn't. Lycanthropes are descended from more than just wolves—canids from all over the world can manifest the energy that triggers transformation. Jackals, coyotes, dingoes—even dogs."

"Hang on. There are were-*dogs*?"

"Dogs are just domesticated offshoots of wolves. Werewolves that bit dogs transmitted the carrier curse to them, and they infected other humans the same way. Similar to a virus—and when a virus jumps from one species to another, it mutates. A human infected by a dog will still transform under a full moon, but now he'll exhibit certain characteristics of the canine that actually bit him—and he'll pass those on to the next person he bites."

Visions of were-Chihuahuas dance in my mind; I think they're doing the Macarena, but it's hard to tell. "So if I have to deal with some yappy little bureaucrat, he's probably just channeling the yappy little dog inside him?"

He laughs. "More than likely. It doesn't necessarily mean he was bitten by an infected dog, either—just that one of his ancestors was. The traits are passed down genetically as well."

"And what's in your family tree, Dr. Pete? No, wait—let me guess."

I mock-squint at him. The shaggy brown hair reminds me of a cocker spaniel, but it's not curly enough. Brown eyes, more soulful than sad—not basset hound, but maybe beagle. Average-size nose, which eliminates the pugs and greyhounds but leaves everything in between. His name doesn't give me much of a clue—Adams is probably British, but it's pretty generic.

"How about a hint?" I say.

"All right," he says, and I can hear the mischief in his voice.

He transforms.

I'm not sure what I expected as far as the actual process goes; probably either the instant morphing you see so often on television, or the extended, bone-cracking version movie directors love to inflict on their audiences. What I get is somewhere in between—not instantaneous, but not three minutes of skin-stretching agony, either. I guess it takes about ten seconds, total, and the most disturbing thing about it is how it *sounds*: kind of like someone squishing raw hamburger in their fist while chewing a mouthful of peanuts with the shells still on.

In the movies, werewolves are always snarling and growling and generally looking vicious. Dr. Pete opens his mouth and *pants* at me, like a—

"Collie," I say. "You've definitely got some collie in you."

He nods agreement, which is a lot cuter than scary; it somewhat offsets the fact that his eyes are a vivid, unearthly yellow. I stare at him, noting that while his head appears pretty wolf-like, the rest of his body hasn't changed that much. His chest is a little broader, his arms a little bigger, and his hands have turned into big, furry things with wicked-looking claws on the ends. I duck my head under the table and see that his legs—sorry, his *hind* legs—now crook backward the way an animal's do. His shoes have fallen off, but he's still wearing socks, which looks faintly ridiculous.

I straighten up. He does something nimble with his hands, but unfortunately I don't speak were–sign language; I'll have to do something about that.

Changing back takes him about the same amount of time. "Collie on my mother's side," he says. "Some black Lab on my father's."

His tone is light, but I can feel the sudden surge of alertness in him. He's worried that seeing him transform will be too much for my fragile psyche to handle.

"I could use some more coffee," I say. I hand him my cup. "Fetch?"

He laughs more like a terrier.

The golem finds us in the cafeteria.

He—it?—isn't what I expect. Dr. Pete's description of "a human-shaped plastic bag filled with sand" had me envisioning something like a lumpy yellow blow-up doll, minus the orifice options. What stands in the doorway is a broad-shouldered figure a little over six feet tall, wearing a very sharp pin-striped suit of dark blue, matching fedora, and polished black leather oxfords. His skin is darker than his shoes, and just as glossy; his features seem sculpted out of black chrome. His tie appears to be alligator skin.

He strides over to us, his movements oddly deliberate but not jerky; he reminds me more of someone performing a dance about walking than someone actually doing so. He stops in front of our table and looks at me. At least, I think that's what he's doing; he doesn't seem to have actual irises or pupils, just eye-shaped indentations. It's like looking at a mask, one with strong, angular features: square chin, heavy brow, Roman nose with a pronounced hump to it.

"Jace Valchek?" he asks. His voice is deep and raspy, sandpaper scraping the bottom of a metal barrel. He holds his hands loosely at his sides, and I note that the skin on them is just as black as his face. He doesn't have fingernails.

"Who's asking?" I say.

"I'm Charlie Aleph. I'm here to escort you to see the Director." Just like Cassius, I can't quite place his accent—Arabic? German? Something with harsh gutturals, anyway—but the coiled tension in his voice is as obvious as a stretched bowstring, while his body language is completely relaxed. The only people I've ever seen able to pull off that combination effectively were lifelong politicians or trained assassins.

I can't tell how much of the wariness I feel is natural caution and how much I'm picking up from him. "Yeah, fine. Do I get to actually see the outside world now, or are we traveling in a hermetically sealed armored car?"

"We'll be driving," Charlie Aleph says. "Whenever you're ready."

I toy with the idea of having another cup of coffee and making him wait, but that's a game I'd probably lose; never try the patience of someone whose family tree includes marble and granite. I get to my feet. "Okay, let's go. Dr. Pete, thanks for the tea."

"Call me if you have any problems," he says, and I get the feeling he's talking about more than just symptoms.

"Sure," I say. I wonder if they'll give me a phone.

Charlie leads me out of the cafeteria and down the corridor to an elevator. His body makes these soft crunching noises as he walks, like he's stepping on fresh snow.

"So," I say as we stop at the elevator. "What's my status? Am I a prisoner or a cop?"

"Neither. You're a consultant of a nonrecognized foreign government, granted Special Agent status for the duration of the case." He doesn't look at me while he talks, which is good. Those eyeless eyes aren't exactly comforting.

"Bureaucratic doublespeak meaning that while I work for you, I don't have any special legal standing. No Diplomatic Immunity, for instance."

"No."

The elevator arrives and we get on. I almost expect it to creak under his weight, but that doesn't happen.

"What happens if I try to run?" I ask as the doors close.

"I'll stop you."

"You don't look too quick."

"You'd be surprised."

"I hate surprises."

"Then don't run."

The doors open. We're in the lobby of an office building, not a hospital; I guess that was Dr. Pete's private practice, or maybe just a facility the NSA reserves for special cases like me. I see a few other people, but nobody out of the ordinary—a paunchy guy in a business suit, a middle-aged woman in a long beige coat. The front wall of the lobby is all glass, and it looks like a gray, overcast day outside. My own internal clock tells me it's early morning, but for all I know the sun's about to go down.

Okay, Scary New World—here I come.

Out the door. Charlie Aleph heads straight for a dark blue Crown Vic parked at the curb. I stop, take a deep breath of air, look around.

The first impression I get is utterly mundane. City street, lots of buildings, businesses, cars. People walking down the sidewalk, driving past in Toyotas, Fords, Chevys. No bats soaring overhead, no howls echoing off the concrete. But there *is* something. . . .

It's the air. It smells, I don't know, *wilder* somehow, as if there were animal musk and wet moss underneath the car exhaust and damp asphalt.

I hesitate for only a second outside the car—I'm not going to run, where the hell would I go?—then get in. Charlie's already started the car, and pulls into traffic before I even get my seat belt on.

I look over at him. He stares straight ahead.

"So," I say. "Golem, huh?"

"I prefer the term 'Mineral-American.' "

"Oh. Sorry. Uh, I don't suppose you're going to tell me—"

"You'll be told everything at the briefing."

Right. Golems aren't big on the small talk, I guess.

I stare out the window as we drive. I start to notice details that would have me questioning my sanity back home—here, they confirm it. Restaurants with names like the Severed Artery or the Happy Leech. Vehicles with heavily smoked windshields and windows. People walking down the street wearing gloves, goggles, face masks, and hoods—no exposed skin at all. And what can only be more golems, with the same shiny skin as my driver but colored white, red, brown, or yellow. I glance over at him and say, "I thought go—uh, Mineral-Americans would all be yellow."

"Different grades of silica. Sometimes artificial color is added."

"Why?"

"Job designations. Clerical, manual laborer, hazardous worker. A few others."

I study him a little harder. Up close, I can see the grainy texture of the black sand beneath his thick plastic skin. "What's the job designation for black?"

"Enforcement."

He doesn't elaborate. He doesn't have to.

Something lopes past us, way too fast. It leaps onto the hood of a cab, goes sideways off the door of a delivery truck, and disappears around a corner. I don't get a good look at it—I get the impression of short gray fur, a streamlined body, long arms, legs, and snout, and a vest of Day-Glo green. I think it was carrying some sort of bag slung over its shoulder.

"Damn couriers," Charlie says.

A sudden thought strikes me. "Charlie, where are we?"

"Grant Street."

"No, I mean which *city*?"

"Seattle. Space Needle's right over there." He jerks a thumb over his shoulder. "You have one of those where you come from?"

"No, we all live in grass huts. Big pointy building *scary*."

He glances at me. His almost expressionless face creases ever so slightly around the mouth, in something that might one day—with careful care and feeding—be called a smile.

"Uh-huh," he says.

The FBI office I work out of is in St. Louis. I've been to Seattle once before, but don't know the city well—which is probably a good thing, as I'll have to unlearn most of what I know anyway.

We don't drive far. A few minutes later we're pulling into the underground parking of a large concrete structure, with the monolithic impersonal architecture of a Federal building. Security seems a little lax to me, but maybe they have some kind of protective voodoo I can't perceive.

The lot's filled with government cars, lots of Crown Vics and boxy sedans. We park and head for the nearest elevator.

"Got any helpful advice?" I ask as we're waiting for the doors to open.

"If the Director invites you out for a drink," he says, "say no."

The elevator lets us off on the twenty-third floor, in front of a security checkpoint. Two large frosted glass doors set into a bare concrete wall, with two of the scariest-looking guards I've ever seen posted on either side: both are lycanthropes, but they bear about as much resemblance to Dr. Pete as a professional wrestler to a jockey. The one on the right has jet-black fur, yellow eyes, and a muzzle big enough to bite my head off in one snap. The other one's fur is a reddish orange, and while he's shorter than his partner, he makes up for it in width. His biceps are as thick as fire hydrants and look about as solid. Both wear chain-mail suits, stainless-steel links covering them from wrist to neck to ankle, leaving their heads and clawed extremities bare. Spiky tufts of fur bristle here and there between the links.

There's some complicated hand motions from the red-furred one, which Charlie responds to. "Yeah, hi, Tony. This is Consulting Agent Jace Valchek."

The black-furred one makes a few gestures of his own.

"She doesn't sign," Charlie says.

Tony taps his own chest with one curving claw.

"Oh, yeah," says Charlie. He fishes in the pocket of his suit and pulls out an ID badge. He hands it to me and I clip it on.

The black-furred one looks me over, then bends over and peers at my badge close-up. When his muzzle is about six inches from my face, he growls. It's possibly the deepest, most threatening sound I've ever heard in my life, and despite the fact that I *know* it's supposed to intimidate me, it still makes my breath catch in my throat and my pulse speed up.

I meet his blazing yellow eyes. Take a deep breath through my nose. "Nice," I say. "Is that aloe vera? I would have guessed you were an oily, not a dry—but split ends are a bitch, either way. You use a cream conditioner?"

He stares at me. Blinks. Then straightens up and waves us through. As the doors shut behind us, I can hear Tony snort. Guess I have a bright future on the werewolf comedy circuit.

The office is large and busy, and I don't get to see much of it; Charlie hustles me down one side and to the far wall, which is made mostly of smoked glass except for the wooden door. He pulls it open and motions me inside.

I recognize the interior: it's Cassius' office. The smoked glass wall is covered by wood paneling on the inside—I'm guessing it can be retracted into the floor or ceiling—and Cassius himself is seated behind his desk. A blond woman in a gray skirt and a high-collared white blouse sits primly on the edge of the leather sofa, hands clasped together on her knees. She looks like she's in her mid- to late thirties, her hair pulled back into a tight bun. She smiles at me with exactly the amount of friendliness a receptionist displays.

"Jace," says Cassius. He's replaced his tie with one of blue velvet, the same deep blue as his eyes. He seems older today than he was yesterday, and it's not just because of what Dr. Pete told me; Cassius' body language is different, his spine straighter, his shoulders back. I realize my initial surfer-boy impression was deliberate on his part, trying to make me feel less threatened. "I hope you're feeling better. I apologize for the inept and negligent way in which you were introduced to our world."

Junior partner in a law firm, I think. Bright, sharp, but still a little inexperienced. Just the kind of person you want to mentor, share your own insights with. "Save it. I know you need my help, and I know why. You want me to cooperate? I want our deal spelled out. In writing."

"Of course." He opens a drawer and takes out a document. "Your employment contract. The terms are very clear—they detail your salary, accommodations, and a generous bonus as compensation for the way in which you were recruited."

"I don't give a crap about any of that. When do I get to go home?"

"At the successful conclusion of your assignment." He places the document on his desk and pushes it toward me. I stride forward, pick it up, and read through it. It's surprisingly void of legalese, stating more or less exactly what Cassius just told me—except for one thing.

"This doesn't define what my assignment *is*," I say. "Just that it will 'be deemed to be successfully concluded with the capture or elimination of the target of the mission.'"

"Yes. The person responsible for at least three murders so far. We believe—"

"What if I don't sign?"

Cassius smiles at me. It's a genuinely likable smile, and I wonder how many years it took him to perfect it. "Who said you have to sign anything? This is simply a description of what we're willing to provide, if you cooperate with us. You're free to turn us down."

He's good. He doesn't bother threatening me—I can figure it out for myself. Homeless, broke, and alone, one of a tiny minority on a world full of predators. *Good luck with that; I'm sure you'll do great in your new career as entrée.*

Still, they obviously need me. This may be the only chance for negotiation I get.

"I want my living allowance increased by fifty percent," I say. "I'm not setting up shop in some cramped little walk-up. The abduction bonus gets doubled, and don't bitch at me about your budget—I can tell you guys don't do this kind of thing every day, and special projects always have deep pockets. And I want my gun back."

He doesn't argue, which irritates me. Instead, he nods, picks up a pen, and writes in the changes.

Then he hands me the pen.

I grit my teeth, take it and sign the contract. At this point, a signed document is probably better for me than for him.

"Welcome aboard," he says, tucking one set of the papers away in a drawer. I fold my own copies and jam them in a pocket. "Your weapon and laptop are being examined, but they'll be returned to you shortly. First, I'd like to introduce you to some of the people you'll be working with."

He nods at the golem, who's been standing motionless as a statue by the door since we arrived. "Charlie Aleph you've already met. He's an Enforcement-class golem with twenty years' experience. Served in the first Persian war as field artillery, decorated twice for valor. He'll be your enforcer."

"Right. Is he going to frisk me for crucifixes and wooden stakes, too? Look, if I'm going to work for you, you're going to have to trust me—"

"I'm aware of that," he says, and his tone stops me cold. It has that unmistakable ring of command, the one that says, *I know exactly what I'm doing so just shut the hell up or suffer the consequences.* I shut up.

"Charlie isn't there to spy on you or keep you in line. He's there to protect you, and inflict serious damage on anyone that gets in your way. He's your weapon, not your babysitter. Got it?"

"Got it."

"And this is Gretchen Petra." He nods at the woman seated on the couch. "Gretchen will be your liaison with our intel division."

The woman rises from the couch and puts out her hand. I shake it; her grip is strong and cool. "A pleasure," she says. Her accent is British and cultured, and she looks vaguely amused. "Please don't judge our world solely by David. A few of us aren't *complete* bastards."

I know I'll be working with this woman, but I'm not in the mood to be gracious. "Oh? What are you, three-quarters?"

Her smile gets a little bigger. "Oh, heavens, no. No more than fifty percent, I assure you." Her eyes actually seem, I swear to God, to twinkle. "Of course, the rest *is* pure bitch." Her voice stays as soft and gentle as freshly laundered flannel. I think I like her.

"Good to know," I say. "Can we start the briefing now, or do I have to sacrifice a goat or something?"

"No thank you, I just had breakfast," Gretchen says. "Sir?"

"Go ahead."

Gretchen nods. "Here's what we know so far. There have been three killings. Each was recorded, using digital equipment. The recording of the first murder was uploaded to the Internet from the site of the second, and the second uploaded at the site of the third. Two of the sites were in remote areas with no readily available Web access; we don't know why the killer went to the time and trouble to establish his own."

"Who were the vics?"

"A researcher, a tour guide, and a waitress. Two males, one female. We've been unable to discover any link between them and think they may have been chosen at random."

"No such thing. How were they killed?"

"That's somewhat . . . involved. Three methods were used, all of them requiring a fair bit of planning. The first victim was killed by sled dogs—"

"Hang on. Sled dogs?"

Cassius clears his throat. "Yes. The murder took place near a small outpost at McMurdo Station—the victim was a government scientist."

I stare at Cassius incredulously. "McMurdo Station? In the Antarctic?"

"Yes."

"What was he doing research on, were-penguins?"

"I can't tell you that, I'm afraid. It's classified."

Of course. This was the NSA, after all, not the FBI. "Okay, sled dogs. Go on."

Gretchen continues. "The dogs were sedated, then had a coat of silver-based paint applied to their teeth. Once they were awake, they were exposed to a stimulant that drove them into a near frenzy. The researcher was placed into their pen and torn to pieces."

"Silver. So he was a lycanthrope?"

"No, a hemovore. He survived until the dogs managed to separate his head from his body."

"All right. Vic number two?"

"Australian tour guide, male, also a lycanthrope. Found locked inside a homemade iron maiden in the middle of the Outback. Are you familiar with the device?"

"I know what it is." A close-fitting coffin lined with spikes that impaled the victim when the lid was closed, a torture device from the Middle Ages. "Silver spikes?"

"Blades, actually. But it was the design of the sarcophagus itself that was particularly cruel—the blades initially penetrated the victim's skin to a depth of less than an inch."

"Not enough to kill him, you mean. How did he die— bleed to death?"

"Not at first—the blades were positioned to miss the major arteries. But the victim was locked in the sarcophagus just before the rising of the full moon—the one time that lycanthropes *must* transform. As his body changed in size and shape, the embedded blades tore deeper into his flesh. Exposure to silver also becomes much more painful to a lycanthrope during a full moon; the resulting agony caused the victim to writhe uncontrollably, literally tearing himself apart." Her voice is clipped and precise, a professional doing her job. "*Then* he bled out."

"And the last one?"

"Took place on the island of Hokkaido, Japan. The victim was a hemovore employed as waitstaff in a blood bar in Sapporo, the largest city and capital of the prefecture. She was bound and suspended by her wrists, approximately twelve feet off the ground. A sharpened wooden pole was fixed to the floor beneath, one end inserted in her rectum. A pulley system transferred her weight slowly from her wrists to the pole. An extremely nasty way to go—the pole eventually emerged from her mouth."

I nod. "Was the pole tipped with silver, or did it have silver embedded in it?"

Gretchen arches one elegant eyebrow. "Yes, there was a silver cap affixed to the top of the pole. Completely unnecessary—sharpened wood penetrates the flesh of hemovores on its own. How did you know?"

"He's killed a vampire using animals and silver, and a lycanthrope by locking him in a coffin and impaling him. These acts are deeply symbolic. Killing a vampire with a wooden stake, even a really big one, doesn't fit the pattern— there had to be some symbolic reference to lycanthropes in it somewhere. Where was the body found?"

"In a forest—a protected reserve, actually."

"Let me guess: it has historical or cultural significance to lycanthropes."

"Yes. Hokkaido is home to a species of wolf found nowhere else."

I nod. "Okay. Antarctica, Australia, Asia. Obviously, he's killing people on continents that begin and end with an *A*— keep a close eye on those places and I guarantee you'll catch him. Can I go home now?"

Cassius ignores my joke, which almost makes me feel at home. Almost. "Gretch, take Jace up to the forensics lab. The physical evidence we've collected is there, plus Damon should be done with your equipment by now. But first, I'd like a few moments alone with Ms. Valchek."

Charlie heads for the door without a word. Gretchen gives me a sly smile on the way out that I'm not sure how to take.

And then I'm alone with my new boss. Again. I hope it goes better than last time.

"Jace," he begins, then stops with a frown.

"I do something wrong already?"

"No. I did." He sighs and gets up from his chair. "Look, I think we can both agree I pretty much blew the whole first-impression thing. You don't have any reason to like me, let alone trust me. But we're going to be working together, and I do *not* want the work to suffer—because the work is saving the lives of innocent people. I *know* you're professional enough to do that—I just wanted to let you know that *I* am, too."

"All right." I bite down on a half-dozen replies, which hurts; they're all sharp and extremely bitter.

He looks at me for a second without saying anything. Maybe it's the Urthbone, but for just an instant he looks in-credibly, anciently tired; like he's been fighting a war for centuries and just doesn't give a damn anymore.

No, that's not quite right. He still gives a damn, but it's buried under so many years and so much psychic baggage that he doesn't quite know where that damn is anymore, or what it's for. My grandfather used to get that look when the Alzheimer's started to set in, the frustrated groping for a word or concept that was tantalizingly close but had no handle to pick it up by; he had the eyes of a wounded little boy when that happened, and it always broke my heart.

"I'll . . . do my best," I say. It's about as conciliatory as I can manage.

The look vanishes, and the junior partner in the law firm is looking at me again. "I'm sure you will," he says, and opens the door for me.

And just like that, we're done. I walked into that office a prisoner, and I walk out an employee. The surreality of it makes me a little lightheaded, and I realize I don't actually know how often I'm supposed to get a dose of Urthbone. I'll have to check the first chance I get.

Charlie and Gretchen are waiting for me, and we head back to the elevator. Gretchen walks as if she's strolling down a runway at Milan, all poise and elegance. Charlie stalks beside her like a pit bull straining against a leash. I wonder how I look to them—fragile? Alien? Hopelessly ignorant?

"Well, what do you think of our fearless leader?" Gretchen asks. She jabs at the elevator button with one red-nailed finger.

"I don't know," I answer carefully. "I just—"

"Don't underestimate him—he's made his career out of people who've done that. He's highly intelligent, Machiavellian to the extreme, and utterly ruthless. If you can get past that, he's not bad to work for."

Her honesty surprises me. "Yeah, he sounds like a real sweetheart."

"He can be—but be careful. He doesn't have many weaknesses, but women are one of them. Especially your type."

"What, O Positive?"

"Really? I would have said B Negative. . . . You're a smart woman, Jace. You're also stubborn, aggressive—and human. That's a combination he finds both rare and irresistible."

"Why?"

She manages to shrug while only moving her eyebrows. "Who knows? It's like the old joke: Why do vampires date humans?"

"I give up."

"Yes, but not without a struggle."

Great. I'm going to have to deal with "human being" jokes, too.

"David is loyal to a fault," Gretchen says. "Give him your best—professionally, I mean—and he'll put his *very* long life on the line for you. Cross him and he'll wait twenty years for his revenge."

"I'm not planning on being here that long," I mutter. "But thanks for the whole carrot-and-stick pep talk."

The elevator shows up, disgorges an agent in a business suit and a golem in a short-sleeved white shirt, his hairless head and exposed arms a dull yellow. His ears are just bumps. He nods at Charlie, but doesn't say anything as he steps past.

"How about you, Charlie?" I ask as we step inside. "Do you agree with Gretch? Is Cassius all she says?"

"The Director knows what he's doing. If that means making sacrifices to get the job done, that's what he'll do."

"Yeah? Sacrificing himself, or just other people?"

"Whatever it takes."

The forensics lab is on the top floor, a warren of rooms both large and small, all lit by fluorescents and as window-less and claustrophobic as a subbasement. My new col-leagues guide me through the maze to a lab the size of a classroom, stocked with equipment that at first glance seems comfortingly familiar: comparison microscopes, glass-doored cabinets, centrifuges and computers. My laptop is on a long, wide table, plugged into an outlet with a new power cord, and my gun lies in pieces on a white piece of cloth next to it.

The man studying those pieces is perched on a stool next to the table, peering intently at a bullet he holds with a pair of forceps. He wears the standard white lab coat, but his hair is even whiter, as short, thick, and bristly as a tooth-brush. His eyebrows are the same, dense and snowy over eyes so ice blue they look artificial. His face is wide and ruddy, and when he notices us he grins and springs to his feet.

"Hello, hello! You must be the new hire!" He puts out an enormous hand, his fingers short and stubby. He's built like a weight lifter, his smock bulging across the chest and at the biceps, his legs just a little bowed. "Damon Eisfanger, very pleased to meet you." He shakes my hand gently, as if afraid he'll break it.

"Jace Valchek. I think that's my property you're vivisecting."

"Hmm? Oh, yes, yes, the weapon. I haven't damaged it, I assure you. I just couldn't pass up the opportunity to examine such . . . *unusual* technology."

"Can I have it back?" Despite what Cassius promised, I didn't really believe they'd ever let me hold my gun again; these people weren't stupid, and the minute someone with an engineering degree understood what they had—

"Yes, of course. It may take me some time to reassemble it—"

"Don't bother." I grab pieces with both hands before he can change his mind. *Click, snap, chunk, click,* and I'm armed once more. Even though I know it'll be ineffective against most of the locals, it still makes me feel better; if someone ticks me off, maybe I can shoot their car.

Eisfanger is looking at me with admiration. "That was quick," he said. "I take it this is a hobby of yours?"

"Not really. All law enforcement officers are expected to maintain their firearms where I come from. That includes field-stripping and cleaning them on a regular basis—I'm just a little faster than most."

"So *all* police agencies use these?" He sounds fascinated and a little incredulous, as if I'd just told him we also fly around and shoot laser beams from our eyes.

"Not just the police. The military, hunters, criminals, ordinary citizens; they're about as common as staplers. You *do* have staplers?"

Eisfanger shakes his head. "No—I mean yes, of course

we have staplers. It's just the idea of a weapon so esoteric being so widespread—"

"Esoteric?" I frown. I've heard guns described a lot of ways: cheap, expensive, evil, fun, sexy, dangerous, scary, sneaky—but never *esoteric*. It's like calling fast food exotic cuisine. Of course, "fast food" here may refer to fresh long-distance runner—

Dizziness surges in my head and gut. It's like that feeling you get when you visit a foreign country and everything seems new but not that strange, and then some little detail jumps out and you realize, you truly *understand*, that the people here don't think the same way you do; that you're a lot farther away from home than you really knew.

Eisfanger doesn't notice. He's already talking about something else, my laptop I think: ". . . I was very careful, especially with the power supply, but it seems our worlds are compatible technologically, which, when you consider the complexity of machine code, is remarkable, quite remarkable—"

"So I can access your systems?"

"Oh, yes. Your account, e-mail, passcodes, they're already installed. Tutorial programs will give you a tour of our databases. And of course, you'll be able to review all the relevant information on the case you're working on."

Gretchen steps forward. "We'd like to take a look at the physical evidence, Damon."

"Where would you like to start?"

"The McMurdo victim," I say.

Throughout this exchange Charlie's hung back, not saying a word, but he makes sure he's right beside me as Eisfanger leads us through the lab and to a refrigerated room behind a large steel door. The corpse of a husky lies on a necropsy table on its back, its legs splayed to either side and held upright with clamps. It's been split open, the internal organs removed and no doubt analyzed. I'm more interested in the murder weapons—the teeth.

I take the gloves Eisfanger offers and snap them on. The room is cold, but the excitement I'm getting off Eisfanger is anything but. He's practically bouncing on the soles of his feet as he slips on gloves of his own—much thicker than mine but still rubberized.

"Take a look at this," he says, grabbing the jaws and pulling them open. The teeth gleam dully, looking more like aluminum than silver, and I realize why Eisfanger's gloves are thicker—he can't handle the teeth directly. "Have you ever seen anything like it?"

"No. So the dogs had to be destroyed?"

"Oh, no. The vic managed to tear this one's throat out before he went down—the others were anaesthetized and had the paint removed. We have samples."

More trouble than my superiors probably would have gone to—but then, they wouldn't have to worry they might be executing a distant cousin. "How were they drugged? Food?"

"No—tranquilizer darts."

I lean in, pull back the black lip of the mouth. "Doesn't look like he was all that gentle in applying the paint, either." I can see cuts and abrasions on the inside of the mouth and the tongue.

"We think he used some sort of clamps to keep the mouth open while the dog was sedated, but something improvised as opposed to medical."

I nod. "So not a veterinarian. The paint is precisely applied . . . he takes pride in his work. Control is important to him, that's obvious."

I straighten up. "Did we recover anything else from the site? The darts, the rifle that fired them?"

Eisfanger looks at me blankly. "The what?"

Oh. Right. "How were the darts delivered?"

"I presume the usual way—thrown."

Great. These people had no idea what ballistics even *were*. "Never mind. What else is there?"

"That's it. No fingerprints, just some snowshoe tracks. The site itself was a modular metal pen, set up literally in the middle of nowhere. The dogs were used as transport there, but we don't know how the killer left."

"It's Antarctica. How many ways could there be?"

Gretchen speaks up. "We're working on that. We believe he may have access to unorthodox transport."

"You mean like the way I was brought here?"

She shakes her head. "Not exactly. That sort of thing is very rarely done, and only by government agencies. No, we think he might be using a shape-shifting spell—transforming into something that can fly, or possibly swim."

"Is that unusual?"

"Extremely. It's a form of magic that both hemovores and lycanthropes are unable to use—and only a handful of human sorcerers have the necessary training."

"Sounds like a good place to start."

"I'm afraid it's not that easy." Gretchen sighs. "Unenhanced humans are not very well documented. Many live in isolation and have virtually no contact with anyone else. We know the number of human animists that could do something like this is small, but we don't know exactly what that number is—or where, in fact, all of them are."

"Oh, this just keeps getting better and better," I mutter. "What next? Are you going to tell me the suspect is short, dresses all in green, and speaks with an Irish brogue? Were traces of shamrocks and breakfast cereal left at the crime scene?"

"Leprechauns are just as mythical here as on your world," Gretchen says. She sounds more amused than annoyed. "We also have an appalling lack of elves, fairies, sprites, pixies, ogres, trolls, hobgoblins, and unicorns. The jury's still out on UFOs, Bigfoot, and the Loch Ness monster."

Charlie's voice rasps from behind me. "There's always Santa."

"If the murder happened near the North Pole instead of the South, I'd agree with you," I say. "Still, I guess we can't rule him out entirely; maybe he used flying reindeer for the getaway. . . ."

Eisfanger chimes in, his eyes bright. "Yes, and maybe the Easter Bunny painted the dog's teeth!"

We all glance at him, but the line falls flat and nobody

laughs. Even lycanthropes have their geeks, it seems, too-bright people with an obsessive interest in their field and slightly off-balance social skills. I've known my share—hell, some people would describe me the same way.

"Okay," I say, "the Australian vic. Do we have the murder weapon?"

"Yes," says Eisfanger. "Unless the gremlins have hidden it." His smile confirms my analysis: the subtle cues that indicate a change in topic are more or less invisible to him.

"Take me to it," I say. Directness usually works.

The sarcophagus is in a corner of the lab, covered with a white sheet. Eisfanger removes the sheet as carefully as if he's revealing a body, and turns on twin spotlights over the table.

About the size and shape of a coffin, but maybe half as deep. Heavy-duty hinges and a thick metal latch, the kind that locks automatically when it closes. I touch the surface with one gloved hand. "So this is the silver maiden, huh? Cheap wood. Looks flimsy."

"It's not." Eisfanger undoes the latch. "Open it."

I grab the lid with both hands, hoping that Eisfanger's sense of humor doesn't lend itself to newbie hazing pranks. It's much heavier than it looks, but I expected that. I open it fully, the lid coming to rest at an angle against the table. The smell that rises from it is rank and animal, blood and excrement and spoiled meat. The blades that jut up from the inside of the lid are caked with dried blood, bits of flesh, and clots of fur; there are nine of them, varying in length.

Eisfanger gives me a quick rundown. "These two went through at the calf, between the tibia and the fibula. These two slid between the ulna and radius bones in the forearms. This pair penetrated the lower abdomen just below the ribs, piercing the large intestine."

"Pinned," I murmur. "Like a butterfly on a board. What about these three on the top?" There was a trio of blades in a row at face level.

"These two would have pierced his cheeks. You can see

that the middle one is shorter than the others, and angled slightly downward; it would have penetrated just above his lip, and not very deeply."

"In his human form."

"Well, yes. When he transformed, it would have been pushed through the muzzle, splitting the nose. The blades on either side kept him from turning his head."

"And the angle is just enough that if he slams forward, it won't push into his brain." I'm thinking hard, in that zone where I let my thoughts turn into spoken words without much of a filter to stop them.

Charlie says, "That wood doesn't look strong enough to hold a thrope, especially one half-crazy with pain."

"That's the idea," I say. I tap the lid and glance at Eisfanger. "Sheet metal sandwiched between thin layers of wood, right?"

Eisfanger nods. "We're not sure why he went to the trouble."

"Incentive," I say. "The wood's there to create the illusion that escape is possible. He was supposed to struggle. He didn't have the room to break free, but he did have enough to carve himself up from the inside out. But even then, note how the blades are positioned: between two bones in all four extremities, because bone will last longer than muscle. The blades are positioned so that the sharp edge faces away from the nearest artery—the killer didn't want the vic to bleed out too soon."

"To what end?" Gretchen asks. "Is this pure sadism, or is there a deeper purpose? Are we looking at retribution or ritual?"

"Too early to say. How about the third victim, the Japanese one?"

"We don't have that evidence yet," Eisfanger says. "The murder only took place"—he glances at his watch—"twenty-two hours ago."

I stare at him. "And you let me lie around in a hospital bed?"

"I, uh, didn't have any say in that—"

"Never mind. Gretchen—this case has leapfrogged three continents so far. Does our mandate cover international jurisdiction, or do we have to sit at home and wait for the phone to ring?"

"We *are* empowered to travel to countries that are signatories to the Transnational Supernatural Crimes and Activities Act," she admits.

"Is Japan one of those countries?"

"Yes."

"Then I suggest you pack your Dramamine, or whatever vampires take to prevent spewing their O-Negative breakfast into an airsickness bag. That crime scene is less than two days old, and I want to see it with my own eyes."

THREE

The inside of the NSA jet looks more like a corporate Lear than a government transport: rich walnut paneling in the main cabin, onboard galley, butter-soft leather seats that recline all the way down. I'd expected Cassius to need some convincing, but he'd just nodded and told me the jet was already prepped; thinking back on it, I realize the reason I was probably zapped to Seattle in the first place was because of its position on the Pacific Rim—Cassius was thinking two steps ahead. When I mention that to Gretchen, she just grins and shakes her head. "Only two steps? My dear, Cassius was thinking two steps ahead when people still considered steam engines to be the epitome of high technology. Now he thinks in terms of the entire dance, not just the first few movements."

Gretchen doesn't come with us, but Cassius assures me she'll be more valuable collating intelligence at HQ than in the field. I'm a little disappointed; she has the kind of sharp, ironic wit that the British do better than anyone else, polished to a fine edge by what must be decades of use. She reminds me a little of a predatory Mary Poppins.

Who *will* be accompanying Eisfanger, Charlie, and me is our Japanese liaison, a lycanthrope already on the plane when we arrive. He quickly rises from his seat to greet us, an Asian man wearing a black business suit with a thin black tie. "Hello," he says, bowing his head gently. "I am Kamakura Tanaka."

Tanaka is elegant in that way certain Japanese men are, his features sharp but delicate, his jet-black hair worn long but pulled back and fastened behind his head with a clip. He reminds me immediately of a praying mantis, alert and hungry.

I bow back. "Thank you. I'm Special Agent Jace Valchek, and these are my colleagues Charlie Aleph and Damon Eisfanger." The forensic animist bows, a little too deeply, and Charlie touches the brim of his fedora with a shiny black forefinger.

"I understand that you wish to see the crime site as quickly as possible," Tanaka says. "I have arranged transportation on the other end, and I will be accompanying you. Your luggage will be taken care of, as well." About all I have is the overnight bag Gretchen gave me before we left, my laptop under one arm and my gun in my pocket, but I don't tell Tanaka that.

The plane is laid out with several seats facing each other near the tail and a small galley and individual cabins up front. Tanaka and I take seats opposite each other, while Eisfanger stows his luggage in a cabin and Charlie heads for the cockpit—could be he knows the pilot, or maybe he's just reconnoitering.

Tanaka studies me frankly as the plane begins to taxi; maybe he's never seen a real, live human before.

"Got something stuck in my teeth?" I ask.

"No. Forgive my curiosity. I have never met someone from . . . another *place* before."

Ah. So that's it. "Cassius told you, huh? Funny, I thought it'd be a bigger secret than that."

He smiles. "It is. But David and I are old friends, and he knows I can do my job more effectively if I understand the situation—as can you. Please feel free to ask me anything, about the case or the world around you. I will do my best to provide answers."

"All right. What's your official status in the investigation? You work for the NSA, local police, what?"

"I am the official security liaison between your NSA and the Nipponese Shinto Investigative Branch. Our agencies perform similar functions in each of our respective countries."

"Not *my* country. . . ."

He nods his head in acquiescence. "I was about to eat. Would you care to join me?"

I notice for the first time he has a tray of *nigirizushi* in front of him on the low table between us. "Are you going to tell me the Batplane has its own sushi chef, too?"

"I'm afraid not. I obtained this from the airport concourse before you arrived. I hope the food is amenable?"

"I'm a vegetarian, but sushi is the exception to the rule." I've already picked up chopsticks and grabbed a slab of glistening tuna on rice. I pour some soy sauce into a little ceramic bowl with one hand while I stuff the fish into my face with the other. It turns out I'm pretty damn hungry.

Tanaka is staring at me with an unreadable expression on his face, but the Urthbone tells me exactly what he's feeling: disbelief.

"What?" I say around a mouthful of raw heaven. "My table manners bother you?"

"No, it's what you said. You . . . you are a *vegetarian*? Does that mean what I think?"

"Well, it doesn't mean that I think God looks like a head of broccoli." I chew and swallow. "It means I don't eat meat—with the exception of anything I can add wasabi to." I grab a big green chunk of it with my chopsticks and drop it in my saucer of soy.

"You must consume a great deal of fish."

I peck at the wasabi with the chopsticks, mashing it into the sauce. "Not really. I get most of my proteins from tofu, beans, dairy, and eggs."

He shakes his head. "That seems very . . . *alien* to me."

"I suppose it would."

"Why do you deny yourself meat?"

I dab another piece of *nigirizushi* in my wasabi and soy. "I'm not denying myself anything. I'm choosing not to kill another being to fill my stomach."

"But . . . that is their *purpose*, is it not?"

I pop the piece in my mouth. "Depends on your point of view, doesn't it? If you think the planet and everything on it is here for your own personal use, then I guess the pain and suffering of other living beings doesn't matter much. But where I come from, we look at things differently—or we're starting to, anyway."

"So no one consumes meat where you are from?"

"No, plenty of people do. I'm just not one of them."

"Without the natural cycle of predator and prey, the natural world becomes unbalanced."

"Sure. But that balance also gets thrown out of whack if one side of the equation becomes too dominant. If everybody eats beef, cattle need lots of room to graze. Forests get cut down to make pasture. Instead of trees absorbing carbon dioxide to make oxygen, we get cows absorbing grass to make methane. I don't know about thropes, but I'd rather breathe air than cattle farts."

He considers this. "That is a very Eastern way of looking at things. Most Americans I know do not think like this."

"Well, most of the Americans you know probably aren't from a parallel dimension."

"That is true."

The food is making me feel better, a little less culture-shocked. Strangely, it's also making the Urthbone stronger; I can feel Tanaka's emotions like an undercurrent in my own mind. It's a bit like being drunk, when your own emotions seem bigger and more important than they are usually; I decide that now's a good time to try to refine the effect, see if I can make it work for me. I try to focus on Tanaka's emotions as opposed to my own, and find it isn't as hard as I thought it would be.

There's just a touch of worry, but hardly any; he's good at his job and knows it. Confident, but not arrogant. And there's something else, something stronger, underneath that—it must be his lycanthrope nature, the wild part of him that he keeps in check. I close my eyes, pretending to enjoy a particularly succulent prawn, and probe the feeling like an invisible tongue searching for a sore tooth.

The result, though, isn't a jab of pain in my mouth—it's a burst of another feeling entirely, and a lot farther south. Warmth spreads through my belly and groin, and the smell and taste of the food is suddenly much stronger. I breathe in sharply, almost inhaling half my ebi roll, and cough, spewing grains of sticky rice and bits of shrimp meat all over the table. Tanaka leans forward, suddenly concerned.

"Are you all right?" He lays a hand on mine, and the feeling of his warm skin against my own makes me a little dizzy on top of the coughing fit.

"Fine," I manage to choke out, and pull my hand back.

I get my share of male attention. I stand five eight, do a hundred crunches a day and have the abs to prove it. I've been told I have the neckline of a goddess, though nobody ever says which one. My hair is long, very black, and full, while my features tend more toward the Slavic definition of beauty than North American. I don't put on a miniskirt unless I mean it, but when I do I can cause car accidents.

But nobody's ever responded the way Tanaka did.

It wasn't just the intensity of his lust that I felt; it was the *depth*. That's the only way I can put it. All men have that automatic hindbrain trigger that fires whenever they see a beautiful woman, but if you could decode that signal and put it into words it would just come out as "want sex now!" in a demanding, Homer Simpsonesque voice.

Tanaka's signal was more like Barry White crooning in my ear. "Hey, baby. I want you. I want you *bad*. I want you all the way, every inch of you, inside and out. I don't care how long it takes; I don't care what I have to give up to get it. I'll do anything, to anyone, just for the chance of spending one minute naked with you. Oooh, baby . . ."

There was more than just desire in that burst of emotion. There was patience, and yearning. There was fascination, and hunger. And most of all, there was this tremendous *focus*, as if I were the last woman on Earth and he'd just gotten out of prison.

"You have some prawn in your hair," he says.

"Uh, thanks," I stammer. *What the hell was that? Did*

this guy just gobble a handful of Viagra, or whatever the werewolf equivalent is?

An explanation occurs to me, but I'm a little too rattled to be subtle about confirming it. "So. You're a lycanthrope. Don't know a lot about you people. Are you more like wolves or humans?"

"That is a matter of much debate. Most consider themselves enhanced humans."

"Enhanced, right." I try desperately to push away the image that comes to mind. "Are you—I mean, is there any downside to that? Disadvantages?"

"I'm not sure what you mean."

"You know, biological stuff. Like having to shave hard-to-reach areas, or midnight cravings for rabbit, or . . . or certain times of the year making you, uh, behave differently."

"Yes, of course. Lycanthropes celebrate their heritage every lunar cycle with the Moondays festival. It's quite the celebration—"

"Do you go into heat?" I blurt out.

There's an endless moment of silence as he considers his response and I wait for the Earth to swallow me up—unlikely, since we're actually in the air by now. Strangely, I don't feel nearly as embarrassed as I should; Tanaka certainly isn't, and his calm amusement seems to be dampening my own sense of discomfort. The lust is still there, but it's not nearly as intense as when we touched.

"Ah. Not as such, no. The tides of the female body, though, are still tied to the moon, much as they always have been. And the males of our kind are . . ."

He hesitates. He meets my eyes. Another surge goes through me, nearly as strong as the last.

"Civilized," he says, "but still wild at heart."

I smile weakly, and change the subject.

After that I retreat to a far corner and spend most of the flight fiddling with the cell phone Eisfanger gave me before we took off and reviewing materials on my laptop. Tanaka leaves me alone; I don't know if he's sensitive to my mood—God, I hope not—or if it's just some Japanese protocol thing, but I'm grateful for the solitude. Eisfanger's doing something strange with chanting and incense in his cabin, while Charlie's disappeared into the cockpit.

There's a lot of data to go over, including the recordings of the two killings the killer made and posted to the Internet. Gretchen's working on that angle, but she told me before we left that she isn't having much luck. "He's using magic to cover his tracks," she said. "Fox virus, looks like. Damn thing keeps doubling back over its own trail."

I watch the recordings, over and over. The first one begins with a simple wire cage, maybe fifteen feet long, five feet wide, and six feet high, against a backdrop so white and featureless, it looks artificial. It's lit by a single bright spotlight behind the camera that throws sharp-edged jet-black shadows on the snow. A chain-link barrier divides the cage in two; one side holds five snarling, barking huskies, their silvered fangs giving them an alien, otherworldly appearance. The other contains the victim.

I freeze the image and study him. According to the file, he's an African-American vampire named Abraham Porter. He looks like he's about forty, balding, with broad shoulders and a bit of a paunch. The way he's dressed suggests late fall in Maine, but he doesn't seem cold. No breath puffs out of his mouth, either, adding to the illusion; I have to remind myself that I'm looking at a scene where the mercury was somewhere around fifty degrees below zero.

The look on Porter's face is just as savage as the dogs; his fangs are extended, his eyes bloodred. I wonder how a human being managed to get him into the cage—brute strength seems unlikely. Could a vampire be drugged? I didn't think so, but I don't know for sure. Maybe it was more magic.

Which I'm really, really, beginning to loathe. I feel like I've been dropped into the last minute of a basketball game, told I have to play by a new set of rules, then had the ball passed to me while the coach promised he'd get that rule book right out to me, yes ma'am, by next week at the latest.

I hit the play button again. A rope attached to the divider leads upward to a pulley on top of a pole, then down and off-camera. Someone pulls on it, raising the divider, and the dogs lunge forward and attack.

The rest is fairly predictable, though Porter lasts longer than I would have expected; if he had more room to maneuver, he might have had a chance. As it is, once two of the dogs latch on to his throat and pull in opposite directions, it's all over. It takes a third to actually sever the spine.

And then the body just kind of falls apart, disintegrating into big chunks that crumble into smaller chunks, until the whole thing is dust. Instantaneous decomp, right down to the molecular level.

First no ballistics, now no body. Frustrating, though I'm slightly mollified by having an actual recording of the murder.

I watch the second one. Same kind of flat, featureless terrain, but this time it's red-brown instead of white, desert lit by the last rays of the setting sun. Once again the murder weapon is center stage, the sarcophagus standing mostly upright—it's on some kind of stand, leaning back at about a seventy-five-degree angle—with the door open to show the victim inside. He's muscular, looks like he's in his thirties, has a bushy red beard and curly hair. He seems groggy. It must be possible to drug a lycanthrope, though I'm guessing it's not easy—their immunity to disease and ability to heal rapidly suggest their bodies' defenses would resist any kind of chemical.

The silver blades on the lid gleam sunset red, looking as though they're already coated in blood. Once again, a pole, pulley, and rope arrangement leads to the door on one end, off-camera at the other. When it's yanked, the door flips shut. There's a wet, punching sound beneath the loud click of the lock, and then the vic screams. The killer's timed it perfectly; the light from the horizon dims just as the lid slams closed, signaling that the sun is down and the full moon is now dominant. The scream turns into a howl halfway through, though the anguish in it remains the same.

Then it's just the silver maiden rocking back and forth on its stand, as the victim inside thrashes and howls. It goes on for a long time. Eventually, dark liquid starts to drip from the base of the casket. Blood always looks black in moonlight.

Both recordings were uploaded to a site called Televisionary, which seems to be this world's version of YouTube. Viewers numbered in the thousands, at first—the footage was assumed to be faked, and the McMurdo site was remote enough to suppress news of the murder. When the Australian clip was released, though, the vic's family recognized him and told the media. Removing the clips from the site didn't help—they'd already gone viral, notoriety ensuring their survival in millions of downloaded copies. I know why the killer staggered the releases the way he has: he's building an audience. The Japanese killing hasn't been released yet, but everyone in the world knows it will be . . .

When the killer's added another victim to his résumé.

I close my eyes and think. Two different methods of killing, both of them savage yet impersonal. A lycanthrope killed in a coffin, a vampire killed by silver and dogs. Almost a kind of homicidal dyslexia, a reversal of methods instead of letters. The staging of the scenes, the preparation involved, suggests a strong element of ritual—but the sadism of the killings seems much more personal. Either the killer enjoys torture, or he has a deep hatred of his victims.

I look through the files on the vics. Not a lot in Porter's; he was some kind of researcher working for the U.S. government near the South Pole. Everyone at the research station had been eliminated as a suspect, and Porter's personal life seems devoid of psychopaths with a grudge.

The lycanthrope was Andrew Fieldstone, a local who made a living running tourists out to Ayers Rock. He was a bit of a troublemaker, had several arrests for public drunkenness and assault—starting bar fights seems to be the equivalent of a sport in the small town he lived in. He hadn't been involved in anything that would provoke this level of violence.

According to the animist evidence, the killer's a human male. According to my new boss, he's also crazy . . . but by Cassius' own admission, vampires and thropes don't have a lot of experience with psychopathic behavior. So why are they so sure the killer is insane? The murders, while disturbing, look more to me like the killer's trying to send a deliberate message—and while that might seem unbalanced to most people, it makes a little too much sense to be definitely attributed to the workings of an irrational mind.

Something isn't right. I'm not being given the whole picture, and it doesn't take a genius to figure out that it must have something to do with the research facility at McMurdo. Besides, I don't think they'd yank someone out of a parallel dimension for a paltry three deaths, no matter how gruesome. No, I'm pretty sure my employers know exactly why Porter was killed; it's the other two deaths that have them uneasy.

And maybe the murders that haven't occurred yet. . . .

The jet prepares to touch down at the New Chitose Airport on Hokkaido, the northernmost of Japan's four islands. It's not as densely populated as the others, big stretches of it still virgin wilderness dotted with remote lakes and the odd volcano. The murder took place in the Hidaka Mountains, at a place called the Ezo Wolf National Park; from what Eisfanger tells me, we'll need a four-wheel drive to get out there.

Charlie finally emerges from the pilot's cabin and makes his way over to my seat. I'm staring down at the city through the window.

"Ever been to Japan?" Charlie asks.

"No," I say. "Not on any world. You?"

"Once. Lots of pires, not as many thropes. In Tokyo, anyway."

"Maybe we should have brought Gretchen."

"Maybe. Most of the bloodlegging trade goes to Japan; they still have a thirst for the stuff."

"Bloodlegging?"

"Black-market human blood. Hear they pay a thousand dollars an ounce."

"Nice to be wanted."

"Nah, you got nothing to worry about. That's for virgin blood."

I wonder how much trouble I'll get in for shooting my own enforcer.

It's just after 2:00 P.M., Hokkaido time. I used the onboard kitchen facilities to brew up some Urthbone tea shortly after we left, then poured it into a little plastic travel bottle I found in a cupboard; I take a healthy swig now. We've been in the air for a little under eleven hours, and all I've had to eat has been the sushi and some cheese and crackers—I stayed away from the raw haunch of lamb and the wax carton of sheep's blood in the minifridge.

The jet lands and rolls up to a gate, where one of those enclosed accordion ramps latches on. We disembark, and I realize I never saw or heard the pilot the entire time. Typical spook stuff: classify and compartmentalize, and never tell anyone anything except what you have to. He probably flew the plane wearing blinders—or maybe Charlie just sat there and glared threateningly at him the entire time.

Unlike most of the airports I've been in, this one seems practically devoid of glass and almost deserted—it feels more like we're in a big subway station at 3:00 A.M., lots of illuminated signs in Japanese and echoey concrete. Then I realize that, for vampires, this is the middle of the night; no doubt the place is much more active when the sun isn't up.

"Okay," I say to Tanaka. "What's next?"

"The train station."

We head outside to an idling taxi. No waiting at customs, either; Tanka simply gives a guard stationed at a turnstile a curt nod, and he lets us through. NSA privileges, no doubt—or maybe Cassius is so well connected he doesn't have to bother with little details like international borders. The cab's built like they are in the UK, two seats facing each other in the back, and Charlie and I take one while Eisfanger and Tanaka take the other.

I glance at my watch. "Crime scene is now thirty-three hours cold. Not great, but better than forty-eight. How soon before we reach it?"

"Two hours by train. Then thirty, perhaps forty minutes by car."

I look out the window. Chitose is supposedly a reasonably sized city, but it seems closed: not many cars on the road, most shops locked up. There's something else about it that seems alien, and it's not that all the street signs are indecipherable.

It takes me a moment to figure it out. Most windows have tight-fitting shutters of plastic or metal, though a few businesses have windows with heavily smoked glass. Combined with the deserted streets, it gives the place a locked-down, fortress-like feel, as if the inhabitants were preparing for some kind of coming battle.

The cab lets us out at the train station, and I almost expect to see tumbleweeds blowing across the empty platform. The train is waiting, a shiny new Shinkansen bullet train, all streamlined chrome and steel. The public transport feels a little low-rent to me—the FBI would have used a chopper—but that feeling vanishes when we board. We have an entire car to ourselves, and it's definitely not coach; in fact, it seems to be a completely outfitted forensics lab.

"I hope these facilities are adequate," Tanaka says. "David was not completely clear on the level of technology you're used to."

Is that a scanning electron microscope? "This'll do, pig, this'll do," I murmur.

"Excuse me?"

"Sorry. Film reference, wasn't meant as an insult."

"Ah. I see." His tone tells me he clearly doesn't. I briefly consider educating him, but explaining a movie about a talking pig who wants to be a sheepdog to a Japanese vampire just isn't all that high on my to-do list.

The train begins to move; I get the impression they were waiting just for us. "Not a lot of service this time of day, I'll bet."

"Very little, and none to Shimukappu. The Hidaka Mountains are sparsely populated, even more so at this time of year. In another month, when the snow begins to fall, there will be many more people."

I try to figure out what attraction snow would have to vampires and werewolves, and fail. "Why is that?"

"Ski season."

Sure, why not. I can just imagine Bela Lugosi shushing down fresh powder while his cape billows out behind him. Do people ski at night? I don't even know.

Charlie's found a seat and sunk into it, staring impassively out the window. Eisfanger's already examining the equipment, making occasional sounds of glee. I look around, find a bare countertop and put my laptop down, then pull out my bottle of Urthbone and take a healthy swallow.

I'm abruptly, intensely *aware* of Tanaka standing behind me. Though I can't see him, I know he's changed into were form. He's staring at me hungrily through glowing yellow eyes, his claws flexing, his gleaming white fangs bared. . . .

I whirl around. Tanaka stands in the same spot he was a second ago, unchanged. He arcs an eyebrow at me quizzically.

"Sorry," I mutter. "Long trip."

"Would you care to freshen up?"

It turns out our little expedition consists of more than just a single car—there's another with living quarters and a third that's just for support personnel. I'm starting to feel a little like we're going into the mountains to hunt Godzilla. Maybe he's into snowboarding.

I make grateful and extensive use of the facilities, which include a shower. By the time I'm done I feel a lot better; I've swapped the turtleneck for a scoop-neck sweater in brown and a pair of black jeans, both of which I'm guessing Gretchen picked out.

Tanaka's nowhere in sight. Charlie's tipped his fedora over his eyes and gone to sleep. Eisfanger, however, is more than willing to talk—just not about anything I care about. When I ask him about the silver samples from the dog teeth, I get a twenty-minute technical dissertation on the molecular qualities of metal pigments. It culminates in the astounding revelation that silver-based paint, while not commercially available, is pretty damn easy to mix up.

Silver occupies a strange kind of niche in this culture, not quite as dangerous or rare as uranium, but more toxic and easier to obtain than mercury. Vampires can handle it without any trouble, and—much like mercury—it's indispensable to certain industrial processes, which Eisfanger is apparently intent on describing in detail.

"Eisfanger," I say, trying to derail him. "Interesting name. German?"

"No," he says, momentarily distracted from an in-depth explanation of silver halides. "It's Icelandic—my father can trace his ancestry back to a pack of Arctic wolves. That's where I get my hair and eye pigmentation from."

"How about your mother? Same thing?"

He laughs. "No, my mother's lineage is a lot less distinguished. Her grandmother was mauled by a wolf-bitten pit bull and survived. Her kids all turned out like me—kind of blocky."

"Stubborn, too?"

"Yes, ma'am," he says with a smile. "Though I prefer the term 'option recognition deficient.' "

"Yeah, I've got a touch of that myself. How about Sleeping Beauty, back there?" I nod toward the back corner, where Charlie hasn't moved since I sat down. "He seems pretty single-minded himself. They use a bull to charge his batteries?"

Eisfanger's eyes widen. "Charlie? A *steer*? I wouldn't let him hear that. . . . Cattle are used mainly to animate low-level manual laborers."

"Okay, then what?"

"Well, enforcement golems are always powered by something carnivorous—usually something big, fast, and mean." His smile widens. "Take a guess."

"Lion?"

"No."

"Tiger?"

"Uh-uh. Think *bigger*."

"Grizzly?"

"Still too small."

I frown. Anything larger wouldn't be a meat eater, would it? Then I get it, or at least I think I do. "Oh, I see. Killer whale?"

His smile turns into a smirk. "Nice try, but it's not aquatic."

"Then I have no idea. This isn't exactly a level playing field, you know." I glare at him. "This isn't my world. I don't know all the rules yet. Maybe you have giant man-eating shrews or dragons or some bizarre creature I've never even *heard* of. The most basic principles of magic probably taught to kids in third grade are a complete mystery to me—I mean, every time I hear the word 'animist,' I think of cartoons."

He looks a little embarrassed. "Yes, you're right. I'm sorry. It's not really fair, is it? Let me make it up to you— I'll give you a quick lesson in animism, all right?"

Maybe Eisfanger's a little more savvy than I thought— he interprets the look on my face quickly enough. He laughs and says, "No long lectures, I promise—I know I have the tendency to talk too much, especially when I'm nervous."

"I make *you* nervous?"

"Well, yes, you do. You're from another world—with all sorts of technology I'm clearly not equipped to fully understand—and you seem utterly fearless. In lycanthropic terms, you're definitely an alpha female."

The idea of pack structure hadn't occurred to me, but it makes perfect sense. I wonder if Cassius got his position by ripping a superior's throat out.

"Okay," I say. "I know I'm not the most gracious woman in any world, but a little Animism One-oh-one would be appreciated. Thank you."

He blushes, which with his fair complexion looks more like an instant rash. "All right. Well, the basic principle of animism is that all things have a spirit within them: people, animals, plants, objects, elemental forces, even geographical features like rivers or mountains. Animist shamans have learned how to communicate with and influence those spirits."

"All things, huh? Even a pair of nail clippers?"

"Sure. Just because they have a spirit, though, doesn't mean they're intelligent. Small, simple objects are analogous to insects—they usually have a single, obvious function. But they do have personalities, of a kind: a tendency toward stubbornness, for example."

That made a certain sense—I'd wrestled with my share of recalcitrant cell phones and hair dryers. "So you can tell anything what to do?"

"Well, yes. But that doesn't mean it'll obey. Animism is more like a spectrum of negotiation; on one end is complete agreement, on the other total refusal. The complexity and success of the negotiation depends on many things: the skill of the negotiator, the natural tendencies of the object or being, the terms being offered."

"And the more complex the object, the more intelligent?"

"Complexity is only one factor. Age is another. But the most important element of all is function. What the object does, more than anything, will determine the nature of the spirit that inhabits it."

"So the spirit of, say, fire, would be what? Hungry?"

"Devouring, yes. Also volatile, passionate, and impulsive."

"How about something recently constructed? Like, say, a silver maiden?"

He shakes his head. "Normally, that's my job as a forensic animist—I talk to objects or bodies, get them to tell me their secrets. But the sarcophagus was too new to have an integrated spirit, and the blades themselves—well, silver just won't talk to a lycanthrope. Same thing with the dogs' teeth.

Silver and magic is like chaff and radar, or putting tinfoil in a microwave."

"So you could have actually talked to the corpse?" None of the bodies had been available for autopsy; the older the vampire the faster they decomposed, even in subzero temperatures. All that was left of Keiko Miyagi was a viscous puddle, and Abraham Porter had simply crumbled into dust once the dogs tore off his head. Andrew Fieldstone's body was still missing—probably to prevent someone like Eisfanger from pulling any clues from it.

"If it was fresh enough, yes. I *did* talk to the dogs, but they mainly remembered how the killer smelled—that's how we know he's human. Unfortunately, we don't have an olfactory database for a more specific ID. Yet."

"Smellprints? You're really working on that?"

"Oh, yes. Our noses, even in nonwolf form, are amazingly acute. We just haven't quite figured out a way to quantify the data."

I try to imagine it, Eisfanger sticking his nose into a device like a microscope, except the two tubes go into his nostrils instead of over his eyes. "Good luck with that. . . . So the dogs told you it wasn't a thrope or a vampire. What makes you think he's crazy?"

Now Eisfanger looks more uncomfortable than embarrassed. "I can't tell you that. It's classified—I'm not even supposed to know."

"Then why do you?"

"It's hard to keep secrets from someone with my job description."

"I guess so." I don't try to pressure him—in time, either he'll trust me or he won't. "Okay, back to animism. How about a little show-and-tell?"

"You want a demonstration? Well, I'm not really prepared. . . ."

"Not something you can do while we're moving?"

"Oh, that's not a problem. I'm just, well, a bit of a perfectionist." He suddenly brightens. "Oh, I know. Just a moment." He digs under his seat and pulls out what looks like an equipment case, one of the aluminum-sided ones with reinforced corners and metal latches. He sets it down on the low table between us and opens it up, the lid preventing me from seeing its contents.

He takes out a small animal skull, sets it down on the table next to the case. "*Rattus norvegicus*, the common brown rat. I use this particular specimen to communicate with local rodents that may have ingested parts of a victim or witnessed something significant. His name is Wittgenstein."

"And he's—what? Alive?"

"Oh, no, he's definitely dead. But animal spirits can be bound to their remains with the proper rituals. Don't worry, he's quite happy; I give him the spiritual equivalent of food and other rewards." Eisfanger picks up the skull and wiggles his fingers rhythmically behind it, as if he were stroking an invisible body.

"What kind of rewards?" I ask, not sure I want to hear the answer.

"Well, he likes to be tickled. All rats do, actually; several spots on their body have been identified as 'tickle areas.' Their response to having these areas stimulated is very close to a human's: young rats enjoy it more than older ones, the ones that are stimulated are more playful, and they emit an ultrasonic squeak that seems to be the equivalent of laughter."

"So, one of your primary forensic tools is a ticklish rat skull."

"He's very useful. I worked on a case where a body had been disposed of in a sewer and almost completely devoured by rodents; without Witty, we never would have made a positive ID."

"I guess that makes sense. Can you make murder weapons talk to you, too, or just dead animals?"

"That depends. Wood is a good subject—something formerly living is always best. Silver, no. Other kinds of metals, sometimes. Geographic features don't always notice what happens around them; they exist in a very different frame of reference and have a very different sense of time. A conversation with a mountain can take a few decades."

"Huh. I guess that's why my pet rock in the corner doesn't say much."

"Your . . . what?"

I sigh. "Sorry, didn't mean to be politically incorrect. Our resident Mineral-American."

He grins. "Mineral-American. That's very clever."

It takes me a second to realize he's never heard the term before. Not because he's clueless, but because he wasn't the target of a particular golem's deadpan sense of humor.

"Yeah, that's me," I say. "Sharp as a bag of hammers. So how does animism turn a two-legged bag of kitty litter into a citizen?"

"Well, usually it's a pretty simple ritual. The spirit of the animal is condensed into a liquid, most commonly blood, and then mixed with the sand or clay that's going to become the golem. Once the golem itself is finished, another ritual activates it. It wakes up with a rudimentary intelligence, but learns pretty quickly. Once they're trained they're sent to work in a factory or office or wherever."

"Enforcers, too?"

He shakes his thick head. "They're different. Separate facilities, special training. They can be a little . . . *volatile* when they first wake up."

"I'll bet. One second you're a polar bear; the next you're a walking sandbox."

"That's not exactly it. They don't retain the memories, the thoughts, of their previous life—what they do keep is the animal's essential nature. That's why they use carnivores for enforcement; hunters have the necessary instincts already in place."

"Right. So what large, aggressive beastie is powering Charlie's motor? The Abominable Snowman?"

He chuckles. "Well, I wasn't being exactly fair with my hints. See, Charlie's a special case; there's only a few like him in existence. The liquid they drew his essence from wasn't blood, and the project shamans needed a whole lot of it before they could find and distill the essence of what they were looking for."

"I'm still not following. If they didn't use blood, what did they use?"

"Oil. Charlie's animated by the life force of a *Tyrannosaurus rex*."

I glance back at the sleeping golem. Suddenly, the alligator-skin tie seems a lot more appropriate. . . .

The rail line through the Hidaka Mountains isn't a heavily traveled route, especially at this time of year, and I'm not surprised to learn that this isn't the regular train. Our rolling crime lab is a special government Shinkansen, a bullet train outfitted with the latest in technology and tasked to bring it wherever needed; Japan's extensive rail network and the train's ability to travel at nearly 200 miles an hour make it almost as fast as an aircraft, and much better equipped. Unlike other bullet trains, this one—named the Shinsou—doesn't need special tracks to travel on, able to switch between regular rails and the special Shinkansen tracks.

That's good, because this rail line is too remote and winding to support a bullet train. The view out the window is beautiful but strange; beneath an overcast sky, the Hidaka folded mountain range looks more like a series of immense, rounded hills than the craggy, irregular peaks I'm used to. Snow-dusted conifers cover them with a patchy fur coat, making me think of mold growing on abandoned anthills. It feels alien and artificial, like part of a theme park on another planet.

When Tanaka reappears I wake Charlie up so we can discuss the case. The only new data Tanaka has for us is on the background of the victim, Keiko Miyagi: apparently the blood bar she worked at has a less-than-savory reputation.

We also get some information on the significance of the murder site. Ezo Wolf National Park is historically important for two reasons: first, it's the only place the Ezo wolf—also known as the Hokkaido wolf—is found, a species that was nearly wiped out in the 1800s when pire ranchers tried to eradicate them to protect livestock. Only intervention by local thropes prevented a complete massacre, and both the remoteness and history of the location made it ideal for what the Japanese government built there in 1942.

A concentration camp.

"The Second World War," Tanaka says, staring out the train window at the mountains flowing past, "was fought over racial purity. At least, that is what the leaders of the Axis countries—Germany, Italy, Japan—professed to their followers. Hitler declared that lycanthropes were being tainted by mongrel blood, introduced by humans deliberately to weaken the race. Mussolini agreed with him, and the Emperor—a hemovore—saw it as an excuse to rid the islands of all lycanthropes once and for all. Most of the camps were in Europe . . . but not all. The Hidaka facility was one of them."

"This wasn't in the original report," I say.

He turns to face me, and what I sense now isn't lust but shame. "My government is not proud of what was done there, and would prefer that aspect of the homicide not be given undue attention."

"I'll decide how much attention it gets. Tell me about the camp."

"The strategy of purification was threefold. First, all dogs were executed. Second, lycanthropes of impure blood were rounded up and gassed. And third, unenhanced humans were arrested and imprisoned, accused of participating in some vast, ill-defined conspiracy. To ensure their loyalty, they were turned against their will."

Eisfanger nods, his eyes sad. "A simple and brutal philosophy: a human bitten by a pire or a pureblood thrope would become one. No chance of so-called 'mongrelization.'"

"Mongrelization, hell," Charlie growls. "It was never about that. It was getting near the end of the meal, and there were only so many pieces of pie left on the plate. The thropes grabbed as many as they could, and the pires did the same."

I got it. Despite the treaties and agreements, in a world of predators human beings were still the prey of choice. And while the supernatural population kept increasing, the

human one dropped. For thropes, that didn't really matter—
they could survive and prosper without humans around.

But vampires couldn't. Once the last human bit the dust,
that would be it for biting, period; no more new bloodsuckers, while the thrope population would keep on churning
out litters. It was the kind of dilemma that persuaded people
to follow madmen.

"So that's it?" I say. "That's why there are less than a
million of us alive today?"

"No," Tanaka says. "The war was fought on many fronts.
The Emperor established camps in India and China, where
there was still a relatively large population of humans left,
and falsified reports as to how many were being turned into
hemovores. When the Reich saw that defeat was inevitable,
Hitler's sorcerers released a plague spell in an attempt to
eradicate the last of the human population worldwide. It was
so virulent that even some lycanthropes were affected; the
bodies of the victims had to be burned. When the spell had
run its course, few humans were left alive."

"Huh," I say. "In my world, India and China fought on
the side of the Allies."

"Yeah?" says Charlie. "Who won?"

I think back to Charlie's "Mineral-American" remark.
"The Canadians, of course. I mean, they are the largest and
most powerful country in the world."

"Canada won World War Two?" Charlie says.

"Well, the Allies won, but they couldn't have done it
without the Great White North. My uncle was in the Royal
Brigade of Mounted Beavers."

"The parallels between our worlds are fascinating," Eisfanger says. "What was your war fought over? Land? Resources?"

"Resources, definitely. Mainly maple syrup."

Tanaka laughs, while Eisfanger just looks puzzled. Charlie gives me a look that might be the distant ancestor of a
grin, and I meet his noneyes and smile back.

It's close to five by the time the Shinsou pulls into the
small station, where we disembark and off-load a vehicle

from one of the cars. It's a blocky, futuristic-looking SUV with enough halogens mounted on it to light a production of *Phantom of the Opera* and big, monster-truck tires and suspension. I have to climb a ladder to get in.

Tanaka takes the wheel and we head off, down a narrow paved road that leads through a small skiing village and then into the mountains proper. We turn off the road onto a winding gravel trail cratered with potholes, scrubby pine crowding both sides. The overcast sky has darkened to twilight, the unseen sun crawling into bed behind the mountains.

The road ends at a large wire gate, set into a rusted wire fence that vanishes into treeshadow on either side. There's no sign, just a sheet of paper in a transparent envelope attached to the fence with plastic ties and a shiny new chain padlocked to the frame. Tanaka gets out and opens it up, then drives us inside.

The camp isn't far down the road. It's a collection of dilapidated wooden buildings, most of them on stilts—to prevent tunnels, I suppose. Two long rows of cabins that must have been for housing, and a larger, two-story building beyond them. We park in front of it and get out.

"This is the processing center," Tanaka says. "It's been largely gutted. Prisoners were taken inside, bitten, then locked in cells for their first change. It was deemed inefficient to wait for the full moon, so transformation was induced by sorcery."

The front doors are gone, ripped from their hinges long ago. There are no windows. Tanaka leads us up a short flight of steps and inside, moving carefully over rubble. The interior is dark, but we've all been given flashlights; the beams play over a large foyer, with two more doorless entryways in the far wall. Bright yellow triangular pylons mark off an area in the middle of the room, where I can see a large pool of dried blood. There's an X-shaped void outlined by a yellowish discoloration in the exact center of the stain, with holes near each of the four ends.

"This is where the pole was bolted to the floor?" I ask.

"Yes. We have it and the other physical evidence on the train, including the body of the victim—or rather, what's left of it." The yellowish stain must have been caused by the physical remains of the vic's body, which had mostly lique-fied by the time it was discovered.

I look around the room. "What's that?" I ask, pointing. There's a six-foot-high wheeled wooden barrier running par-allel to the wall on my left. It looks a little like a mobile bar, except it's too high and too narrow, no more than six inches wide.

Tanaka pulls on a pair of latex gloves and walks over to it. He grabs one end and pulls it aside, revealing a series of holes in the wall behind it. They're all about the same size, maybe six inches in diameter, and are at different heights; most are about three feet off the floor, though some are lower.

"This is the processing queue," he says. "Inductees were required to place their arm through the wall, up to the elbow. This partition was wheeled closely enough to press against their bodies, then locked in place to prevent them from with-drawing. A purebred lycanthrope on the other side would bite each forearm in quick succession."

I tried to imagine what it must have been like. Marched in by guards like the ones outside the NSA offices, their animal musk overpowering. No words, just growls and snarls, long clawed fingers pointing where you were supposed to go. The vulnerability of shoving a limb into a dark hole, wondering if the next thing you were going to feel was fangs tearing it off. The hard wood of the barrier pressing against your back, your face pushed into the wall like a child being punished. The people on either side of you, some of them weeping, oth-ers stoic. Some of them praying as they said good-bye to their humanity forever.

I look down. Some of the holes are no more than two feet from the floor.

"Yeah, this is a crime scene," I murmur. "But I'm a little unclear on something. I thought you said the Japanese camps were used mainly for turning out hemovores?"

Tanaka nods. "That is true. But the Emperor still had to

maintain appearances with his allies; this site was one of the few which also produced lycanthropes. German personnel were in fact stationed here as well."

"Huh." Once again, the killer was sending mixed signals; he'd picked a place that was significant in more than one way, to more than one species.

And maybe to more than just himself.

"Tanaka, when did Keiko Miyagi become a vampire?"

"I don't know; we don't keep official records of that. I can find out, of course."

"Do that. I'm betting it was right here, in this very room. This is where she stopped being human and became something else. And I'm betting we'll find the same kind of connection with the previous vics, too."

I look up, see the spot where the block and pulley was attached, directly above the bloodstain. I can almost see her there: suspended, violated, literally dying by inches. Killed by her own weight the same way the tour guide was killed by his struggles.

But the scientist didn't fit. A vampire killed by sled dogs with silvered teeth? The other two murders seemed almost as if the killer was denying responsibility, placing some of the blame for the deaths on the victims themselves—but what had the scientist done to contribute to his own demise?

I walk in a slow circle around the bloodstain. "Damon," I say. "Can you use your abilities on this?"

"Our own forensic animists have already investigated," Tanaka tells me. "They found little of note."

"I'd still like to have my guy give it a shot." If there's one thing I've learned working for the Bureau, it's never trust the locals; there's always a buried layer of nepotism, incompetence, or interdepartmental hostility that you'll be completely unaware of, no matter how pleasant and cooperative your liaison may seem. Tanaka might genuinely be trying to help, but that second cousin of his immediate superior who's sleeping with Tanaka's ex-wife might decide to misplace an important file just when I need it. Eisfanger, on the other hand, I can yell at.

He's already opened his case and taken out a few items—some small bones, a rattle, a number of stoppered vials. "I'm going to talk to the bloodstain," he says. "Hemovore blood is powerful stuff. It may still have an echo of the victim's persona in it."

And then I pick it up, just a twinge from Tanaka's general direction: he's upset. I can't quite make out if it's nervousness, irritation, or both, but he doesn't like what Damon's about to do.

I walk back in Tanaka's direction, pulling out my Urthbone at the same time. I take a long swallow while pretending to study what Damon's doing.

Yeah. There we go. Tanaka's not just annoyed; he's worried.

"Before you proceed," he says, "there's something you should know—"

Eisfanger's already drawn some runes on the floor with a dark liquid. He tosses the bones onto the bloodstain halfway through Tanaka's warning.

And then everything goes crazy.

FOUR

A whirlwind of screaming light rises from the stain like a special-effects-heavy commercial for a demonic kitchen cleanser. Eisfanger's eyes roll up in his head and he pitches over backward, out cold.

Abruptly, there's a wall in front of me. A tall, pin-striped wall, with a fedora on top of it. I guess a golem's first priority is to protect his . . . whatever I am, but right now he's just getting in my way.

"Aleph! Move your rocky—"

By the third word I've been picked up by the waist and set down ten feet away. Charlie may be made of sand, but he moves more like quicksilver.

"—ass," I say.

There are faces in the whirlwind, distorted but still recognizable as men and women—some Asian, some not. They all seem to be in pain, some howling, some weeping.

"Ghosts," I breathe. "Are they dangerous?"

"No," says Tanaka. "They are merely echoes, not true spirits."

I step past my overprotective bodyguard and kneel by Eisfanger. He's already propped up on his elbows, blinking woozily. "My," he says. "My, my, my. Head. Hurts."

"You all right?"

He blinks a few more times, then seems to focus. "Uh. Yes, yes, I am. Wasn't prepared for a multiple, that's all—overloaded my wards."

"Multiple. You're saying there's the blood of more than one victim here?"

Tanaka's nervousness increases, but he says nothing.

"No," Eisfanger says. "The forensics report was quite clear—only Miyagi's blood was found here."

"Then what?" Charlie asks. "Local spooks, hanging around since they were executed?"

Tanaka shakes his head. "This was not an extermination center—people were turned, not killed."

"I've got an idea," I say. "Why don't we ask them?"

I help Eisfanger to his feet. "Just give me a moment," he says. He bends down and rummages in his case, takes out a necklace made of bones, and drapes it around his neck. He dabs a few markings on his face from one of the vials and mutters something beneath his breath.

Then he thrusts his hand into the whirlwind.

His whole body goes rigid. Orange and red light flashes from his eyes like there's a fire in his skull. His mouth opens and a voice speaks, but his lips don't move. "Cold. Always cold," the voice says. It sounds female.

Another voice follows the first, then another and another. Some are men, some women. They speak in Japanese, in French, in German, and in English. I can't understand all of it, but from the words I can pick out, the gist seems pretty clear.

Cold. Empty. Life, draining away.

Eisfanger pulls his hand out convulsively, staggers back a step and then catches himself. "Right," he says, his own voice now all business. "One blood source, multiple spiritual essences. This little lady was more than just a waitress."

"A feeder," says Charlie.

"Yes. She's been drinking human blood, from more than one person. Highly illegal, even in Japan."

I turn to study Tanaka. He looks composed, but he feels anything but. "Amongst certain groups," he says, "there is still a fascination with human blood. It commands a very high price, so high that many humans sell it willingly. While such businesses are still technically illegal, the law is seldom enforced."

"Of course not," I say. "After all, the only people who suffer are us mere humans."

He looks pained. "Excuse me, but such is not the case. Those who provide their blood are highly valued, treated well and paid most handsomely. They are not victims."

"No," I say coldly. "They're whores. But at least they get a nice paycheck, right?"

"They—"

I cut off his reply. "Save it. If human blood is that valuable, there's no way a waitress could afford it. She was probably dealing—you said she worked in a blood bar, right? I'm guessing she offered the right customers something that wasn't on the regular menu."

I turn back to Eisfanger. "Can you pull any kind of details from these echoes? We need to find these bloodleggers and question them."

"Sorry," Eisfanger says. "They're not intelligent, just single-emotion patterns. All they project is what their source was feeling at the time of the transfer."

"I see. Cold, emptiness, life draining away—does that sound like the people were treated well, Mr. Tanaka?"

He bows his head. "No. No, it does not. I will do my best to locate them."

"No," I say. "*We* will do our best. Eisfanger, I want you to go over every square inch of this place. Then we're going back to the train, and we're going to review all the physical evidence."

"I've already looked at that, on the way up—"

"Then you'll look at it again, with me peering over your shoulder. Tanaka, I want everything you have on the blood trade and who controls it locally."

"Of course," Tanaka says. His voice is soft, but I can *feel* the growl hidden inside it. Figures. Wolves or local law enforcement, they all react pretty much the same to newcomers in their territory. And I just peed all over Tanaka's. . . .

"Nothing of note? *Nothing* of *note*?" I'm not quite yelling, but I'm getting warmed up.

"That is not what I said." Tanaka still appears calm, but he's not; I can feel his temper rising.

We're back on the train. Charlie, Tanaka, and I are in the same car, Eisfanger's back in the lab going over the original report. I intend to join him—but first I'm going to find out why Tanaka withheld evidence from me.

"What I told you," Tanaka says, "is we found *little* of note. I was about to inform your animist of our own findings, but he began the ritual without any warning—"

"Oh, so it's *his* fault? He was just doing his job, Tanaka."

"As am I."

"Of course. Tell me, how many of your superiors like to indulge in a little human hemoglobin now and then? Hmm? A nicely aged '45 from California, maybe—or do they prefer a more exotic vintage? A perky, blue-eyed blonde from somewhere Nordic, or an earthy, robust Australian—"

"I don't care for your tone."

"Too bad. There's no mention of Miyagi being a feeder in your files, and there's only one reason for that I can think of. Someone told you to hold back that information, and you wagged your tail like a good little doggy—"

It happens so fast I almost fall over backward. One second Tanaka and I are arguing toe-to-toe, and the next—well, his toes are suddenly a lot hairier. He goes from simmering five-foot-eight Japanese man to furious six-foot werewolf in the blink of an eye. It stops me in mid-rant.

But only for a moment.

I have to look up to meet his eyes—now a blazing yellow—but I refuse to take a step backward. "—and buried it like, like a goddamn *bone* you didn't want me to find! Well, I *did* find it, it's *mine* now, and you can go *piss up a goddamn rope*!"

Okay, I admit it—I sort of lose control. Not as bad as the time I broke an associate's jaw, but I'm definitely seeing the world in shades of red. Considering what I've been through in the last twenty-four hours, I'm surprised it didn't happen sooner . . . but it's still a big mistake.

I'm about to discover just how big.

I should have known better. After all, I've dealt with homicidal animals before—I'm just not used to them being on the same side of the law that I am.

Tanaka's got me by the throat and off the ground in one smooth motion. I have my gun out and jammed under his own chin a heartbeat later.

"Let me go or I'll blow your brains all over the ceiling," I manage to get out through clenched teeth. He ignores me, of course.

Damn. I hope thropes really do heal as quickly as Dr. Pete claims—

"Hold it."

Something whizzes between us and shatters a train window. Tanaka yelps and puts his free hand up to his long, pointed ear—the object must have clipped him on the way past. Charlie Aleph has one arm cocked behind him like a pitcher about to let loose; he's holding something shiny, round, and a little smaller than a golf ball between his thumb and two fingers, rolling it lazily back and forth.

"Next one goes between your eyes," he says. "Drop her or I drop you."

Tanaka's rage is like molten metal flowing down his arm, through my throat and into the base of my brain. The wind howls through the broken window like a crazed beast. If he doesn't let go in the next second I'm going to empty the clip into his skull.

He lets go. I hit the ground on rubbery legs and topple over backward, springing up again instantly. Tanaka has backed away, already changing back, though much slower. His immaculate black business suit has ripped at the shoulder seams, and several buttons have popped off his shirt.

"I apologize," he says as soon as his mouth can form words again. He has to speak loudly to be heard over the rushing air. "I am not used to being challenged by . . . one such as you."

"You mean a woman?" I say, trying to get my breath back.

"No. A human."

"Get used to it," Charlie says. He's lowered his arm, but he's still playing with the oversize ball bearing.

"If you will excuse me?" Tanaka mutters, his head bowed. His body is trembling. "I would like to . . . reorganize."

"Go ahead," I say. "Don't forget to comb your hair."

He retreats to the door at the far end of the car, his gait shaky, and goes through it. I nod at Charlie and say, "Thanks, but I had the situation under control."

"Yeah? Thropes and pires tend to forget how easy humans die—they usually slash first and make up later. Figured you'd rather have your head than the apology, but hey—you're the boss." He pushes back the sleeve on his right arm, revealing a leather tube strapped to his forearm. He pushes the ball bearing into the end of the tube, which is obviously spring-loaded.

"You really are a gun," I say. "How many shots does that thing hold?"

"Twelve per side."

"Per side? So you're double-barreled, too."

"Pardon me?"

"Never mind. Solid silver?"

"Nah, too expensive. Silver sheath over an iron core."

"How much stopping power?"

He pulls the sleeve back down, smooths the fabric carefully. "If I want something to stop," he says, "it stops."

"Can't dispute that. Looked like you really shook him up, too."

"Doubt that was my fault. Changing that quick takes a lot out of a thrope; I've seen some keel right over."

Like adrenaline shakes in a human, but probably worse. "All right," I say grudgingly. "Good job, I guess. But next time, wait until I *ask* for your help, okay?"

"It's your funeral."

Charlie drops into a nearby seat, tilts his fedora over his eyes, and reverts to being an inanimate object. I sit down myself, thinking about what just happened and how it's probably going to make my job harder.

But that's not all I'm thinking about. During the confrontation, on some level I knew Tanaka wasn't going to hurt me—because what I felt beneath his rage was something else entirely. Something just as dangerous, and just as intense.

Something just as passionate . . .

"Please," Tanaka says. He's changed his clothes—into a suit that looks exactly the same—and seems much more composed. We're talking on the upper deck of the train's observation car, a streamlined Plexiglas dome that would let me appreciate the beauty of the landscape we're speeding through if it weren't heavily smoked and night hadn't fallen. All I see is my own reflection and the impression of darkness streaming past.

"You've already apologized," I say. "Forget about it."

"You deserve an explanation."

"You're right, I do. Got one?"

"As I told you, my government finds the subject of the camps distasteful. The practice of *ketsueki gouin*—blood drinking—is an equally sensitive topic. I do not wish to impede your investigation; I was simply trying to spare my employers further embarrassment."

"Sure. Because if our guy follows his pattern, this next killing is going to be on the Internet pretty soon, and Japan isn't exactly Stone Age when it comes to technology. You know, I'm starting to think this is exactly what the killer wants."

"What do you mean?"

"Let's just say that there are political considerations in at least one of the other killings. I think this guy wants more than just attention—he wants *outrage*. Not sure how the Australian vic fits in yet, but I'll bet the location turns out to be more important than the victim. He's using the murders to focus public awareness on something he thinks is important."

"The plight of his race, perhaps."

I glare at him. "You think? I mean, 'his race' is only on the verge of extinction. 'His race' is basically used as either raw material or gourmet meals for yours."

"We are not solely to blame."

"No, the bloodsuckers are just as guilty. Lucky for you, our boy believes in spreading the blame around. And in case you've forgotten, Tanaka, 'his race' is also 'my race.' "

"I have offended you again." The regret and shame in his voice is real.

I sigh. "No, that's okay. Look, this is difficult for both of us. I know what it's like to have the brass leaning on you. But we both have the same objective in mind—to catch this guy, and stop the killing. Right?"

"Yes." He pauses. "I will do my best to provide you with uncensored information. Will you trust me on this?"

I want to ask him if I have a choice—but instead I say, "Yes. But withhold something from me again and I'll show you just how dangerous a 'human being' can be."

"I understand."

All things considered, he takes his reaming-out with good grace, which gives him high marks in my book; in my experience, men have a hard time apologizing, let alone admitting they were wrong—or maybe that's just the ones I work with. Or sleep with.

Or both. Which is a very small group under the heading "Roger" and the subheading "Complete and Total Bastard." There are additional sub-subheadings, but they're not worth repeating unless I'm about to shoot something.

Roger. As in "affirmative," if what you're affirming is that you can give someone your heart and he can throw it in a wood-chipper while you watch. As in "the Jolly Roger," the skull on the pirate flag with the big white grin, almost as big as the one on my ex's face when he dumped me and stole my promotion. As in to give someone a good Rogering, as the British say—which he did to me, in more ways than one.

The memory of his body that suddenly surges into my mind is just as sharp as that of his betrayal. His skin, his smell, his taste . . . I shake my head and try to focus on what Tanaka's saying.

"—the blood bar she was employed by. I will make enquiries, and determine which *shateigashira* is responsible for the blood trade in her area."

"I'm sorry? I don't know that word."

"It refers to the leader of a criminal gang—or, more precisely, to a level of management in a much larger organization."

"Which organization?" I ask, though I'm pretty sure I know the answer.

"The illegal blood trade is very profitable, and counts high-ranking officials among its participants. In Japan, there is only one organization that dares to involve itself in such matters."

I'm really hoping the answer has something to do with the Sailor Moon Fan Club. No such luck.

"The Yakuza," Tanaka says.

The Sapporo station is as busy and crowded as the mountains were empty, Asian men and women dressed mostly in black. They hurry from one platform to the next, clutching briefcases and newspapers and *manga*, talking on cell phones or sipping from large paper cups with red plastic lids. I wonder what's in them—the cups, not the commuters.

I guess it doesn't matter. One will be in the other, soon enough.

Tanaka hustles Charlie and me out through the crowd and into another taxi, while Eisfanger stays with the train. If what Charlie told me is accurate, then almost all the people around me are pires, as indestructible and immortal as Cassius. I look for signs of ageless wisdom or invincibility in the faces around me, but all I see is a kind of cold, ruthless efficiency; no one seems to have a cold, or be half-asleep, or look drunk. It doesn't mean anything, of course. It's only a rushed first impression, a bunch of strangers on their way to work, seen through a foreigner's eyes. I might get exactly the same feeling in the same train station on my own world.

Just not at one in the morning.

Sapporo itself is full of neon and skyscrapers, the streets crowded with tiny vehicles with smoked-glass windshields that make it impossible to see into them. From the inside looking out, the glass makes the neon a little dimmer, the shadows a little deeper; it doesn't seem to bother our driver, though. I guess supernatural beings have more acute senses. It's just one more reminder that this world isn't designed for my kind.

I wonder what's happening, back in my own universe. Is there a massive manhunt going on for a missing FBI agent? Is CNN providing hourly updates? Or has Cassius pulled something devious, leaving behind a dead doppelgänger or using magic to cover up my disappearance? That train of thought leads to other stations, including the idea that maybe he just had me completely erased from my own reality. It wouldn't take much, really; I don't have a lot in the way of family or friends. Both my parents are dead, I've been engaged to be married once (*wish* he were dead) and spent most of my time at work alienating my co-workers (who would probably cheer if they thought I *was* dead). Tanya, my one good friend, would definitely miss me—but she'd get over it. Tanya's a social butterfly, and while she's sweet, her memories are short. Give her a year and she'll have a new best friend.

I make an effort and focus on what Tanaka's saying. He's set up a meeting with the local *oyabun*, the head of the Yakuza family that runs things in the city. He tells me this is considerably higher up the chain of command than he expected to deal with, and warns me to be careful.

"Don't worry," I say. "I'll be extremely polite. And you'll let me know if I make any serious blunders, right?"

"If such a thing happens," he says, "you will not need me to tell you."

"Terrific."

He's nervous, and it's not just my inexperience with

proper protocol that's bothering him. "You're not happy with that arrangement. Tell me why."

"It is most unusual for an *oyabun* to deal directly with those of lower rank—especially a human. It is . . . troubling."

"I'll be fine. Human or not, I represent the NSA, and by extension the U.S. government. The fact that the local boss wants to see me is a good sign—either he wants something or he has something to trade. Either one could be useful."

He nods in assent, but he's still worried.

The cab takes us to a neighborhood I recognize, even though I've never been there before and can't even read the street signs. I don't have to; the groups of young, tough-looking guys hanging around doorways, the run-down look of the many bars that line the street, the overall feel tells me where I am. This is the rough part of town, where the more respectable citizens come to buy whatever they can't get legally.

"Stay close," Charlie says as we get out of the cab.

"Don't fastball anyone unless I say so, okay? We're here for information, not confrontation."

"I'll keep that in mind when you're down a quart."

Tanaka accompanies us inside. The place is long and narrow, with a dark oak bar stretching down one side and booths separated by rice-paper screens along the wall. It's dimly lit by red paper lanterns overhead and candles on the tables. A bald, obese man with thick, rubbery lips is tending bar, his white apron splotched with vivid crimson stains. Aside from him, the place is empty. We sit down in one of the booths.

"Is this where Miyagi worked?" I ask.

"No. This is merely a workingman's bar. They mostly serve animal blood mixed with warm sake."

"Yeah? Wouldn't that clot?"

"It is diluted with anti-coagulants."

"How about the booze? Technically, alcohol is a poison—it shouldn't affect pires, right?"

"Magic is used to fuse the life essence of the blood with the alcohol—it allows for an intoxicating effect."

Hmm. So a vampire *can* be drugged—I'll bet that's how

the killer subdued his vic at McMurdo Station and maybe Keiko Miyagi, too. "Tanaka, did your people do a toxin screen on Miyagi's remains?"

"There was no point. They had decomposed to little more than an inert liquid."

"Yeah, but the bloodstain on the floor *hadn't*—it was generated by her injuries *before* she expired. Get Eisfanger to run some tests on the samples he took, okay? I'm looking for a strong sedative or hypnotic." Telling Tanaka that makes me feel better; when it comes to old-fashioned forensics, at least I know the rules.

"I shall do so."

The bartender comes over to our table. He's got a thick roll of fat around the base of his skull, like his neck used to be three feet long until someone sledgehammered his head down to its current height. His eyes are puffy, suspicious slits. He grunts a few words in Japanese and jerks a thumb like a sausage toward the back.

I nod and we all get up. Behind a curtain at the end of the bar there's a narrow hallway with a bathroom to one side. At the end of the hall, a dented metal fire door is propped open. I let Charlie go through first.

There's a long, black limo parked outside in the alley. A gull-wing door hums opens like a mechanical mouth, an invitation to be devoured. We accept.

The interior of the limo is empty, a smoked-glass partition separating us from the driver. The door closes itself with a soft *chunk* and the limo glides down the alley as smoothly and quietly as a shark.

I take a deep breath and let it out. "Okay. Here we go. . . ."

The car drives for at least an hour. I don't know the city at all, but that doesn't matter; we get on some kind of freeway and head for what I assume are the ritzier suburbs. By the time we get there, we're practically back in the Hidakas, or the foothills at least. The limo turns off the freeway and onto a private road, which winds through woods and up to a tall chain-link security gate. We pause there while the driver identifies himself, then roll through when the gate slides open.

The driveway is almost as long as the road leading to the estate, and ends at an honest-to-God castle: tall, white stone walls with guardhouses atop each corner, and a huge, red-lacquered gate that currently stands open. We drive inside and park in the courtyard, in front of a five-story pagoda-roofed tower. L-shaped wings connect to the tower at either side, enclosing the courtyard in a deep U with the tower at the bottom.

I can't see any guards. That worries me.

The limo door swings up and we get out. It occurs to me, somewhat belatedly, that I don't speak Japanese. I hope I can count on Tanaka to translate; I really don't want to negotiate with a Yakuza boss through charades. I try to imagine what that would look like and almost burst out laughing—I have a bad habit of thinking wildly inappropriate things when I'm nervous.

The driver stays where he is, invisible and anonymous. The limo door swings shut at almost the exact second the front door to the tower opens, giving me the eerie sensation that I'm on some kind of automated ride. *Enjoy the Fabulous Yakuza Blood Flume—you will have happy much good time! No refunds!*

Shut up, brain.

To my surprise, it's a woman who comes out to greet us. She's dressed in a loose silk robe of brilliant blue, her glossy black hair in a ponytail and her feet bare. She smiles and says in perfect English, "Welcome. This way, please."

She turns and goes back inside. We follow.

The interior is minimalist, sparse without being stark. The floor is darkly varnished wood, the walls white and un-adorned. Two terra-cotta statues of warriors stand on either side of a polished wooden staircase that leads upward, but the woman doesn't take it; instead, she goes to the left and through another door.

Long corridor, doors on either side. No windows. One piece of art, a bronze sculpture of a man in full samurai armor, his sword held in striking position, the blade level with his eyes.

Large door at the end of the hall, looks like teak. The woman pushes it open without knocking, motions us inside. She stays in the hall, closes the door behind us so gently it makes no noise at all.

It's a study. Leather-bound volumes line bookshelves, a large globe in one corner, heavy drapes closed behind an enormous desk. The chair behind it is empty, the surface of the desk bare. Flames crackle in an enormous fireplace that dominates one side of the room, silhouetting the man who crouches there, adjusting a log with an iron poker. He finishes what he's doing, then straightens up and turns to face us.

He's a slight man, a little over five feet tall, balding, his remaining hair worn long and loose. He's dressed in a black silk kimono with a scarlet dragon on the back, and brown leather slippers.

Tanaka bows from the waist. The other man doesn't respond, which I figure is a calculated insult. Tanaka begins to say something in Japanese, which the man cuts off with a wave of his hand.

"You do not belong here," he says, looking straight at me. He sounds more regretful than annoyed.

"I was invited," I say.

"To this house, yes. To this world, no."

"That's my problem. Yours is entirely different, and considerably more urgent."

"Oh?" His voice is mild. If I had to guess, I'd say he learned his English at Oxford.

"Yes. The U.S. is investigating a string of international killings. The latest victim worked for you. I need to know why she was killed."

"How is that my concern?" He holds the poker as if it were a walking stick, both hands clasped on the end of the handle, the tip resting on the floor.

"Because I'm not from here and I don't care how many people I upset to get to the answers I require. That could cause you a great deal of unpleasantness."

"I see. And if you were to learn the facts behind the demise of this presumed employee, you would simply go away."

"I might."

"I doubt that." He smiles. "However, I'm being rude. My name is Isamu." Isamu bows his head, ever so slightly. "And you are Jace Valchek, are you not?"

He says something in Japanese to Tanaka, then laughs. I let it pass. Isamu ignores Charlie completely, which somehow irritates me more.

"Yeah. So how about helping us out, Isamu? After all, it was one of your own that got killed."

"She was a person of no consequence. Were this a family matter, I would deal with it myself; but as the persons responsible are outsiders, I am willing to let outsiders eliminate the problem."

Persons? "Thank you," I say cautiously. "What information can you give us?"

His answer surprises me. "I can tell you who killed her—and why."

"And in return?"

"We will discuss that later."

Tanaka switches to English and interjects, "We will not enter into such an ill-defined agreement—"

It's my turn to cut Tanaka off with a gesture. I agree with him, but I want to hear what Isamu has to say. "I'm listening."

He turns back to the fire and places the poker back in its stand. "The blood trade is very important to my people, not just for reasons of profit and influence—though it generates both—but for reasons of tradition. The *sakazuki* ritual is how members of a clan declared loyalty to their leader; in times past, the *oyabun* symbolically shared his blood by sipping from a cup of sake and then passing the cup to his second-in-command."

His chuckle is a small, dry rasp. "Once we became *kyuuketsuki*, that ritual changed. Now, we drink human blood mixed with sake. The vintage and quality of the blood is important, as a sign of both respect and status. They say that humans will never become extinct in Japan, because then the *gokudou* will have nothing to drink."

He pauses, as if waiting for me to comment. I don't. After a moment, he continues.

"Human blood commands a very high price in Japan. Fresh is always best, of course, so the local supply is much coveted. Clans guard their sources jealously, perhaps even with a bit too much zeal."

"You keep them prisoner."

He shrugs. "A valuable commodity must be protected, sometimes from itself. To produce a fine wine you must tend the soil, nurture the grapes, choose the correct time for the harvest. Sometimes you must add things to the equation; other times, you must subtract."

"You take away their freedom and their blood. What's left?"

He meets my eyes and smiles. I realize that, unlike Tanaka, I can't read him at all . . . and then I start to understand what he's talking about.

There are all kinds of things a human dairy cow doesn't really need. Eyes. Ears. Hands . . .

A quick glance at Tanaka's face is all the confirmation I need. The horror in my eyes produces only a satisfied nod from Isamu. "Efficiency is something of an obsession with my countrymen. How to generate the highest-quality product at the highest volume? There was much experimentation in diet and exercise regimens. To an outsider these experiments might seem cruel, but they were being done in the interest of the greater good."

His smiles vanishes. "*We* are the greater good now, Miss Valchek," he says. "*You* are merely the remnants of a failed species."

"You're telling me the killer was one of your . . . *donors*."

He chuckles again. If he does it one more time I may push him into his own damn fireplace. "Ah, if only! No, I'm afraid he has never been within our grasp. He is a member of a terrorist group known as the Free Human Resistance; we acquired an entire cell of them, without knowing what they were. He alone escaped, and somehow managed to later locate his comrades. By that point, though, they had already been . . . *modified*."

"I'm guessing he didn't take that well."

"No. He slaughtered fifteen of my men and then executed every one of his former colleagues. I'm sure he thought of it as a mercy."

"I can't imagine why. His name?"

"His true identity is hidden. He is known in the human underground as the Impaler."

"Catchy. Let's see if I understand this, Isamu. You want me to catch some local maniac who's robbed you of your own personal blood bank, because you haven't been able to catch him yourself. That about right?"

"He is the same man who killed Keiko Miyagi."

"Maybe. You said '*persons* responsible' earlier. Who else is involved? Any chance they might also belong to this Free Human Resistance?"

He frowns; he probably isn't used to anyone talking to him like this. "It is very likely, yes."

"Sure. Except I doubt the guy I'm chasing is a local, and he seems to hate thropes just as much as pires. If he *is* this Impaler, I don't think—"

"He is working with a shape-shifter."

That stops me. Isamu is no doubt very well connected, but I doubt if he's seen the case file from the McMurdo killing.

"Also," he continues, "I did not say he was local. The FHR is international in scope."

"It's true," Tanaka says, not meeting my eyes. "But in Japan their activities are modest. Nothing high profile, not like this."

"Maybe they've decided to get a little more proactive," I say. "Most serial killers commit their first murder after an inciting event—often some kind of trauma or loss. You think putting a group of maimed brothers-in-arms out of their misery qualifies, Isamu?"

"I think," he says quietly, "that I have had enough of your insolence."

"You sure? 'Cause I've got plenty to spare."

"I do not think that you do." His voice is colder now, no pretense of being polite. "You come into my home, asking for assistance, and repay me with disrespect. I am your superior in position, in age, in species, and in gender. Your grandfather's grandfather was soiling his diapers when I was feasting on my hundredth virgin, and I am a thousand times more powerful now than then. *You have no idea who you face.*"

His eyes have gone bloodred. I really hope Charlie's faster than this guy.

"I have never tasted animal blood," he hisses. "And for every life I have taken, I have mixed their blood with ink and recorded it on my body."

He drops the silk robe around his feet. I know about the Yakuza tradition of full-body tattoos, but the pictures I've seen have always been intricate and colorful: tigers and dragons and demons, from mid-calf to neckline to elbow.

Isamu's are different.

They extend over the same regions, but that's where the similarity ends. The ink is black, the lines delicate, and they portray only one thing over and over.

Faces.

Men, women, children, each one wearing an expression of horror, pain, or fear, a tapestry of suffering captured in flesh. The tattoos are staggered by size, smaller faces in front of larger ones and smaller ones in front of those, and somehow I know that these are actual layers added over the years, not a single design. The layering gives the faces depth, and the one feature that is never obscured is their eyes: their eyes, screaming and pleading and weeping. It's like the whirlwind I saw at the crime scene, magnified a hundred times and frozen in place.

"I know exactly who I'm facing," I say. "That's kind of what I do. And you don't impress me any more than the other monsters I've put away."

"I'm not the one you should be worried about. Didn't you wonder about the absence of guards?"

Oh, crap.

"Ryuu was born—by the Western calendar—in the year 1508. He studied the art of *ninjutsu* from the time he was fifteen until his thirty-first year, when he joined the ranks of the *kyuuketsuki* and ceased to age. He continued to practice his craft, first for any *daimyo* who would pay him, then exclusively for us. He has spent five centuries perfecting his skills. Do you really think your two-legged beast or your man of sand can protect you?"

A five-hundred-year-old ninja. Don't know why I didn't see that one coming. "That sounds like a threat."

"I have changed my mind. You are far too impulsive and ignorant to accomplish anything; your best use is as partial compensation for the loss of my stock. I can only hope your blood is sweeter than your tongue."

I glance back at Charlie. He doesn't look worried.

"Bring it on," I say. "Ring your ninja-summoning gong or whatever the hell it is you do."

Tanaka takes a step forward, holding his hands out imploringly. "Please. There is no need for this to become adversarial—"

"There is no need to summon him," Isamu says. "Ryuu has been here all along. . . ."

My gun is out and pointed at Isamu's head before he can finish his sentence. He stares at me more or less the same way I'd stare at someone brandishing a trout.

I glance at Charlie. He's got one hand inside his jacket, like he's going for a gun himself. There's a man dressed all in black standing behind him, holding a three-foot-long sword in exactly the same pose as the samurai statue in the hall.

I'll never forget the sound it makes when it slices into the back of Charlie's neck.

FIVE

You know the sound a golf club makes when it hits sand? That kind of dry, chuffing noise as metal strikes silicon and then sprays everywhere? That's what I'm expecting—but that's not what I hear. Instead, there's a muffled *thwang*, and the *katana* stops dead no more than an inch into the back of Charlie's neck.

Charlie spins, pulling something from inside his jacket at the same time. The *katana*, firmly embedded, is yanked out of Ryuu's hands—leaving him nothing to counter the eighteen-inch blade Charlie's now swinging in a tight backhand arc toward the ninja's own neck.

Poor Ryuu. I mean, I can only see his eyes, but in the second before his head topples to the floor and explodes into dust, he sure looks surprised. Guess a five-century-old ninja doesn't really expect to be outstrategized by a walking bag of sand—even one in a pin-striped suit.

I've got the drop on Isamu, but of course that doesn't mean anything to a target who isn't afraid of guns. He leaps straight at me, probably intending to rip my arms off and beat me to death with them, and I shoot him many times. Many, *many* times. He refuses to explode in a disgusting display of gore and instead is merely propelled backward to his starting point. This produces a look of intense irritation on his face, which just doesn't work for me. I was hoping for something a little more satisfying—fear, horror, maybe the dawning realization that he is well and truly hooped.

Oh, well. You take what you can get.

Something large and hairy launches itself through the air past me, heading for Isamu, and I realize Tanaka has stepped up to the plate. He lands on the *oyabun* in a snarling tangle of claws and fangs, and then comes flying past me an instant later going the other way. Isamu's not just irritated, he's a lot stronger than he looks.

But now he's facing an angry thrope, a grim golem, and an extremely pissed-off Federal agent. One who's busy reloading her .454-caliber irritant, granted, but still. Which is when he obviously realizes now is the time for plan B and dives under his desk. Maybe that should be plan C, for "cower."

But then the desk starts to sink into the floor, and I realize it's B after all—B for "basement" and "buh-bye." The old elevator disguised as a desk trick, of course.

White vapor starts spraying from overhead vents. Charlie doesn't hesitate—he scoops me up with one arm, hits the top of the sinking desk running, and vaults straight at the heavy drapes on the other side. I have time to hope Isamu doesn't believe in shutters, and then I'm being smothered by musty velvet while glass smashes all around me. Charlie lands on his back and I land on him, which knocks the breath out of me but is vastly preferable to the other way around.

I quickly untangle myself. A white mist curls out of the shattered window behind us—I don't know what's in it, but it can't be healthy. Charlie stands up, the sword still embedded in the back of his neck, and yanks it free by the handle. It makes a sound like a rusty nail pulling out of an old board.

"You all right?" I say. Tiny grains of black sand are spilling out of the tear in his plastic skin.

"Yeah. Lemme see about getting us a ride outta here." He looks around. "Where's Tanaka?"

The sound of more smashing glass answers us. Tanaka's over by the limo, dragging the chauffeur out the window by his hair. The driver's putting up a struggle, but stops when Charlie strides over and lays the blade of the *katana* against his throat.

"Tell him he's driving us back to town," Charlie growls.

Tanaka raises two wolfy eyebrows in a question, and Charlie frowns. "Oh, right. Well then, just put him back in the driver's seat and keep this handy. He'll get the idea."

Charlie hands Tanaka the *katana*, still holding his own weapon in his other hand. I get my first good look at it as he slides it back into its sheath in the lining of his jacket; it's a *gladius*, a Roman short sword.

"Hail, Caesar," I say as we get into the backseat of the limo and Tanaka and the chauffeur get in the front. "You got Colosseum sand in your family, Charlie?"

He's got one hand clamped on the back of his neck now, but I don't know if it's because he's in pain or is just trying to keep from leaking. "Standard Enforcement golem issue, rookie. What, you think all I'm good for is standing back and throwing silver? A pitching arm ain't much good in a toe-to-toe brawl."

The limo starts up and we roar away. From the acceleration, I'd guess Tanaka's providing the driver with plenty of incentive. "How about your indestructible neck? That standard issue, too?"

"Nah. I stick a piece of rebar in there if I think a situation might go sideways. Makes it a little hard to move my head up or down, but at least it stays attached. Had a guy break a meat cleaver in half on it once."

"How do you—I mean, do you have a zipper back there or something?"

"Something like that. I'd show you, but I'm trying not to hourglass all over the seat."

"What happens if—"

"I die. Lose too much of my internal body mass and the spell that brought me to life pops like a soap bubble. It might be black and grainy, but it's still my blood."

That stops me for a second. I'd only known Charlie for a day, but I'd already started thinking of him as indestructible. "You'll be okay, though, right?"

"Sure. Just take me to the nearest beach for a quick transfusion."

Asshole. "How about we work on stopping the bleeding first?"

He digs something out of his breast pocket with one hand and hands it to me. "You mind? I can't really see what I'm doing."

I stare at the gray spool in my hand. "This is duct tape."

"Yeah. Unfortunately, we don't have any ducks with sword wounds back here."

I've got a partner who fixes himself with duct tape. More accurately, I've got a partner who needs *me* to fix him with duct tape. I sigh and peel off a strip. "Lean over, Daffy. You want one layer, or two?"

I half-expect us to be attacked on the way back to Sapporo by armored hearses full of vampire commandos, but I make it without incident. I get Charlie patched up, and he tells me the gas Isamu released was probably a nerve agent laced with silver—deadly to thropes and humans, debilitating to pires. "Might have even done me some damage," Charlie says. "Depends on what kind of voodoo it was mixed up with. Lems don't breathe, but there are some nasty spells out there. Mess with your mojo, you know?"

We let the driver go a block away from the train station and he doesn't even waste our time with the obligatory death threats before leaving in a squeal of tires. We walk back to the train and get on board. Tanaka wants to tell the engineer to take us to Tokyo; he obviously thinks it's a good idea to keep moving, an idea it's hard to argue with.

I do anyway.

"Look," I tell Tanaka. We're standing in virtually the same spot the last time we argued, and he's reverted to nonwolf form. "If we run, we're actually more vulnerable. At the station we can get local enforcement to back us up in case Isamu tries some kind of frontal assault. But train tracks are just too easy to sabotage."

"Which is why we should leave quickly. He will require time to prepare; despite his anger, he will not act rashly. I promise you, once we are out of his immediate sphere of influence, he will wait and plan. If we stay, he will see it as a further affront and will attack simply to save face. Leaving is our wisest option."

I glare at him. If there's one thing I hate, it's backing down to a bad guy. Every cop instinct I have says you never, ever let them think they have the upper hand: it's not pride, it's a matter of leverage.

But sometimes you have to pick your battles. And standing this close to Tanaka, I can *feel* the conflicted anger coming off him—he wants to stay and fight just as bad as I do, maybe even more so because this is his country and his culture. Hell, it's his biology.

And despite all that, his own experience is telling him we should run.

I let out a long, frustrated sigh. "Okay. You're the expert in this situation, I'm going to listen. We go."

He leaves the car to tell the engineer, and I throw myself down in a seat. It's where Charlie finds me a few moments later, staring out the window.

"Where we off to now?" he asks, sitting down beside me.

"Tokyo, apparently. Tanaka says leaving Isamu's territory is our smartest move."

"And you decided to do it anyway?"

"How's that hole in your head? You need another one?"

"I'm fine, thanks. I always carry some replacement soil with me, so I'm all topped up."

"Yeah? You have some kind of valve under that fedora, or do you stick a funnel in your heel and stand on your head?"

"Something like that. What's the plan once we hit Tokyo?"

I get up, rummage in a cupboard until I find the bottle of sake I noticed earlier. "Well, I'm planning on nursing a hangover. Any pire biting me between here and there better be able to hold his liquor. You want some?"

"I don't drink. Anything, I mean. Or eat, for that matter."

"Yeah, you're perfection on two legs. Too bad you have to hang around and put your plastic neck on the line for a mere human, huh?" My voice is a little more angry than I intend.

"Without my neck you'd be dead right now." His own voice is flat and uninflected. The fact that he's absolutely right makes me want to smash the bottle over his head.

"Yeah? Well, if you were in my world, you'd be a big plastic bag full of nine-millimeter holes by now, and Mr. Pointy-face would be showing off his tattoos to the rest of the losers in genpop." The logic there didn't exactly parse, but I never let sense get in the way of a good rant. "I took care of myself just *fine* in the FBI, and I don't need an oversize Glad bag stuffed with *dirt* to pull my ass out of the fire here, *got it*?" By the end of the sentence I'm yelling.

"Got it," is all he says.

I didn't know it was so hard to slam a door on a train. Maybe it's just the Japanese ones.

Okay, so drinking in the middle of a case isn't exactly smart. In my defense, I was frustrated, stressed, stranded in a parallel universe, and suffering from RDT. I was also extremely pissed off that Charlie had saved my life; irrational and ungrateful, I know, but I had spent my whole career proving I could take care of myself and now I had to start all over again. A little alcohol therapy is a time-honored tradition in my profession, and I'm not going to climb into the bottle, anyway—I've got too much work to do. I just plan on knocking back a few while I'm doing it.

One of the cars is a sort of lounge area, with a kitchenette and a row of small tables alongside a long couch. I locate a corkscrew, a glass, and my laptop and settle in. I'm deep into the files on the Free Human Resistance and halfway through my second drink when Tanaka enters the car.

"I have alerted my superiors to Isamu's actions," he says. "He will shortly be too busy to entertain any immediate thoughts of retribution."

"Too bad. I was really looking forward to a raid on the train by vampire ninjas in hang gliders."

"It is a much more serious issue than perhaps you understand. You have destroyed a valuable asset of—"

"Look, I get it, okay? A guy that survives for five hundred years in his business is a serious badass, and we just took out what I hope to *God* was his top enforcer. He's well-connected, he's smart, and he can afford to be patient when it comes to revenge—about all I have going for me is the fact that I plan to be in another universe before he gets around to paying me back."

"Ah. My apologies. I feel responsible for negotiations going as badly as they did."

"Don't. We gained some valuable information—we'll worry about the price later. I initially thought he was just trying to get us to take care of a problem for him, but that detail about the shape-shifter makes me think he was telling the truth." I lift the bottle of sake and wiggle it at Tanaka. "Want some?"

He hesitates, then says, "Yes, thank you." He gets up and finds a small ceramic cup for himself, and I fill it. He knocks it back more like a shot of whisky than wine, and I fill it up again. He nods in thanks, and for just a second I don't feel like a stranger in a strange land, surrounded by monsters; I'm just a cop, sharing a drink and a tough case with another cop.

"The information about the FHR is interesting," Tanaka says. "We had not foreseen their involvement."

"What can you tell me about them? You have any personal experience?"

"A little. They are a political group dedicated to securing the rights and safety of human beings. The organization is global in scope, but chapters vary widely in their methods. In Japan, they take mainly a political stance—in other places, they commit acts of destruction or personal attacks. Even murder."

I'd already gotten that from the files. "Yeah, but have you had any dealings with them yourself?"

He drinks some sake before answering. "Only once. They

staged a demonstration in front of the Chinese consulate in
Tokyo to protest their immigration policies—humans are not
permitted to leave the country. The group was not large, perhaps forty people. The ones I dealt with were vocal but neither irrational nor violent. They dispersed peacefully when
instructed to do so."

Like good little blood banks I wanted to say, but didn't.
Bad enough I'd taken out my frustration on Charlie; I didn't
want to add another future apology to my list. "I take it this
Impaler wasn't among them."

"If he was, I was unaware of his presence. The Impaler is
something of a legend; some say he does not exist at all,
that he is merely propaganda created by the FHR, a symbol
of human resistance."

"An underground hero? That might explain the lack of
information on him in this file. It practically calls him an urban myth. Says 'no firm evidence of his existence has been
produced, though several unsolved killings in widely dis-
tributed locations have been attributed to him.'"

Tanaka shakes his head. "And yet he never publicly
claims credit for his victims—odd behavior for one who is
supposedly a symbol."

"Maybe he was waiting for a bigger audience."

"Such as the one he commands now? Then why has he
still not identified himself?"

I frown and pour myself another drink. "Yeah, it's
strange. You think he'd be shouting it from the rooftops, letting everyone know he's striking a blow for humankind."

"Perhaps he's waiting for something else."

We kick some ideas around for a while, but there isn't
much more to say. Eventually I notice I haven't had any
Urthbone tea in a while, and I pull out my flask. That leads to
a discussion of what it is and why I'm taking it, and then to
Japanese tea and its many merits and history.

Then more sake.

The constant, almost subliminal movement of the train
has become a soothing, rhythmic backbeat to the buzz in my
head, and the more I relax into my surroundings the more

aware I become of Tanaka. The effects of Urthbone, it seems, are heightened by alcohol, a fact Dr. Pete neglected to mention. And the more aware I become of Tanaka, the more aware I become of just how aware he is of me. I wonder out loud just how sensitive his sense of smell actually is, and just what it can tell him.

He lets me know.

A rice wine and Urthbone hangover is not an experience I would recommend to anyone. But then, neither is waking up next to someone you don't really remember going to bed with.

And yeah, there he is right next to me. A naked and thankfully nonhairy Tanaka, snoring away on the narrow futon we're both wedged into, in a small compartment with a single bed and a shuttered window. We're still on the train, but something's different.

We're no longer moving. Which means we're either in Tokyo or under attack, and either way I really can't be caught in bed with—

Oh my God. I slept with a werewolf.

I don't know if it's shame, some primal anti-bestiality instinct or just last night's overindulgence, but I leap out of bed and bolt for the bathroom, a tiny cubicle I dimly recall using last night. Which brings back a few other memories, and then I'm getting rid of the sushi I had for a late-night snack.

By the time I'm finished, Tanaka is up and miraculously dressed. He asks if I'm all right and I mumble something in the affirmative. He tells me we've arrived in Tokyo and that he has to meet our local contact. I tell him to go, and try not to make it sound like an order.

And then I get myself cleaned up, put on yesterday's clothing, and try to think of the most devastating retort I can use when Charlie opens his mouth. It depends on what he says, of course, so I run through a few preliminary predictions: *Well, you've really screwed the pooch now. Hey, Grandma, I thought you'd been eaten by the Big Bad Wolf. 'Scuse me, Boss, I think you've got some fur stuck between your teeth.*

And let's not forget the whole health issue. I have a sudden thought, rip all my clothing off again, and make a thorough search for bites, claw marks, or hickeys. None. The contents of the wastepaper basket beside the bed confirm that we weren't so wasted we didn't take precautions—three times, apparently—and the total absence of shedding on the sheets gives me hope that I wasn't quite as adventurous as I can be.

I get dressed again. Okay. Now all I have to worry about is the personal and professional fallout from sleeping with a colleague I just met, and the inevitable mocking of my peers. Sure. Just another day at the office, which is currently a bullet train parked in a vampire-populated Tokyo. I sigh, and stop mentally beating my head against a wall. *Cut yourself a little slack, girl. Considering the circumstances, you're doing a hell of a lot better than many others would.* I know it's true, but it doesn't improve my mood much.

I head for the dining lounge, hoping I can at least find coffee before the ordeal begins. No such luck. Both Charlie and Tanaka are there, Tanaka digging into what looks like a rice omelette, Charlie sitting across from and staring impassively out the window. It's daytime, but the light is cold and gray.

"Morning," I say.

"Good morning," they say simultaneously. Charlie ignores the coincidence, Tanaka immediately looks embarrassed. I walk past them and start looking for coffee. Can't find any. I finally settle for tea, plugging in an electric kettle.

"Isamu's compound was raided this morning," Tanaka says. "There was no one there."

"He's not stupid," I say, leaning against the counter and crossing my arms. "I'm sure he has lots of places to go to ground."

"Eisfanger finished his workup of the tox screen of Keiko Miyagi," Charlie says. "Found something call quinaxalone. Powerful sedative. Says it was magicked up to work on pires."

I give him a hard look, but he's playing it close to the vest. Waiting for the right moment, I'm sure; after all, he's a hybrid of mineral and lizard. He could probably give lessons in patience to Ryuu, if the ninja still had a head.

"Okay, so she was drugged. Let's follow that up, see if it takes us anywhere."

"I already have," Tanaka says. "Charlie and I were just discussing it. Quinaxalone is currently only available in the U.S."

"Which gives further credit to an international outfit like the FHR being involved. The question is, where are they going to strike next?"

"If this Impaler is the one we're after," says Charlie, "we'd have better luck hunting him on our home turf. The Free Human Resistance started in the States, and that's where their power base is. I know a few guys could maybe help us out."

Tanaka looks relieved. "Yes, that is an excellent idea. Considering the killer has struck on several different continents, it's almost certain he's no longer in Japan—"

I cut Tanaka off coldly. "So I guess I should just leave the country, huh?"

Silence hangs in the air. Charlie goes back to looking out the window, while Tanaka seems to be considering jumping out it.

"Charlie, you mind if I talk to Tanaka alone for a few secs?" My choice of phrasing is deliberate.

Charlie doesn't take the bait. "Sure, boss." He gets up and leaves the car without another word.

I stare levelly at my one-night stand. *Nicely done, Valchek. Only been on the planet a few days and you're already racking 'em up.*

Shut up, brain.

"Look, Tanaka—what happened last night was a mistake."

"I'm sorry you think so."

Not really the response I'd expected. "I'm—well, I'm

flattered, but this is not really normal behavior for me, you know? I don't just— I mean, okay, sometimes I do, but not with . . . with—"

"Members of another race?"

Ouch. "I was going to say 'professional colleagues.' But it's not my *fault*, all right? It was that damn tea."

"Excuse me?"

"The Urthbone. I told you, it increases empathy—what I'm feeling isn't really what I'm feeling. And then the booze loosened up both our inhibitions, and . . . well, no offense, Tanaka, but from what I can remember you feel things pretty strongly."

Now he looks irritated, though he tries not to show it. "You are saying I am not in control of my emotions, is that it?"

"No, no. It's my fault, not yours. You were just . . . just being *you*—"

"I see. And I can't help what I am." His voice is cold.

I shake my head. I can tell anything else I say will just make things worse. "I'm sorry, Tanaka. Let's just pretend this didn't happen and go back to work, all right?"

"Very well."

Twelve hours later I'm back in the U.S. Tanaka doesn't come with us.

I've learned all I really can in Japan, and the longer I'm there the bigger the bull's-eye on my back gets. Tanaka stays behind because he's more useful there—it's possible he might learn something on his own he couldn't while I'm around.

I'm not running away. That's just what it feels like.

And Charlie, damn his featureless eyes, doesn't say a thing about me and Tanaka. Neither does Eisfanger, though I think that's because he has no idea.

I decide to stop taking the Urthbone. Maybe what

happened with Tanaka won't happen again, but I can't take the chance. Investigators have to rely on their instincts, and I can't trust mine if my hormones go into overdrive every time I'm around someone who finds me attractive. I could stop brushing my teeth and hair and dress in baggy sweatsuits, but then I'll just be emotionally overwhelmed by disrespect with a touch of pity. Besides, I don't need the tea to keep me grounded—the case will do that just fine. Once I get my teeth into one, it kind of consumes me; if that kind of total immersion doesn't bind me to this world, nothing will.

I spend the flight going over data with Eisfanger, avoiding Charlie entirely. He doesn't seem to mind. I know I'm just putting off the inevitable; I finally grit my teeth and broach the subject just before the plane touches down on American soil. Eisfanger's at the other end of the cabin, playing with his rat skull; Charlie's reading a newspaper. I sit down across from him and say, "Hey. We should talk."

He doesn't put the paper down. "What about?"

"You deserve an apology."

"I deserve a lot of things, but I still drive a secondhand Ford. Write me up an IOU."

"Not gonna make this easy, are you?"

"I'm not really an easy kind of guy."

I wait, but the punch line never shows. I groan. "Jesus, you're either a real sadist or have a blind spot the size of Cuba. Look, I'm sorry I reamed you out for saving my sorry, promiscuous ass. You did exactly what you were supposed to and you did it really damn well. I can be a real jackass at times and you better get used to it. That's about all I got. Okay?"

He puts down the paper and looks at me. "Okay. No sweat. You don't have to make a big, hairy deal out of it."

"All right, then."

"Unless, you know . . . you have a *thing* for big, hairy deals."

Ah.

"There was no deal, it wasn't that big, and it *certainly*

wasn't hairy," I say, and grab his newspaper so I can try to hide my smile.

The three of us debrief Cassius in his office. Gretchen gives me a warm smile from where she's perched on the sofa when we enter and sit down.

"The Impaler," Cassius says. He doesn't look happy. He makes a fist with one hand and taps it lightly on the desk as if he's considering smashing it in two. "That's . . . unexpected."

"So he's real?" I ask.

"Oh, yes. Very good at staying out of sight, though—no photograph of him is known to exist, and I've had varying reports of his physical description: young, old, short, tall. Some people even claim he's a vampire or a lycanthrope, though I'm sure that's not true. But I also heard he was dead."

"According to Isamu, he nearly was. The rest of his cell wasn't so lucky."

"Hmm. Well, this alters our investigation considerably. The Impaler has access to resources and contacts worldwide, from crime families to arms dealers. He's a dangerous opponent. Only—"

"Only he's not crazy. He's a well-known international terrorist that's smart enough to not get caught. And what he's doing makes perfect sense from a terrorist POV: he's using the media to create an atmosphere of uncertainty and increasing fear. So here's the question: what the hell am *I* doing here?"

"You're here because our killer is insane," Cassius says.

"How do you *know* that? Because so far, despite a definite pattern of sociopathic behavior, I'm not seeing a lot of signs of out-and-out psychosis—hell, from a military point of view, what he's doing almost makes sense. Sow fear and confusion in the enemy, pick your kills for maximum social impact—"

"No. If he truly wanted to terrify, he'd hit targets in

heavily populated centers, not isolated areas. And the killings would be less elaborate and more brutal; in the case of the silver maiden, the death wasn't even visible."

I sigh. "Okay, those are good points. There's a certain artistic quality to the murders that doesn't make much sense. But that just points to a different motive, not necessarily mental illness."

Gretchen clears her throat. "I'd like to point out that you've discovered more in two days than our investigators have in two weeks, Jace. That suggests to me that your approach and expertise are exactly what we need, despite your misgivings."

"Absolutely," Cassius adds. "Don't underestimate yourself. Insight that seems obvious to you is not to us; you come from a culture that has madness so firmly entrenched that you take it for granted. I could give you a list of terms our researchers discovered, apparently commonplace to you but meaningless to us." He shuffles a few papers on his desk and pulls out a single sheet. " 'Nut job.' 'Rubber room.' 'Off his rocker'?"

I shake my head, I can't argue with him, but his explanation still doesn't ring true. I let it go for the time being. "All right, let's say the Impaler is losing his marbles—"

"That one I find kinda offensive," Charlie says. I shut him up with a look.

"—he's still what we call an organized killer. He plans very carefully, even though his thought processes may be based on delusional thinking. If he's operating on a timetable, I don't know what it is; there was a nine-day period between the first two killings, and an eleven-day gap between the second and the third. A killer like this, I'd expect him to stick to a rigorous schedule or the gaps between murders to decrease—neither appears to be true. Which means that though he's almost certain to strike again, we don't know when; could be two weeks, could be two months."

"But at least we know who we're looking for," Gretchen says. "I can generate a list of known associates and past sightings. Perhaps one will lead us to our quarry."

"I may have a lead," Eisfanger pipes up. "The drug used on Keiko Miyagi—I have a list of pharmaceutical distributors in the U.S. It's a lot of data, but maybe I can cross-correlate to something else."

"I know some guys with connections to the FHR," Charlie says. "We'll go talk to 'em."

"Good," Cassius says. "Let's get going."

That signals the end of the meeting and we all stand up. Once again, Cassius says, "Jace? Just a moment."

I glance at Gretchen, but she just gives me a bland smile; somehow, that says more than a raised eyebrow could.

"What's up?" I ask.

"Just want you to have this." He pulls a small vial out of his breast pocket and hands it to me. The others are filing toward the door, but Eisfanger is hanging back.

I take the vial and examine it; it's got a few ounces of a yellowish fluid inside. "What is it?"

"Wolf pheromones. Dab a little bit of this anywhere you have hair; it'll make you smell like the alpha female of a Siberian pack."

"And I want to smell like a Russian wolf why?"

Eisfanger steps forward. "It'll get you in certain places you wouldn't be able to otherwise. And a certain amount of respect."

I scowl at the little vial. "I thought my badge was supposed to do that."

"Only to a point," Cassius says. "Especially when dealing with wolves. Pack structure is very important to them, and even the lowest-ranking wolf will be treated better than a human."

Great. The olfactory equivalent of passing. I slip the vial into my pocket. "Okay. Anything else?"

"Yes. I want you to be careful. Let Charlie do his job and keep you safe. You're no good to us dead."

"No?" I say as I head for the door. "Thanks for letting me know—I forgot to check my contract for a zombie extension clause."

"Talk to the receptionist on your way out. She's got

details on your accommodations and some paperwork for you."

While Gretchen works on her list, I take some time to get settled. The receptionist hands me an envelope with a key card and a cash voucher in it; apparently I've already got a place to stay within walking distance of the office. I half-expect Charlie to tag along when I say I'm going over there to check it out, but he just nods and says he'll see me later.

I find it with no problem. Concrete high-rise, security entrance, reasonably sized one-bedroom on the third floor. Furnished with bland, motel-style furniture and a double bed, even a few pots and plates in the kitchen. I'm not crazy about staying there for any length of time—it has all the earmarks of a safe house, which means it's probably bugged out the wazoo—but it'll do for now. The fridge is empty, which I'm grateful for.

Then I do some shopping. I could probably sign a car out of the motor pool, but there's a mall a few blocks away. I make my first foray into the big bad world of supernatural commerce, taking care to dab on some wolfy underarm charm first.

Seattle seems to have a pretty even mix of pires and thropes. It's evening by now, so I see both kinds out and about. It's often hard to tell them apart; the paler ones are probably pires, but that's hardly definitive. The thropes that are in full-on hairy mode stand out, of course, but there are fewer of them than I expected. I guess it's just more convenient to stay in human form, since it's the base model for both races. Lowest common denominator rules.

I see more wolf children than anything else—running around, sniffing everything, yelping and snapping at each other. It's unbelievably cute. Here I am on the Planet of the Monsters, and it feels more as if I'm stuck in a remake of *101 Dalmations* done with wolf cubs. Makes me wonder what their version of Disney World is like.

I find myself thinking about Tanya and what she would make of all this. She's a tiny blonde with a big goofy smile and a habit of sleeping with married men. "Keeps the complications to a minimum," she says, and then finds herself in the middle of some huge family drama that usually winds up in a bitter divorce and a restraining order. She seems to thrive on it.

Yeah, she'd probably like it here. In fact, the hardest decision she'd probably have to make is which one to pick, thrope or pire. Pire, probably. She'd never have to worry about gaining weight again.

Thinking about Tanya makes me a little melancholy. I decide to splurge on some music—you can't enjoy a good funk without a sound track—go into the first music store I see, and head for the blues section.

Where I get smacked in the face by a cultural difference that makes perfect sense in retrospect. I don't recognize any of the artists. Technology and even history can evolve along parallel lines in different worlds, but music is a *cultural* artifact—and the cultures I'm dealing with are very different from my own. I listen to a few samples and some of it's very good, but I'm not in the mood to experiment. I want something *familiar*, dammit.

Most people would have a ton of music stored on their laptop, but I have a rule about using mine strictly for work— no games, no tunes, no time wasters. I spend the next two hours looking through every CD in the store. I wind up with a bunch of classical—it figures the further back I go, the more similarities I find—one jazz recording, the National Anthem, a country-and-western album, a collection of novelty songs and a movie sound track. Not exactly consistent, but it's a start.

Then I get some clothes, some food, some bedding and towels and toiletries. The money has way too many pictures of full moons on it, but the clerks take it happily enough.

I go back to my new residence—and find Gretchen waiting for me.

"Uh . . . hi," I say. "What's up?"

"Nothing on the case, I'm afraid. I simply thought I'd come by and say hello. Let me help you with those." She grabs a few of my bags as I fumble for my keys.

"Thanks." We go inside, and she follows me onto the elevator.

"I have to say, Jace, that you seem to be taking all this extremely well. If I were in your shoes, I'm not sure I could."

"Well, it's not like I have a choice. When I catch the Impaler, I'll take my frustrations out on him. Until then, I'll just shoot Cassius. You know, to stay in practice."

The elevator stops and we get off. "Yes, I heard about that. Still not entirely clear on how your weapon works, but at the very least you got his attention." Her grin tells me I've got hers, too—or at least her amusement. "I wish I'd been there to see it."

"Yeah? The next time I shoot him I'll tell him it was a personal request."

I unlock my door and we go in. I put my bags on the kitchen counter, and Gretchen helps me transfer things to the fridge. "The Impaler," I say as I stuff some TV dinners into the freezer. "I've been thinking about his name. Any relation to Vlad?"

"As in *Dracula*? No, I'm afraid he's strictly fictional here. Popular, though."

"I'll bet. So I'm guessing he acquired the title from what he's done to pires."

"And thropes, though he doesn't stay with that one particular method. Nicknames are a funny thing—once one sticks, it doesn't seem to matter what you do afterward." She pauses, then says, "You have one already, you know."

Somehow, that doesn't surprise me. "Which is?"

"The Bloodhound."

I frown. "There's at least three different ways to take that, none of them terribly flattering. But it could be worse, I guess. I'm going to pretend it's on account of my tenacious nature and tracking ability."

"What else could it be?" Gretchen says with a knowing smile. Yeah, I definitely like her.

She tells me she has to get back to work, but makes sure I have her cell-phone number in case there's anything she can help with. I was going to check out some TV, but after she leaves I realize I've got the beginnings of a headache; I decide to take some painkillers and go to bed instead. Curious as I am, seeing the vampire equivalent of *Seinfeld* reruns can wait.

And then my cell phone rings.

"Jace? It's Cassius."

"Hi. What's happening?"

"Nothing in particular. I just wanted to see if your new accommodations were all right."

"They'll do, I guess."

"How are you feeling? Dr. Adams said you were having some trouble with RDT."

"I'm fine. The stuff he gave me works like a charm. Symptom-free." I wonder if he's about to bust me on the subject of Tanaka—a boss like Cassius always knows what's going on—but he doesn't.

"And the wolf pheromone? Have you used it yet?"

"Yeah, I put some on before I went shopping. Nobody tried to take a bite out of me, so I guess it works."

"Good, good."

"Look, there's something I've been meaning to ask you about. What happens to my life while I'm gone? I mean, what am I supposed to tell people about where I've been?"

"That won't be a problem, Jace. Because you're from an alternate reality, we can do things with time as well as space. We can put you right back on the night we took you."

"Really? That's a relief; I was starting to think I'd have to make up some kind of alien abduction story."

"I hope I've put your mind at ease." He pauses. "Well then, try to get a good night's sleep. I'll see you tomorrow."

"Thanks." He hangs up.

That was a little strange. Was he just checking up on me, or—

Hmmm.

A good night's sleep does wonders—too bad I don't get one. My headache lingers for far too long, and it's still nagging me in the morning. I go on the offensive, clubbing the damn thing with aspirin and then finishing it off by drowning it with coffee. It helps a little.

Walking to work improves my mood further. It's a wonderful day, blue sky and bright sun, the air crisp and cool. It smells better than most cities, too—but then, a large proportion of the residents have very keen noses.

Something shoots past me in the street, and for a second I think it's one of those couriers that bounced off the car when Charlie was driving. But it's moving even faster and in a straight line; my second impression is that it must be a motorcycle, except there's no engine noise. By the time I figure out what it is, it's almost out of sight.

Sure. I've seen bears ride bicycles in the circus. Why not wolves?

It was more quad than bi, with four pedals and a long, low-slung seat—more of a harness, really. He didn't seem to be wearing a helmet, but I guess safety is less of an issue when you can heal from pretty much anything.

I find a corner kiosk and get some more coffee before heading into the office. Tony the were-guard gives me a gruff nod, and I nod back. It all feels weirdly normal. They haven't assigned me a cubicle yet, so I just head for Cassius' office and knock on the door.

"It's open."

Cassius is behind his desk, studying something on a laptop screen. He barely glances up when I enter. "Jace. Get down to Intel Analysis; Gretchen's got that data you wanted."

"Sure. Where—"

"Third floor." His voice is brisk, and he goes back to working on his laptop immediately.

I take the hint and do an about-face, then pause with my hand on the door. "Uh, I'm going to need a desk at some point—"

"Talk to Reception. They'll assign you one."

Right. Guess my assumptions last night were off-base. Or that's what I *would* think, if I were in high school. . . .

Please. The old attentive-one-minute, distant-the-next routine? That's the very first lesson in Bad Boys 101 or How to Act Like a Dick and Drive Jane Crazy. Well, I don't need any more crazy at the moment, thanks. I head for the third floor and hope for some good news.

Intelligence Analysis is a large, bustling room, full of desks, monitors, and people with intent looks on their faces. There are no windows. Though everybody seems to be talking—on the phone, on a headset, to each other—they all seem to be using low, calm voices, giving the place a kind of subdued intensity.

I spot Gretchen in a corner, talking to a bearded Middle Eastern man wearing glasses. Something about him is unusual, and it takes me a moment to realize it's the glasses. Nothing odd about the specs themselves—but he's the first person I've seen actually wearing a pair. Not a lot of astigmatism in the supernatural set.

Gretchen notices me and waves me over. "Good morning, Jace," she says. "This is Agent Mahmoud. He may have discovered something useful to you."

Mahmoud nods. "Hello. I believe that your subject may have had some dealings with a gang known as Los Colmillos del Demonio. They mainly distribute Bane, but lately they've been branching out into other areas."

"Bane?"

Gretchen nods. "Street drug used by lycanthropes. Wolfbane cut with PCP—heightens aggression, reduces sensitivity to pain, impairs impulse control. Nasty stuff."

"Yes," Mahmoud continues, "and also highly profitable.

But it's only one market, and Los Colmillos have apparently decided to expand into another. Four members were arrested last week with a significant amount of Cloven in their possession."

"Garlic-infused methamphetamine," Gretchen says. "Also called Stinkfoot, Devil's Hoof, and Sicilian Speed. Administered to a pire, it causes euphoria, mania, and increased bloodlust. Quite addictive, as well."

"What's the connection to the Impaler?"

"This." Mahmoud hands me a sheet of paper. "The FHR funds many of their activities through the smuggling of drugs. We got a tip that they're the ones supplying Los Colmillos—and according to our source, the one who set up the deal is someone very high up in the FHR chain of command."

I read the sheet. It's a transcription of a recorded conversation between an anonymous informant and an NSA operative, detailing what Mahmoud just told me. "The source seems to think the drug push is to finance some kind of large-scale project," I say. "Could be what we're after."

"There's just one problem," Gretchen says. "All known FHR members have gone to ground. We don't have eyes on any of them. If we want to track the Impaler through the Resistance, we'll have to find *them* first."

"So we take one step back," I say. "If we can't find the wholesaler, we talk to the retailer. Los Colmillos del Demonio."

I hand the sheet back to Mahmoud. "My Spanish is a little rusty. What's that mean?"

"The fangs of the Devil," he says.

SIX

I sit down across from the thrope and regard him levelly. He's in wolfman mode, six and a half feet of black-furred, fanged, clawed muscle. His gang's symbol is dyed and shaved into the fur on his back, letting people know he stays in this form all the time. The heavy iron collar around his neck is chained to a secure bolt in the concrete floor, and other than the chair I'm sitting in, there's no furniture in the room. He growls at me, letting me know my alpha female status doesn't mean squat to him.

It's taken us three weeks to nail this guy. Three weeks of chasing down leads, shaking down his pack, staking out thrope bars. His name is Eduardo Hermano Lopez, and he's the leader of Los Colmillos del Demonio.

Charlie's watching on a video monitor—one-way glass uses too much silver, so it's not that common. He'll step in if I bungle the interrogation, but it's important to me to try to do it on my own. The growling hairball doesn't make me nervous—as far as I'm concerned, a bad guy in a cage is exactly as dangerous as an angry hamster—but this *is* my first time.

I flex my fingers and begin.

You big leader no more, I sign. *You my puppy now.*

My presentation is still a little shaky, but my comprehension's good. *I will rip your throat out and feed your tonsils to my pack*, he signs. I feel absurdly proud that I remember the sign for "tonsils."

No. You go to kennel twenty-five years. Having, selling drugs. Unless you make deal now.

What kind of deal?

FHR.

What's that mean? Female Hair Removal? He makes the snorting equivalent of laughter.

Funny. You know what me saying. Your supply giver, I want.

Me not heard of supply giver. Me think you stupid in head. It's surprising just how well sarcasm comes across in sign language; I look forward to trying it out myself when my skills are better. *What's wrong with you, anyway? My five-year-old cub signs better than you, and he's only got eight fingers.*

I ignore the question. *Why protect them? They only humans. Sheep. Dumb, weak, slow. Not pack, not gang. You not owe them loyalty.*

He considers this. *True. But no one trusts a traitor. Bad for business.*

Me not hunting business. Hunting one human only. Give him, you go free.

Who?

The Impaler.

The name brings a snarl to his lips. *Him? Good luck. I'd give him to you if I could, but no one hunts him. He hunts others.*

Then you stay in kennel.

I don't know where he is. No one does. He's a [something]; he leaves no tracks. He contacts us, we don't contact him.

I sigh and shake my head. Not a good idea—my skull already aches, and the motion actually makes me nauseous. I mutter, "Then enjoy the obligatory delousing, fleabag," get up, and leave.

Charlie's in a room down the hall, sitting in front of a video monitor with Gretchen. "Perhaps he'll be more forthcoming in a few hours," she says.

"I doubt it," Charlie rumbles. "From what I hear, he's lost more than a few pack members to the Impaler himself. Guy's the FHR's main enforcer, after all—if half the stories are true, he's killed more thropes than Hades Rabies."

But none of those killings inspired them to yank somebody out of their home dimension. Or am I not the first cross-universe tourist they've set on his trail?

The question's been bugging me more and more lately. I'm not being given the whole picture, and Cassius refuses to answer any of my questions about the McMurdo research station.

And my headaches have been getting worse.

"Got a possible new lead, anyway," Charlie says, getting to his feet. "If it doesn't pan out, we can come back here and work out our frustration on our guest."

"Sounds like a plan," I say. "We finally locate an FHR cell?"

"I'm afraid not," Gretchen says. "They've gone deep underground—we're not picking up any chatter at all. But with all the pressure we've put on Los Colmillos, other business ventures are attempting to take their place."

"La Lupo Grigorio," Charlie says. "The Gray Wolves—and that's Italian, not Spanish. Old-school Mafioso family, got their claws in all sorts of pies. Looking to move in on the Colmillos turf."

"And that helps us how?"

"With their regular customers under close scrutiny," Gretchen says, "the Resistance can't deal with them. We have intelligence that says the Gray Wolves are negotiating to bring in a rather large shipment of Cloven, and it doesn't appear to be through their regular sources. It may be coming from the FHR."

I shrug. "Worth a shot. Eisfanger have anything new to report?"

"I'm afraid not. He's been unable to pinpoint the source of the quinaxalone; there are simply too many possible avenues of distribution."

That's not really a surprise, but you never can tell what'll break a case open. "Okay. Just give me a second to visit the little agents' room and we'll go rattle a few cages."

"Sure. I'll get the car."

In the bathroom I dig out my daily supply of painkillers and swallow four with a handful of water from the tap. Ever since I stopped taking the Urthbone my head's been pounding like an angry landlord on a deadbeat's door. Still, it seems to have leveled off—or maybe I've just reached the point of self-medicating where I'm successfully managing to mask my symptoms. Either way, I can handle it—

"I'm not so sure you can," Roger says.

I whirl around—hearing a man's voice in a woman's bathroom is bad enough, but hearing your ex is far worse. Especially when that ex is supposedly in another universe.

Except he isn't. He's standing right in front of me.

He looks exactly the same as the last time I saw him. Tall, broad-shouldered, slicked-back dark hair, wearing a black business suit that's practically the FBI uniform. He's giving me his Serious Look, which I used to find incredibly attractive and now makes me nauseous. And boy, do I feel nauseous. My head feels like it's about to split open. The world spins, gravity goes sideways, and the floor takes a swing at my shoulder. It connects, too.

Everything dims to a swirling, blurry gray. The last thing I hear Roger say is, "They're lying to you, Jace. Just like I did."

And then the gray fades to black.

I wake up next to a puddle of vomit. Pretty sure it's my own, but I'm not willing to send a sample to Forensics. I'm really getting tired of upchucking; I've barfed more since I got to this world than I have since I was in diapers.

I can't have been out long—I'm still alone in the bathroom. I pull myself together, clean myself up, and get the hell out of there.

Not sure what that was all about. A hallucination, brought on by RDT? Or something else, something supernatural?

Either way, whether the message is from my subconscious or the astral plane, something is trying to warn me. Of course, I passed out before any information that might actually be useful was offered. But then, both the subconscious and the supernatural are notoriously cryptic, so I guess I shouldn't really expect a detailed description of exactly who is lying to me and about what.

But I still want one.

Charlie's waiting outside in the car. He's stuck pretty close since the incident on Hokkaido, but he seems to know when to hang back and give me my space, too. He doesn't ask if I'm all right, though he gives me a long look when I slide into the passenger seat. I ignore it. "So . . . tell me about the Gray Wolves."

"La Lupo Grigorio," he says as he pulls into traffic. "Big-time organized crime. Came to national prominence in the twenties, during Prohibition. They're into loan-sharking, drug-running, hijacking—anything that turns a profit."

"We call 'em Cosa Nostra where I come from. Pretty much the same deal, but with more guns."

"Just because they don't carry glorified peashooters doesn't mean they don't use weapons. Knives, swords, throwing axes, javelins, compound bows—these guys are dangerous."

"I'll keep that in mind."

A twenty-minute drive later we arrive at our destination, a wrecking yard near the airport. The rusted sign on the chain-link fence reads: Salvatore Salvage. A few weeks ago I would have expected guard dogs to greet us as we walk through the entrance and toward the beat-up trailer that houses the office, but I know better now. Even the meanest pit bull doesn't stand much of a chance against your average thrope or pire—not unless its teeth have been coated with silver.

The door to the trailer is open. Inside, a short man with greasy black hair sits behind a metal desk, watching porn on a portable DVD player that's balanced on a stack of catalogs. He looks up when we come in, and taps a pause button. How considerate.

"Somethin' I can do for ya?"

I show him my badge. "NSA. We've got a few questions for you."

He doesn't look impressed. "NSA? What the hell is that, an insurance company? I ain't interested."

"National Security Agency," Charlie rumbles. "We're Feds, Sal. Pay attention."

"Okay, so you're Feds. What you want?"

"We want your contact in the FHR," I say. "Give him to us and we'll forget about the Cloven you're trying to move." I don't have the authority to make a deal like that, but so what? The only thing I care less about than a bunch of pires burning out their neural synapses is violating the trust of their dealer. You can't do that kind of thing normally, but normal dumped me without a note nearly a month ago. These days, I'll happily set fire to a bridge the second after I've crossed it—I don't plan on being around for the consequences to catch up with me.

"That's real generous of you," Sal snorts. "Not that I got any idea what you're talking about. So unless you got a warrant—"

"We don't need a warrant, Sal," I say. "*National. Security.* Understand? I can throw your hairy ass in jail until it turns white and your fangs fall out, because I'm looking out for the interests of the country. Your whole blood-latte-sucking, full moon–worshiping, Creature Feature *country.*"

"Yeah? So go ahead." He gets to his feet. "I got the best pire lawyer in the state—"

And then he does something I don't expect; he grabs the edge of the desk and yanks upward, flipping it over in our direction. He darts through a doorway and slams it shut behind him, a bolt *thunk*ing into place a second later.

I curse, loudly and explosively. If I were still on the Urthbone, I would have sensed he was about to rabbit. Charlie leaps the desk and charges the door, hammering at it first with his shoulder, then with kicks. It withstands two before it comes off its hinges.

The other room holds a long table stacked with lumpy white bundles of tightly wrapped plastic. Charlie and I just got very, very lucky.

But it's not the Cloven we're after; it's Salvatore. He's not there, having escaped through a window while Charlie was knocking down his door. I follow the same route while Charlie sprints for the way we came in.

I spot a hairy form disappearing behind a tower of stacked wrecked cars. Sal's transformed, which means I'm chasing someone much larger, faster, and stronger than I am—not to mention the sharp bits at five out of six extremities.

That's all right. I've got an actual secret weapon—and I'm not talking about Charlie.

The junkyard is an acropolis of columns made from crushed vehicles, an open-roofed, jagged-edge maze of twisted metal and fiberglass. Safety glass crunches underfoot as I silently motion Charlie to the left and I take the right. Salvatore's got two big advantages already—he knows the territory and he can move really fast on all fours. Following him in there would actually be incredibly stupid on our parts.

So, of course, that's exactly what we do. There's no time for anything else, and more than likely our furry friend is just going to bolt out the other side while we're getting turned around and we'll lose him anyway.

I know Charlie will just charge straight ahead and assume he can handle whatever Sal throws at him. I slow down, take the stealthy approach, try to figure out which way he'll most likely go. I take the path to the right, leading me between a wrecked Greyhound bus and a two-story-high pile of tires.

I figure out why Salvatore took off like that. He thought I was a thrope—I smell like one, after all—and I had to be picking up on the garlic next door. I wasn't—even when I ran through the room all I got was a faint whiff—but to his sensitive nose it must have been as obvious as a smoking gun lying on the desk between us. If he had any idea what a gun was, that is, or why it would be smoking.

But I'm not a thrope and I'm not a pire. I can't see in the dark or tell what you had for lunch from a block away. I'm an evolved ape, and if I want to catch this guy I'm going to have to start thinking like one.

I start climbing.

It's not that hard. There are plenty of handholds, and I've done enough rock-climbing to know a few tricks; I make it to the top of the column in under a minute. Sal could be long gone by now, but I wasn't going to catch him on foot anyway. I'm hoping he's more territorial than smart.

My view isn't as good as I'd hoped—too much junk in the way, too many places to hide. I can see Charlie, though, crouching down and examining something on the ground next to a tall column of stacked metal cubes that look like giant dice. No sign of Sal.

Because I'm not looking in the right place. There's a twitch of movement and a creak, not from below, but at the same height I am. The column of metal cubes next to Charlie is moving, the top starting to lean like a tree in a high wind. The column is right beside another stack of wrecked vehicles, and I'm not the only one who can climb.

I holler, "Charlie! *Timber!*" as the column topples, revealing Salvatore in the bed of an old truck on top of the neighboring stack. He's pushed the cubes over with his feet, bracing himself against the tailgate and hanging on to the bumper, but now he's wide open.

The Ruger Superhawk is already in my hands. I put a bullet in each of his shoulders.

He gives a howl of anguish and surprise and lets go of the bumper. The fall won't kill him, of course, but it knocks the wind out of him. I put another bullet in the back of his left knee to make sure he doesn't run.

I make it to the ground as fast as I can, hoping Charlie's all right. By the time I reach the bottom I have my answer— he's already got the cuffs on Sal, who's started to revert to human form.

"What—what the hell was *that*?" he says as soon as he has lips again.

"Carved teakwood bullets with silver tips," I say. "Pack a helluva punch, don't they?"

"Bullets? What is that, voodoo?"

"Yeah," Charlie grunts, hauling Sal to his feet. "Angry white girl voodoo. Let's talk inside, Sal. You can bleed all over your shipment."

"Hey, how the hell's a thrope throwing silver without wearing gloves? And what was that thing she pointed at me?"

"Answer a few of our questions," I say, "and maybe we'll answer yours."

We haul him back to the trailer. He's lost a fair bit of blood and is going into shock, but I can see the bleeding is already slowing. Silver-based wounds can kill a thrope, but I hadn't hit any vital organs.

"Happy with your new toy?" Charlie asks as we prop Sal up in a chair.

"It'll do. Think we should get Sal to the hospital?"

"Nah. Easier to just kill him."

"What?" Sal blurts.

"True," I admit. "Less paperwork, no chance of a lawsuit. But look—he's stopped bleeding."

Charlie draws his short sword. "Easy to fix."

"You guys are a barrel of laughs."

"Think we're kidding, Sal?" I ask. "Think about it. That's a whole lot of Stinkfoot you've got here. Worth a lot of money. You die, we take it, who's going to know?"

That's not the answer he was expecting. He swallows, then says, "So take it. But don't kill me—I'll tell them Los Colmillos took it. They'll believe that. Takes the pressure off you, right? And injured like this, they got no reason to think I'm lying."

"Depends on if they believe you," Charlie says. He puts the point of the sword against Sal's Adam's apple, and a little wisp of smoke sizzles up from where the silver edge of the blade makes contact with skin.

"'Course they'll believe me. It's my pack, they know I won't betray them. And it won't be a betrayal, 'cause the

Colmillos are our enemies anyway. Just shiftin' the blame a little—"

"No," I snap. "That doesn't work for us. We're *Federal*, dimbulb. You think we want to get dragged into some local turf war? The only ones we want between the crosshairs are the FHR—they can get hold of enough product to make this look like the back room of a bootleg pizzeria."

"I . . . I could tell them the FHR took it. Double-crossed us, took it back and decided to sell it to the Colmillos."

"Not bad," Charlie says. "Puts the heat on the Resistance, takes it off us. But not good enough."

I pick up a bag of Cloven, heft it experimentally. "See, all the pressure in the world doesn't do any good if we don't know where they are. We need a contact, Sal. Give us that, give us a point of entry—and once we're concentrating on him, we'll forget all about you."

He thinks about it. "Yeah. Yeah, okay. Only it's a her, not a he; human woman named Selkie, Maureen Selkie. She's the one we deal with. I got no problem with giving her up, but getting in touch is gonna be tricky—the FHR is real cagey. Usually they get in touch with us, we don't contact them."

"Usually?" I say.

"We like to know who we're doing business with, so after the last meet I had her followed. She's good, almost gave my guy the slip, but he's got a nose like you wouldn't believe. Followed her even after she changed into a bird—"

"A what?"

"A bird—seagull, I think. Finally lost her when she went out over the water, but she made a stop beforehand. Irish pub named the Green Lily in the University District. Lotta ORs hang there."

"That's it? The name of a bar?" Charlie asks.

"It's all I got. It's all anyone's got—ask around."

"We have," I say, "and you're right."

"So . . . we're good?"

"Charlie?"

"I'm fine."

"Me, too. Thanks for asking. You, though, still don't look so good."

"Nah, I've had worse. That thing you used on me hurt, but try getting your teeth knocked out with a silver hammer."

"Ouch." I pull out my cell phone. "Still, you really should get checked out. I'll have the radio car bring you to the hospital first."

"But . . . I mean, how are you—"

"Oh, all this?" I wave my hand at the drugs and then shrug. "Not my department. Local cops will confiscate it, I guess."

Sal still looks confused. In my experience, wiseguys aren't all that wise.

The first thing Charlie says to me after the patrol car takes Sal away is, "Crosshairs?"

It takes me a second to catch the reference. "What, you don't have scopes here? I mean, you've got crossbows, right?"

"Never had much use for one, myself."

"You wouldn't. And you're welcome, by the way."

"For what? Yelling something about lumber? I spotted that falling stack on my own."

"It's *timber*, sandman. And don't try to tell me you don't have lumberjacks here."

"If we did, wouldn't they be called timberjacks?"

"Good point. I'll bring that up the next time I talk to Paul Bunyan."

"No idea who that is. But I do know the name Maureen Selkie."

So did I. She was a high-ranking FHR member, but little was known about her other than she was an Irish national. Now we knew who our shape-shifter was.

"I know that bar," Charlie says. "Didn't think it was an FHR hangout, though—just a human joint."

"We'll check it out, but I want to talk to Gretchen first,

get the full work-up on Selkie. She's the best link we have to the Impaler so far, and I don't want her to know we're after her until we're ready to move."

We drive in silence for a while. "Charlie?" I say. "Salvatore said the bar was a place where ORs hang out. What's it stand for?"

He hesitates, then says, "Original Recipe."

Yeah. It'd be funny if my entire species wasn't on the menu.

Ordinarily, taking that big a shipment of drugs off the street would make me happy, give me a feeling of accomplishment. Right now, it doesn't seem to matter worth a damn. So I prevented a bunch of pires from OD'ing or passing out in a sunbeam—so what? They're more likely to eat me than thank me. The ungrateful undead, that's what I'm dealing with.

By the time we arrive back at the NSA offices, I'm in an ugly mood. We find Gretchen in the cafeteria, sipping a cup of Blood orange Pekoe and studying a laptop.

"Congratulations on the Cloven," she says. Gretchen becomes aware of important events outside her immediate vicinity approximately four seconds after they occur, less if they happen on the same continent.

"Thanks. Think Cassius will give me time off for good behavior? Didn't think so." I take a seat across from her. "We have a possible lead. Maureen Selkie."

Gretchen gets right to work, hitting keys so quickly it sounds more like a burst of rattling than tapping. "Ah. Quite the busy girl. Involved in a number of terrorist actions in the last decade, including planting silver-laced meat in supermarkets in London and the staking of a high-ranking official in Belgium. Whereabouts currently unknown."

"We have a report she visited a pub in Seattle called the Green Lily."

More rattling. "Yes, that would make sense. It's owned by her brother, James Selkie. If she were in town, she might drop by to see him."

I nod. "We've also been told she's a shape-shifter."

Gretchen arches an eyebrow. "*Very* interesting. An Irish werewitch—that would explain her name, I suppose. A Selkie is a mythological Celtic creature who can assume different forms."

"But she's still human, right?"

"Absolutely. That sort of magic can't be done by the other races—thropes are limited to one particular kind of change, and pires by their nature are unchanging. Golems—"

"Let me guess—lems are too *stubborn* to change."

"Nah," Charlie responds. "We just don't see the need. Why mess with perfection?"

"Golems' largely inorganic nature excludes them," Gretchen continues. "It's something of a trade-off for all of us. We're protected from transformation spells, but unable to perform them ourselves."

"Right. But Selkie can." A sudden thought strikes me. "Any chance she's whipped up something to do her dirty work for her? You know, turned a crocodile into a manservant, that sort of thing?"

Gretchen frowns. "I would think it unlikely, but you should really ask Eisfanger. You think that perhaps the Impaler is a magical construct of some kind?"

"I don't know. Maybe." My headache has returned, and I rub my temples with both hands. "We need to talk to Selkie, in any case. I'll need surveillance on the pub, covert, twenty-four-seven. And some way to bring her down if she turns into a bug or a bird or something."

"I'll talk to Cassius and arrange it."

"Don't bother. I need to talk to him, anyway."

Gretchen gives me a *be careful* look. She's been invaluable in the last few weeks, showing me around, introducing me to people, helping me settle in. Charlie's been around a lot, too, of course, but he's not really the kind of person you can talk to. Not about some things, anyway.

"I know, I know," I say. Cassius and I haven't said more than a few words to each other since he gave me the wolf pheromones—and no matter how busy he is, I know when someone's brushing me off. Either I was completely wrong about his bad-boy act, or he just thinks on a different timescale than I'm used to. Ignoring someone you're interested in for three weeks is probably completely sensible behavior when you're a few centuries old.

Not that I care. Maybe I'm demanding, but the one thing I insist on in a man is a pulse. And I don't care how charming, intelligent, or attractive he may be.

I tell Charlie I'll be back and march up to Cassius' office. He tells me to come in before I knock on the door—his teeth aren't the only thing that are sharp—and looks up from his computer when I walk in. "Yes?"

I don't bother filling him in. Anything to do with this case is flagged and sent directly to him, and I'm sure he knew the details a split second after Gretch did. "Going to need some extra manpower. And weapons."

"Already assigned. See Eisfanger about equipment."

"Uh-huh. You know, I've finally figured out something."

"What?"

"In extraordinary situations, ordinary rules don't apply. And this is definitely far from ordinary."

"It is an unusual case."

"I'm not talking about the case. I'm talking about my employment status."

He frowns. I've seen twenty-five-year-olds with more wrinkles. "Is this about the terms of your contract?"

"Not exactly. It's about what the contract *doesn't* say."

"I don't—"

Call me petty, but interrupting him gives me a great deal of pleasure. "See, I'm not really an employee. I'm a freelancer, an independent contractor. No pension plan, no 401(k), no dental. And despite having me at a colossal disadvantage, you *need* me."

Now he smiles. Negotiation is something Cassius understands the way a woodpecker understands trees. "It's a little late to revisit your contract, Jace. And you'll find I don't respond well to extortion."

I smile back. "Not my point at all. What I'm saying is that you can't *fire* me."

His smile changes. It's not a smirk anymore; it's the grin of someone who's just gained a measure of respect for his opponent. I like it a lot better.

"And how do you plan to explore this newly discovered freedom?"

"Insults, I think. Possibly insubordination. Oh, and insolence—that worked really well for me in Japan. I'm sure I can come up with a few more, but for now just assume that if it starts with 'in,' it's on my list."

"Insufferable? Inept? Intransigent?"

I refuse to be drawn into a vocabulary showdown with someone who's older than most words. "Don't get me wrong—I want to catch this guy as badly as you do, and I'm not going to do anything to screw up my chances of going home. But as far as I'm concerned, I don't march to your drummer. I see a No Smoking sign, I'm gonna fire up a cigar. Chain of command? Gonna yank it whenever I can. And you can forget about a dress code."

"Every day is casual Friday? Going to start coming to work in your pajamas?"

"I don't wear pajamas, Cassius. But maybe I'll show up in nothing but high heels and my underwear, just to make a point. Add another 'in' to the list. . . ."

"Well," he says softly. "As you said. There's really not much I can do."

"Not yet, anyway . . . but I'm sure you'll think of something."

"Good-bye, Jace."

"Seeya later, Caligula."

He chuckles as I walk out the door.

———————————✦———————————

"This should incapacitate her," Eisfanger says.

Charlie and I study the contraption dubiously. We're in the tech lab, looking at something Eisfanger's cobbled together to take down Maureen Selkie, if and when she pops up.

"It's a tether," Eisfanger says. It looks more like the off-spring of a deep-sea fishing rig and a stuffed octopus: a short rod and reel tipped with a black rubber bulb and a dozen thick rubber cables dangling from that. "You activate it by jabbing her with the end. The cables snap around and entangle her—they're lined with superglue pods, so they'll adhere and stay in place."

"What if she changes into something tiny?" I ask. "She could slip right between the cables."

"Well, you have to nail her before she does that," Eisfanger admits. "But once you do, she's stuck. The cables are infused with Anaconda and Chameleon spirit—they'll actively wind around her and squeeze. More important, they'll attach to her on a *metaphysical* level, too; no matter what she shifts into, the cables will shift with her without losing their strength."

Charlie hefts the thing. "How about the line?"

"Braided nanofiber. She might yank your arm off, but the line won't break. And she'll need a lot more than an ordinary blade to cut it."

"Let's hope she's not carrying Excalibur around in her purse," I murmur. "You've only got the one?"

"It's a prototype. Try not to break it."

My phone chimes. "Valchek. Yeah? Okay, we're leaving now." I hang up. "Selkie just showed up at the Green Lily."

Charlie props the tether against his shoulder like a rifle. "So let's go fishing."

Back home, we'd take down a suspect like Selkie fast and hard: tactical strike team, body armor, sniper support. That won't work against someone who can turn into a housefly or a cockroach, though Eisfanger tells me that the further away from human form and mass the more difficult the transformation is to maintain. Still, she only has to maintain it long enough to get away, which means we have to get close to her before she sees us coming.

The Green Lily isn't strictly a humans-only bar, but I don't see any obvious pires or thropes—there are, however, a number of golems, including a table full of workers with orange hard hats on the table in front of them. I wonder what they're doing there—lems don't eat or drink. Maybe they're fans of Celtic music.

The bar itself is brightly lit, loud, and smoky. The air smells of beer and garlic. There are prominent crucifixes on every wall, and I get more than a few suspicious looks when Charlie and I walk in. I walk up to the bar and order a beer, scoping out the situation. Charlie sits beside me.

"That's her at the table near the end of the bar," I say.

"Yeah. That's her brother with her. Don't know the other two guys."

"No, me either. FHR, or just locals?"

Charlie glances in that direction. "Associates or potential recruits, I think. Hard to say—could be bodyguards."

"We'll assume they're muscle. Don't spook them. I think I can get close enough to nail Selkie without help, but hit 'em hard as soon as I've bagged her—not before. Got it?"

"Yeah. You planning on just strolling over with that thing in your hand?" The tether was in a black bag slung over my shoulder—a little awkward, and not exactly designed for a quick draw.

"That's where you come in, big guy. You're going to sit right here and strike up a conversation with the bartender. About fishing. Complete with show-and-tell, understand?"

"I got it."

"When the moment arrives, I'll signal and you toss me the rig. I know your arm's good, but how's your patter?"

"I spend all day talking to you, don't I?"

"Oh, so you're just going to start a fight?"

"Not unless he insults my casting technique."

"Let's hope it doesn't come to that."

I grab my beer and stroll up to Selkie's table. She's a slender, pale-skinned redhead with her hair cut short, wearing a leather bomber jacket over a green T-shirt. Her brother's a chunky man with the same complexion and hair, wearing a pair of glasses with heavy black frames. The two unknowns are a skinny guy with scraggly black hair and a bony face, and a shaved-skull bodybuilder in a sleeveless black T-shirt. They both check me out as I walk up, and their gaze is a little too professional for my liking; definitely bodyguards.

"Hi," I say. "You guys like sex toys?"

It's probably the second-weirdest thing I've ever said to start a conversation, but I figure it's strange enough to at least get a response. And with three men at the table, my offer of a free demonstration should fog their radar long enough to get the tether in my hands. This maneuver would probably get me shot in my own world, but here I just might be able to pull it off—

"Are you saying I'm fucked, Officer?" Selkie asks. My stomach clenches like a fist.

"Have a seat," the skinny man says. He's got dark hollows under his eyes you could hide bodies in. "We've been waiting for you."

"I'll stay on my feet, thanks. You know who I am?"

"That we do," Selkie says. Her accent is lovely. "I came here for a reason, you see. To deliver a message."

Messages from terrorists are often signed with high explosives. I realize I'm a little unclear on exactly how advanced that particular technology is on this world; no guns doesn't necessarily equal no bombs. I have the sinking feeling I'm about to be educated.

"We know about you," Selkie says. "That you're from another world, one with no vampires or werewolves in it. Is it true?"

I swallow. "Yes."

She leans forward, her green eyes intent on mine. "Good God in Heaven above. What I wouldn't give to see a place like that."

My head hurts. My stomach hurts. For the first time in my career, I find myself wondering if I'm doing the right thing. I have no idea what to say to this woman.

"But that's neither here nor there," she says. "There's

bigger things at stake than what either of us wants, isn't there? And what you want is the Impaler."

"You know where he is?"

"Have you been here long enough to get a sense of this place? I'm sure your masters have kept you on a tight enough leash, but even so, the truth is hard to hide."

"I think I've got a pretty good idea what's going on."

"Do you now? You know about the Purists, and the camps? You know about how pires procreate?"

"I know about the camps."

She nods. "That's more than we expected. Tell me, have you given any thought to the kind of human being that exists in this world?"

"I don't know what—"

"There are no weaklings in the human flock. The wolves and the bloodsuckers, they do a damn fine job of weeding those out. But then, there aren't a lot of fighters, either; they're eliminated as being too dangerous. The fighters that do survive have to be tough enough to not be picked off and smart enough to stay off the monster's radar."

"And that's you, right?"

She smiles and shakes her head. "Me? I'm not what you think. Just another sheep tired of standing in line at the slaughterhouse, that's all. But the Impaler is different."

Her eyes narrow. "He wants you to know who he is. He's not some faceless killer, not some myth dreamed up by the Resistance. He's the strongest, fiercest free man on the planet. His family's been staking pires and killing thropes for more than a hundred years, and he's not going to stop. His name is Aristotle—tell that to your bosses, and see what kind of reaction you get."

"I'll do that," I say. "Mind if I get another beer, first?" I wave in the general direction of the bar.

Charlie puts the tether right in my hand. I whirl and jab with it, not really expecting success; she was far too prepared, and any of her colleagues has enough time to get between me and her.

But they don't. None of them move a muscle, including

Selkie. She stays exactly where she is as the black tentacles whip around her and tighten. She looks more resigned than shocked.

And then she changes. Not into another form, just another face. An older woman with salt-and-pepper hair and an ugly scar under her right eye.

The men at the table have all placed their hands very carefully on the table, palms up. None of them make eye contact. It has the feeling of a routine they've been forced to perform many times before.

I feel like I'm going to throw up, again. I've been had.

The question is, how many times . . .

"Aristotle," Cassius says carefully. "Are you sure?"

Charlie, Cassius, and I are in Gretchen's office on the intel floor. Gretchen and Cassius exchange a glance that tells me this is not good news.

"He's supposed to be dead," she says quietly.

"He's supposed to have been dead for fifteen years," Cassius replies. "Thoughts?"

"I think it explains a great deal."

"Doesn't mean it's true."

"Excuse me," I interject. "Who the hell is Aristotle, and why should I care?"

Gretchen looks at Cassius. He nods.

"Aristotle," Gretchen says, "is descended from a rather infamous historical figure, one I believe has a well-known counterpart in your own world. But regardless of his ancestry, Aristotle was one of the most ruthless and hunted humans of the last fifty years. No photograph or reliable description of him exists; the only thing we can say for certain about him is that he's very, very smart. It's thought he was one of the central planners of the FHR until he was assassinated by one of his own in an internal coup."

"So is it possible? Could he be the Impaler?"

"It would make a certain amount of sense," Cassius says. "Considering his family tree."

"Enough with the hints. Who's he related to?"

Cassius hesitates, then says, "Aristotle's last name is Stoker."

It takes me a second to process, then I burst out laughing. "Stoker? As in *Bram* Stoker, the guy that wrote *Dracula*? Oh, that's great. That's too good."

"In a world without vampires he created his own," Gretchen says. "And destroyed them. On this world, he wasn't limited to his imagination."

"Bram Stoker was known by another name here," Cassius says. "The Whitechapel Vampire Killer. Or as he called himself in letters to the press—"

"Jack the Ripper," Charlie growls.

"Why not?" I say. "I'll bet he and Dr. Frankenstein shared a dorm room in college, right?"

"Sure. Make jokes," Roger says. "That's what you always do when you know you're screwing up."

He's standing right behind Gretchen. Nobody else reacts to his presence—in fact, they all seem to be frozen in place. "You're on the wrong side, Jace," Roger says reasonably. He always sounded reasonable, even when he was dumping me. "And you know it."

Then something explodes behind my eyes, and the last thing I see is a brilliant flare of red.

SEVEN

When I open my eyes, I'm back in a hospital bed. There's an IV in my arm and a bandage on my forehead.

"You gave us quite a scare," Dr. Pete says. He's sitting beside the bed on a chair, studying me intently. I wonder how long he's been there, and if he gives this much attention to all his human patients.

Then I think about how many of us are left, and wonder if he has any other human patients.

"I'm fine," I say, sitting up in bed and wincing. "I just— what happened again?"

"You had a severe dissociative episode, brought on by RDT. You haven't been taking your Urthbone."

There's no point in lying to him. "I didn't like the side effects."

"Oh? Maybe you'd prefer a cerebral hemorrhage? Or to go into convulsions and die?" He sounds a little angry.

"Are those my choices? 'Cause all of them suck."

"What other symptoms have you been having?" Yeah, that's a definite growl in his voice.

"Headaches. Nausea. Hallucinations—though I'm not too sure about the last one. Kinda hard to tell in your world, you know?"

"Look, you can't stop taking your medication. I know you hate depending on anything or anyone, but this isn't up to you. Take it if you want to live."

"Yeah?" I blurt. "And what if I don't?"

Okay, *that* was unexpected. I realize how close I am to crying, and try to get myself under control. "You've already given me some of the damn stuff, haven't you?" I say, sniffing back tears. "That's why I'm so damn emotional."

"Of course we did. When Charlie brought you in here you were bleeding from the ears and having trouble breathing. Or would you have preferred we just let you die?"

I don't say anything.

"Suicidal ideation is part of RDT," he says, his voice softer. "I told you, Jace—your body and this universe aren't a match. They're trying to reject each other."

That provokes a bitter laugh. "Yeah, I know all about rejection. Got my own personal demon showing up to jeer me on, as a matter of fact."

"Don't listen to it. I promise you, RDT does fade with time. I know you're tough enough to hang on until it does."

"You don't know anything *about* me," I say. "You don't know about trying to crack the glass ceiling in the Bureau. You don't know what it's like to have your mother call you on your birthday and beg you, in tears, to quit your job. You don't what it's like to be yanked out of your world and into a nightmare. So stop pretending you do."

He regards me calmly and waits. After a moment he says, "Feel better?"

"A little."

"Maybe I don't know everything about you, Jace, but I know you're not shy about expressing yourself. I want you to promise to do that—tell someone about what you're going through, don't just lash out in frustration."

"Who? I'm kind of a peer group of one."

"Me, if you want. Call me anytime. We can go for coffee, talk about anything that's bothering you. Just because I turn into a wolf under a full moon doesn't mean I don't know what it's like to be human."

"I'll think about it."

"Or you could try talking to your partner."

"Charlie? You want me to have a heart-to-heart with a walking statue?"

"He's more than that, and you know it. He's also been standing guard outside your room ever since he brought you in."

"Sure he isn't just asleep? It's kind of hard to tell."

"You can ask him yourself." He walks over to the door and opens it. "She's awake—you can come in."

Charlie walks in, holding his fedora in both hands. It's the first time I've seen him without it, and it makes him look oddly vulnerable. "Hey, lazybones. Done goofing off yet?"

"Sure. Let's get back to work." Even to my own ears, my voice sounds as flat as roadkill and about as enthusiastic. I find I don't much care.

"Charlie?" Dr. Pete says. "Can I have a word with you?"

Charlie nods and follows him out into the hall. They're only gone a few minutes, and I spend the time wondering what'll happen if I don't catch the Impaler. Will they fire me, just turf me out on the street? And how long will it be before Isamu or one of his men shows up in my bedroom one night and I just vanish? Not that they'll kill me, of course . . .

Maybe suicide is actually the smart option.

Charlie comes back in with a wheelchair instead of Dr. Pete.

"I don't need that," I say. "Besides, I can't go anywhere. I'm having dinner." I motion to the IV drip in my arm.

"We'll get it to go," he says. "The stand's on wheels. Now climb aboard—I got something I want you to see."

I can tell by the tone of his voice he isn't asking. I sigh and give in.

He takes me down the hall and to an elevator, then up to the fifth floor. The sign on the wall identifies it as Long Term Critical Care, which seems like a contradiction in terms to me; people in critical condition either get better or die.

"Why are we here, Charlie?"

"Consider it a field trip."

He pushes me down the hall and up to the door of a private room. I can hear the steady, low thrum of a motor; it gets much louder when we go inside.

The noise is coming from the structure that dominates most of the room, a platform about three feet high and the size of a double bed. A corpse floats about eighteen inches above it, suspended in mid-air by the powerful air jets in the platform. The body is horrifically burned; in places, there are only clumps of charred flesh clinging to bare bone. Much of the skull is exposed, no lips or nose left. And the eyes—

The eyes are watching me.

My whisper is swallowed up by the motor's noise, but Charlie hears me anyway. "It's . . ."

"Not dead," Charlie says. "No. This is what happens when you mix napalm with silver fulminate. It sticks and it burns. For a long, long time."

"What happened?"

The eyes are fully formed. They stare at me, unblinking. It has no eyelids.

"You know where lems come from?"

"Uh—a spell. Some Chinese sorcerer."

"He wasn't Chinese. He was Jewish." Charlie's popped one of his silver ball bearings into his hand, and he plays with it idly as he talks. "China was where the spell was introduced, but the sorceror—Ahasuerus—was a Jew. Nobody knows exactly why he decided to spread that spell around the world, but that's what he did. Pretty soon you could find lems almost anywhere: Asia, Europe, South America . . . and the Middle East.

"It's funny how many human preconceptions and prejudices just won't go away. Sometimes I wonder if the thropes took over the Catholic Church or if it was the other way around. . . . Anyway, in the Middle East it was Islam and vampires. Maybe in your world it's different and all the big religions get along—but not here. Pires and thropes are one thing, but Catholic thropes and Muslim pires can work up a hatred for each other you wouldn't believe."

"I think I might."

"Yeah? Well, the only thing a pire extremist hates more than a thrope fundamentalist is a Jew of any type. And since lems were created by one, we're all considered Jewish by default."

"I don't know where you're going with this—"

"Certain Islamic vampire sects like to use golems in an unusual way. They implant one with pressurized tanks of napalm, cut with silver to make sure any burns are permanent. Multiple nozzles hidden just below the surface of the skin, pointing in every direction. Then send it into a crowd of Catholic thropes in a church or on a bus and activate it with a remote—the napalm sprays and ignites at the same time."

I shake my head. "We have those, too—we call them suicide bombers."

"Yeah? We call them sandtraps."

"Why are you showing me this, Charlie?"

"Golems were created to be protectors, Jace. It's in our basic nature. Yeah, we're weapons, but we're weapons that think and feel. Weapons that can choose. To create one of us and take away that choice, to give someone a life that lasts a day and ends in mindless slaughter? That's evil, Jace." He stares at the burned body hovering before us. "That, right there, is evil."

I realize that I'm not picking any emotions up from the burn victim, despite the Urthbone in my system. "Wait. This guy's a pire, not a thrope."

"I'm surprised you can tell. Yeah, see, making sandtraps is a tricky business. Silver fulminate and napalm is an unstable combination, can ignite prematurely. This guy here had one go up while he was still building it."

My emotions do a somersault, and pity turns to anger. "Son of a—"

"Makes me wonder, you know? Pires are immortal. They take a few basic precautions, they can live forever. But clowns like this put their very long lives on the line, just for the chance to kill a few thropes who like to go to Sunday Mass."

"There's evil everywhere, Charlie."

"Not my point. The doc said you were thinking about offing yourself."

His bluntness almost makes me smile. "That's not—"

"Don't do it. Guys like this, they're willing to die to kill other people. We want to stop them, we have to be willing to die, too. So, you want to die? At least go down fighting. Job like ours, you'll get your chance soon enough."

He stops. "That's it. End of sermon. You want to go back to your room?"

"Uh, yeah. Thanks."

Once we're back in the hall I ask, "Charlie? I can't believe that guy is still alive."

"Pires are tough, but fire and silver are a nasty combination; his body'll grow back, but it'll take a long, long time. Years, maybe even decades. And it'll hurt like hell, every second of every day."

"Good. Let's get out of here, okay? Hospitals depress me."

Someone else is waiting for me when we get back to my room. Gretchen. She's sitting on a chair beside my bed, reading a magazine. When Charlie wheels me in, she looks up, seeming entirely unconcerned.

"Well. How's the invalid?"

"Grumpy."

"Not surprising. Your physician tells me you're lucky not to be in a coma." Her tone is light, but there's an undercurrent of concern in her voice. In my present sensitive state, it almost makes me tear up again.

"Dammit, cut that out," I blurt. "This stuff turns me into a leaky emotional sponge."

"I thought you couldn't read pires."

"I can't," I sniff. "So shut up."

She smiles at me gently, and I abruptly realize she's probably old enough to be my grandmother, at the very least.

She reminds me a bit of her, too, what I can remember; she died when I was nine. A very sweet little old lady who liked to sneak cigarettes and coffee no matter what her doctor said. She could curse a blue streak, too.

"Perhaps this will cheer you up," Gretchen says. "They have a pool going down at the office."

"How long before Cassius fires me?"

"No, method of suicide. It's leaning heavily toward jumping off a bridge, but deliberately getting yourself killed in the line of duty is gaining ground quickly. People see you as self-destructive, but with a strong work ethic. And a sense of drama, I suppose."

I glare at her. "Okay, three things. First, I'm getting out of this chair, marching down to the office and setting fire to it. Second, you totally made that up, and third, thank you. Now go get me a damn coffee, please."

"Your wish is my command, O serene one." She gets to her feet and glides out of the room.

Okay, she could teach Granny a thing or two.

Dr. Pete agrees to release me on one condition: that I start taking my Urthbone again. He says that since the tea was obviously too strong, he's giving me a weaker, powdered form that I can just add to a liquid.

Gretchen leaves after a short visit, citing work concerns. Charlie wants to take me home, but it's the middle of the day and I insist on going back to the office. "I'm fine," I say. "What am I going to do at home—watch thrope operas and play solitaire?"

"Being alone might not be such a bad thing. Let you get used to that stuff you're taking again."

"Ah, I'll be okay as long as I avoid overhormonal thropes—lems and pires don't seem to register. Anyway, I want to talk to our suspect as soon as I can."

"Good luck. The woman we snagged is named Brigitte

Sullivan—she was using a disguise spell called a glamour to pose as Selkie."

"Damn. I was really hoping that was just a hallucination." *Like Roger*, I add silently. *Who is apparently trying to make up for being a lying scumbag in real life by becoming a spokesperson for the Truth in my head. But is he right? Am I on the wrong side?*

"Aristotle Stoker," I say. "Descendant of Bram. Tell me about him."

"One of the big movers and shakers of the FHR. Raised and educated in secrecy, brought up to hate all thropes and pires. Supposedly a genius. Also supposedly dead, killed in a suspicious fire fifteen years ago. The Impaler showed up about five years after that."

"So maybe he faked his own death, went even deeper underground."

"Why?"

"To train. To take his campaign to the next level." It was starting to make a kind of sense to me. "He's a human being living in a supernatural world. To compete, he had to turn himself into something mythic. Something the monsters would fear."

"The Impaler's got an impressive rep, sure. But why not use that off the bat?"

"In show business, timing is everything. That's what the killings are about—he's building an audience. The revelation that the Impaler is behind them will drive the numbers even higher."

"But why tell the person hunting him his real name?"

"He wants to create a connection between us. I don't know how he knows about me—magic, maybe—but I've seen this before. Serials often view their crimes as a game, and a game is always more enjoyable with a good opponent."

"Same kind of thing his great-great-granddaddy did."

"Bram, yeah. Tell me about him."

"Victorian London. Pire hookers started getting killed in

the Whitechapel district. Decapitated, mainly, but a few of the younger ones that didn't turn to dust were cut up with a silver blade. Letters were sent to the newspapers, the killer claiming he was going to murder a vampire prostitute every week until they were all gone. Police finally caught him when he bragged about what he'd done while drinking in a humans-only pub. One of his own turned him in."

"What happened to him?"

"Hanged. But before that—when it got out that he wasn't a pire or a thrope—there were riots. Two hundred and sixty-two humans were torn apart by mobs."

"Christ." I stare out the window. "So Junior's got a legacy to live up to. Probably sees himself as some kind of savior."

"Yeah. Except he's more into getting other people nailed to pieces of wood."

"He hasn't used that one yet, but I wouldn't be surprised. . . ."

I pretty much expect to get hauled on the carpet by Cassius, so I'm not really surprised to have the receptionist tell me he wants to see me. I consider blowing him off—I was serious when I laid down my attitude toward rules and regs—but decide I may as well get it over with.

I march in without knocking. "So I had a little episode. Big, hairy—"

Tanaka's standing there, in front of Cassius' desk. He stares at me with an unreadable expression on his face.

"—deal," I finish. Now would be a good time to have another fit, fall down, and pass out.

Or maybe just have the earth swallow me up.

———————————————

"Mr. Tanaka," Cassius says, "has uncovered some intriguing information about your suspect. This information was important enough that he felt he had to deliver it in person."

"Ah," I say. "Good. Okay. Right." I stay where I am and hope I'm far enough away.

"Agent Valchek," Tanaka says formally, inclining his head. "I fear that my information is not as vital as Director Cassius makes it sound. Rather, my superiors felt that I could do more good here than in Japan."

"International treaties work both ways," Cassius says. "One of the crimes happened in their country, after all. If the suspect is on U.S. soil, they have every right to search for him here." He keeps it out of his voice, but I can tell he's not happy. Maybe the Urthbone works better on pires than I thought.

"I'll debrief you," I tell Tanaka. A microsecond later, when my brain informs me what it's just tricked me into saying, every ounce of blood in my body surges into my face. I'm hoping it kills me quickly.

"Yes, good idea," Cassius says flatly. "Bring him up to speed. You and I will talk later."

"Come on," I tell Tanaka. "Let's get a drink. Of coffee, I mean."

He nods and follows me out of the office. I try to stay ahead of him on the way to the elevator—

Oh, God. The elevator.

He doesn't question my decision to take the stairs. I lead him down to the cafeteria, put him in a chair, grab two cups of tea from the counter, and sit down across from him. So far, so good.

"I must confess my motives are more personal than I admitted," Tanaka begins. Not so good.

"Look, Tanaka—what happened between us shouldn't have."

"I know. You were in a vulnerable position, which I took advantage of. I am deeply sorry."

Huh. While that's technically correct, nobody likes to hear that someone's *sorry* they slept with them. I don't, anyway. "Apology accepted. I guess. So what's the news?"

"I believe the Impaler knows that you are hunting him."

"That would have been useful to know a few hours ago." I tell him about the fake Maureen Selkie and what she told me. "The question is, how?"

"Ironically, I believe through Isamu himself. The Impaler has numerous resources in the criminal world, as I'm sure you've discovered. Isamu's anger at the death of his best assassin has reached the ears of many, both allies and rivals."

"That wouldn't tell him who I am."

"Perhaps not, but he knows all the same. That is the true reason I came: to warn you to be careful. Someone close to you may not be who they seem."

I groan. "Great. I can throw paranoia in with all my other mental health issues. Got any news that *won't* make me crazier?"

He hesitates. "No. However, I did bring something of a more practical nature."

"Practical, great. I'm all about the practical."

"I will have to retrieve it from my hotel room. This facility has a gymnasium, correct?"

"Yeah, Gretchen showed me where it was. Worked out there a few times."

"Can you meet me there in an hour?"

I can't see any reason to say no, so I don't. He nods good-bye and leaves. I completely and totally forget to give him one very vital piece of information—and no, it isn't where the gym is.

He's already there by the time I show up an hour later, changed into a white *gi* outfit, his feet bare. He's over by the sparring mats, limbering up—guess even thropes can strain a muscle.

"Didn't know this would get physical," I say, then mentally slap myself across the face. "I mean, I didn't know you wanted to spar."

"Would you like to change?"

"No," I say. "In my experience, opponents in the field generally don't make that kind of offer before attacking. If I can't fight wearing this, I shouldn't be fighting."

"Of course." He pads gracefully over to a low bench against the wall, where a long, thin case rests. He picks it up and brings it over, presenting it to me with a little bow. "A gift. Following our . . . *conversation* on the train, I thought these would be of some use to you."

I'm almost afraid to open it, but I'm too curious not to. I undo the clasps and raise the lid.

Two *eskrima* sticks, made of polished ironwood and about thirty inches long. Unlike most batons, these have a sharpened silver tip at one end.

Now I remember the conversation he's referring to. Before things got too intimate—or maybe it was somewhere in the middle—we got into a discussion of martial arts. I told him I practiced a Filipino fighting style often called Kali in the U.S., and that one of the most common weapons used in that style was twin fighting batons. He wasn't familiar with it, and I made some kind of joke about it probably being suppressed by pires because it would lend itself handily to ramming wooden stakes into the chests of the undead.

"The silver tip makes them effective against both thropes and pires," Tanaka says. "They have another unusual feature, as well."

I lift one out of the padded box and study it. There's a thin line of silver running straight down from the tip to around the halfway point, but only on one side; the other has a small, recessed stud.

"If you'll allow me?" Tanaka says, holding out his hand.

I give him the baton. He holds it about halfway down the shaft, presses the stud with his thumb, and flicks his wrist. A foot-long blade snaps out and locks into place, turning the stick into a scythe. The cone-shaped tip swivels to the side.

"Silver over steel," he says. "Sharp enough to decapitate a foe." He hands it to me, careful not to touch the blade itself. "Note that the blades also have a strip of ironwood embedded in their center, making them effective as impaling weapons against pires, as well."

Not many guys give me a giant switchblade on the second date, let alone a matching pair. And even if this isn't technically a date, Tanaka's obviously still interested; if traveling a few thousand miles to give me an expensive gift wasn't a big enough clue, I can feel the desire radiating off him. It's not as intense as it was last time, but my body is starting to remember things that are still kind of blurry in my mind. Sweaty, sticky things.

"Nice heft," I say. "Lot heavier than rattan." I try to keep my voice steady—right now, every thing I say feels like a double entendre.

"I hope they are not too heavy."

"You kidding?" I set the case down and pick up the other baton. "That damn Ruger's given me wrists of steel. These feel about perfect. . . ."

I'm already testing them out, seeing how easy it is to snap the blades in and out, spinning them around. Despite the blades, they're perfectly balanced.

"Forgive me, but I have little faith in your own weapon," Tanaka says. "It may be effective in your own world, but here it is not. It did little more than annoy Isamu—I thought these would prove more effective, especially in close quarters."

"You'd be surprised to see just how effective my boom-stick is now," I murmur, but I'm not really offended—a gun is just a tool, after all, and you should always use the right tool for the job. Here, stakes and silver were the Black & Decker of weaponry.

"Thank you," I say. "These'll be useful, I'm sure. At least I'll get more than a blank stare when I pull them out. . . ."

"Would you care to test their effectiveness?"

I realize he's talking about sparring. "That sounds a little dangerous."

"Not at all." He kneels beside the case and slides down a panel, revealing two more blades in a recessed nook. "These are for practice. Steel, no silver."

"Practice blades in Kali are usually made from wood."

"Wood, I find, does not hold much of an edge."

"But if they're still sharp, how can you call them—oh." Steel may cut, but it won't kill—not a thrope, anyway. "Let me get this straight. You want me to spar with you, using these."

"Correct."

"And if I, say, accidentally stick one in your eye, you won't mind."

"On the contrary—if it's an accident I will be disappointed. I expect you to do your best to harm me, and to do it with *purpose*."

I sigh. "I'm not making any promises. But I'll try."

He shows me how to swap out the blades, using a polishing cloth to prevent his fingers from coming in contact with the silver, and then we move to the mat.

"So, where are your weapons?" I ask.

"Right here," he says, and transforms.

Okay, so sometimes I'm a little slow. I was so busy concentrating on ignoring the Urthbone-generated feelings in my gut that I missed the obvious—Tanaka wants me to see what it's like to fight a thrope using these things, and like any good teacher he wants the experience to be as authentic as possible.

I don't have the blades out yet, wanting to get used to the feel of the sticks themselves first, but I drop into a defensive pose automatically, both sticks at the ready.

He swings at me open-handed, trying to slap me in the side of the head, but doesn't connect; I use an inside sweep to nail his wrist and break his motion, then backhand him across the skull. He shakes it off in a microsecond and swings with his other hand. I slam his forearm down with an *abineko* move, but momentum carries the strike past me. I know his backhand is going to come at me like a freight train and try to counter with a hard shot of my own to his upper arm, but it hardly slows him at all; the back of his fist catches my own shoulder and I go flying off to the side.

I get up carefully, the sticks in a defensive posture. He stalks forward and tries to grab one. I let him, then smash his carpal bone with the *punya*, the butt of the other stick. He doesn't let go. I hit him again as he starts pulling the stick upward. He growls. The stick's up to head height and I switch tactics, bashing him with the end of the stick hard enough to break bone. I hear something snap, but he still doesn't let go—so I swing low at the kneecap.

He howls in pain and anger but doesn't go down. Fine. I strike, pull through, strike again, whipping the *eskrima* back and forth until the leg buckles. He collapses, releasing my stick as he does.

I step back into a ready stance, my right hand forward. "How's that?" I ask.

He pulls himself up and tests the leg. I know I turned the kneecap to pulp, but he seems to be able to put weight on it already. He comes at me again, jabbing and feinting but favoring the leg. I counter, bat his strikes away or block them.

Then he pivots and slashes with a foot, faster than anything else he's done. His claws catch my slacks and tear them open.

Did he draw blood?

And I become abruptly, sickeningly aware of the situation I've put myself in. That this guy that seems a little too attached after a one-night stand can *literally* make me his bitch with a single scratch.

I snap both blades out. I might not be able to kill him using stainless steel, but I can sure as hell disarm him, in every sense of the word.

There's an attack method called *siniwali*, using both sticks in a continuous, weaving pattern of high strikes known as the Heaven Six. I use it now, pressing forward hard, turning the zone in front of me into a meat grinder.

He backs off, puts his hands up in surrender.

I stop, breathing hard, wondering if I can trust him. He transforms back into a man, and the look on his face is one of confusion.

"I don't understand—," he begins.

"Yeah, well, I do! *Jesus*, Tanaka! What were you going to do, claim it was an accident and apologize again?"

"You are angry because I have torn your clothing?"

He seems genuinely puzzled. He's not stupid, so there's something I'm not getting—

An explanation clears its throat in the back of my head. It taps my paranoia politely on the shoulder, then steps forward and whispers in my ear.

The wolf pheromone. I didn't mention it to Tanaka.

"Crap. You think I'm *already* a thrope."

"You . . . are not?"

"No. Artificial scent, supplied by Cassius. For undercover work, you know?"

"Ah."

There's a moment of awkward silence.

"I was wondering why you did not transform," he says. "I thought that as a new lycanthrope you were simply being . . . private."

I sigh. "Thanks for the scythes, Tanaka. I'm sorry I tried to chop you into little pieces."

"I'm sorry I gave you reason."

He bows, then excuses himself to go and change into street clothes. Yeah, I really know how to show a guy a good time. . . .

"What do you mean, she's been released?" I ask Gretchen.

"Not just her. The others arrested with her, as well." Gretchen leans forward and puts her elbows on her desk. "Cassius' orders. Don't ask me to explain, because I don't know why."

"But . . . they were our only lead! They could have led us to the Impaler!"

Gretchen shakes her head. "No, they couldn't have. They were planted in that pub to relay a message to you, and they have no more idea where Selkie or Stoker is than we do. Cassius may have released them in order to keep them under surveillance—but Aristotle's too smart to fall for that."

She's right, but it still annoys the hell out of me. My suspects, my case—I should have at least gotten the chance to talk to them, and I tell Gretchen that.

"Perhaps that's one of the reasons they were released," she says quietly. "To prevent you from doing so."

"What? That makes no sense."

"It would to Cassius. I think he's afraid you might wind up identifying with them instead of your employers."

"That's ridiculous," I mutter.

"Is it? You know what's it's like to be the underdog. To be isolated, alone, outnumbered. And of course, you're human. Just like they are."

"They're terrorists," I snap. "I'm nothing like them. And more to the point, I don't want to stay here a second longer than I have to. Cassius *knows* that."

"Yes, I suppose he does," Gretchen says. "But you don't survive in his occupation for as long as he has by not maximizing your chances."

I groan and lean back in my chair. "So back to square one."

"Not quite. Knowing the Impaler's identity significantly grows our database. Given time, it's sure to increase our chances of catching him."

"Yeah? Feels like we just traded one set of rumors for another. We still have no idea where he is, what his plans are, or even what he looks like."

"Patience, dear girl, patience."

"Easy for you to say. You're immortal."

Law enforcement, regardless of organization, department, or universe, consists of long periods of boredom punctuated by adrenaline-charged bursts of activity. Well, maybe not in the accounting department, but for the most part it's a rule that holds true across the board. This case is no exception.

After that workout with Tanaka, I'm feeling restless, hyper, and on-edge. There's no new information to go over, and

I've studied what we already have until my eyes threaten to bleed. I finally give up and go home.

Where I feel even worse. It's Friday, so the whole weekend stretches out before me. Back home—real home—I would have called Tanya, probably wound up going to a bar or something. Not really an option here—Gretchen will be at work until late, and I'm not in the mood to trade barbs with Charlie. What I'm really in the mood for is . . .

No. And no bar, either. Maneuvering myself into position to drunk-dial Tanaka is not the smart option.

I channel-surf for a while, watch a few minutes of a buddy-cop drama called *Toothe and Fanng* about a pire and a thrope as a pair of mismatched detectives. About as mediocre as you'd expect, though they do drive a cool car. Find a sitcom about a family of golems that's funny but blatantly racist; no wonder Charlie seems pissed off all the time.

I finally settle on a football game. Not usually a sports fan, but you haven't seen any sport until you've seen it played by seven-foot-tall werewolves who can run at 60 miles an hour and jump a dozen feet straight up. No pads or helmets, either.

The sheer novelty holds my attention for a while, but I've had my fill before too long. There's a lot of blood; thropes heal so fast that little things like getting your face half ripped off are only inconveniences. One guy even disembowels another, which is apparently not only frowned upon but also a ten-yard penalty.

I turn off the TV and stare at the blank screen for a while. Not very entertaining, but at least it's less violent. I pick through my ragtag music collection and listen to some Beethoven, but it just doesn't suit my mood. Neither does "Achy Breaky Heart," the theme to *The Jeffersons* (about a thrope family that's movin' on up), or the sound track to *West Side Story* (in which the Jets and the Sharks become the Bats and the Wolves). Nothing feels satisfying.

I finally surrender and pick up my phone. Dial the number. Think about hanging up before it's answered.

"Hello?"

"Hi, Dr. Pete. It's Jace Valchek. Got a minute?"

"Sure, Jace. What's up?"

"Too much and not enough. I'm feeling kind of jittery."

"Taking your medication?"

"Yeah, yeah."

"And the side effects?"

"Better. But I still feel kind of . . . I don't know. Disconnected."

"That's because of the lower dose. You're going to have to do other things to compensate."

"What . . . *kind* of things?"

"Socialize. Get involved in things other than your work. Start a hobby that involves meeting other people and interacting with them."

"That was never really one of my strong points when I *wasn't* living in a world filled with thropes and pires."

He laughs. "Not a big people person, huh? Well, there are other alternatives—the main thing is to put down some roots, some links to the world around you. You can even take that literally by planting a garden—"

"My thumb is so far from green it's not even a color. If it and something *actually* green came into physical contact, there would be an explosion."

He laughs again. It's a nice sound, one I haven't heard often enough lately. "Okay, I get the point. I'm going to suggest something. It's a little radical—even dangerous—but it might be just what you need."

"Bring it on."

"How'd you like to meet my family?"

I blink. "What?"

"You need some localized, earthy experience—and there's nothing more earthy than my family. Of course, if that prospect scares you—"

"Cut out the cheap psychology, Doc—remember what I do for a living. Anyway, your family couldn't be any scarier than mine, and that includes factoring in the whole were thing. My aunt Cynthia alone would probably send half your relatives howling for the hills."

"All right, then. I'm going over there tomorrow afternoon for lunch—I'll tell them I'm bringing someone along."

"This isn't about shocking your parents, is it? Bringing home a human?"

"Oh, it takes more than that to shock my parents. You'll see."

He hangs up, leaving me to wonder just what I've got myself into now.

EIGHT

Dr. Pete picks me up at eleven in a white minivan. It occurs to me that I don't even know if he's married; thropes don't wear rings, for obvious reasons. I take a quick look in the back as I'm getting in, and notice a definite absence of toys, fast-food wrappers, and car seats. Not definitive, but indicative.

"Morning," Dr. Pete says. He's dressed in jeans, a plaid shirt, and loafers. I'm wearing an oversize blue sweatshirt, track pants, and sneakers; on my days off I like to go for comfort over style.

"Morning. Where are we headed?"

"The depths of suburbia," he says with a grin. "Bellevue, to be exact."

"Where I come from, that's not only a suburb but the name of a famous mental hospital."

"From what I understand of the term," he says as he pulls into traffic, "that's a pretty fair description of what you're about to experience."

He fills me in as we drive. I can't really keep track of all the aunts, uncles, cousins, nieces, and nephews, but I try to remember the major players. The sheer size of his family answers the age-old question of what you get when you cross a Catholic with a werewolf: a small country.

He also gives me the rundown on the difference between a thrope's family and his pack, which is not always the same thing. You're born into your family, which is also your pack until you come of age. Then you can choose to join another pack—based on profession or lifestyle, usually—or can marry into one. If you don't want to choose right away, you can be an independent until you make up your mind.

"Not too many lone wolves, though," Dr. Pete says. "Most thropes choose a pack, sooner or later."

"And if they don't?"

"Then they don't. There's no penalty—not an official one, anyway."

He doesn't have to elaborate. Certain doors simply wouldn't open to a loner; certain invitations wouldn't be offered.

That's how it is on any world.

Dr. Pete, it turns out, isn't married—the only one of his seven brothers and six sisters who isn't. He is, however, the favorite uncle of many of his nieces and nephews. "Which is a mixed blessing," he admits. "I love all of them dearly— well, most of them—but sometimes when I visit it's a little overwhelming."

"I see. You're just bringing me along as cannon fodder?"

He gives me a puzzled look.

"An expendable hostage. Human shield. Sacrificial decoy."

"Oh. Yes."

I laugh. "Well, this should be interesting. . . ."

His parents live in a big house in the south end of the city. There's what appears to be a thrope riot going on in the front yard; when we pull up, it transforms into a furry tidal wave that surges against the minivan with a crash.

"Watch the paint!" Dr. Pete hollers. "No claws! No claws!"

The thropes surrounding us are in permutations from wolf cub to humanoid, sporting many different colors of fur: blond, brunette, redhead, pure white or glossy black and every shade between. Some are cute, some are terrifying—in other words, children. I understand the terrifying ones are sometimes called "teenagers."

We get out of the van. All the thropes that currently have hands are signing furiously, which makes me feel like I'm in some kind of surrealistic performance art piece or maybe a live-action version of a Muppet movie on bad drugs. I can only catch about one word in three, but I get the general gist—who is she, is she your girlfriend, did you bring me anything, and a request to either drive his van or lambaste his camel.

"Peter!" a voice booms out. "Ah, the prodigal cub returns!"

The fur flood recedes to let through a big, burly man with a considerable paunch and two wiry gray tufts of hair protruding from his head like an aging Bozo the Clown. He's got a wide, smiling face, canines so prominent they look artificial, and eyes as black as chips of coal. He's wearing a bright yellow polo shirt and baggy black shorts with sandals, and carrying a struggling child under one arm.

"Hey, Pop," Dr. Pete says. "This is Jace Valchek, the one I told you about. Jace, Leo."

"Hi," I say.

"Hello!" he says, and gives me a hearty, one-armed hug. "Welcome! It's a pleasure to meet you."

"Thanks."

Dr. Pete leans down to address the child under Leo's arm, who's mostly stopped kicking and is regarding me suspiciously. He's got jet-black hair, gray eyes, and he's wearing a T-shirt with a smiling moon on it. "Hey, Nicky. In trouble again?"

"Nah. I'm wrestling Grampa."

"How's that going?"

"I'm winning!"

"Excellent. Come see me later, I'll tell you where all his weak points are." He straightens up and says, "Okay, okay, I'll come out and see all of you in a minute. Now back off and give her some breathing room."

Pop Leo turns around and leads us toward the house while the kids disperse with no apparent decrease in enthusiasm. "How you holding up so far?" Dr. Pete stage-whispers.

"Better than Nicky," I whisper back.

"I heard that!"

The house is a monster, three stories high and sprawling, painted a bright green. It doesn't look like a mansion, though, just big and lived-in. Extended family, extended living quarters.

The noise diminishes slightly once we're indoors. It's still definitely in the "din" category, but there's less screaming and more banging, with a backdrop of flamenco guitar. Three swarthy men are doing intricate and stirring things with guitars in the front room, while a toddler standing on a piano bench pounds solemnly on the keyboard. They're good enough to not only keep up with her but make it sound like she's the performer and they're just the backing band.

The house also smells wonderful. I may be a vegetarian, but I still get a guilty jolt of pleasure from certain aromas; roasting lamb is one of them. I try to pretend it's just the spices, and hope they serve something I can actually eat.

I needn't have worried. The table is slightly smaller than a soccer field and holds enough food to feed a dozen teams: eggs, bacon, muffins, salad, fish, bread, sausages, lamb, potatoes, fruit, pancakes, juice, coffee, milk, pastries. A rough head count of the clan puts it somewhere around thirty, though so many people keep coming and going it's hard to keep track.

It's chaotic, confusing, and oddly soothing. I find myself grinning, passing various dishes, and eating a lot. The fact that I don't eat meat is the subject of much discussion, but it's more along the lines of genuine curiosity than anything else. Several of the women come to my defense, citing recent diets they've read about that are good for your figure, and point out that their men could stand to lose a few pounds. Everybody eats in human form, even the children, which makes eating and talking at the same time a lot easier.

Afterward, everybody helps clean up and the whole party moves into the kitchen. When that's done, people break up into smaller groups all over the house and the backyard, which has a pool. I decline the offer of a swimsuit, but join Dr. Pete in a lawn chair at poolside.

"So, what do you think?" he asks with a grin. "The clan try to buy your soul yet?"

"They don't seem so bad."

"They'll wear you down with relentless hospitality. I'm surprised they didn't offer you pack membership before dessert."

"You're kidding, right?"

He chuckles. "Only partly. Joining a pack is serious business, but I can tell my folks like you. They were a little thrown off when I told them about the artificial pheromone, but I explained it was a security precaution for your work."

"Wait. So they know I'm not one of them?"

"Well, the adults do. The kids think you're an alpha female, which means they'll give you some respect. With the others you're on your own—but you seem to be doing pretty good so far."

Something was tugging at my memory, but it wouldn't quite surface. "How does that work, in a legal sense? When a human gets turned into a pire or a thrope?"

"Depends on if it's voluntary or not. If it is, witnesses are usually required and documents have to be signed. If not, the transformed party can sue the other party for damages and have them criminally charged."

"So with consent it's like a marriage. Without, it's rape."

"More or less. Why?"

"Just wondering what my options are if things go wrong."

His face turns serious. "I suppose that's a possibility. But it's not something you have to worry about from most of the population; neither pires nor thropes have any reason to transform a human against their will. It's a truly rare occurrence."

Besides, it's not so bad, is what he doesn't say. *Just look around you.* Kids running around and splashing in the pool, adults laughing and joking, everybody out enjoying the sun . . . it all suddenly feels a little forced.

I shake my head, and the feeling passes. When you start

wondering if the whole world is a play put on to manipulate you, that's the time to look up "paranoid" in the dictionary and check for your picture.

"You all right?" Dr. Pete asks.

"Fine. Just not used to this much—glee, I guess."

"Oh, they're just getting started. You don't want to see what they're like when they're actually celebrating something."

There's a long table, shaded by patio umbrellas, at the other end of the pool. A half-dozen or so females, ranging from ten-year-olds to grandmothers, are gathered around it and busily working on . . . something.

"What are they doing?" I ask.

"Making decorations for Moondays."

"Moondays?"

He shakes his head. "Sorry. Some things are so ordinary you just take them for granted. Moondays is the festival that takes place every month during the three nights of the full moon. You think this is a lot of food, wait until then."

"Shouldn't it be called Moonnights?"

"Well, it's pretty much a seventy-two-hour-long event, day and night. Daytime events are spent in human form, and are more family-oriented. At night, everyone changes into were-form—it's the one time we don't have a choice. Then the party really starts."

Despite the sunshine, despite the laughing children and Dr. Pete's relaxed smile, I still feel a chill go down my spine. "Yeah? And exactly how do thropes like to party?"

"Lots of drinking, lots of dancing, lots of team sports. Lots of, uh, amorous entertainment. Lots of food."

I put the next question as delicately as I can. "Is it . . . safe?"

"You mean for non-thropes? Sure. Mostly."

He sees the look on my face and hastily adds, "I mean, any large event has its troublemakers, but the Moondays of today aren't anything like they used to be. The whole idea behind them is to *control* our animal nature, by finding socially acceptable outlets for our instincts."

"That sounds suspiciously like something regurgitated from a first-year university textbook."

"Maybe so, but it's still true. Look, lycanthropes used to be a very different race. We'd hide our true nature from everyone around us, then go on a wild carnivorous spree once a month. Everybody knows how unhealthy that is now."

"Oh, absolutely. I don't care what anyone says, you have to get a few carbs in now and then."

"These days, people split their times as lycanthrope or human about fifty-fifty. When Moondays roll around, there's much less pent-up aggression to be released. We've turned it into a celebration as opposed to an explosion of primal urges."

"Sounds like it's still pretty primal to me."

"Not in Seattle. New Orleans, Rio de Janeiro, Anchorage— those are places that can get out of hand. But—" He stops himself.

"But what?"

"Nothing. Hey, you should see this." He gets up and motions me to follow him.

I do, making a mental note to pursue the topic later. He walks up to the table where the women are working and says, "Ah, making *mirositors*, I see." The women are taking chunks of beef jerky and dried apricots, sprinkling them with herbs, and wrapping them in small, brightly colored squares of cloth.

"It's for the young ones," a woman who must be in her eighties says. "We sprinkle some herbs on the treats, you see? With a strong smell. Then we hide them and they must search them out with their nose."

"Like Easter eggs," I say. The woman smiles at me and nods, but I can tell she has no idea what I'm talking about.

"You help?" she asks, motioning to a chair.

"Uh—sure." I sit down and pitch in.

"I'm going to go catch up with some of the kids," Dr. Pete says. He leaves before I can protest.

Not that there's anything to protest, really. Putting the

little packets together—the cloths have to be folded just so, and then tied with a little piece of colored string—is relaxing in that monotonous, mindless way that certain tasks are. The women ask questions about me and Dr. Pete, some sly, some blunt. I inform them that he's just my doctor, then have to defend that position when they begin to detail the many, many fine qualities he possesses and why he would make a perfect husband.

It's all right, though. I've had to use the same arguments before, with my own mother. In its own way, it's as rhythmic and repetitious as the folding of the cloths, and almost as soothing.

Almost.

It makes me think about Roger, which is not a subject I tend to embrace. Still, he's the closest I ever came to walking down the aisle—well, *thinking* about walking down the aisle—and the fact that my professional ability to recognize sociopathic tendencies completely failed me when it came to the person I was sharing a bed with screwed me up for a long time. The first casualty of that particular psychic battle was any thoughts of matrimony, ever. When you have your trust violated on the level that he violated mine, it's hard to imagine ever having that level of emotional intimacy again.

So why is Roger the one who's trying to warn me?

I refuse to consider that he might in any way be real. I'm suffering from a condition that causes hallucinations; therefore, he has to be a hallucination. Never mind that the aforementioned condition was brought on by supernatural weirdness—I can't just toss out the rules of deductive logic because the occasional natural law gets bent. Roger being more than a hallucination opens up a whole can of worms labeled: PARANOID SUSPICIONS—CONTENTS UNDER PRESSURE. Is Roger really an evil wizard? Is an evil wizard posing as him? Did an evil wizard send a demon to pose as him and get inside my head? Does Roger have an evil twin who is, in fact, an evil wizard? And why am I so obsessed with evil wizards when I've got vampire ninjas, Mafia werewolves, and Irish shape-changers to choose from? Maybe it's an evil *witch* that's getting into my head—Maureen Selkie in ex-boyfriend drag?

No. If she were trying to contact me, she wouldn't pick an image from my brain that I associate with treachery. Unless maybe my own mind applied that as some kind of filter, trying to let me know the sender wasn't trustworthy. . . .

Argh. It's like trying to build a house out of wet spaghetti. I make a mental note to talk to Eisfanger about astral projection and telepathy later and whether they even exist in this world. I still don't know everything that's possible or impossible here. . . .

And then the zombie sits down next to me.

Half her face is rotted away. She looks like she was around seventeen when she died, and the undertaker who did her makeup used too much. The exposed, lengthened canines tell me she was a thrope, and the hole in her skull tells me how she was probably killed. I can see her brain.

"Hi," she says. I'm surprised how good her enunciation is with only half her lips.

"Hi," I say cheerfully. Some stubborn inner resolve has kicked in, a grim refusal to be freaked out by anything else. Mummies, giant spiders, flaming skeletons, whatever you got; bring 'em on.

"I'm Alexandra," she says. "I'm, um, Uncle Peter's niece? And I was wondering if I could ask you a few questions?"

"I'll answer yours if you answer mine."

"Okay, I guess so." The other women at the table don't seem fazed at all by Alexandra's appearance—though a few of the older ones don't seem to approve, either—so why should I?

"Are you dead?" I ask. It seems like a reasonable question, but it produces giggles from most of the kids at the table.

She smiles at me, which is a truly horrifying sight. "No. My turn. Are you really from another world?"

"Yes. If you're not dead, why does your face look like that?"

"It's called corpsing. It's just a fashion thing, lots of people are into it. Is it true there aren't any thropes or vampires where you come from?"

"Not real ones. But there are people who imitate them, fashion-wise."

She frowns. "They dress like us? But we dress *normal*."

I can practically hear the cultural gap yawn between us. "No, they dress like they think vampires would—lots of black, makeup to make their skin pale, artificial fangs. Like you imitating a corpse, I guess."

"Oh. We have those, kind of. Except their fangs aren't fake and they like to speak weird." Unlike the very mundane conversation we're having at the moment, of course.

"Is corpsing painful?" I ask.

"No. It uses a charm, see?" She holds up her wrist, which has a small purple pouch tied to it with string. "And it's just temporary. I take the charm off, everything grows back really fast."

"Cool." And it actually is, in a creepy kind of way. It's actually less of a commitment than a tattoo.

"So, what's it like where you're from? I can't imagine."

"A lot like here, actually. We drive cars, we shop in supermarkets, we live in cities. Sometimes being here feels like I've just gone to another country instead of another universe."

"So you don't have Moondays?"

"Not as such."

"God, you are so *lucky*," she moans in that self-indulgent way only a teenager can really do justice to. "I *hate* having to change every month. I can't wear any of my clothes, it makes my joints hurt, and I totally eat like a *pig*."

"Bah!" the oldest-looking woman at the table says. "You should be proud of who you are! Not complain all the time!"

She glares ferociously at Alexandra, who sighs theatrically and says, "What*ever*." She gets up and slouches away, probably to go find her socially unacceptable boyfriend and make out with him. Those lips will make it difficult, but I'm sure they'll find a way. Teenagers are inventive.

I notice that the Urthbone effect is much more subdued

than it was previously. I can feel the emotions around me, but they don't seem to be affecting my own mood nearly as much. Perversely, at the moment I kind of regret that; the women around me are happy, surrounded by people they love and preparing for something they're looking forward to.

Me, not so much.

It's a nice illusion, sitting here and doing family-type things, but it's not my family, it's not my culture, it's not my world. For every comforting detail I can identify with, there's some bizarre off-kilter factor that makes the familiar horrible and strange. As if to underscore the point, a small child trots by, his mouth bloody, holding a dead rat between his teeth. His parents congratulate him, of course.

My phone rings, a number I don't recognize. I answer anyway.

"Hello?"

"Hello. It's Kamakura Tanaka. I realize that it's the weekend, but I was wondering if we could meet."

"You have new information?"

"Not . . . exactly. I simply feel that it would be productive to discuss the case. To share our perspectives."

He sounds sincere but a little hesitant. I realize he's probably sitting in a hotel room, maybe nursing some too-expensive minifridge scotch and wondering what the hell to do with himself.

"I'm kind of busy at the moment, Tanaka. How about to-morrow?"

"That would be fine. Where should I meet you?"

I'm not that familiar with my neighborhood yet, so I just give him my address and tell him to ring the buzzer at noon. He thanks me and hangs up.

Dr. Pete finally returns, bearing two large glasses of iced tea.

He tells me he wants to show me something, and I excuse myself from the table. He leads me into the house and down to the basement, where I find . . .

Comic books.

"These are mine," Dr. Pete says, opening up a cardboard box filled with them. "Had 'em since I was a kid. Worth a lot now—or would be, if they were in better condition—but I prefer to leave them here as a kind of library. Let the younger generation discover them, if they ever take a break from playing video games."

"Here." He pulls one out and hands it to me. "Check this out."

The cover shows a woman in a skintight outfit and a pair of aviator goggles, striking a pose on a rooftop while lightning flashes behind her. She's got a wicked-looking crossbow in one hand, and a curving scimitar in the other. The logo reads: "*Amelia Earhart, Aviatrix.*"

"You're kidding. Amelia Earhart was a comic-book heroine?"

"Sure. They called human adventurers 'underheroes.' They fought all sorts of bad guys, could do things thropes or pires couldn't—endure sunlight, ignore the effects of garlic or silver or the full moon. Me, I liked the fact that they usually had to use their brains to get out of trouble as opposed to brawn."

I study the cover, note that it's dated 1939. "In my world, Amelia Earhart went missing during an attempt to fly around the world, in 1937."

"Not here. She succeeded, and it made her an even bigger celebrity than she was before. She died piloting a paratrooper transport over North Africa in 1941."

Congratulations, I think to myself, staring at the blurred image of the woman in her heroic pose. *You did something no one else had ever done—then died four years later in a war over the scraps of the human race.*

"I guess these comics are where it started," Dr. Pete says. "My interest in nonsupernatural humans."

I know what he's trying to do, and it's sweet—showing me a piece of his childhood, trying to demonstrate that I have value in this world, no matter how outnumbered or outpowered I am. But it still feels a little too much like a veterinarian explaining to a particularly smart dog how proud he is of her.

I hand him back the comic and force a smile. "Yeah, lucky me—not only do I get to be your patient, I can do double-duty on weekends as your hobby, too."

I can feel his hurt without even looking at his face. "Jace, that's not true—"

"I know, I know," I say, my voice tired. "I'm sorry. I think I'm just a little overwhelmed, okay? Thanks for inviting me out and everything, but I think I'm ready to go. Back to my apartment, I mean."

"Of course. I'll drive you."

It takes a while to make the rounds and say good-bye to everyone. Most express sincere regret that I have to go and tell me I'm welcome back anytime. They mean it, too, and I start to feel like an ungrateful brat. Alexandra wanders out when I'm almost done, now using headphones to insulate herself from the party. She sits down on a lawn chair, nodding her head to whatever she's listening to. It sounds like she's really got it cranked, whatever it is—

No way.

I tap her on the shoulder. She jumps a little, then stares at me accusingly. "What?"

I sign for her to turn the music down, which she does grudgingly.

"What are you listening to?"

"It's this Irish group, Sons of Vox. Why?"

"I've never heard of them."

"Well, duh. You're from another world."

"No, I mean I spent a couple of hours in a music store the other day and I don't remember seeing them."

She shrugs. "They're kind of underground, I guess. I really like them, but they're not big or anything."

"Not big." I blink. "Where I come from, they're pretty well known—by a different name, though."

"Really?" She sounds interested, now. "What?"

"U2."

"Oh." She thinks about it for a second. "I think I like Sons of Vox better."

Dr. Pete interjects. "Sounds like *you two* have something in common."

Alexandra rolls her eyes. "*Please*, Uncle Pete—not with the puns."

I punch him on the shoulder. "Yeah! We're trying to discuss *serious music* here."

"Okay, okay. Are you ready to go?"

"Give me a minute, all right?"

He shrugs. "Sure, yeah. Come find me when you're ready, okay?" He walks off, a little irritated by my sudden about-face but trying to hide it.

"So," Alexandra says, "how many albums have they done on your world?"

We spend the next few minutes comparing notes. I give her my e-mail address and she promises to send me some music. I leave the party feeling a little better: not exactly cheerful, but not as depressed as I was. I don't much feel like talking, though—I spend the trip back mostly in my own head, deflecting Dr. Pete's attempts at conversation with mutters and noncommittal replies. I've got the opening riff to "Where the Streets Have No Name" running through my head, powerful but a little melancholy.

We pull up in front of my building and stop. "I'm sorry if I gave you the wrong impression—," he starts, and I cut him off.

"Not your fault, Doc. I *know* you're just trying to help— I'm full of Urthbone, remember? And I actually had a pretty good time."

"You still feeling jittery?"

I stop and consider the question—I'd kind of forgotten about the reason Dr. Pete had asked me to come with him.

"No, not at all," I say. "I feel a lot better. Thank you."

"Well, that's the main thing. Make sure that you—"

He stops, staring past me. I glance in the direction he's looking, feeling a little surge of adrenaline, and see a pair of bright yellow eyes watching us from the shadows of the alley that runs beside my building.

"What?" I say.

"I'm not sure. Probably just a homeless lone wolf—but they can be dangerous, especially to humans on their own. Maybe I should escort you to the door."

"That's really not necessary—"

He's already out of the car, though. I sigh and follow him; I'm in no mood to argue with the male protective reflex, no doubt magnified in this case by the doctor/patient relationship.

We're halfway to the entrance when the wolf stalks out of the alley and cuts us off.

He's gray, shaggy, and large, his head at least three feet off the ground. He's in full wolf form, no evidence of humanity at all, and his lips curl back in a snarl of warning as we approach.

"Jace, stay back." Dr. Pete doesn't sound worried, just firm. Those are the last words he says to me as he quickly shifts to half-wolf form himself.

The wolf stares at me. I stare back. There's something familiar about him. . . .

"Doc, hold it," I blurt out as Dr. Pete lets out a menacing growl. "I know this guy."

The gray wolf sits, transforming to half-were form as he does. When he has hands, he signs to me. *Hello, Jace. Please forgive the intrusion.*

I don't bother signing back. "Tanaka. What the hell are you doing here?"

I came to make amends. And I was . . . His paws pause. *. . . concerned for your safety.*

"That's not necessary. I can take care of myself—unless you know something I don't?"

No. I have heard of no new threat. I was simply worried . . . and perhaps a little restless. I went out for a run and found myself in your neighborhood. I will leave. His ears droop, which make him look more like Eeyore than a vicious supernatural beast.

"No, hang on a second, okay?" I turn to Dr. Pete. "You can take off. Thanks for a great day, really."

"You're sure?" He eyes Tanaka with open mistrust and just a little hostility.

"Yeah, yeah, I'll be fine. I work with him. I'll call you if I'm having problems, all right?"

"Well . . . all right. Good night." He nods curtly at Tanaka, then goes back to his car.

I watch him drive away, then turn to Tanaka. He's waiting, with that hangdog expression canines get when they know they're in trouble, no doubt expecting another visit from Hurricane Jace.

I shake my head. "I'm not angry. Really. I appreciate the sentiment."

He makes a single fluid gesture with one clawed hand. *But?*

"But this would have been a bad idea even if I had joined the Hair Club for Humans. You're a great guy. Honestly. But long-distance relationships are tricky at the best of times, and the distance between me and you stretches from species to country to universe. The more invested in a case I am, the more focused on it I become, and I don't think it's possible for me to *be* any more invested in a case than I am right now. It's just not going to happen, Tanaka. Wrong time, wrong place, wrong woman. I'm sorry. You should go home."

I understand. I should not have come—not here, not to America. Thank you for your honesty. I wish you well.

He reverts back to full wolf mode, and pads off into the night.

———————◆———————

I sleep a little better that night, so I guess Dr. Pete's treatment has some merit. Even so, it takes me a while to drift off; I keep thinking about Tanaka. I mean, I know I did the right thing, but sometimes doing the wrong thing is more enjoyable.

From what I can remember, a *lot* more enjoyable.

But the idea's ridiculous. Even forgetting about the whole man-into-beast aspect, I don't think a man like Tanaka's my style. He's got the whole Japanese culture thing going, which doesn't have a good track record as far as gender equality is concerned; the comments Isamu threw in my face, while insulting, didn't really come as a surprise.

Which brings up the question of who my type actually is.

Roger? On the surface, he seemed to have it all: brains, ambitions, looks, charm. Great in bed. But let's face it, that's not a type—that's a fantasy. Guys who have that much to offer up front tend to be self-centered and shallow underneath. Actually, I'm pretty sure that particular analysis isn't limited to the male gender, or even the human race. The more desirable you are, the more power you have, power corrupts, and absolute power corrupts absolutely. Of course, by that definition Marilyn Monroe must have been a cannibal, but who knows. Maybe she was from another universe, too.

I guess I've always been attracted to powerful men. I read somewhere that the two universal attractors in human beings, regardless of culture, are power and youth—specifically, power for women and youth for men. Which explains why aging rock stars date eighteen-year-old models but doesn't answer my question at all. Isn't there something less generic that I'm looking for in a man?

Well, how about Dr. Pete? Nice guy, doctor, clearly a family man. Compassionate, sense of humor, intelligent. The resemblance to a young Indiana Jones doesn't hurt, either. Of course, he isn't so much interested in raising a family as a litter—no, that's not fair. Putting aside all questions of his wolfiness, would I date this guy if I'd met him in my other life?

Yes.

The answer surprises me, and my brain immediately goes to work building a viable defense. *It would never work: doctors work even longer hours than agents, a family would be nice but there's no way you're having eight kids, the in-laws seem pleasant but your folks would eat them alive—*

Shut up, brain.

As long as we're on hypotheticals, how about Cassius?

Fresh-faced California surfer-boy good looks with the experience and intelligence of a spymaster. James Bond as played by a young, bloodsucking Robert Redford.

I'm tempted to say Cassius is too much like Roger, but I can't. Despite the surface similarities, there's a depth to Cassius that makes Roger seem like a game-show host. Yes, Cassius probably gave Machiavelli lessons in manipulation; yes, he's no doubt capable of utter ruthlessness—but he's not heartless. Maybe it was just the high levels of Urthbone in my system at the time, but I could sense the kind of pain Cassius carries around. He's one of those rare bosses, capable of making the hard decisions and willing to accept the emotional consequences of his actions. Conversations I've had with Gretchen since meeting him have confirmed this.

Still, it's all moot. I'm not going to be sticking around long enough to get involved with any of these guys.

I'm not.

***

I spend Sunday doing laundry, shopping, mundane apartment things. One of the things I still find spooky is what I call daytimers—pires who, for whatever reason, are out and about while the sun is up. The outfits they wear cover every square inch of skin—hood, gloves, black bug-eyed goggles, mask—and white or red seems to be the color of choice, usually something smooth and gleamy. Pires don't have to worry about heat or perspiration, so artificial fabrics like polyester or rubber work just fine. Some of the pires I see look like they've painted their entire bodies in liquid latex, wearing only shoes, gloves, and goggles. A lanky, crimson-skinned woman wearing a streamlined helmet zips past me on Rollerblades, sucking on a hemaccino through a straw.

Charlie calls me up to see how I'm doing on Sunday night, and hangs up after I tell him I'm fine. Straight and to the point, that's my partner. I keep checking my e-mail, but that music Alexandra promised me never shows up. Ah, well— she's a teenager, she probably just forgot.

By Monday morning I'm itching to get back to work. I arrive at the office a half hour early and plan to head for the intel division to see if Gretchen's dug up anything new— but the receptionist tells me Cassius wants to see me as soon as I get in. Uh-oh.

Turns out he just wants to go over the case, see where we are and what we're doing. This kind of general recap of events is pretty much SOP for most intelligence agencies, especially with cases that drag on for extended periods of time; it keeps details fresh in the agents' minds and often stimulates a new insight or connection. Strangely, neither Gretchen nor Eisfanger is present—not even Charlie.

"—so that's about it," I say. "Aristotle Stoker knows we're looking for him."

Cassius nods. "And that's all Tanaka had to tell you?"

I hesitate. "He also seems to feel that our investigation has either a leak or someone with a hidden agenda. No specifics."

"A hidden agenda in a case involving national security agencies from more than one country? What a strange and unusual conclusion."

"Yeah. Anything you can share with me?"

He raises an eyebrow and stares at me. I shrug. There's a whole conversation right there, one that starts with: *You realize I can't even admit to knowing about such things, let alone discuss them*, and ends with *I know, but I had to ask*.

"Look, there's something that's been bothering me," I say. "Why me?"

"I'm not sure I understand the question."

"Out of all the profilers you could have picked, why me?"

He hesitates just long enough to let me know he's hiding something. "I'm afraid it's both more technical and less personal than you might think. The number of variables involved in a cross-universe transfer are immense; it's like hitting an orbital launch window. You just happened to be available—in a metaphysical sense—when that window was open."

"Gee, thanks. I feel so much more valued now."

"You're very valuable, Jace. Tanaka certainly seems to think so, wouldn't you say?"

Here's where normally I'd brace myself for a reading of the Riot Act concerning interoffice romance and agent conduct—but as I made it abundantly clear to Cassius in a previous rant, I'm going to disregard little subtleties like that. Apparently it sank in, too, because the tone of his next question is cautious.

"Is this an . . . *alliance* you intend to pursue?"

"I think the word you're groping for is 'relationship.' And no, I don't intend to take things any further." I'm deliberately vague, wondering just how much he knows.

"Ah." He's quiet for a moment, studying my expression. I look as neutral as I possibly can.

"I just wanted to let you know that I have no problem with that, myself. You're in a difficult position, and I don't intend to make things any harder for you than they already are. Isolation is an occupational hazard in intelligence work; I'm glad you're making friends. And I hope you're discovering that we're really not that different from you."

"And if you told me anything else, I'd ignore you anyway, right?"

He smiles. "Am I that transparent? Here I thought I was doing a pretty good job at finessing you."

"Is that what you call it? You got the first letter right, anyway."

"That's a little harsh."

"No, underage scotch is a little harsh. What you've done to me has to be measured on a different scale entirely."

"You want another apology?"

"How many until I have the full set?"

"Getting one from me in the first place makes it a collector's item."

"Great. I'll put it up on eBay and see what I can get."

The last remark provokes an unexpected burst of laughter. "What?" I say. I can banter with the best of them, but that wasn't much of a punch line.

"I'm sorry," he says, shaking his head and grinning. "I

think we have a little cultural dissonance going on. What's eBay in your world?"

"A public auction site, where people buy and sell practically everything—why, what is it here?"

"Online porn for thropes. There's this thing they do called baying, which involves releasing as long and loud a howl as possible at the moment of orgasm. EBaying is doing the same thing over the Internet."

I frown. "That explains a lot. And here I thought he'd pulled a muscle in his back or something. . . ."

Okay, I just made that up. But it provoked another burst of laughter from Cassius, and he had one of those infectious laughs that could cause giggles at a funeral. I started laughing, too. And then I thought of this scene I'd seen in a movie once—I think it was *Porky's II*—where a woman with the nickname Lassie is having sex in a school equipment room. The sex itself is offscreen; what the audience sees is the reaction of the high-school boys trying to play basketball in the gym next door as the woman does exactly what Cassius just described: lets loose with a long, mournful howl as she hits her peak. It goes on and on and on, getting funnier and funnier, but what's really hilarious is the reaction shots of the boys as they struggle—and fail—to keep straight faces. When I saw it in the theater, it provoked the same kind of building crescendo of laughter in the audience, leaving them literally gasping; the humor may have been juvenile, but the setup and delivery was genius.

And that's what happens to us. The harder I try to keep my own laughter under control, the harder I laugh. So does Cassius. I don't know if the Urthbone is affecting the equation, but every time I think I'm done I hear this desperate *Ow-wooooooooooooooooooooh* in my head, and I'm off again.

"Okay," I gasp. "*Damn.* I think I needed that."

"That's probably what he said," Cassius says, and we both start all over again.

When it finally, finally winds down, things are different between us. Laughter is something we take for granted, because everyone—old, young, dumb, smart, good, evil—

laughs. But you can't share the kind of release Cassius and I just did without a certain level of intimacy, whether you acknowledge it or not.

It doesn't last. The monitor on his desk chimes three times, and his attention is instantly fixed on it. "Jace," he says. "The Miyagi video just went up on the Net."

He swivels the monitor so I can see it, too. Sure enough, there's a bound Keiko Miyagi, suspended by her wrists, her ankles fastened to the pole that's slowly killing her. Any laughter left in me dies as she does. It's gruesome to watch . . . but it's also my job.

Cassius is already on the phone to Gretchen, trying to pin down the server that's hosting the site. I can tell it's not going well, but that's hardly a surprise. I study the footage intently, looking for revelation. She's nude but not gagged, and a steady stream of loud, angry Japanese is pouring from her mouth. She's not going quietly. The first two vics didn't do much more than howl or scream; Fieldstone went from being drugged to wolfing out, while Porter was too busy fighting drug-crazed huskies to utter anything coherent. I wonder what she's saying.

"It's originating in Alaska," Cassius tells me. "Get to the airport—Charlie and Eisfanger will meet you there." I'm already on my feet and moving.

And wondering who's dying at this very moment.

NINE

"Well, here we are again," Eisfanger says, taking his seat. The plane starts to taxi down the runway. "How was everyone's weekend?"

"Outstanding," Charlie grunts, staring out the window.

"Interesting, in the Chinese sense of the word," I answer, flipping open my laptop.

"Yeah? I spent mine—"

"Gretch's nailed down the location," I say. "Same as last time, a satellite link broadcasting from a remote area, in this case a river delta in Alaska. Local law enforcement are being advised, but they're going to wait for us until they move in. We'll have first eyes on the site."

"Unless the natives beat us to it," Eisfanger says.

I frown at him. "I thought local authorities were onboard."

"Not talking about the law. I mean natives, as in Alaskan packs. You ever seen an Alaskan timber wolf?"

I shake my head.

"Well, they mass a little less than a grizzly and are a lot less friendly. There are bloodlines in that state that go back thousands of years, and some of them have never even bothered taking full human form."

"Great. Hillbillies with fangs. How about pires?"

"Tourists, mostly. Get a lot of them during the dark season—you know, hardly any daylight. Anchorage has a lot of casinos."

That made sense. Dr. Pete had said something about Anchorage, but I couldn't quite recall what it had been. Something about Moondays?

"We'll be flying in to Anchorage," Eisfanger says, "then transferring to a floatplane. The nearest town is Bethel, a glorified fishing and hunting village with the only government offices for hundreds of miles. We'll touch down on the river, then take a boat to the site itself."

"He's not making it easy for us, is he? Every one of his killing sites has been in the middle of nowhere. Serials that pick remote spots usually do so for one of two reasons: to conceal their crimes, or because the location isolates their victims, letting them hunt without interference. The first definitely isn't true—he's publicizing his crimes, not hiding them."

Eisfanger scratches his wide jaw. "So maybe the second reason? A human being is at a physical disadvantage against a hemovore or a lycanthrope; maybe he's trying to even the odds."

"Possibly, but I don't think so. Two of his victims were large and strong, and one worked for a powerful criminal organization—if anything, he's flaunting the fact that he's not afraid of anyone. No, the locations are important in and of themselves—I'm just not sure how."

"The Japanese site had historical relevance."

"True, but the Australian one didn't. And the McMurdo site is a big unknown—unless you'd care to enlighten me?"

He hesitates, then looks around as if he expects someone to leap out from behind a seat, even though we're the only ones on the plane. Charlie's still staring out the window, but he abruptly gets up and walks to the rear of the plane without saying a word.

"Where's he going?" I ask.

"Out of earshot," Eisfanger says. "Guess he thinks I don't trust him."

"Do you?"

"Of course!" Eisfanger says, sounding offended. "But I'm not going to *force* him to listen to something that could get him in trouble. Plausible deniability ain't just a river in Egypt."

"Okay. So what can you tell me?"

"Not that much, really. The McMurdo site is a weapons research facility—that's why it's located in such a remote region."

"Weapons? You mean like nuclear weapons?" From the confused look on his face, I can see he has no idea what I'm talking about.

"Right," I say. "No nukes. Well, that's good news, anyway."

"I don't know what nukes are, but I doubt they're as dangerous as what they test at McMurdo. I don't have any details, just rumors—but they're quite disturbing."

"Tell me."

"Diseases that target only thropes or pires. Orbital mirrors that could focus sunlight on any part of the globe. Golems that mimic thropes or pires perfectly."

"Bioweapons, space lasers, and androids?"

His eyes widen. "You're familiar with these things?"

"Only in fiction. My world hasn't gotten any further than the rumor stage with those ideas, either—most of them, anyway."

A weapons facility and an old concentration camp. Stoker's trying to tell me—to tell the world—something, but there's more to it than the sorry plight of the human race. Is the weapon the government's working on maybe something designed to solve the human problem once and for all?

But the human problem means two different things for pires and thropes. Pires need human stock to replenish their own, while thropes don't; therefore, it's ultimately in the thropes' best interests for the human race to die out, and in the pires' for it to survive.

The first victim was a pire scientist at McMurdo. If the pires were working for the survival of humans, why kill one?

I think about it all the way to Anchorage—and wonder how much I can trust my own boss.

I don't get to see much of Anchorage beyond the airport. About the only difference that really stands out in the terminal is the aroma; there's a certain rank gaminess to the air, probably caused by the preponderance of thropes. I don't see many in were form—air travel is really more comfortable for the two-legged—but I can sure smell them. Still, a New York bus on an August night is worse.

I've never been a fan of small planes, and adding pontoons doesn't make it any better. I try to take my mind off the choppiness and sudden drops in altitude by studying the terrain below. It's beautiful, raw and wild and green, and being high above it almost makes it seem like I'm home again.

The pilot is a black man—well, a dark-skinned thrope—with a French-Canadian accent and gold-rimmed aviator glasses. His name is Francis Duvalier, and apparently he's not only our ride but also the local Sheriff. I get a sense of relaxed amusement from him, that kind of been-there-done-that confidence you find in highly independent people. He fills us in on the local political landscape and what we can expect as far as cooperation from the locals goes: not much.

"This place, it is very much like the Wild West," he says loudly over the roar of the engine. "The locals, they do not like to be told what to do. They keep to themselves, and solve conflicts with their fangs and claws."

"They do that a lot?" I ask.

"There are many packs, each with its own territory. Border disputes happen often, but war between packs almost never. Most disputes are settled one-on-one."

So—not so much hillbillies as street gangs. Lucky I packed my switchblade.

"Is there a local boss?" I ask. "The leader of the strongest pack?"

Duvalier grins at me. "How do you think I got this job?"

The flight takes a few hours—Alaska is a *big* place. We finally touch down on the Kuskokwim River around 4:00 P.M. and I can get out and stand on solid ground again. The air is cold, barely above freezing, and I'm not really dressed for it. It doesn't seem to bother either Duvalier or Eisfanger, and Charlie of course ignores it completely. I wrap my arms around myself and try not to shiver.

Duvalier tilts his head back and sniffs the air. "First snow of the year coming, I think. Maybe mess up the crime scene."

"Then we better get going," I snap. Being cold makes me grouchy.

"Of course. But we can get there faster traveling as *loup*, no?"

He has a point, but I'd rather not tell him I'm a mere human unless I have to. "Good idea. You and Damon go on ahead; Charlie and I will take the boat with our equipment."

"Maybe I should ride with my gear—," Eisfanger begins, but a glare from me shuts him up. "Oh. Right. You know, I could use a good run."

"I'll try not to lose you, city boy," Duvalier says with a grin.

He helps us lug our bags to a flat-bottomed skiff moored next to the plane; we've got a lot with us, since we won't have Tanaka's high-tech train to help us out this time. We do have GPS coordinates thanks to Gretchen, and once Duvalier sketches out our route on a map we're good to go. He and Eisfanger shift into four-legged mode—Eisfanger looking slightly embarrassed as he strips down first—and I get my first look at the techie as a wolf. He's pure white, his pitbull heritage giving him a wider head and shorter snout than most wolves.

Duvalier is long and lean, jet-black fur with just the barest bit of curl to it that gives him a tousled, rakish look. He winks at me and then takes off down the dock at a strong lope with Eisfanger right behind him.

"Mind if I drive?" Charlie asks.

"Sure. I'll navigate." I climb aboard.

Bethel is in a region known as the Yukon Delta, a huge and mostly unpopulated area that's mainly subarctic tundra and marshland. It's flat and muddy, the riverbanks lined with scrubby black spruce and balsam poplar, with lots of ducks and geese paddling through the frigid water. The docks themselves are oddly deserted; I wonder where all the locals are. Charlie revs up the outboard, and the small village and its docks are very quickly out of sight.

I dig a parka out of our bags and put it on, along with some gloves and a toque. It helps a lot. Fortunately, the site is only about an hour away by boat—we should be able to make camp before nightfall. I would have preferred to take a helicopter, but this is actually faster—there's no chopper in Bethel, and the closest one that's available is five hours away. Hopefully we'll be picked up by one when we're ready to leave, but for now the quickest way to get there is by boat. Unless, of course, you can run on four legs.

It's cold and desolate and mostly bare, not like the Alaskan forest I'd imagined at all. Of course, we're right on the edge of the Bering Sea, home to polar bears, walruses, and killer whales; we're about as far north as you can go and still be in the USA. Not quite the fifty-below temperatures of McMurdo, but still a barren and hostile environment.

The sun is low on the horizon, gleaming off the water as we motor down the river. I wonder how cold it'll get once the sun sets.

And whether the locals prefer hunting during the day or the night. . . .

Eisfanger and Duvalier are waiting for us when we arrive at the site, an outcropping of rocky tundra covered with patchy gray-green moss, bordered on two sides by marsh and one by the river. Eisfanger is in half-were form, while Duvalier is still fully lupine.

Charlie brings the boat to a sputtering halt and beaches

it. I jump out, already replacing my warm leather gloves with sterile latex ones.

At first glance, I can't tell if the vic is a thrope or a pire—what I see is a naked male body, lying on his back and wearing what seems to be an old-fashioned diving helmet, the kind that looks like a metal sphere with a window in the front. As I get closer, tugging paper booties over my own shoes, I see that's exactly what it is. The helmet itself is a dull, tarnished gray, the glass of the faceplate tinted a deep red. A grid of four thin silver rods has been welded across the window, sealing it shut. A few feet away, a compact satellite dish sits on top of a wooden crate, broadcasting the Hokkaido killing to the world.

Eisfanger begins to sign as soon as he sees me, but he's moving too quickly and using lots of words I don't recognize. "Whoa, slow down."

Sorry. Vic's a thrope—cause of death is drowning. I think.

I frown and crouch beside the body. Up close, I can see little silver sparkles in the red of the glass—and then I realize it isn't the glass that's red.

I turn back to Eisfanger. *Helmet's iron, rods are silver. I think the liquid is—*

"Blood," I finish. "Laced with silver of some kind." I examine the helmet critically, note that a heavy clasp and padlock has been used to seal it around the neck. "There's no entry point for adding a liquid. The blood's probably his own."

Could be a variation on the silver maiden—silver blades that cut open an artery when the helmet closes.

I nod. "Doesn't tell us how the silver was introduced, though. We'll know more once we get it open."

I'll start setting up.

Charlie's already begun unloading the boat, and Duvalier changes into half-were form to help. I go over and examine the satellite dish cautiously, but it doesn't seem to be booby-trapped. I turn it off.

Before too long we've got an enclosed tent structure around the body, though a stiff wind has sprung up and threatens to tumbleweed the whole thing across the tundra. Both Eisfanger and Duvalier have been very careful where they stepped, so the crime scene is relatively undisturbed. The wind is a problem—there's no telling what evidence it's already blown away—but there's little I can do about that. We set up our own tents around the crime scene tent, managing to do so just before the last of the daylight slips away.

In the tent, under the harsh glare of the electric lights, the rising wind competes with the snapping of the fabric and the throaty purr of the generator. Eisfanger has his gear, both scientific and mystical, set up on two folding tables. You'd think there would be a clear delineation between them, but no—he has a feathered rattle right next to a bone saw, which magnifies the creepy element of both. The body is on another folding table.

He uses bolt cutters to shear off the padlock, and a bowl to catch the blood that spills out once the helmet's seal has been cracked. The helmet may have started out as a piece of diving equipment, but it's been heavily modified: as Eisfanger predicted, there are razor-sharp silver blades where it snugs against the neck, spring-loaded so they'll slash the wearer's throat once the helmet is in place.

The victim's face is revealed, a man in his forties with a thick blond beard now dyed red with his own blood. The skin of his face is pocked with hundreds of small black dots with glittering centers, contact burns from tiny bits of silver flake.

"Look at the interior," Eisfanger says. He runs a gloved finger against one curving red surface, and it comes away with a thick, silvery sludge tinged with red on it. "Some kind of paste—silver mixed with a gel, probably water soluble."

"Yeah. The helmet starts filling up with blood, he's thrashing around in panic, the paste and blood mix together. Once it gets up past his nose, he has no choice but to breathe it in. That gets the silver into his lungs."

"Which kills him, but not right away. Nasty way to go."

"And not good for forensic magic, right?" I already know the answer.

"No. Too much silver, same as the Australian vic. But I might be able to get something from the surrounding terrain."

"Like the Miyagi bloodstain?"

"Similar. The building she was killed in had too much psychic residue from its activity as a camp—like too many fingerprints smudging the one you want. Both the Australian and Arctic vics were in deserts—one hot, one cold, but both essentially lifeless in the immediate area around the body. This, though—this has lichens, and moss. I'm going to see if I can have a conversation."

He says it'll take a while; vegetation is usually friendly but doesn't talk terribly fast. It's not like I have anyplace else to go, so I huddle in a corner and take turns staring at Eisfanger and the corpse. Eisfanger's mumbling and running his hands gently in circles over the ground, occasionally stopping to sprinkle something from a small pouch.

The corpse doesn't do anything at all, for which I'm grateful. Not that it suddenly coming back to life would surprise me, but it's been a long day and I really don't feel like shooting my evidence in the head. Assuming that would work on zombies here—or even if they *have* zombies here. Maybe teenage punk thropes with a gangrene fetish are as close as they get.

The quality of the wind-noise changes, in a way that's hard to define. I wonder about it and get my answer a moment later as Charlie and Duvalier—now fully human again, and dressed—enter the tent, both of them flecked with white.

"Starting to snow," Duvalier says. "Got this tent up just in time, I think."

Charlie takes his fedora off, knocks it against his leg to remove the snow. "Be a long night," he says. "I'll take first watch."

Duvalier shrugs. "Fine by me. Wake me up when you want to switch—"

"I've got something," Eisfanger says.

He's got my immediate attention. "What is it?"

"The moss remembers an incident from yesterday. Something large and heavy, rolling over the surface of the land. It stopped here, then left again."

"Sounds like a vehicle," Charlie says.

Duvalier frowns. "Nobody drives out here. Ground's uneven, marshy in some spots and rocky in others. Four-wheel drive might make it, but I didn't see any tracks."

"I think I can answer that," says Eisfanger. "The moss says it was 'spring-fed' afterward, which means artificially invigorated. I think a spell may have been used to repair any surface damage to the tundra and cover up tracks."

"Can you—I don't know—unspell it?"

"Not as such. But the spell was probably only used to affect the moss itself—the ground beneath it might still hold a pattern." He gets up, goes over to his gear, and selects a bundle of dried herbs and a small flask. He returns to where he was squatting and sprinkles a few drops from the flask, then lights one end of the herb bundle. He douses the flame by waving the bundle briskly through the air, then makes intricate passes over the floor with the bundle. The smoke flows downward, creating a miniature fog bank hugging the ground, then slowly dissipates.

"Gotcha," Eisfanger says with satisfaction.

The moss has turned perfectly transparent, like a delicate ice sculpture crafted by insects. Beneath it, pressed into the thin soil, is the clearly visible print of a tire tread.

"Find the other one," I say. "It'll give us a wheelbase to work with."

"Well, there's a problem with that—"

Duvalier is crouched down, studying the track. "You won't find another one," he says, straightening up.

"How did you know that?" Eisfanger asks. "That's what the moss said, too."

"What, now we're after someone on a unicycle?" Visions of trained circus bears—white ones—wearing pointy hats and balancing on one-wheeled contraptions zip through my head. They're juggling fish.

"Not one wheel—two," Duvalier says. "One in front of the other, leaving a single track."

"You recognize this?" I ask.

"I don't recognize the tread itself, but I know what it is. It's a blizzard bike—a motorcycle designed to operate in the winter. Wide, studded tires, powerful motor with an engine block heater and antifreeze system. It's the only kind of vehicle that could get around out here, but I didn't think there were any zerkers in the area."

"Zerkers?" I say. "Like in . . . 'zircus'?"

"No, like in 'berserkers.' You know the term?"

"Where I come from it referred to Vikings—Nordic raiders in longboats who spent most of their time pillaging, looting, and raping. They'd drive themselves into a battle frenzy beforehand, so they seemed more like beasts than men."

Duvalier nods. "An apt description. Zerkers are thropes too wild to join a civilized pack, but not so wild they reject technology. Their bikes give them greater mobility and independence; they often carry everything they own with them. Subzero weather on a bike can produce temperatures of a hundred below, but they ride in half-were form and ignore it. They work as mercenaries, thieves, smugglers—whatever's illegal and dangerous. And they wear homemade armor."

I revise my opinion of the locals once again; not hillbillies with fangs, not street gangs with fur, but knight-Viking bikers. Better than those damn polar bears on unicycles, anyway.

"So what was one doing way out here?" Eisfanger asks.

"Could have been hunting," Duvalier says. "Plenty caribou round here. Zerkers don't give a damn about pack boundaries."

"Or he could have been giving our killer a lift," I say.

"Stoker's got plenty of criminal contacts—these zerkers sound exactly like the kind of people he'd be mixed up with."

"Forgive me for saying so," Duvalier says, "but that's hard to believe. The only use zerkers generally have for human beings is to eat them. Hell, they've been known to eat each other."

I shake my head. "The guy we're dealing with is no ordinary human. If anybody could forge an alliance with cannibalistic, Harley-riding lycanthropes, it'd be him."

No ordinary human. The words are accurate, but as soon as they're out of my mouth they're replaced by a bad taste. It sounds like the kind of thing a thrope or a pire would say—not a member of the same species.

And then something odd happens; both Eisfanger and Duvalier snap their heads in the same direction, then freeze. It'd be funny if it weren't for the intent, focused looks on their faces.

"Whoever this zerker is," Duvalier says, "I believe he's coming back."

"Yeah," says Eisfanger. "And this time he brought some friends along."

And now my merely human ears can hear it, too: the rising, grinding roar of a number of motorcycle engines, getting closer.

"And here I thought first watch would be boring," Charlie says.

━━━━━◆━━━━━

There are five of them.

They roar out of the wind-whipped snow like lunatics, treating the bikes they're riding more like motocross vehicles than anything designed to drive down a highway: doing wheelies, using boulders like ramps and launching themselves into the air, bouncing off the rocky ground like armored kangaroos when they touch down. The wheels on their bikes are wider than auto tires and spiked for extra traction.

"You're the top dog around here, right?" Charlie asks Duvalier. The Sheriff nods, but his earlier good humor has vanished; I can feel deep apprehension behind his serious demeanor.

"That I am," he says. "But that doesn't mean *they* know that."

We've all come out of the tent to greet—or maybe "confront" is a better word—our visitors. They pull up in a line and kill their engines. The leader is clearly the one in the center, pulled up just a little closer than the others. I study him carefully.

He's the only one not in half-were form, presumably so we can talk to each other using words instead of signing; I note that this also leaves his hands free, and slip my own hand inside my jacket to make sure the Ruger's safety is off. He's a big man, broad-shouldered and muscular; I'd estimate his weight at around 230, his height when standing close to seven feet tall. He's got a rugged, craggy face, with a brow like a cliff and a jaw as square as a sledgehammer, bristling with stubble. His hair is a long, tangled brown mane, reaching past the shoulders of his armor.

The armor they're wearing is straight out of *Mad Max*: shoulder pads made from old steel-belted radials, held on by thick-linked chains bolted to the rubber. Thick fur pelts with bits of gristle and meat still clinging to them, stitched together with wire. One guy's outfit looks like he murdered a leather couch and a chain-link fence, then wrapped himself in the remains. The rider on the far left is wearing a steel helmet clearly designed for a thrope skull, with a dozen or so six-inch butcher knives welded into a crest across the top. He lifts his lips in a silent snarl when he notices me glance at him.

I'm starting to regret the quick slug of Urthbone I took before leaving the tent. It isn't so much the hostility coming off them that's unsettling; it's the hunger. And the total lack of anything that could be called fear.

The leader stares at us calmly. He gets off his bike and strides forward, stopping about a yard away from Duvalier and ignoring the rest of us completely.

"Hey," the giant says. He sounds very, very at ease; a man in his own living room, talking on the phone.

"Hey," Duvalier says. He sounds almost as calm, but there's still no humor in his voice. "I'm Sheriff Duvalier. First Hunter of the Longjaw Pack."

"Bearbreaker. Independent—though I do have friends." He grins, a huge, teeth-baring smile that reveals the longest canines I've ever seen in a nonfurred face.

"I see that. What do you and your friends want?"

"Nothing much. We were passing through on our way to the Lunatic Ride and thought we smelled fresh meat."

Duvalier's eyebrows go up. He's surprised, though he tries not to show just how much. "The Ride? I hadn't heard anything about that."

Bearbreaker chuckles, a low rumble that sounds more like a growl than laughter. "Sorry. Guess your invitation got lost in the mail."

I have no idea what's going on, except that Duvalier seems tense and Bearbreaker doesn't. "What's the Lunatic Ride?"

The biker seems to notice me for the first time. "Mmm. And who might you be?"

"Special Agent Jace Valchek, NSA. This is a crime scene, Mr. Bearbreaker, not an open buffet. I'm in charge of the investigation."

"For an investigator, you're fairly ignorant."

"For a barbarian, you're fairly polite."

He smiles. "True—so I'll *politely* answer your question. The Lunatic Ride is a gathering, held on an irregular basis, of those who swear allegiance to nothing but freedom. It's rarely in the same place twice, and only those invited know about it. We come together to celebrate our independence, to trade stories and gear and information, to settle grudges and get drunk and challenge each other, to do a little partying and a little business. This year we're setting up camp just outside of a place called Bethel, where I'm sure the locals will welcome us with open arms. Isn't that right, Sheriff?"

"Your money's as good as anyone else's."

"Good attitude. Should be a few hundred of us, and we're real generous to our friends. Hope the bars are well stocked—meat, we can take care of on our own."

I can tell that doesn't sit well with Duvalier—it's probably his pack's caribou that'll wind up in the Ride's hairy bellies—but it's entirely possible they'll pay for what they hunt and kill, too. I was at the aftermath of a biker rally in Sturgis, once, and while there was enough vomit, smashed glass, over-flowing trash cans, and cigarette butts to swamp a landfill, the locals all came out of it with bulging wallets and a minimum of property damage.

"A few hundred, huh?" I say. "Any of them pass this way recently?"

"Could be. Why, you got one inside that tent?" The idea doesn't seem to bother him particularly.

"We haven't identified the victim yet."

"Want some help? I could take a few bites and see if the taste's familiar." That brings a chorus of wolfy, barking laughter from the others.

"Thanks, but I don't think you'd appreciate the flavor. He's got enough silver in him to support the Lone Ranger." That gets me a confused look, but I think he understands my overall point. He meets my eyes—

The jolt I feel is completely unexpected. Something passes between us, something tense and charged and some-how familiar. It takes me by surprise, but he almost seems to expect it. It lasts no more than a second before he looks away.

"Okay. Guess we'll be on our way, then. Drop by the camp if you're in the mood, Valchek—I can show you a bet-ter time than *this*, anyway." More feral laughter.

"That's not saying much," I tell him, feeling a little stunned, and he grins and gets back on his bike. A few sec-onds later they're all roaring off into the snow without a backward glance.

Eisfanger clears his throat. "That was a little . . . unset-tling."

"And it's over," I say. "Let's get back to work."

Which we do. Eisfanger prepares the body for transport; I snap some pictures of the tire track he uncovered while the moss is still see-through.

Somehow, I'm not surprised when it matches the tracks outside in the snow.

TEN

Duvalier heads straight for the radio in the boat as soon as the bikers leave, which is how he finds out that his people have been trying to reach him for the last few hours. Seems there is a large group of zerkers setting up camp a mile or so out of town, and what exactly did the Sheriff plan to do about that?

What he does is make his apologies to us, morph into wolf form, and take off into the snowstorm. We stay put, processing the site and the body as thoroughly as we can with what we brought with us. We get both hair and fiber samples as well as the tire track, though we have no luck with foot- or fingerprints.

And we finally have a suspect.

"You think Bearbreaker will lead us to Stoker?" Eisfanger asks. It's just after 2:00 A.M. and we're finally done; all we have to do in the morning is break camp.

"I don't know." I hesitate, then ask the stupid question that's been on my mind. "You said Selkie was a shape-shifter. Is it possible—"

"That Selkie's posing as Bearbreaker?" Eisfanger shakes his head. "The same thought occurred to me after he left. I took Wittgenstein out and let him sniff around; he's got a keen nose for changeling sorcery. He couldn't find anything, and to add that much mass to Selkie's frame would have required a lot of mojo—enough to leave plenty of traces behind. He's not using that kind of magic."

"So Stoker has a zerker ally. I wonder what he needs him for—can't be transport; he's got Selkie for that. Muscle?"

"Could be. Zerkers often work as mercenaries or body-guards."

"Only when the client can't afford golems," Charlie says, ducking under the tent flap. He's covered in snow, which is apparently just wet enough to stick to his dapper olive-green suit, but not so wet it melts from body heat—which I'm pretty sure Charlie doesn't have, anyway.

"Yeah?" I say. "What's it cost to rent a golem merce-nary?"

"Depends on the war. We're willing to work cheaper in certain locales."

"Like what, for instance?" Eisfanger asks.

"Desert campaigns."

"Why?"

"Local cuisine."

"But golems don't—" He stops as he realizes Charlie's referring to sand, and as filler instead of food.

I shake my head and say, "I'm going to bed. Wake me when it's my turn to stand watch."

I stumble outside and to my tent, where I remove my boots and some of my clothing before crawling into the sleeping bag. The wind has died down, and the soft patter of snow on the fabric of the tent lulls me to sleep within min-utes.

My last thought before I drift off is of Bearbreaker. I'd felt something when he met my eyes, some sense of con-nection that I couldn't define.

But I got the feeling he could. . . .

I wake up in the morning, cold and headachy; a quick shot of Urthbone helps one, but I'll have to wait for hot coffee for the other. I ask grumpily why no one woke me for my shift, and Charlie informs me he heard noises coming from my tent that seemed to indicate either demonic possession or my having sex with a chain saw and he didn't feel it was safe to interrupt either one. I inform him that my snoring isn't anywhere near that bad, and anyway, shut up.

It's stopped snowing, and the wind has died completely. The snow makes the landscape look pristine instead of barren, and the early-morning sun breaking through the clouds turns the whiteness up even higher. Eisfanger hands me a pair of sunglasses and I put them on gratefully.

A quick breakfast—peanut butter and bread for me, ham sandwich for Eisfanger—and we're ready to pack up and leave. The one thing we haven't examined thoroughly is the satellite broadcaster; we'll ship that to Seattle and let the techs there take it apart.

The trip back is uneventful, though the landscape now looks completely different due to the endless white blankness of the snow on either side of us; it feels not so much like something was added as erased.

Duvalier is there to greet us at the dock in Bethel along with a few other locals, who are marginally less hairy and better dressed than the zerkers we met last night. He tells us the Lunatic Ride is camped to the east of the town and so far they haven't made any trouble.

"That'll change, though," he tells me. "Moondays start tonight."

Moondays. Right. Now I remember what Dr. Pete told me about Anchorage, how it was one of the places that could get out of control during the monthly festival. And if that was how urban thropes behaved in Alaska, what would a bunch of feral Hell's Angels do out in the middle of the tundra?

"Your plane is all fueled up and ready to go. I'm getting Willy here to fly you instead; you understand I'm a little busy at the moment."

A pire bundled in bulky, grease-stained rain gear—big black gum boots, yellow rubber slicker, ridiculous wide-brimmed hat, and a face mask that seems to be made out of duct tape and welding goggles—shuffles forward and nods hello; he reminds me of Paddington Bear after a horrible car accident.

"Much appreciated," I say, "but only Eisfanger's leaving. Charlie and I are going to hang around, do a little sightseeing."

The look on Duvalier's face makes it plain he thinks this is a very, *very* bad idea, but he doesn't protest. He's going to need all the help he can get over the next three days, and he knows it. He nods and says, "I'll see you have a place to stay."

"Thanks. Can you get me a vehicle to use, too? I'd like to go out and take a look at that camp."

He hesitates; the look on his face now says this is a *much* worse idea than the previous one, and maybe he should also supply me with the number of the local undertaker to save time.

"Okay," he finally says. "You want a snowmobile, or something on four wheels?"

"The second one." I turn to Eisfanger. "Tell Cassius I'm playing a hunch, and I'll keep him apprised of the situation."

Eisfanger looks apprehensive, but he just shrugs and says, "Will do." He and Count Paddington board the plane, it roars to life, and a minute later I'm watching them get farther and farther away in the sky.

"Let's go," I tell Duvalier, and he leads us off the dock and into town.

Bethel is mainly an Inuit village, people who make their living from hunting and fishing. Hunting is largely a thrope endeavor, while fishing is the mainstay of the local pires, who trade their catch for caribou blood. I wouldn't have thought of vampires as being especially able fishermen, but apparently it's just as feasible to catch fish after the sun's gone down. The long winter nights coincide with the fishing offseason, which gives the local pires lots of free time to spend in the great outdoors, under a sky lit only by the stars and the aurora borealis.

And the moon.

The village has lots of children, which shouldn't surprise me; in small communities like this the concentration is usually on family. Sure, it has the untamed, dangerous feel of the frontier, but the frontier has always been defined by its colonists, and colonists mean children. So there are children—all thropes, at the moment—running around the streets, making snowmen, and having snowball fights. What's disturbing is that almost all of them are barefoot, half of them are wearing shorts, and quite a few are riding bicycles with smaller versions of the wide, spiked tires on the zerkers' bikes. Some of the kids are in were form, of course, running and rolling in the snow and snapping at each other playfully. Not as many of them are in half-were form as I would expect—I guess they don't actually need fur to be immune to the cold, which would explain why Bearbreaker seemed perfectly at ease conversing in a blizzard while dressed for Arizona.

Duvalier finds us rooms in a small lodge on the outskirts of town, full of thrope tourists in the summer but almost empty now. It's a nice place, a small restaurant and roomy lounge with a big fireplace on the main floor, seven or eight rooms on the second. Duvalier says he'll get someone to drop off a vehicle, and I tell him to contact me when he knows the situation and what he'll need in terms of additional manpower.

"Thanks," he says. "Hopefully that won't be necessary. We'll see, I guess."

"Uh, there's one more thing you should probably know." I pause, then steel myself and say, "I'm not a thrope."

Duvalier frowns, his nostrils flaring as he checks my scent a little closer. "But—"

"Artificial. I'm . . . unenhanced. But I can still handle myself in a fight, and I have these." I show him the *eskrima* sticks, flash the blades.

He sighs. "That's just great. You know what zerkers like to fight with? Other than their claws and teeth, I mean?"

"Biting sarcasm?"

"Axes. Custom-made battle-axes, with stainless-steel heads that weigh ten pounds or more and sport twelve to eighteen inches of striking edge. When they're *serious* about fighting they bolt an extended, razor-sharp silver blade to that, but for you they won't have to bother. They keep their ax heads dull—they cause more damage that way—but I've seen one chop through a parking meter with a single stroke. I don't think your little hand scythes are going to be much good against that."

I don't even bother telling him about the gun. "I'll keep that in mind."

He nods, and then he's gone. I get the feeling I haven't exactly put his mind at ease, but better to tell him now than have him throw me into a situation unaware. Still, his attitude annoys me; the underlying assumption that brute force always ultimately wins out is just a little too gendercentric for me. Or maybe it's speciescentric or just Alaskansheriffcentric. Or it could be I just like the suffix "centric" too much.

It doesn't take either Charlie or me long to get settled, though Charlie does change his clothes. When he leaves his room and joins me on the railed catwalk that runs around the perimeter of the second floor, he's put on a simple pair of jeans, boots, and a navy blue windbreaker that hangs loose enough to conceal his sword and ball-bearing holsters.

"Dressing down?" I ask.

"Trying to blend in. Not a lot of lems around here."

"Your people don't like the cold?"

"My people don't feel the cold."

"But you still wouldn't live here if you had the choice."

"It's not exactly a thriving hub of sophistication. And me, I like a little sophistication."

I lean back on the polished wood of the railing, cross my arms, and frown. "Really? Fine wines, French cuisine, exotic women? Doesn't seem your style."

As soon as the words are out of my mouth I know they're a mistake. Too late—he gives me a look that's colder than the temperature outside.

"Doesn't seem within my abilities, you mean. You're right. I don't eat, I don't drink, I don't have sex. But my eyes and ears and brain work just fine. And exactly what do you think "my people" fill their time with, since we don't have to deal with the constant entry and exit of various substances into and out of our bodies?"

"Uh . . ."

"I like art. I like music. I like books. I've even been known to loosen up and enjoy a laugh or two. But I guess to you I'm nothing but a weapon on loan."

"Not true," I snap, and now I'm the one who's irritated. "Maybe I haven't been exactly touchy-feely when it comes to getting to know you, but I've had a lot on my mind. Plus, I have *no idea* what you do when you're not at work—you're the first golem I've ever met, remember? For all I know, you stand in a closet and turn yourself off. Any attempt I *have* made at asking questions of a personal nature you've either deflected with an answer of one syllable or tried to see how gullible I am."

"That's not exactly—"

"But that's not what *really* pisses me off." I'm on a roll, now. "Maybe you're not used to this, but where I come from we don't have living weapons that follow us around and keep us from harm. What we have are *partners*. A partner is a person who watches your back, points out when you're screwing up, trusts you completely and occasionally saves your life. They do that for you . . . and you do that for *them*."

We glare at each other for a long moment.

"Problem is," he says at last, "we're here, not there."

"Doesn't make a damn bit of difference to me."

He considers this. "You know, that'd be a lot more reassuring if you weren't so damned fragile."

"I'm fragile? At least I don't burst into tears when I'm feeling underappreciated."

"True. You're more likely to shoot something."

"I find it therapeutic. You should try it sometime."

"No thanks. I'll stick to knitting tea cozies and sobbing into my pillow."

"We done?"

"Pretty much."

I nod and head downstairs. Charlie follows, close behind.

My plan is to drive out to the zerkers' camp, find Bearbreaker, and intimidate him into giving up Stoker.

Sure.

My backup plan is to challenge Bearbreaker to single combat, defeat him, become Queen of the Zerkers and spend the rest of my life riding a giant motorcycle over frozen tundra.

Much more likely.

My backup backup plan is to hang around, talk to as many locals and zerkers as I can, and see if I can dig up any evidence that Stoker was here. That one is at least half-doable—assuming the locals are more friendly than the zerkers—but the person I really want to talk to is Bearbreaker, and I have no idea how feasible that will actually be.

I get my answer a few minutes later. Bearbreaker's motorcycle is parked outside the Sheriff's office and he's leaning up against it, drinking a beer and looking very relaxed. When he sees Charlie and me walking toward him, he smiles and waves.

"Hey there," he says.

"Hello," I say. I stop in front of him and meet his eyes. "You here to talk to the Sheriff?"

"Actually, I was hoping to talk to you."

"Yeah? Funny, I was planning on doing the same thing."

"I won't make the obvious joke about you talking to yourself."

"Think you just did."

"I wasn't talking to you."

I grin despite myself. "What do you want, Bearbreaker?"

"Same thing you do. Conversation."

"I talk better when I'm drinking coffee."

"Me, too. If by coffee you mean beer, and by better you mean louder."

"How about we sit down together and do both? You can yell at me and I'll pretend to listen."

"Okay. There's a diner up the street, but the booths are kinda small." He flicks a glance at Charlie, who looks back as impassively as a glacier.

"I don't drink," Charlie says. "I prefer standing a stone's throw away and watching."

Bearbreaker nods, noting the threat but not responding to it. He motions us to follow him and heads up the sidewalk, leaving his bike where it is.

We get our share of looks on the way, from the merely curious to the downright hostile. I imagine I can hear doors slamming and bolts sliding into place all over town, and wonder just how wild tonight is going to get.

The diner is small, with booths of cracked red vinyl and Formica-topped tables edged in peeling chrome. Bearbreaker slides into one and nods at the waitress, a wrinkled Inuit woman who looks neither impressed nor hostile. She shuffles over and takes our order—two coffees, surprisingly. Charlie's elected to stay outside, hands in his pockets, staring through the window at us like a wooden cigar-store Indian facing the wrong way.

"Nice statue," Bearbreaker says. "Does it do tricks?"

"A few. Usually pretty hard on the audience, though."

"I'll bet. How about you? You talented, too?"

I stare at him, trying to gauge where he's going. He's trying to provoke me, that much is obvious, but in which direction? I can feel his interest in me, but it's more than sexual—it's both less intense and more complex than Tanaka's lust.

"Oh, I'm hell on wheels. Or do your people already have that trademarked?"

He chuckles. "We're not that bad, really. I mean, there's the random acts of violence, the total disrespect for the rule of law, the cannibalism . . . but other than that we're real sweethearts."

"Uh-huh. Well, sweetheart—you know a guy named Aristotle Stoker?"

He cradles his coffee just below his chin, blowing on it to cool it down; his massive hands make it look like one of those tiny Japanese teacups.

"Maybe I do," he says. "Or maybe I just know a guy who might be this Stoker character. Wouldn't want to get the wrong man in trouble."

"Who said he was in trouble?"

"If he isn't there yet," Bearbreaker says, pausing to drain half the cup in a single swallow, "I get the feeling he'll find himself in downtown Disaster after talking to you."

"I can't be that bad. You're talking to me."

"I got a thing for dangerous relationships."

"Is there any other kind?"

He leans back in the booth, resting the elbows of his massive arms on top of the padded back. "Let's say I know this Stoker. Why would I tell you anything about him?" He meets my eyes, his grin turning into a lazy smile.

That's a damn good question, and there's only one answer I can come up with. "You want something."

"Everybody wants something."

"Yeah. I want Stoker."

"And I want . . ." He pauses, long and slow and deliberate. "An ice-cream cone."

"Funny time of year for it."

"I'm a funny guy."

"Vanilla?"

"Not since I was thirteen."

"Do I have to run through all thirty-one flavors?"

"Oh, there are a lot more than that. Guess you're not from around here."

That sends up warning signals, but it's a little late for caution. "This is fun, but I have things to do. I'll get you a banana split sprinkled with cocaine and doused in brandy if you'll tell me where Stoker is now."

"Offering cocaine to a thrope? Interesting approach, but I prefer my nose to function, thank you—and I've never cared for brandy." His tone is gently chiding, as if I've made a mistake but not a serious one. "Tell you what—we're both strangers here, right? But the locals don't cross themselves and spit when you walk past. Spend some time with me, let the natives see us together, and maybe their hackles will go down."

"Hang out together? In public?"

"Wouldn't be much point doing it in private."

"Long as you don't mind an escort." I motion with my head toward Charlie.

"Fine with me. But he buys his own ice cream."

Bearbreaker won't commit to giving me any definite, specific information on Stoker, but he's serious about the ice cream. We wind up wandering across town—well, to the other end of the street, which is pretty much the same thing—to a general store. The locals are busy setting up booths lining the thoroughfare; people stare at us but don't say anything.

The store yields a surprisingly good flavor of blackberry from a large cardboard tub in the same freezer they keep frozen bait. The owner, an Inuit man with long, jet-black hair, is busy hanging crescent moon–shaped lanterns from the eaves when we arrive, and he goes back to it after serving us. We stroll down the street, shadowed by Charlie.

"Moondays in Alaska," Bearbreaker says between licks of his cone. "Ever done it here before?"

"Uh . . . no."

"It's fantastic. The snow, the smell of the tundra . . . really talks to the hindbrain, you know? All the stuff they do in the cities to celebrate seems kind of silly and pointless when you're out here."

"Sure. I know what you mean."

"Yeah? Where'd you grow up?"

It's an innocent enough question, but I have to consider it carefully before I answer. "The Midwest. Small town you wouldn't have heard of."

"Try me."

"Roadside."

"You're right; I've never heard of it. Whereabouts is it?"

"I don't mean to be rude, but I kind of thought I'd be the one asking the questions."

He shrugs, a movement that reminds me of boulders shifting. "I don't mind rude. Ask away."

"This guy who may or may not be Stoker—what's he look like?"

"Oh, you want proof I'm not just stringing you along? Okay. He's a little guy, maybe five four. Sharp face, like a weasel. Real smart, heart like an ice cube. Dresses like crap."

Bingo. Our first description of Stoker—I've finally got something to work with. I keep my face and voice neutral. "Might be our guy, might not. Know where I can find him?"

"Not now. But he said he'd get in touch during Moondays, and that starts tonight. You could hang around with me, see if he shows up."

Right. When the full moon comes out tonight, every thrope beneath it is going to go full, all-out hairy—all except yours truly. Who, despite what she smells like, isn't a thrope at all and would like to keep it that way.

"Sorry, but partying with a pack of zerkers isn't really my style. I'll be in town, but my wild time is my *own* time." The last remark is out of my mouth before I have time to think about it, but it feels right.

He smiles. "I can understand that. Maybe I'll run into you out on the tundra—I like to spend at least one night on my own under the stars, too."

"Maybe you will." Good. If he's spending his nights roaming around out in the wilderness, he won't be searching for me in town.

"Then I guess I'll see you tomorrow," he says. We've strolled back to where his bike is parked. "Thanks for the ice cream."

He gets on, fires it up, and takes off. He nods at Charlie as he passes him, but doesn't look back at me.

Charlie walks up and joins me. "How'd it go?"

"Hard to say." I frown. "But the next three days are going to be interesting."

The first night is incredibly boring.

I'd kind of expected a whole Wild West thing—you know, where the saloons are filled with bar brawls that spill out into the streets and result in drunken gunfights, with guys being shot off balconies and into horse troughs? Except there'd be blizzard bikes instead of horses, axes instead of guns, and all the yee-hawing would be replaced by growls, howls, and the occasional yip.

That doesn't happen.

The first night the zerkers keep to themselves. From my room I can hear faint, bass-heavy music and see the glow of a bonfire on the horizon, but that's about it. Duvalier drops by and tells us they've bought up pretty much every drop of liquor in town, but he's been assured they prefer their own company. He doesn't know how long that'll last and neither do I, but I tell him he can count on our assistance if he needs it. He nods, tosses me the keys to a half-ton truck parked outside, and says he'll let me know.

Charlie and I stay indoors. I get on my laptop and spend the next few hours getting as much data from Gretchen and Eisfanger as they can give me, which isn't much. We were right about the cause of death; the satellite broadcaster was exactly the same as the others and had been stolen from a container ship in Perth. I send Cassius an e-mail letting him know about the Bearbreaker situation and how I'm handling it; he congratulates me on getting a description and says he'll have Gretchen try to find a match in our files.

Then I go to bed.

"Morning, Jace."

"Mmnnuh."

"You have a visitor."

"Fwah. Go 'way. I have a gun."

"He has coffee."

I lift my head from the pillow and blink at Charlie blearily. "Then I'll let him live. Whozit?"

"Prime suspect number one. I've got him cooling his heels downstairs."

I'd expected Duvalier, but somehow I'm not surprised. "Tell him I'll be there in a minute."

I get up, throw on some comfortable clothes, run a brush through my hair and make sure I have my gun. Then I go downstairs, where Charlie and Bearbreaker are having an old-fashioned staring contest, with the newfangled twist of trying to look casual and vaguely amused at the same time. I think Bearbreaker might have been winning, but Charlie could probably take him in the long run.

He offers me the coffee, which I politely decline. I may be a caffeine addict, but I'm not stupid. "Didn't think you'd be awake yet," I say, trying to sound alert.

He shrugs and drinks the coffee himself. "Haven't been to bed yet."

"Talk to your friend?"

"Not a lot of talking going on last night."

For a second I think that's some kind of sexual remark, then realize that with all the thropes wolfed out, none of them would be *capable* of talking—not vocally, anyway. "You know what I mean," I add quickly.

"Sure. And yeah, I did. Buy me breakfast and I'll tell you what he said."

"You pick the place."

He grins. "I was hoping you'd say that. . . ."

Main Street is blocked off and lined with booths, filled with every person in town and probably quite a few from the surrounding area. There's a number of pires wrapped up like mummies, but none of the thropes are in were form; I gather that during Moondays it's tradition to only transform at night.

There's a comforting kind of sameness to festivals, no matter where you are in the world. There are endless cultural variations, of course, but certain things seem like constants: there's always food, performers, music, and games. The music and performance is currently being supplied by a small but funky bluegrass band twanging away on a small stage in front of the post office, the most popular game is a weird variant of volleyball played in an empty lot with a giant inflated sphere and no net, and the food seems to be, oddly enough, all vegetarian: candy apples, corn on the cob, lots of pastry and deep-fried starchy stuff.

As if reading my mind, Bearbreaker says, "Hope you got enough meat last night. I know the whole idea is to celebrate our human side during the day, but some months I just don't eat at all until the sun goes down."

"Yeah, I know what you mean," I say, though I obviously don't. From what Dr. Pete told me, I thought the whole idea of Moondays was for thropes to embrace their wolfiness; either I missed a few details or this is a regional variation. After all, Mardis Gras in New Orleans and Mardi Gras in Rio are two very different things.

Bearbreaker takes me to a booth selling something I've never seen before, some kind of mushroom dipped in batter and deep-fried. I'm a little wary, but I try a bite and discover it's delicious—reminds me a little of prawn, somehow.

We take our food and wander down the street, Charlie keeping a discreet distance behind us. It's both comforting and kind of embarrassing how he's always present, like having your dad along as a chaperone.

"So I got a message from this Stoker guy." Bearbreaker finishes his mushrooms and licks the grease off the ends of his fingers with a tongue like—well, a bear's. "A message for you."

He knows I'm here. It only verifies what I already suspected, but the statement still has an emotional impact. I don't know where Stoker is—probably hundreds or even thousands of miles away—but there's also the distinct possibility he's looking at me right now through a pair of binoculars.

"Let me guess. I'm working for the wrong side."

"It was a little longer than that. I wrote it down." He fishes a folded piece of paper out of the back pocket of his pants and hands it to me. It reads:

Hello, Jace.

My condolences on being kidnapped from your home. I wouldn't wish this world on anyone, least of all on someone who fights monsters. This place must be your worst nightmare; I know it's mine.

They're lying to you, Jace. They're not the only ones that can send you home—I can, too. Human beings can do magic that vampires and werewolves find difficult or impossible, and that includes using your RDT to trigger a kind of slingshot effect; basically, eliminating the wards that are keeping you here and letting Mother Nature pull you back where you belong.

You don't know how much I wish I could go with you.

I hope we get the chance to talk, face-to-face. I'm intensely curious to hear firsthand about a world where a human being can walk down a street without fear of being kidnapped and turned into a blood factory, or having their very humanity stolen by a bite or a scratch. It sounds like Heaven to me— but Heaven is not where I belong. I am a creature of Hell, sentenced there since birth, and I am sworn to fight the demons that rule it until my dying breath. I would be honored if you would join me in that fight, but it is not your battle and I do not expect you to make that kind of sacrifice for a world that is not yours.

We are not enemies. Can you blame me for fighting for the survival of my—of our—species? If my methods seem brutal, remember that this is a war. I do what I have to, not out of sadism but necessity. It is not your fight, but I ask you out of simple humanity to not hinder me. By your inaction you will save countless human lives, and earn our eternal gratitude.

And I promise I will get you home.

It's signed *Aristotle*. Two seconds after I finish reading, it consumes itself in a quiet *whoom* of flame, making me blurt, "What the hell?"

"Sorry—warlock paper. Wasn't my idea—guess he wanted to keep his offer private."

"He dictated this to you?"

"Not in person. Rather not go into details."

"Of course." I study him, reevaluating. He must be one of Stoker's most trusted lieutenants to be the go-between for something like this—or maybe he's just a mercenary that's being extremely well paid for his loyalty. "What's your take on this, Bearbreaker?"

"Me? I'm just a soldier—kind of like your sandy shadow, behind us. I get paid for my skills, not my opinions."

"Humor me."

He doesn't hesitate. "I think you should look out for your best interests. Works for me."

"Despite his politeness, I don't think your boss has my best interests at heart."

"Who said he was my boss? Just a guy I'm passing along a message for."

"Sure. This guy—you trust him?"

Bearbreaker stares at me for a moment, not saying a word. When he finally speaks, he looks away first. "In my business, bad instincts will kill you. Fast. My instincts say he's a man of his word—otherwise I wouldn't be here. But he's got a real hate on for every pire and thrope alive, and I don't think he'd hesitate for a second if he had the chance to wipe us all out."

"If that's true, why are you helping him?"

He turns back to me and grins. "Girl, I'm a zerker. I ride a bike in thirty-below weather bare-chested—you think I'm gonna let a little thing like a genocidal OR slow me down? Hell, running into him is the most interesting thing to happen to me since that riot down in Mexico. I'm sticking around just to see what happens next . . . but I gotta say, I kind of see the man's point."

"How so?"

"I know what it's like to be an outsider. To know the rest of the world doesn't understand or give a damn about you, to know most people would be just as happy if you dropped dead tomorrow. I get that." He shakes his massive head. "But like that Nietzsche guy said, whatever doesn't kill you makes you stronger. And this Stoker, he's a tough customer—the world's been trying to kill him for a long time, and it hasn't done it yet. Me, I think the guy's just trying for a little payback."

"The world's trying to kill him, so he's going to kill it first?"

Bearbreaker shrugs. "Hey. Whatever works for you . . ."

And then he ditches me.

He excuses himself to duck into a nearby shop to use the john and never comes back. Charlie strolls over just as it's beginning to sink in and says, "He stick you with the bill, too?"

"Go check on him, will you?"

He does, and confirms my suspicions. "Back door," he says. "Bet his bike's gone, too."

"No doubt."

"What was that paper he handed you? The one that flash-fried?"

I hesitate. "Message from Stoker. Same thing the Irish decoy told me—I'm on the wrong side, I should be working for him instead of against him, yadda yadda."

"Doesn't give up easily, does he?"

"Neither do I."

I contemplate taking the truck out to the zerker camp and arresting Bearbreaker—I can tie his bike to the murder scene; that's enough to bring him in—but decide against it. First, I don't have the manpower for that kind of operation, and second, putting pressure on Bearbreaker will just piss him off—he won't roll over, and I'll be severing the one link I have to Stoker. Better to keep the zerker in play and see what happens.

Charlie and I return to the inn and check in. Gretchen's ID'd the vic as Elliot Dennison, an oil-rig worker from Anchorage. A number of previous arrests, mostly for public drunkenness and assault, similar to that of the Australian vic, Andrew Fieldstone. As far as the location goes, Gretchen hasn't found any particular historical significance.

It's frustrating. I can connect any two of the murders by type of victim or site, but they make no cohesive pattern when viewed overall. So far, two of the vics were thropes, two were pires. No consistency there. The one thing that does hold true is the methodology—killing a thrope with blood is a clear reference to vampirism.

I'm still thinking about it when I go for dinner downstairs. Charlie's up in his room, but there's another woman eating in the small restaurant—one of the other guests, I assume.

I suppose I should say "dining" rather than eating; she's obviously a pire, sipping blood from an oversize brandy snifter. Could be red wine, I suppose—but her pale skin and sharp incisors tell me otherwise. Besides, the Urthbone has given me a sensitivity to the emotions of thropes and humans, and she doesn't broadcast at all—even when she looks up from the book she's reading and smiles at me.

"Hi," she says. She's got just a touch of a southern accent. "And here I thought I'd have to have supper all by my lonesome."

I study her for a second before replying. She's got long, oil-black hair, a face with the kind of high cheekbones and long jaw that can look either striking or odd. On her it's definitely striking. She's dressed in a loose-fitting black silk blouse and a dark purple skirt, with high-heeled black leather boots that go all the way to the knee.

"Hi," I say, taking a seat. "Hope I'm not disturbing you."

"Not at all—glad to have the company. I'm Mona."

"Jace."

"You mind if I join you? I hate eating alone."

I shrug. "Sure, fine by me. You a local or a tourist?"

She closes her book and joins me, her glass of blood in hand. "Oh, I'm just visiting. Thought I'd surprise an old friend of mine, but it seems she's out of town. Bad planning on my part. Figured I may as well look around a bit while I'm here. You familiar with the place?"

"Afraid not." Too bad; a local contact might have been useful. Still, maybe she can provide me with some information. "I'm from Seattle, flew in by seaplane. How'd you get here?"

"There's a Coffin Express—you know, one of those buses where you can sleep the whole way? And it's an *awfully* long way from Anchorage, I'll tell you that."

"Yeah, I'll bet. How long have you been here?"

"I just got in a few hours ago."

Strike two. Mona wasn't going to know anything I didn't—

"This town has a fascinating history, if you're into humans."

"Excuse me?"

"Oh, sorry. That's my field of study—humanology. I know it's kind of trendy now, but I've *always* been interested in unenhanced people. My best friend when I was a child was one."

I'm dying to ask her what a pire means by "when I was a child" but don't want to blow my cover. "Really. What happened to her?"

"Him. Died of a human disease—cancer. Such a shame. Of course, he only would have lived seventy or eighty years, anyway—but that's one of the reasons I find them so intriguing."

"I have to admit, I really don't understand the fascination. Aren't they just inferior versions of us?"

She shakes her head, smiling. "Oh, no, not at all! They're amazingly resilient, especially when you consider the fact that they have no supernatural abilities—well, not inherent ones, anyway. They're the forerunners of both the pire and thrope races—we wouldn't exist without them—and they basically created civilization as we know it. We should respect our progenitors, don't you think?"

Damn straight. "I suppose, when you put it that way. What were you saying about the history of this town?"

"Oh, yes. It was the site of a massacre, some three hundred years or so ago. A clan of pires and a pack of thropes both approached it simultaneously, and fought to see who would own it. Legend has it that the Inuit who lived here— it was only a fishing camp at that point, and not a permanent one—negotiated a peace between the two by using the only bargaining chip they had: their own lives."

"You mean—"

"I mean the spoils the two groups were fighting over were the humans, who all loaded their parkas down with rocks and threatened to jump into the sea if the fighting didn't stop. The residents knew they were going to lose either their lives or their humanity, but they demanded to be able to pick which one. The pires and thropes agreed to the deal—but by that point, they were all *very* hungry."

"So become dinner for a pire or a thrope. Not much of a choice."

"In a way, it's the very essence of being human. Knowing they're going to die one day, and fighting for the only real power they have—the power of choice."

I nod, trying to look nonchalant but actually pretty impressed. This woman's summed up the most basic difference between my race and hers: when you know life isn't forever, the decisions you make *matter*. You don't have the next hundred years to try to fix a mistake.

"Funny," I say, "I have a friend who's a history buff, and she's never mentioned that story."

"Oh, I doubt she's heard it unless she's a humanologist; it's not a very well-known tale." Mona finishes her blood and gets to her feet. "I'm going to see what's keeping our waiter—while I've been yammering on, you've probably been thinking about food."

"Oh, you don't have to—"

But she's already on her way. The waiter shows up a few minutes later and apologizes for not having noticed me.

Mona doesn't come back.

The second night is a little wilder. I can hear motors revving in the street, and some howling. Still, I don't get any urgent messages from Sheriff Duvalier, so I decide that as long as the town isn't going up in flames he can handle it on his own.

Besides, I have a lot to think about.

Stoker's offer bothers me on several levels. He may or may not be telling the truth, but what's really disturbing is how well-informed he is. Am I dealing with a leak, or is it just more magic?

I'm not going to take the deal, of course. For one thing, all professional ethics aside, it would require me trusting someone who's demonstrably a sociopathic killer. Just not that desperate, thanks.

Not yet, anyway.

I think about what Mona told me and the fact that Gretchen didn't mention anything like it. Oversight? Or is it just an old story with no great significance? For that matter, is Mona really who she says she is?

I'm starting to jump at shadows. Tomorrow I'm going to nail a few of them down and make them talk.

"You know," I say to Charlie, "I think I'm going to stop making plans. Just go straight from objectives to total chaos, save some time."

Charlie and I are standing back-to-back, so I can't see his face. But I can *hear* the *T. rex* in his growled reply: "Yeah. Time's kinda short at the moment."

Two zerkers in front of me, three in front of Charlie. We're standing in the middle of an alley, while Bethel's entire population seems to be busy partying a mere two blocks away. We were taking a shortcut from the inn to the middle of town proper—only someone, it seems, was waiting for us.

None of them are in were form, but that hardly matters. The three facing Charlie are on their bikes, the two facing me on foot. All are armed: the three riders with nasty, long-handled axes, the other two with a weighted chain and an honest-to-God scythe. From the way the thrope's handling it, I'd say he knows his way around a wheat field.

I recognize the zerker with the scythe by his helmet, with the long crest of butcher knives along the top; he was with Bearbreaker at the crime scene on the tundra. His human form is lanky and weak-chinned, with squinting black eyes.

"Well, if it isn't the local Fed," Squinty says. "You smell good enough to eat, in more ways than one."

"Sorry, but you just stink," I say. I've got the Ruger aimed squarely between his eyes. "That's not even an insult, just a description. Seriously, invest in some soap and burn your clothes."

"I like alpha females. It's so much more satisfyin' to break 'em."

"I don't break easy—"

I'm drowned out by the roar of another blizzard bike at the end of the alley. Full throttle, tires squealing, barreling toward us like a bat out of Hell.

Bearbreaker. Going for the dramatic entrance, no doubt. I wonder what he'll have to say when—

He's not slowing down. And even more bizarrely, he's riding sidesaddle.

The other three bikes more or less take up the width of the alley. He can't go around, and unless his bike can fly, he can't go over. So what—

Charlie and I both realize what his plan is and flatten ourselves against one wall of the alley. The zerkers on the bikes don't have enough time—or maybe they just don't believe what they're seeing.

Down to ten feet away and moving like a rocket, Bearbreaker twists the bike sideways, hard. It broadsides the backs of the other three bikes simultaneously, but without its rider; he kicks off against the frame an instant before impact, using the bike's momentum to launch himself into the air.

The crash is amazingly loud. Blizzard bikes are large, heavy, and have many chromed bits that break off easily. This all goes tumbling down the alley toward Squinty and his friend a split second after Bearbreaker soars over their heads like a flying squirrel who's been pumping iron for twenty years.

The zerkers on their feet are both fast enough to get out of the way. Two of the riders aren't so lucky—they wind up as the filling in a motorcycle sandwich. The last one manages to leap clear, leaving Charlie and me facing three *extremely* disgruntled thropes who are already shifting into half-were form. Guess tradition doesn't count for much when your most important possession has just been trashed.

Charlie fastballs some silver at the one in the lead, but the ball glances off a piece of armor. I have my gun out and leveled at Squinty, who's charging straight at me. He's not quite as fast as Cassius, but there's no time to think, no time to do anything but react.

I shoot him.

The slug takes him high in the chest, punching through his chain mail like it isn't there. He skids to the ground at my feet, his snarl rising to a high-pitched whine as his brain figures out that his heart has just exploded. One of the butcher knives on his helmet clips my shin, but I barely feel it. I'm staring at the dead man at my feet. The man I just killed.

His features revert to human, just like in the movies. His eyes are wide open, and look more confused than anything. If he could still speak, I bet he'd be saying, "What the hell was *that*?"

"You all right?" Charlie's voice. Sounding concerned, not tense. Fight must be over.

I look up. Another thrope sprawled on the ground—

Charlie's second pitch must have been in the strike zone. The third one is nowhere in sight—guess he hightailed it when he realized the odds were against him.

"Yeah, yeah. I'm fine." Farther down the alley is a twisted pile of metal, rubber, and fur, which is already starting to curse.

A little past that is Bearbreaker, facedown on the ground and motionless.

"Looks like he broke his fall with his head," Charlie says. "Knocked himself out. Funny, I always thought that was just a saying."

I walk, none too steadily, over to where Bearbreaker lies. "Give me a hand," I say. "We've got to get him out of here before the others pry themselves free."

Louder cursing, sprinkled with dire promises and ungrammatical threats. "Yeah, all right," Charlie says. "But he's not staying in *my* room."

We—well, Charlie, mostly—get Bearbreaker back to the inn. As soon as he dumps Bearbreaker on my bed, Charlie heads out the door.

"Where are you going?" I demand. The adrenaline is starting to wear off and I'm feeling a little shocky.

"Roof. If the zerkers decide to storm the palace, I'd like to have some warning. And the chance to pick off a few before they get too close."

"And you're okay with leaving me alone with *this*?"

"Hey, it was your idea. You want to adopt a stray, *you* walk and feed him." And then he's out the door before I can come up with a clever reply.

I look down at the giant sprawled on my bed. Knowing how quickly thropes recover, I can't imagine he'll be out for too long. I hope not, anyway.

Because the longer he's unconscious, the more time I'll have to think about what just happened.

I don't have to worry—no more than a minute passes before he groans and his eyelids flutter. He opens his eyes and stares at the ceiling for a second before saying, "Where am I?"

"The exotic Jace Valchek Suites, where Your Comfort Is Our Extreme Inconvenience. You might want to consider a helmet in the future."

"Why? It's not like I own a bike. Anymore."

"Sure you do. It's just gotten married to three others."

"I think the word is 'welded,' actually. . . ."

"Why the *hell* did you *do* that?"

He winces. "Please don't yell. And you're welcome."

"We could have handled it. All you did was force a confrontation."

"No, I delivered a pre-emptive first strike. Maybe you could have taken those five, maybe not, but they *were* going to attack, no matter what you said—"

"*I could have handled it!*" I shout. "It didn't have to . . . *I* didn't have to—"

He's looking at me strangely. Why is my face wet?

Everything's gotten all blurry, and I quickly sit down on the edge of the bed, afraid I might be having another RDT episode. I'm not dizzy, though; it's just hard to *see*, with all this stuff in my eyes. . . .

And then I just let it go, all at once.

I don't break down like that very often, and when I do I kind of lose track of everything outside of my own head. I don't cry very loud, but I cry *hard*; afterward my ribs are always sore and my throat hurts.

I gradually become aware that I seem to be leaning against a wall. A big, musky wall that has a catcher's mitt gently pressed against the small of my back. I take a deep breath, already scripting the verbal barrage I'm going to unleash to show him I don't need his sympathy.

"I've never killed anyone before," I say. I can barely hear myself.

"I'm *sorry*," he says. And the most amazing thing is, he

sounds sorry; they aren't just the meaningless words you repeat to comfort someone when you don't know what else to say. He sounds even sadder than I do.

"You wrecked your bike." I don't want to talk about my own pain, so I try to bring up his. Zerkers carry everything they own on their bikes; they treat them like their own children, they—

"It's only a bike," he says. "Was, I mean."

I pull back and stare into his eyes for a second. A little part of my brain is whispering that maybe this isn't such a good idea.

Or maybe it is, counters a different part of my brain. *Maybe exactly what you need right now is a good old-fashioned mattress dance, with no strings attached.*

Getting involved with a thrope biker isn't—

Isn't what? Responsible? The last thing you need right now is more responsibility. This is about pure release, not hearts-and-flowers. He's here, he's hot, and he definitely won't call you in the morning.

Unlike Tanaka?

That stops me. It's a little soon to be contemplating another bad decision. And besides, Bearbreaker's connected to the suspect—and not as a member of law enforcement.

That doesn't mean he's guilty of anything. But he was *at* the crime scene—

"Oh, the hell with it," I say, and there's a knock at the door.

"Jace?" It's Charlie. I'm suddenly on my feet, feeling as guilty as any teenager busted by her parents.

"Yeah, come on in."

"The door's locked."

When did I do that? "Just a second."

Charlie strides into the room, glances at the bed. "Still out cold, huh?"

I look over, see that Bearbreaker is lying motionless with his eyes closed. I utter a silent thank-you and say, "Yeah, hasn't moved a muscle."

"Thought I'd let you know I just talked to Duvalier on

the phone. He says he's got the situation under control and we probably won't see reprisals."

I frown. "Why not? I mean, we wrecked three of their bikes and *killed* two of them."

"Yeah, there's going to be paperwork on that. I don't do paperwork."

"I'll do the damn paperwork. Why no reprisals?"

"Zerkers aren't organized like a regular pack. Each one takes responsibility for their own actions. Even when they ride together, it's just for convenience—the only loyalty they have is to their own individual survival."

"So the ones we busted up have had enough, and the others don't give a crap?"

"More or less."

I'm not sure how far I trust that assessment, but right now it's a gift horse I have no urge to perform exploratory dentistry on. "That's good. Uh, I still think it's a good idea to keep watch, though—you mind playing lookout a while longer?"

He studies me for a second more than I'm comfortable with. "Sure. Give me a call when I can come down, all right?"

"What? No, I mean, just give it a few more minutes, that's all—"

He's already gone, closing the door softly behind him. I sigh.

"Smooth," Bearbreaker says.

"You should go."

"Sure. Mind giving me a lift? My wheels are in the shop."

"Oh, crap."

"And by 'shop' I mean 'graveyard.'"

"I'm sorry about that. Looks like you'll just have to do the four-legged thing—I think the sun's almost down, anyway."

I stride over to the heavy drapes and pull them open. The moon has been up for hours, but it looks like the sun only set a few minutes ago.

It takes a second for it to sink in.

Bearbreaker is up off the bed and halfway to the door by the time I get my gun out. "Hold it!"

He stops, looks back. It's the first time I've pulled my gun in weeks that anyone's even hesitated, though he doesn't seem exactly frozen in fear.

"Why haven't you transformed?" I demand.

"Why haven't *you*?"

Neither of us answers—neither has to. Same question, same answer.

"You're not the only one with access to artificial wolf pheromones," Bearbreaker says.

"You're no pire."

"I'm as human as you are, Jace."

"Who are you?"

"You already know." He grins. "Call me Aristotle, please."

My God. I've got him. My ticket home, right here in front of me. "Get down on the floor."

"No. I wanted to meet you, Jace. Talk to you, get to know you. Now that I have, I'm going to leave. I have things to do . . . and you have things to think over."

"The only thing I have to think over is where I'm going to shoot you."

"You'll have to kill me, Jace. I won't let them take me alive. And somehow, I don't think you'll do that."

I stare at him, my gun aimed squarely at his chest. He stares back.

Oh, crap.

ELEVEN

Afterward, I feel kind of sick.

It's understandable, I guess. I mean, I almost made out with the guy. I didn't know who he was at the time, but—

None of that matters now.

I go to the bathroom, clean up a little. Wash my hands and face. Stare at myself in the mirror and think about the fact that I'm not the same person I was when I got up this morning. I talk pretty tough, but a wolf that snarls doesn't have to bite.

Can't remember who told me that—probably a thrope. Anyway, it means that as long as I had a gun to wave around, I didn't have to actually shoot anyone. That worked pretty well until I came to a world where they weren't afraid of guns . . . until someone called my bluff and forced me to lay down my cards.

I did. Turned out I was holding a dead man's hand.

"A dead thrope's hand" would be the more accurate turn of phrase, but I don't think the zerker I killed would care much about that. He's beyond caring about anything but what they carve on his tombstone.

Not Stoker, though.

I couldn't shoot him. I don't know why, exactly—partly because I was still in shock over my first shooting I guess, partly because I realized that if he were dead, I might have one hell of a time proving to Cassius he was Aristotle Stoker. Bye-bye, ticket home.

But it *was* Stoker. I knew it in my gut. And even though I don't want to admit it, the last part of the reason I couldn't shoot him was simply my refusal to reduce the human population of this place by one more soul.

So I let him go, and now I don't know what the hell I'm supposed to do. What am I going to do next time, wave as he rides off into the sunset? Shoot him in the leg and hope he survives after the Ruger's blown open his femoral artery? Or hope *I* survive when he hops over, takes my gun away, and uses it on me? He said he wouldn't be taken alive—and after what he went through at that Yakuza blood factory, I believe him.

No. Next time, it's him or me. I can't let him keep slaughtering thropes and pires. They're people, dammit, people with kids and families and friends. They're not monsters, and I have to get my head in the game if I want to save any of them.

When Charlie comes back, I tell him Bearbreaker felt better and left. I don't tell him anything else.

"I can't believe you let him go," Cassius says. His voice is around the same temperature that the tundra was back in Alaska.

I meet his eyes defiantly. "I didn't think he was a flight risk. His bike was totaled; we were in the middle of nowhere. I'd established a relationship of trust and planned on using it to gain more information."

If my Urthbone mojo worked on pires I could tell just how angry Cassius is, but this subzero routine is like watching a glacier and trying to figure out how fast it's moving. He taps a few keys on his computer without taking his eyes off me, which is a little unnerving. "You should have brought him in."

"I could have," I admit. "But I didn't think he'd give us anything. He's a professional hired gun—mercenary, I mean—

and I doubt even an accessory-to-murder rap would scare him. I figured the cautious approach was better."

"You were wrong. Learn from it, do better next time."

He looks down and starts typing. After a moment I realize that he's done talking to me. I get up and leave, hoping I haven't come down with frostbite in the last five minutes.

Two days later there's another victim.

I can't help but wonder if it's because of me. True, serial killers almost always escalate—but Stoker has a specific agenda, and he's organized enough to stick to it. So did he move his timetable up because of me?

If so, he needn't have bothered. I haven't told anyone about his posing as Bearbreaker, mainly because I'm not sure it would do any good. Yeah, a seven-foot muscleman tends to stick out, but he's got a werewitch on his payroll and she could probably make him look like anything. Well, anything but the bogus description he gave us in the first place.

The one thing I do know is that what I saw wasn't a trick. Eisfanger's little ghost rat told him Bearbreaker wasn't using any kind of glamour, so I guess he really is that . . . large.

The next victim is a lot closer to home—Montana, to be exact. By now I've got it down to a routine: study the video of the previous vic on the way there, try to get as much data as possible from local law enforcement already on the scene, have Gretchen crunch the numbers and look for patterns on the fly.

This time, though, it's a little different. For one thing, Cassius and Gretchen come with me.

The message is clear: I've screwed up and need supervision. I wish I could argue with that, but I can't. I'm kind of glad, actually—Gretch is the closest thing I have to a female friend in this world, and I could use someone to talk to.

Not that there's a lot of talking on the way there. We're

taking a chopper this time, and since it's daytime we're basically flying inside a sealed, windowless bubble separate from
the pilot—who apparently thinks that a helicopter ride should
duplicate the experience of a roller coaster as closely as possible. It's extremely noisy, too; I feel like I'm in a barrel going over Niagara Falls again and again.

"Here's the situation," Cassius says. I have to ask him to
speak up; my hearing isn't as keen as Gretchen's. "The signal
is coming from a small cabin just outside of Missoula, Montana. It's not as isolated as the previous sites. We have the
cabin surrounded by agents, but nobody's gone in yet. Windows are sealed; nothing's visible from outside."

"He's deviating from his pattern," I say. "Getting closer to
population centers. There's an implied threat, there. And this
is only the second time he's left a victim inside a building."

"The first time the vic was a pire," Gretchen says. "Perhaps this one is, as well—the local population leans heavily
toward hemovores."

"We'll see when we get there," Cassius says.

———

We touch down in the field directly beside the cabin. Both
Cassius and Gretchen have put on their daywear gear, long
black gloves of shiny plastic and tight black masks that tuck
into their collars. Smoked-glass goggles finish the outfit.
Gretchen is wearing pale green slacks and a yellow blouse,
while Cassius is dressed in his usual black suit with a dark
red tie. Together, they look a bit like yuppie terrorists. I'm
dressed in typical Bureau style, a black suit pretty much a
match to Cassius', while Charlie's wearing a charcoal-gray
two-piece, with matching snap-brim, alligator-skin shoes,
and a pair of dark shades—he makes all of us look shabby.

We climb out of the cabin and into a sun-drenched field of
yellow wheat stubble, with the cabin no more than a hundred
feet away. Four thrope agents are stationed around it, holding
crossbows at port arms and generally looking menacing.

The agent in charge, a thrope with reddish brown fur in

chain-mail body armor, lopes over and gives Cassius the rundown in sign language. Cassius nods and motions us to follow him.

The cabin itself is no more than a shack, peeling tarpaper roof and unpainted wooden walls gone gray with age. The windows I can see have little glass left, but all that shows behind them is black.

Cassius pulls the rickety door open. Behind it is a wall of black plastic, no more than three feet from the door, sealing off the rest of the room. It has a hatch of sorts set into it, a zippered flap probably taken from a tent and duct-taped into place. The flap's been reinforced with more black plastic.

Cassius doesn't hesitate. He unzips the flap. Bright, golden light spills through the opening, followed immediately by the stench of burned meat.

The room has been sealed, every square inch, with black plastic and duct tape. A car battery sits in one corner, wires trailing from it to the satellite broadcaster nearby and to a metal cot in the center. The cot is bolted to the floor, and the victim is bound spread-eagled to the cot; the second set of wires lead into the vic's mouth.

Gretchen hands out paper booties for everyone to put on over their shoes, and the three of us enter. Charlie stays outside.

The body is of a young female pire. She's naked. Cause of death appears to be—well, the middle of her body is gone. It looks as though someone took a blowtorch and burned a swath from her groin to the center of her face. And lying right in the very center of that swath is a long, flexible tube, no more than a half inch in diameter, giving off the soft golden glow that's illuminating the room.

I put my hand over the tube without touching it. It's not giving off any heat. "What the hell is this thing?"

"Fiber-optic light pipe," Gretchen says. "Tuned to the precise EM frequency of sunshine."

Cassius nods. "Inserted down her throat. Burned her alive from the inside out."

I frown. "Wait a minute—are you saying she was killed

by a magic flashlight? Because if it's that easy to make, I don't understand why every FBI agent doesn't carry one in their pocket."

"It's not useful as a weapon," Cassius says. "Any light pollution at all eliminates the effect, so it can only be used in complete darkness."

"Killing a vampire with sunlight," Gretchen says. "Where's the lycanthropic element?"

"Not sunlight," I point out. "*Secondhand* sunlight. Which is also an accurate description of—"

"Moonlight," Cassius finishes. He's examining the broadcaster. "Telltales have been covered with tape." He turns it off.

"The body's in pretty good shape," I say. "There's a lot more left than at the Hokkaido site."

"Yes," Gretchen says. She's pulled out a camera and is taking pictures. "Normally, exposure to this kind of light should produce complete incineration of the corpse. The fact that it didn't tells me she's Bloodborn."

"What's that?"

Gretchen hesitates and glances at Cassius, who gives a barely perceptible nod. It's so quick I'm half-convinced I imagined it. "The Bloodborn are hemovores who are conceived biologically as opposed to being sired. They are identical to other pires, except they are that way from birth."

"What? How can that work if pires don't get any older?"

"We don't, true—unless we choose to have children. In that case, it's a direct exchange; the child ages a year for every six months each parent donates. When the child has reached the desired maturity, the spell that allowed the birth is dissolved, and aging stops for both parents and child."

Cassius nods. "The decomp level of a pire's body depends on the time debt it's acquired—the length of time between now and when it made the transition from human to hemovore. An older pire will turn to dust—a younger one might skeletonize or become a rotting corpse. There's no decay here at all, just the burns. She was still aging when she was killed."

"Which means parents to notify," I say. "Maybe they can"—I'm about to say *shed some light on this* and catch myself just in time—"tell us something useful."

Gretchen lifts and turns the head gently to one side. "I can tell you something already." The throat is almost completely burned away, but the spine has protected the skin on the back of the neck from incineration; there's a symbol at the base of skull in scarlet, a circle with a line through it at an angle and a single red dot on either side of the line. Like a No Smoking sign with two periods instead of a cigarette.

"Is that a tattoo?" I ask. "I didn't think pires could do that."

"It's painted on," Cassius says. "Same concept, different method. It means she isn't just Bloodborn, she's a Pureblood."

"Which means?"

"Political extremists," Gretchen says. "A movement that sprang up after World War Two, in the wake of the pire population expansion. Pires that have never known what it was like to be human, and have no desire to."

"Not just pires anymore," Cassius adds. "Thropes, too. Ones from bloodlines uncontaminated by any canine influence other than pure wolf—they think they have more in common with the Bloodborn than their own kind."

On my world, we got Baby Boomers—here, they got Baby Biters. And Wolf Supremacists, it sounds like. I understood the meaning of the faux tattoo now: *never been bitten.* "Just how extreme are they?"

Gretchen gently sets the head back down. "They believe that nonpure thropes should be sterilized, and all humans captured and treated like cattle."

"Nazis, in other words."

"Worse," says Cassius. "The Nazis simply wanted to turn as many humans as they could. Purebloods want to create a culture devoid of human presence or influence."

"That's absurd," I say. "What are they going to do, tear down every city in the world and live in caves?"

"That's closer than you might think," Gretchen says.

"But not relevant at the moment—we have a site to process. Shall we?"

When we're done, we head for the nearest town, Missoula. We ride in separate vehicles, Cassius and Gretchen with the evidence in one, Charlie and me with the local agents in the other. The message is clear.

I'm beginning to wonder why I'm even here. I have no idea where Stoker is going to strike next, or at who. The latest victim bothers me more than I care to admit—the second young, attractive woman killed using a method with sexual overtones. They were both pires, too—is it because he sees vampirism as more inherently seductive than lycanthropism? Or is it something more blatant, just hostility toward women?

That's not what's really bothering me, of course. This isn't a faceless killer anymore; this is someone I've met. Someone I've talked to. Someone who's either a murdering psychopath or a champion of a dying race—possibly both. I know what he looks like, and I've kept that knowledge to myself. Thinking about him produces feelings of shame, revulsion, pity, and a kind of admiration—not for what he's done but what he's survived. There are other feelings there, too, but I push those away stubbornly and pretend they don't exist. I've got enough problems—and a decision to make, soon.

Missoula is a cow town, a little prairie city surrounded by ranchland. It more or less rolls up its sidewalks when the sun rises—the population's mainly pire with the odd thrope cowboy or lem farmhand. It also seems to be stuck somewhere around 1947.

That's not a typical small-town put-down—I don't mean the place is backward, I mean it's a literal, physical reproduction of an earlier time. The theater downtown is sharing a double bill of *Casablanca* and *Arsenic and Old Lace*; most of the cars date from the forties; and people dress the part, too, right down to hairstyles and hats. I haven't seen a thrope in a zoot suit yet, but I'm pretty sure I will.

I nudge Charlie, who's sitting in the backseat next to me. "Hey, Rocky—this the place they chiseled you out of or something?"

"Nah. Lots of towns like this. No matter how old pires get, they got a soft spot for the time they were turned—kind of a permanent nostalgia thing. Plenty of pires got created during World War Two, so when the boys came marching home, a bunch of 'em decided to keep things just the way they were. They weren't getting any older—the ones that didn't have kids, anyway—so why should the place they grew up in?"

It makes sense. Small towns have always resisted change, and a town full of unaging pires would be practically set in cement.

Which would drive the children—no pun intended—batty.

Cassius has booked us rooms at a local bed-and-breakfast. He believes that Stoker will attempt to either contact me or leave me a message, as he has before. My role in this investigation is now mainly as bait.

I'm starting to wonder if that wasn't always the case. If so—why me?

The town comes alive after the sun sets. Restaurants and shops open, people on the streets, kids playing in yards. Pretty normal, if you ignore the whole time-travel aspect. Charlie and I wander into a local bar for a drink—well, a drink for me, anyway. Cassius and Gretchen will meet us later; my orders are to stay in public and visible. I wonder how many agents are surveilling me at the moment, and how. Can't spot them, anyway.

"You must be loving this," I say to Charlie, glancing around the place. It's big, lots of oak paneling, antlered deer heads on the wall and flat-screen televisions showing sports over the bar. I'm drinking a single malt and wondering how it would mix with Urthbone.

"Yeah, I'm a big outdoorsman," Charlie says. "Nothing like spending the weekend in a duck blind, dressed like a tree."

"Not the hunting gack, the forties stuff. Come on, you fit right in."

"Do I? I hadn't noticed."

"What's with you and the Dick Tracy style, anyway?"

He shrugs. "There's just something about the decade, I guess. I like the clothes, the music, the films—the noir ones, anyway."

"Tough-guy stuff, huh? Yeah, I can see that. I'm a little surprised you don't go in for the hunting, though."

"Why's that?"

"You know—your origins. The non-mineral-based ones, I mean."

He doesn't seem surprised I know, just nods and studies a moose head with an immense spread of antlers mounted over the entrance to the men's room. "Yeah, I tried it once. Went bow-hunting for grizzlies in the Rockies. Didn't get much out of it."

"No luck?"

"No satisfaction. I killed three of them, all pretty big from what I understand. But the experience was . . . disappointing."

I'm pretty sure he's about to yank one of my legs right off, but I play along anyway. "How so?"

He's silent for a moment, looking thoughtful. Finally, he says, "They just weren't big *enough*."

My leg stays where it is. I blink, and keep my mouth shut.

"So yeah, I like the forties. It's as good a decade as any."

"I like the music. I used to go swing-dancing to keep in shape."

"Yeah? I've been known to cut a rug or two myself."

I goggle at him. "You? Lindy-hopping?"

He stares back impassively. "Sure."

"Hollywood or Savoy?"

"Both."

"If you're bluffing, you are *so* busted. In this town I can find a jukebox in about thirty seconds."

"In this town you can find a big band on a Friday night. Which it is."

"Is your dance card full?" Cassius says as he and Gretchen stroll up to our table. "Or is there room for one more?" I hadn't even noticed them come in; pires have this way of dropping off your radar, as if all the subliminal clues that tell you you're not alone are masked.

"If I'd known this was going to turn into a dance party, I'd have brought different shoes," I say. "*Et tu*, Cassius?"

"I promise not to step on your feet."

Like you're not stepping on them already. I think it but don't say it. "Didn't figure you for a dancer, either."

"I do have a life outside the office, you know."

"Yes," Gretchen adds with a knowing smile. "A rather long one, too."

"Anything new on the case?" I ask.

"We've identified the victim," Gretchen says. "Natasha Champlain. The office is trying to reach next of kin—her parents are traveling."

"Glad I don't have to make that call," I say. "Worst part of the job."

"Yes," Gretchen says. Cassius and Charlie both nod. Some things about being a cop hold true no matter what universe you're in.

"Ready for the wild nightlife of Missoula?" Cassius asks.

"After Alaska? Absolutely."

"Then let's go," Cassius says, getting to his feet. "I'm sure we can find someplace a little livelier than this."

Someplace with more eyeballs, he means. Someplace Stoker can spot me. Of course, now I can spot him, too— unless he's disguised or hidden by magic. And Cassius has to be smart enough to have that angle covered.

I grit my teeth and make it look like a smile. Out on the town we go.

Charlie, it turns out, is one helluva dancer. Quick, nimble, co-ordinated. I'm a little rusty myself, but he's one of those dancers who always make their partner look good, no matter how inexperienced she might be. I do my best to keep up. There are a number of places to go to, more than I would have guessed. I keep an eye out, but if Stoker's around he's staying out of sight.

One of the joints does in fact have a live band with a full horn section. Charlie and I have been doing all the dancing so far, but Cassius finally asks me to join him on a slow number, "What a Wonderful World." The guy singing even does a passable version of Louis Armstrong, and I make a mental note to add the song to my collection.

It's the first time I've touched a pire since I shook Gretchen's hand. His hands are cool, not cold, one holding mine and the other on the small of my back.

"How am I doing?" he asks. He's no Charlie, but he's pretty light on his feet.

"I was going to ask you the same thing."

"I'm worried about you."

That's a little more honest than I was expecting. "I'm fine."

"I don't think you are. You've been through one trauma after another ever since you got here."

"Yeah, you're right. Maybe I should see a shrink. Oh, wait—you don't have those here."

"Doesn't mean you can't talk to someone. Me, for instance."

"I think I've done enough damage to our professional relationship, thanks."

"I'm not interested in a professional relationship."

My eyebrows go up, but I keep dancing. "What?"

"You were right—what you said about our rules and how

they don't really apply to you. So let's forget about you calling me boss. It isn't accurate, and we should both acknowledge it."

"Uh—this feels suspiciously like being fired."

"Not at all. Think of it as a promotion."

"So if you're not my boss, you're . . . what?"

His eyes meet mine. Blue as a Caribbean sea. "An ally. A friend, I hope."

"And if I say no?"

He smiles. "You are, without a doubt, the most difficult woman I know."

"Thank you."

"You're welcome."

He's a little closer than he was a second ago. He's still looking into my eyes. I really should look away, and don't.

The song comes to an end. Our feet stop moving, but we stay where we are. Any second now he's going to lean toward me. . . .

The crowd applauds for the band. It jolts both of us out of the moment, and we use the excuse of turning toward the stage and clapping to pretend nothing just happened. Which it didn't, but still . . .

Hoo-boy.

I excuse myself and go looking for the ladies' room. For a minute I'm worried I won't be able to locate one—after all, what would pires need a bathroom for?—but then I find it hidden in a hallway that parallels one wing of the stage. It's neat and clean, but there are no mirrors.

Gretchen comes in a moment later behind me. "Well, well," she says. "I see you've decided to ignore Aunt Gretchen's advice."

I sigh and wash my hands. "Not my idea, Gretch. Cassius thinks I suck as an employee, and not in a socially acceptable manner."

She leans against the wall and crosses her arms. "So he thinks you'll be easier to manage as a girlfriend? My, he *is* overconfident."

"Thanks for your support."

"It was meant as a compliment, dear girl. How are you holding up, otherwise?" Her tone is gentle.

I shake my head. "I keep seeing the look on that zerker's face after I shot him. It was just so—"

"Anthony Krabowski."

I stop washing my hands and stare at her. "What?"

"That was his name. He was seventy-two years old. He had three previous convictions for rape, one for attempted murder. That was the life you ended." She studies me, waiting for my reaction.

I nod, slowly. "Yeah. That was what I did."

I process for a minute, wonder if I'm going to cry, and realize I'm not. "Thanks, Gretch."

"We pires may have a different relationship with the Grim Reaper, but death is never easy to deal with. Some problems get worse the longer you put them off."

"Really? 'Cause I'd of thought that after a few centuries of life, you might get tired of the whole thing."

She laughs softly. "That's how it is for some of us. For most, though, life becomes like blood itself—an addiction. No one will fight harder to survive than an old pire who refuses to kick her habit."

"Or the bucket." I hesitate, then ask, "Is that how it is for you?"

"Oh, I'm not that old—not by pire standards, anyway. And my reaction to my increasing age is disappointingly small town, I'm afraid."

I frown. "You're going to buy a rocking chair and take up knitting?"

"Possibly—but not for the reasons you're thinking."

I plainly don't get it, so she spells it out. "I'm thinking of having a child."

"That's, uh—congratulations?"

"I'm only considering it. The commitment required is obviously enormous. But the desire to create life, rather than simply prolonging your own—even in a pire, it's powerful."

I smile. "The most powerful urge there is, Gretch. I think you'd make a terrific mother."

"Well, that goes without saying. But for now, let's concentrate on finding our quarry, shall we?"

When we get back to the table, I see two other people standing by our table and talking to Charlie and Cassius. I don't need an introduction to figure out they both must be Purebloods.

The thrope is smaller than most, maybe six feet even in his were form, and dressed in nothing but gray fur. Most thropes wear at least a pouched belt or bandolier to carry things in, but not this guy. He's got an oversize mug of beer in one paw, which he laps at like a dog from time to time.

The thrope isn't the only one who doesn't feel the need for clothes. The pire beside him is around the same height he is but skeletally thin; I can see every rib through his ghost-pale skin. He's wearing a bloodred loincloth and nothing else. His finger- and toenails are long and curved, his hair long, black, and unkempt.

He's also obviously the spokesman for the group that's lurking a table over, six more Bloodborn and another thrope. They must have come in while Gretchen and I were in the bathroom.

"—someone of your age *must* see that," the pire says. He sounds a little drunk. "You've been a blood drinker for far, far longer than you were ever a mere human."

Cassius looks vaguely amused. "And how would you know how old I am?"

The pire grins, exposing fangs that seem a little larger than normal. "Oh, we Bloodborn can tell such things. And I can *also* tell that after having outlived so many ORs, you couldn't possibly view them as anything more than temporary pets—"

"Hey there," I say.

Skin-and-fangs turns to look me over. I guess there's something to his claim for extrasensory abilities, because he wrinkles his nose and says, "You smell like a wolf. But you're not—you're *human*."

"And you're a mosquito with an annoying buzz," I say. "But I won't hold that against you."

The thrope growls at me, plainly expecting me to be terrified. I probably should be; one swipe from those claws and either I'm dead or I join the Bark of the Month Club.

"Piss off, Fido," I growl back. "In fact, why don't you go find yourself a hydrant and check your p-mail?"

In retrospect, insulting a drunken, racist werewolf in a bar full of his friends might not have been such a good idea.

The thrope lunges forward, his jaws going for my throat. He gets halfway there and his trajectory is abruptly changed by Charlie's fist slamming into the side of his head. That sends the furball smashing into his friends' table—and they all leap to their feet and charge us.

Here's where I should be describing an extremely vicious free-for-all. But the thing about bar fights is they happen very fast and all at once, and when you multiply that by the strength and speed of the parties involved . . . well, I really couldn't keep track most of the time. Try to imagine a bunch of angry cats in an industrial-size tumble dryer and you might get the idea.

I do remember Charlie hitting someone with a piano. And I don't mean he decked a piano player—I mean Charlie picked up a baby grand and hit someone with it.

Myself, I mainly try to stay out of the way. Spraying bullets in a crowded bar is not a good idea, and I'm not packing my scythes at the moment. So, as much as it galls me, I find some cover behind an overturned table and try to be inconspicuous.

And that's where she finds me.

For a second I think it's just someone else taking shelter from the brawl. But then I realize that the woman crouching next to me is Mona, the pire I met in Bethel. She's dressed exactly the same as she was then and doesn't look at all surprised to see me. "Hello, Jace," she says.

I've got the Ruger out and jammed in her ribs before she

can say another word. "Hello, Maureen," I say. "That is you, right?"

"Indeed," she says, her southern accent replaced by an Irish one. "I'm sorry for the deception. But if you'd like some truth to counter it, I can provide you with answers. *Real* answers, not the shite they've been feeding you."

"Where's Stoker?"

"Not here. But I can take you to him—just you, you understand."

I know what she's proposing, and it's probably a very bad idea. But then, that's kind of my stock-in-trade—it wouldn't make much sense to change my strategy now. "Okay. How?"

"Follow me."

She leads me to an emergency exit in the back and out into an alley. She's got a car waiting—a little more mundane than I expected, but maybe that's why she chose it. It's a vintage Chevy, with huge tail fins and a chrome grille so big it's like a whale wearing braces.

We get in. I still have the gun on her, but I don't know what good that'll actually do; she's a witch, after all. She doesn't seem worried by it, but that means nothing—

"Please, point that elsewhere while we're driving," she says, starting the car. "I wouldn't want to hit a bump and have you blow a great messy hole in my guts."

I lower the gun as we drive off. "You know what this is?"

"I know a great many things, lass. About you, about your world, about what's really going on. Shoot me, and you won't learn a single one of them."

"Where are we going?"

"Patience. We'll talk as I drive, how about that?"

We pull out of the alley and down a street. Pires walk past, many of them dressed like they just walked out of a Bogart movie; I half-expect Selkie to change into Lauren Bacall and ask me if I know how to whistle.

"How much have they told you about magic?" she asks.

"Just the basics. Animism, everything has a spirit in it. And humans can do magic that pires and thropes can't."

"That we can, lass, that we can. Shape-shifter spells, for

one. But there's another kind of magic entirely, one they don't like to even admit exists, let alone talk about. HPLC. High Power Level Craft."

"I wouldn't have guessed mystics were big on acronyms."

"We're not. But the government is—and that's just what HPLC is all about. Ruling the world. Power on a global scale."

We're headed out of town. I put my seat belt on without taking my eyes off Selkie. "Go on."

"HPLC is our version of nuclear weapons. But in magic, there's always a cost; for instance, it takes a year off my life every time I change shape."

That wasn't something Eisfanger had mentioned. "So?"

"So what do you think the cost was to bring you from another world?"

That hadn't occurred to me. I'd been treated more like an agent transferred from another detail than some precious resource they had a lot invested in. Now that I thought about it, it was obvious Cassius had been reinforcing that attitude from day one.

"I don't know myself," she says, "but I'm sure the cost was dear. Using HPLC always is."

"So how does it work, this kind of magic?"

"Through gods, of course. Ancient, terrible beings, who can be bargained with if you don't mind risking death or insanity. Which, if you hadn't noticed, both pires and thropes have a certain immunity to."

"So that's what all this is about? Sacrifices?"

"In a manner of speaking. But the sacrifices you should be asking about aren't Stoker's victims—they're all the human beings who died so this abomination of a race could go on. Do you know what the Purebloods believe, Jace?"

"I've got a pretty good idea."

"Is that so? Did they tell you how many of them there are? That they're trying to get legislation passed to tag humans with Radio Frequency Identity chips? It's all for our own good, of course. To protect an endangered species."

She laughs, a high, wild sound. "How *noble* of them, don't you think?"

"This can't go on, Maureen. You can't—"

"But we *can*, lass. We can and we are. This isn't random slaughter, or some pathetic attempt at revenge. Aristotle knows what he's doing. He has a plan, and he wants you to join us. It's not too late, you see. We can still take this planet back. We can have our world again."

She slows down, turning off the highway and down a dirt road. We bump over a cattle grate, one of those metal grilles with the bars spaced so that hooves slip between them. Handy for keeping the livestock where you want them without inconveniencing the ranchers.

She stops. The lights of Missoula are no more than a mile away, but it's still very quiet and very dark. Selkie's face is lit by the green glow of the dash's indicators and nothing else.

"Is Stoker meeting us here?"

"No. Before I take you to him, I need your answer. And don't even think about lying to me; I'll know."

"I need more details."

"You'll have them. But you have to choose your side, first. For us or against us, Jace."

God *damn* it.

TWELVE

"Well," I say to myself, "*that* could have gone better."

I'm limping down the road toward Missoula. Behind me, the car burns brightly, surrounded by curious cows that have apparently never heard that A) cows are supposed to come home after dark, thereby upholding a time-honored cliché, and B) dumb animals are supposed to be scared of fire. Guess they're a little *too* dumb.

Yeah. Just like me.

I've reached the outskirts of town when a large, black vintage car—a Packard, I think—pulls up beside me with a screech. Two blocky guys in crew cuts jump out. One asks me if I'm okay, while the other cups his ear and says, "I've got her. Alive but injured, not seriously."

"You guys are agents?" I say. "Where were you twenty minutes ago?"

Crew cut number one says, "Sorry, ma'am. Mystic blackout, knocked out all our eyes and ears. We've been looking for you ever since you disappeared."

"Well, you found me. Give me a lift, huh?"

Five minutes later I'm back at the B and B, where Cassius and Charlie are waiting, along with a swarm of agents, all in period clothes. Too bad the bait didn't have the sense to stay in the trap and wait.

"What the hell," I say, stalking up to Cassius. "I stalled her as long as I could. Where *were* you guys?"

"Are you all right?" Cassius says.

"Yeah, yeah, I'm fine. Got knocked over when she blew up the car. Pretty sure I put a bullet in her shoulder before she vanished, though."

"She blacked us out," Cassius says. "Some kind of large-scale glamour, affected the whole town. It was like you fell off the planet."

"Well, I'm back, now. Didn't do too well on the landing, though."

A large and extremely strong hand grips the back of my neck.

"Uh-huh," Charlie says. "When we first met, what did I tell you was the politically correct term for a golem?"

And *now* my brain decides to shut up.

"Look, it really is me," I say. "Just give me a second to think, dammit—"

"Sure. Maybe you are, maybe you aren't. If Selkie could mystically black out a whole town, doing a glamour-based impression of another human probably wouldn't be that hard, would it?"

"Thanks a lot, beach-breath. Let's see you come up with a piece of meaningless trivia while your boulder-brained partner cuts off your oxygen supply—"

He lets go. "It's her."

I turn around and glare at him. "Mineral-American! I told you I'd get it, you pebble-headed pigeon attractor—"

"You use a lot of alliteration when you're upset, have you noticed that?"

"Jace," Cassius interrupts. "What did she say to you?"

"Nothing new. She wanted me to join her and Stoker, I was betraying the human race, yadda yadda yadda. And she had some kind of magic lie detector, so I couldn't just bull-shit her. Things went downhill from there."

Cassius stares at me. "I'm amazed you're still alive, frankly."

"Thank Han Solo," I said. "I shot first."

That gets me a blank stare, but I don't really care. A medic comes over and takes a look at my leg, which is bleeding but not broken.

"You were lucky," the medic says.

"Yeah," I say. "That's me."

We leave town immediately. No point in staying, and I think Cassius wants to get me as far away from the Purebloods as possible. I kind of feel the same way.

On the way back to Seattle, I keep to myself. I've got a lot of thinking to do before they debrief me.

I got into law enforcement for a pretty simple reason: I was angry. It seemed to me that the world had too many bad people in it, and I wanted to A) understand why they were the way they were and B) stop them. Not fix them, just stop them—ergo, a criminal profiler as opposed to a psychiatrist.

Ultimately, I suppose I wanted to make the world a better place. Or at least make the ones who made the world a worse place pay a price for it. Either way, I thought I recognized the difference between right and wrong, and I was pretty determined to kick wrong's ass.

Here, the whole world is wrong. So much so that it's completely replaced right, and now the people I should be protecting are the people I'm trying to stop.

I hadn't been completely truthful with Cassius. Maureen Selkie didn't tell me exactly what Stoker was going to do—but she had told me what the pires had done, and why they'd done it. The knowledge was sitting in my head like a big malignant tumor, demanding that I do something about it. I had to do something, that was for sure—I just didn't know what.

We go straight from the airport to the NSA building and Cassius' office. Gretchen and Charlie don't come along—Cassius wants to talk to me alone.

I don't let him get behind his desk—he's going to have to deal with me on his feet this time. I put a hand on his shoulder as soon as the door closes and say, "Before you start asking questions, I have a few of my own."

He turns around and faces me. His expression is smooth, unreadable, all his defenses up. I'm looking at several centuries' worth of poker face, and it's like staring at something carved in stone. Even Charlie would be impressed.

"Go ahead."

"Tell me about HPLC."

No hesitation at all. He's anticipated this conversation and he's prepared for it. "High Power Level Craft. The strongest and most dangerous kind of magic, restricted to government use only. It's the kind of magic we used to bring you here."

"At what cost?"

"A life. A human life, in fact—a man named Clarence Mills. Multiple rapist and child killer, sentenced to death. The Elder Gods literally don't give a damn about the condition of someone's soul—a monster will do as well as a virgin."

I nod. "Okay. How is it that vampires can conceive?"

"It's not that complicated, actually. The spell involved transfers—"

"I know about the process. Where did this spell come from?"

And for the first time he hesitates, just slightly. "I'm not a shaman; I don't know the details—"

"You're lying. Don't do it again."

He stops, considering. He wants to know exactly how much I know, and suddenly I'm sick of all the fencing back and forth. "I know exactly how it works, okay? Selkie told me. The deal you made, the price you paid. The whole rotten, stinking thing."

He sighs. I never realized just how theatrical a gesture that is in someone who doesn't need to breathe. "We had no choice, Jace. For pires to survive as a race, we had to be able to reproduce. Otherwise, the thropes would simply outnumber us. That's why the official policy of the Axis nations in World War Two was to slaughter all humans—if they could do that, it didn't matter in the long run who won on the battlefield."

"The plague at the end of the war. It wasn't *Hitler's* sorcerers that created that, was it?"

"No. They were ours." He shakes his head. "You have to understand, Jace—we needed a global metaphysical shift. Do you know how much power something like that takes? We were, essentially, rewriting a supernatural law; the only way to do that was with extradimensional assistance."

"And you killed six million people to do it!"

He stares at me, and slowly the mask drops away. No defiance, no brittle defensiveness, no denial. It's the face of a man who's done something terrible, and has been staring that fact in the face for a very long time. He hasn't come to peace with it; he's simply accepted the horror and forced himself to live with it. "Yes," he says, and his voice is as hollow as an empty grave.

Mine isn't. I feel like I'm choking on the anger of every one of those corpses. "On my world, it was concentration camps. Gas chambers, mass graves. But not here—here people just got sick and dropped dead. A disease so virulent you had to burn the bodies."

He says nothing. Looking into his eyes, I can almost feel sorry for him. Almost.

"Except they *weren't dead.*"

"No. No, they weren't."

"And all the crematoriums the government set up, they were more than that. They were altars. Altars to that—that *thing* you made a deal with."

"Its name is Shub-Niggurath. An ancient fertility god, sometimes called the Goat with a Thousand Young. It demanded sacrifices that were . . . aware."

I can't even begin to wrap my mind around this. Six million people, paralyzed but still conscious, and burned alive. It made the Nazis on my world almost seem merciful.

"So Selkie told you what we had to do. Did she tell you what they were going to do in return?" He sounds a little more like his old self now, but still grim and resigned.

"Of course not. They want me to switch sides, but they're not stupid. Unlike me."

"You're not stupid."

"No? I'm working for a genocidal government, betraying

my own species, and for what? The chance to *run away*. Not power, not riches, just a ticket back to Kansas and good old Auntie Em. Who cares about all the dead Munchkins I'm leaving behind, right? Not my world, not my problem, just give me my thirty pieces of silver and I'll get out of Dodge."

"Jace. You aren't a traitor. You're a savior."

"What?"

"What we did was monstrous, but we're no different than any other species fighting for survival. Every pire child born since then, every new pire life, has been a direct result of that. Those people have a right to live, too. I may be a monster, but they are not."

"No. Except for the ones who want the remaining humans turned into cattle."

"That's not going to happen. Regardless of what Selkie may have told you, the Pureblood movement is a small, radical fringe element—"

"I'll verify that for myself, if you don't mind. Your credibility isn't real high at the moment."

"I meant what I said about you being a savior. I don't know what Stoker has planned, but I know it involves HPLC. He stole an artifact from the McMurdo Station, one that could conceivably be used to contact an Elder God. These are beings that have the power to obliterate the planet, Jace. That might be exactly what Stoker is planning to do—unless you help us stop him."

This is what it all comes down to. Save a planet from a madman, or condemn everyone on it to Hell for the crimes they've committed. My head feels like it's going to explode and save me the trouble of making a decision.

"I'm sorry to put you in this position," he says. "None of this is fair—not what we did to them, not what we've done to you. But this isn't about fairness. It's about life. No matter what you may think of the decisions we've made, it was always in the name of life. Ultimately, Stoker is on the other side of that equation. I don't believe you are."

"You think you *know* me, don't you? You think you can just play me like a goddamn banjo."

"That's not—"

"How do you feel about me, Cassius? What *am* I to you, exactly?"

We've been having this whole conversation on our feet, and now I step closer to him, get right into his personal space. His pupils dilate and he tenses up, more uncomfortable than I might have expected.

"You're—" He stops, and looks a little angry. That's good; that's honest. He's mad at himself for not knowing the answer, mad at me for asking it.

"We had a moment, back in that bar in Montana. Was that real, or just more manipulation?"

"I wasn't trying to manipulate you."

"That's too bad."

He frowns. "I don't understand." I get the feeling it's a phrase he doesn't use very often.

"If you were, I could write you off completely. But, crazy as it sounds, I think you have some genuine feelings for me. I just don't know what that means, or where I rank in terms of importance. Probably not very high."

"There are bigger issues at stake."

My laugh has more than a little bitterness in it. "I can't believe a world half-full of vampires still uses that phrase." I step back, then head for the door.

"Where are you going?"

"Home. I want a long, hot bath, a cold, stiff drink, and some solitude. I've got some thinking to do."

What I said about what I wanted was true. What I told him about where I was going wasn't.

There's a technique profilers use called geographic profiling. Simply put, it uses data about where a killer strikes to figure out where he lives or works. In a global case like this, it wasn't very useful—but something Cassius had said had gotten me thinking about the killings in geographic terms.

A global metaphysical shift, he'd said. On a map, the

killings are widely spaced and with no clear pattern. But on a globe, they form an arc: an arc that begins at the bottom of the world and curves around to the top. The distances between each killing aren't exact, but they still form a basic pattern. Following it won't give me the exact spot of the next murder, only a general area hundreds of square miles in size—but that area fell in the middle of the Pacific Ocean, where there is only one significant landmass for several thousand miles.

Easter Island.

I don't go home. I catch a cab to the airport and use the forged passport Selkie's given me to book a flight to Chile. I do some research at an Internet terminal and some shopping for supplies at the duty-free. I have no trouble getting my gun through security, but my scythes have to go in my packed luggage.

It's a long trip, fifteen hours in the air, every minute of it spent wondering if I'm doing the right thing. I'm now officially off the reservation, in intelligence terms. I didn't agree to join them and Selkie didn't reveal their plans, but I did accept her offer of some resources in case I change my mind. She told me I'll be able to mask my trail using a spell attached to the passport itself, but I'm not so sure. Fifteen hours is forever in the intelligence community, and I'll have Gretchen's team scouring the planet for me. If I can figure out Stoker's next target, so can they; the one advantage I have is that Easter Island is a legal territory of Chile, and Chile isn't a signatory to the Transnational Supernatural Crimes and Activities Act. So even if they figure out where I've gone, they'll still have to deal with a certain amount of red tape before they can come after me—unless Cassius decides stopping Stoker is worth causing an international incident, which could very well be the case.

I pull out my flask and slug back some Urthbone, then try to get some sleep—who knows when I'll have another chance. This turns out to be a bad combination, as the emotional spectrum of every thrope on the plane seems eager to seep into my psyche as I drift off. I have disjointed, savage dreams, where every person I've ever known transforms into a werewolf and then chases me down an endless hallway lined with coffin-shaped mirrors. The one that catches me is Roger, and he keeps saying, "I told you so. I *told* you so," over and over as he claws me apart. . . .

No one's waiting to arrest me when I get off the plane in Santiago. I don't even leave the airport, booking a charter flight straight to Easter Island. I run into some difficulty there, as it turns out the place is in fact a protected human sanctuary, one of the last such places on the face of the Earth. Thropes and pires traveling there have to have a special visa, and the thrope at the counter won't take my booking without one until I go to the bathroom and scrub off every trace of the wolf pheromone. She sniffs me carefully, even transforming into a half-were state to hone her acuity, but finally accepts that I am in fact not a thrope.

Easter Island—or Rapa Nui, its Polynesian name—is extremely isolated. In the past, the Polynesians have also called it Tepito o he Henua and Mata-ki-te-rangi; the first means Navel of the World, the second Eyes That Talk to the Sky. The latter is probably a reference to the giant stone figures, the *moai*, that guard the coastline.

I don't know much about the Easter Island of my world, but here it's a place with a nasty history: slave raids, tribal wars, cannibalism. Virtually the entire population was massacred at one point, and disease from the mainland has decimated them more than once.

But not the sorcerous post-war plague inflicted by the Allies. That didn't kill a single person there.

I don't know why, but I suspect Stoker does. I also think this might be his last ritual murder; it completes the global loop he's established, and the site obviously has some kind of major arcane significance. The other locations were all remote, a few were important in a historical or political way, but this place is different. It's a specifically *human* outpost, full of human history, and I know that's no coincidence.

The pilot of the floatplane I charter is human too, a grizzled old man named Diego with more white stubble on his cheeks and chin than hair on his head. He doesn't want to know why I want to go to the island, he doesn't want to know why I want to leave immediately, he doesn't want to talk much at all. He communicates mainly in grunts, nods, and a few rapid-fire words in Spanish, and as soon as the plane's in the air it's like I cease to exist.

It's over two thousand miles from the Chilean coast to Rapa Nui; the little chunk of volcanic rock I'm heading to is one of the remotest places on Earth. Only about five hundred people live there, but it's still one of the largest human settlements left. It's a five-hour flight from Chile, and by the time we get there I've been traveling for almost twenty-four hours; I'm relieved to finally see the triangular shape of the island appear beneath us, a dormant volcano at each of the three points.

The plane taxis to a stop at a wooden pier jutting out into the bay. Several small boats and one large motor launch are tied up there already, but no one comes out to greet us. With a population of only half a thousand people, I would have figured visitors would be a bigger deal—but from what I can see, nobody's even noticed we've arrived.

Diego starts refueling immediately. I get the impression he'll be leaving about thirty seconds after he's finished.

I shoulder my pack and head off down the pier. Despite the long trip, I feel weirdly pumped up; there's something about the atmosphere, some kind of building charge in the air that makes me want to break into a run or maybe climb a tree and beat my chest. Not that there seem to *be* any trees; one of the disasters that befell the place was an ecological collapse that followed its complete deforestation. Others included bloody civil wars, famine, and the rise of strange religious cults that promised salvation from the island's problems. It was like a weird little microcosm of humanity itself, running through a condensed version of all the bad decisions the rest of the world made.

At the base of the pier is the island's only village, Hanga Roa. The buildings are all one story, quarried stone with wooden roofs. The roads aren't paved.

And it's utterly, completely empty.

No dogs, no birds, not even insect noise. It's like walking onto an elaborate movie set inside a sealed building, one that just happens to contain the Pacific Ocean. I walk down the main street and hear the roar of the seaplane starting up behind me—Diego isn't sticking around, either.

One of the giant stone heads that Easter Island is famous for stands in the middle of town. I look up into his obsidian eyes and ask, "Okay, big guy—where am I supposed to go now?"

There's a rumble of distant thunder, even though the sky is clear. I realize that it's neither thunder nor distant; the sound is coming from the stone head itself, and forming into words.

"The one you seek waits for you at Orongo."

Right. Considering who my partner is, I guess I shouldn't be surprised by a talking statue. "Okay. I guess that's where everyone else is, too?"

"No. They hide in the caves on the other side of the island. They do not wish to be destroyed by the powerful forces about to be unleashed."

And now the stone head—which actually has a body, too, just a much smaller one—does more than talk. It moves from its hands-on-knees crouching position to fully upright and takes a step toward me.

"Come. I will take you to Orongo."

"After you."

It takes a step past me, moving more like something made out of foam rubber than solid rock. The fist that catches me on the side of the head doesn't feel like rock either, but it definitely isn't foam rubber.

Out go the lights. Nap time.

I don't know how long I'm out for, but I open my eyes to the flicker of firelight. My head, oddly enough, doesn't hurt. I half-expect to find myself tied to a wooden post with a bunch of kindling at my feet, but only the upright part is accurate. I'm on my feet, hands at my sides, not bound but for some reason unable to move. It feels as if I'm wrapped in invisible cling wrap.

"I thought you'd rather be standing," Aristotle Stoker says. He's sitting cross-legged on the ground before me, dressed in khaki shorts and leather sandals, his chest bare. There's a small fire blazing beside him, and my knapsack a few feet away from that. He's got my gun in his hands and is inspecting it carefully.

"A chair would have been nice, actually."

He shrugs his massive shoulders. "Sorry. Creature comforts are in short supply out here."

I try to move, find I can turn my head and wiggle my fingers. That should be enough to escape and overpower him, sure. "I suppose I have Miss Selkie to thank for my involuntary tree impersonation?"

He cracks open the Ruger's chamber and extracts a bullet carefully before closing it again. "Yeah. She's sorry about clocking you, tried to make up for it with a healing spell. You feel all right?"

"Dandy."

"I'm glad you came. Didn't know if you'd figure it out, but I'm not that surprised you did." He holds the bullet between thumb and forefinger, studying it. The silver glints in the campfire's glow. "*Really* glad you came alone."

"And if I hadn't?"

"We wouldn't be having this conversation. You wouldn't be saying much of anything to anyone, come right down to it." He sounds more regretful than threatening.

"Where's Selkie?"

"Around. It's a shame you didn't wake up sooner, Jace; now that it's dark you can't really appreciate the view." He drops the bullet to the ground, then tosses the Ruger onto my knapsack and stands up. "Let me describe it for you. We're on the lip of the Rano Kau crater, at the southwestern tip of the island. One side slopes down into the bowl of an extinct volcano, the bottom mostly filled by a freshwater lake. The other ends in a sheer cliff three hundred feet above the ocean. You can't really see them, but there are over fifty stone houses around here, left over from when this was the focal point of the birdman cult."

"Are you going to kill me, Aristotle? Because if you aren't, I'd appreciate it if you'd turn off the quadriplegic force field."

"I'm not going to kill you, Jace. Still not quite sure what *you* have in mind for *me*, but I don't want you dead. With our numbers the way they are, killing someone like you would literally be a crime against humanity."

In some ways, that's the nicest thing anyone's ever said to me. Strangely enough, it doesn't improve my mood. "Stoker—"

"Bear with me. You should know that Selkie's sealed off the entire island. No supernatural creature—not thrope, pire, or lem—can come within a mile of the coast. If you've got some kind of last-minute rescue planned, you can forget it; for now, this is a humans-only zone."

"I came on my own."

"Why?"

"To get some answers. So far, you've given me more of the truth than the people I'm supposed to be working for."

"Truth. Truth is a nasty drug, Jace. Might seem like what you want, until you've swallowed it. By then it's too late— you can't unlearn it. Ignorance is a lot less painful."

"Spare me the philosophical bullshit. Six million people burned alive to pay off an extradimensional deity—I don't think it can get much uglier than that."

"No?" He sighs. "I wish that were true. But all those people were strangers who died a long time ago, Jace. They're history, not reality. You want to join my cause, you're going to have to get a lot closer than that."

He steps behind me, grabs me by my upper arms, and

lifts. My feet leave the ground. I wonder for a second if he's about to throw me off the cliff, but he's just turning me around. He sets me back down facing the other way, and now I can see the stone altar that was behind me. There's a man tied to it in a spread-eagled position, obviously Stoker's next victim.

It's Roger.

THIRTEEN

It can't be.

I gape. I should probably pretend I don't know him, that he means nothing to me, but the shock of seeing him is just too unexpected. At least I keep myself from blurting out his name.

"Like Maureen told you, we can do all sorts of things." Stoker still has me held by the upper arms; his hands are very warm, probably from the fire. "The next sacrifice has to be human, Jace. What do you think of who we picked?"

"That's—that's not Roger."

"No," Stoker admits. "It's not. The sacrifice has to be a native of this dimension, for one thing. And it takes a huge amount of energy to yank someone from a parallel universe; bringing them here just to kill them seems like a waste of resources to me. Of course, you may feel differently."

"He's from here. He's this universe's Roger."

"Yeah. This is a very different world from yours, Jace, but synchronicity is one of those metaphysical principles that reach across universal boundaries. Not everyone in your reality has a twin here, but Roger does. He's not an FBI agent, though—he was working as a car salesman in California. Also dealing high-grade Bane to thrope high schoolers, but that was strictly a sideline."

I swallow a dozen obvious questions. Selkie is the answer to all of them, of course. They've used sorcery to spy on my world, my history, my life—and come up with a victim they think I might actually approve of.

"He has to die, Jace. Not him, specifically, but definitely a human being. That's just how the spell works."

"That's what this has all been about? A spell?"

"Not just any spell. A High Power Level Craft spell, very similar to the one the Allies used to contact Shub-Niggurath. But the call I'm placing is to a very different entity."

I shake my head. "And how is that supposed to save the human race? You planning on taking us all to another planet? Turning back time? Or am I way off-base and you're planning some completely *different* kind of impossible weirdness?"

He lets go of me and moves toward the foot of the altar, where he's got a video camera on a tripod. I don't see the satellite broadcaster, but it has to be around someplace.

"You sound frustrated. It must seem like there are no rules here, that anything's possible." He adjusts the focus on the camera critically. "I wish I could do any of those things. But those are all just fantasies, Jace; I can't undo all the evil that's been done. All I can do . . . is make them pay."

He doesn't sound angry, or resigned, or determined. He sounds distracted, as if he's not really paying attention to what he's doing. It's a symptom I've seen in schizophrenics; it happens when their own personal reality is running a movie in their heads that's more interesting than the one playing outside.

"What are you going to do?"

He shakes his head, as if to clear it. "The Elder Gods are powerful on a scale we can barely imagine, but they have conflicts of their own. The being I'm contacting is called Ghatanothoa; it and Shub-Niggurath don't get along. The enemy of my enemy is my friend, right?"

"And what's this . . . Ghatanothoa supposed to do?"

Stoker doesn't answer, just keeps fiddling with the camera. And after a sickening moment of thought, I realize that he doesn't know.

That's it. That's the sum total of his plan. Summon an impossibly powerful alien god in the hopes that it'll pick a fight with another impossibly powerful alien god. Hope that some remnant of Earth is still habitable when the smoke clears. What Selkie told me, that humans could reclaim the Earth, was just a lie to persuade me to join them.

Cassius was right all along. Stoker is insane.

He moves behind the altar, bends down and starts doing something there, out of my direct line of sight. He keeps talking as he works.

"Ghatanothoa is already here, you see. Sealed in an underground temple on the continent of Mu—which itself is currently at the bottom of the Pacific. For now."

I have to get free. I try to shift my arms and think I feel a little more movement than I did before.

"See, I'm actually going to raise the continent itself—or part of it, anyway. Wake the old guy up. I figure that an Elder God physically present trumps one that actually resides in another dimension. And then the fun begins. . . ."

I see what he's doing. He's setting up bags of plasma on IV poles.

"Roger's death is going to be especially unpleasant, I'm afraid. I don't know if anyone's told you this, but there's no such thing as a vampire/werewolf hybrid—it's physically impossible, it can't be done. The two kinds of supernatural energy are like oil and water, they just don't mix. But nobody's ever tried this little experiment before."

He examines a small needle critically, then plugs it into a plastic tube trailing from an IV bag. "I'm going to add thrope blood and pire blood to his body at the same time. That alone should cause convulsions as the two forces battle it out. But I'm also introducing two other elements."

He pulls out a small glass vial. "Colloidal silver. I'm going to add it to the mix at just the right moment . . . as the sun rises."

"Transform him and kill him all at once. Am I supposed to be impressed?" I put as much contempt into my voice as possible. "I can't believe you'd kill one of your own. If this world's Roger is anything like mine—and it sounds like he is—nobody's going to miss him much. *But he's one of us.*"

"Sacrifices must be made." Stoker's voice sounds strange again, off-kilter and a little hesitant. "That's why they're called sacrifices. . . ."

He puts three needles in place, two for blood and a separate one for the silver, into a vein in Roger's leg, near the ankle. The sky is lightening already—I guess I was out for the whole night.

"All right," I say.

"Hmmm?" Stoker doesn't look up from what he's doing.

"I'm in. If somebody like Roger has to die for your plan to work, okay. I don't agree with it in principle, it's not a choice I would make, but I can see how you're working on the bigger picture. And that involves saving the human race, right?"

He doesn't answer.

"Come on. You're a smart guy, maybe the smartest human being left, so don't tell me you haven't thought this through. If you don't want to share your plan, you still don't trust me completely, fine. I'll take it on faith. But I don't believe for a *second* that you're doing all this out of some glorified death wish."

He finally looks up, gives me a look that makes shivers run down my spine. It's the same sad expression he wore when I told him I'd never killed anyone before. "Oh, Jace. Of course I have a plan, and I'm glad you understand why I can't tell you more. I am sorry Roger has to die, believe it or not. But someone does; that's just the hard, brutal truth. You'll understand, eventually. You're pretty smart yourself."

"You think you might show a little faith yourself? By, say, letting me out of the invisible mummy wrap?"

He chuckles but doesn't move. After a moment he says, "Look. The sun is coming up."

And it is. The far rim of the crater is now outlined in orangey pink. We're still in shadow, but that shadow will get shorter and shorter, until it reaches the top of Roger's head.

Stoker has a surgical clamp locked on each IV tube. He releases them simultaneously.

The reaction when the plasma hits Roger's bloodstream is immediate and violent. His back tries to arch, his limbs try to writhe; his bonds won't let him. I can see patches of hair sprout and then wither all over his body as the lycanthropic and vampiric energies vie for dominance. His eyes fly open; one's bloodred, the other a feral yellow. He shrieks, a horrible half scream, half howl.

"*For God's sake!*" I blurt.

"No," Stoker says calmly. "For humanity's." He depresses the plunger that pushes the colloidal silver into Roger's bloodstream, just as the first rays of the sun creep over his face.

It's horrifying, but I can't tear my eyes away. Roger's hair bursts into flames, then grows back thicker and bushier as the fire consumes it. The skin on his legs goes dead white, but his veins turn black as the silver spreads. The front lines of the war in his body retreat toward each other, thrope blood running from silver, pire blood from sunshine. Stoker's timing is a little off—they meet at around the middle of Roger's chest.

The body chars and blackens from the heart downward, but he's dead long before it reaches his feet. Thropes revert to human form when they die, so his upper torso and head look almost normal, other than the skin being very pale and a thin tracery of black veins barely visible on his neck. The fire went out when his fur vanished, but the harsh stink of it still hangs in the air. I feel like throwing up, but I refuse to lose control. I make a bad joke out of sheer psychic self-defense: "Well done. Part of him, anyway."

"You don't have to do that, Jace. I know it's horrible. I don't enjoy this, believe me."

I am *not* having a heart-to-heart with this man. "So this is part of a spell? I would have expected more mystical mumbo jumbo."

He shakes his head. "The forces I'm dealing with are beyond that. To get their attention, you need more than rattles and incantations. They respond to power, pure and simple, and death—*shaped* death, you could say—has plenty of that."

Stoker shuts off the camera. Then he reaches down and adjusts something on the other side of the altar—the satellite broadcaster, of course, transmitting the recording of the Montana killing.

"Why the transmissions?" I ask. "Is this supposed to inspire your followers or something?"

"Actually, this little theatrical presentation is for the enjoyment of the ones who replaced us, Jace." He smiles. "As opposed to your performance, which was strictly for my benefit. Maureen?"

One of the boulders changes shape, flowing into the form of a seated woman with her arms clasped around her knees. She gets to her feet and says, "She lied about committing to the cause."

Crap. Busted by the human lie detector.

The werewitch walks toward me, moving a little stiffly. "You told me you'd consider joining us, and that was the truth. One little murder and you lose your bottle? We're better off without you."

"I did consider your offer, Maureen. If you two had managed to convince me you actually had some kind of plan to *help* humanity, I might even have gone along with it. But so far, all I see is a couple of fanatics out for revenge."

Her response unsettles me. No angry diatribe about her cause, about how justified she is in doing something terrible because of all the terrible things done to her. No, she just looks disappointed, and a little resigned. "Then we'll have to do it without you. You were never that attractive an ally, Jace Valchek; our priority should have been simply to prevent you from hindering us. But a human being—a *person*—deserves the benefit of a doubt. We've given you that."

"Sorry I failed the test. Does this mean I have to take Apocalypse One-oh-one again next year?"

"It means," Stoker says, "that you'll be our guest until our plans are complete. After that—well, after that, things will be different. I don't think you'll have much interest in chasing us after that."

So they aren't going to kill me. I'm both relieved and somehow ashamed, as if mercy from a pair of killers somehow makes them better than me. Stockholm syndrome with a side of guilt.

Stoker's already packing up the video equipment. "I have to go, Jace. Selkie will escort you to a safe location until this is all over. Not long, I promise."

"Oh, good. I look forward to spending a little girl time with her."

Selkie ignores that and helps Stoker pack up. Wisps of smoke rise lazily from the corpse and through the bright early-morning sunshine. I can see the bright blue of the Pacific past the edge of the cliff and some seabirds wheeling in the air. Beautiful place for a horrific murder.

Stoker doesn't waste time on good-byes. He and Maureen are as efficient as soldiers behind enemy lines, and in a few minutes he's gone and I'm alone with my jailer. She studies me for a moment, then makes a pass through the air with one hand while muttering something beneath her breath. The invisible hand gripping me opens, and I take one staggering step forward before I catch myself.

"Just like a guy," I say, rubbing my upper arms. "Throws some meat on the grill, then expects the womenfolk to clean up."

She smiles. "I like you, Jace, truly I do. Please, don't make me kill you."

"You have no idea how many times I've heard that."

"Do anything foolish, and you'll never have to hear it again."

I stretch, trying to get the stiffness out of my arms and legs. "You promised me some answers, Maureen. About how you know about my world, about how I can get back there. Is that off the table now, since I've decided not to join your little group? Because, frankly, I think you'd rather I go back where I came from."

She's kneeling and rummaging through my pack, now. I can't imagine why—she and Stoker must have searched me thoroughly while I was out for bugging or tracking devices. I don't have any—I was telling the truth when I said I did this on my own.

She finds what she was looking for and pulls it out: the leather case holding my *eskrima* scythes. She pops the latches and opens the lid. "Ah. Nice pieces of work, these." She picks one up, hefts it. "Heavy, though. I don't think I'd be much good, whipping these about. I'm more of a fey lass than a feral one."

"You can keep them both, if you send me home," I say. I know I should be asking nicely, but the fact that I have to ask at all makes it come out angry.

"Calm down. I've had no qualms with telling you the truth so far, have I?"

"I guess not," I admit grudgingly.

"These are nice—but what I was about to say is that they're no more than toys compared to that bloody great hand cannon you brought with you." She motions to my gun, lying unattended in the dirt next to the dying remains of the camp-fire. "Have you not wondered why no one pays it any heed? Why, even when you've shown what it can do, how simple a machine it is, that not one of all the supposedly intelligent people you work with has given it a second thought?"

I have, actually. It's weighed on my mind more than once, but I've had too many other things going on to pursue it. "Yeah, I've wondered."

"It's because they *can't*. A spell to affect every pire in the world is powerful, but it's not the first spell to travel round the planet; one such was cast in the year 1100, by a most fear-some sorcerer indeed."

"*Please* don't tell me his name was Merlin. I don't have time to find a sword stuck in a rock."

She laughs, that lilting sort of laugh that Irish women do so well; I wonder if it's genetic or if they take lessons.

"He's well known, in fact, for his connection to stones

that hold swords—but not the kind you're thinking. He was the very same mystic that disseminated the spell which brings golems to life."

I thought about it. A.D. 1100 was around the time the Chinese were experimenting with what they called fire lances, the very first crude guns. And China was where the first golems came into being, too. . . .

"The spell is a magnificent thing," she says. "The gun spell, I mean, though the golem-conjuring is impressive as well. It has three layers to it, and they work, not on the laws of physics, but on the mind of any thinking creature. The first layer tells the mind that using explosions to power weapons is a concept not to be taken seriously. Not that such a thing is impossible—for it's not—and for a spell to last, it mustn't collapse under the weight of internal contradiction. This just places a blind spot in a being's thoughts, a prejudice more emotional than rational.

"The second layer is more insidious. It says that the first idea is perfectly fine and acceptable and thinking about it is a waste of time. It ensures that not only does no one think guns or bombs are viable weapons, but also that no one should ever question why."

She pauses. "And the third layer?" I prompt.

"A warning system. Should the first two be breached, should someone hammer away relentlessly enough at the spell to break it in another's mind, it would alert the caster of the spell to such an event. Presumably so they could locate the disturbance, and end it."

"You and I don't seem to have any trouble talking about it."

"You are from another universe, and thus immune. I am not. To me, a gun is an absurdity, an improbability I am unable to believe in. The only way I have to counteract this effect is a spell which continually reminds me that my opinion in this matter is unreliable." She smiles, but there's pain in her eyes. "A disturbing sensation, to be sure. Somewhat like being a little crazy, all the time."

"How do you know this?"

"From spying on your world. From seeing what guns can do, and how they've shaped your entire society. Detecting the spell itself was much more difficult . . . but I am a powerful witch. Powerful enough to open a window onto your world, powerful enough to concoct a solution, of sorts. But even I wouldn't risk trying to break the spell, even in myself; I have no wish to meet its creator."

"Wait. So this sorcerer is a pire? Because if he's still alive—"

"He is no pire, nor is he a thrope. He is . . . something else."

"Spying on my world. Does that mean—"

"We should eat before we leave."

She's avoiding my question, but I suddenly realize how hungry I am. The last food I ate was a sandwich I bought in the Santiago airport, and that must have been at least twelve hours ago. "Hope you have enough for two, because I kind of forgot to bring anything to this barbecue."

She puts aside my scythes, pulls a small pack from behind a boulder, and rummages inside. "Here."

I catch what she throws me. Cheese sandwich, wrapped in cellophane. I tear it open and devour it; I never thought that white bread would taste so wonderful. The body reacts in primitive ways to primitive situations, and apparently witnessing a murder is one hell of an appetizer. My previous nausea has abandoned me like a blind date in a restaurant with a back door, and when I'm done Selkie tosses me an apple as well.

"Thanks," I say, and pitch it back at her as hard as I can.

It's a Granny Smith apple, which is good. Decent weight, solid, nice hard crunch to it. It catches her just over the left eye, producing a loud *thwok* and a startled yelp of pain. She stumbles backward a step in surprise, trips over a rock, and goes down on her backside.

I'm already moving. If I could get to my gun in time, this fight would be over, but it's too far away. I dive for the scythes instead.

I have barely enough time to grab them before Selkie's

back on her feet. Right about now is when I should be toast, except—thanks to Eisfanger—I know a little more about magic than when I first arrived. Dispelling an enchantment like she did with my bonds can be done in a second, but it takes a little longer to prepare to cast it in the first place. Likewise for most magical attacks—you can't just point your finger and zap someone with a fireball. I have no doubt she has something nasty all charged up and ready to go, but I don't intend to give her time to use it.

She gets the first two syllables out before I break her jaw; I don't have the luxury of being nice. Her head snaps around and a tooth flies out of her mouth. Ouch.

That's not gonna do it, though. She's a threat as long as she's conscious, which means my second strike will have to knock her out. I smack her just over the ear—

And my stick hits something a lot more solid than a human skull.

She hisses at me from a mouth full of sharp teeth. Muscles bulge under skin turning scaly and gray. Her fingernails bulk into long, curving claws. All her hair falls out as her skull elongates to form a blunt-nosed, reptilian snout. I guess she doesn't need to talk to shape-shift.

She takes a swipe at me with a claw and I dance back, wanting to see just how fast she is. I'm pretty sure she can't use any other spells while in another form, but I don't intend to test that—I have to keep her busy enough that she won't have the opportunity.

She stalks toward me, a six-foot lizard-woman complete with tail. I snap the scythe blades out and meet her attack.

She's fast. The transformation has apparently fixed her jaw, too, because she snaps at me with a mouthful of yellowy fangs. Her breath smells like a dead pig left in the sun for a week—and I realize what form she's shifted into.

I saw a documentary on the Komodo dragon once. Largest lizard in the world, with the habit of swallowing entire goats—up to 80 percent as large as themselves—the way a boa constrictor gulps rats. The thing that stuck in my head was the image of one particular dragon that was having a little difficulty getting the whole goat down his throat, so he was ramming it against a boulder, over and over, forcing a little more into his gullet every time. That and the fact that so many virulent microbes live in their filthy mouths that any bite will probably kill you within days through infection.

She hasn't transformed into an actual Komodo dragon, more like a were version of it—probably drawing on the essence of the dragon through some kind of fetish. But I'm sure her claws are just as sharp and her bite just as deadly as the real thing.

I've got the reach on her, but she's got more weapons than I do—she can tear me apart with her jaws while I'm busy parrying slashes from her claws. I can't use the blades to stab, I can't risk them getting stuck in muscle or bone. With a pire or thrope, the silver would probably let me slice right through a limb, but it's not that hard a metal; her scales—reinforced by subdermal bony plates, if I'm remembering correctly—will be a lot harder to chop through.

She pivots, turning her back to me, and I step back in anticipation of a kick. Nope. Forgot about her tail—and there goes my reach advantage. It slams into my shoulder, knocking me sideways, but I somehow manage to stay on my feet. Selkie completes her spin and is facing me again.

I go on the offensive, slashing furiously with both blades, weaving a pattern of destruction in front of me. She hisses and retreats.

There's no way this will end well.

I don't want to kill her. But I don't think I can just incapacitate her anymore, and I'm pretty sure she's trying to kill me.

She tries the tail stunt again, but this time I'm ready for it. I step in as she spins and slash across her spine with both scythes. She screams as momentum carries her around, and the tail smashes into my belly an instant later. I double over, the breath knocked out of me, as my vision goes gray and I try to stagger backward out of range.

I force myself to straighten up. She glares at me from the

ground where she's fallen, and from the way she's lying I can tell her legs don't work anymore.

That doesn't stop her.

Ever seen a crocodile run? They can move amazingly fast on land with their muscular little legs. Selkie may be down to half of hers, but she scuttles straight toward me on the remaining two, moving so much like a real lizard it's unsettling. She gets within grabbing distance and snags my ankle with one hand, yanking hard and knocking me down to the ground with her.

At that point, I really have no options left.

The way a real Komodo dragon kills its prey is by pinning it down with its claws and tearing it apart with its teeth. As long as she's holding on to me, Selkie can do exactly the same thing, meaning I'll probably bleed out as soon as she rips open my femoral artery.

She latches on to my leg with both hands and drags me toward her jaws. I spread my arms as wide as they'll go, then swing them together like a pair of mandibles closing.

The blades slam home on either side of her head, about where her ears should be. I swear I feel the ends of the blades click against each other in the middle.

She slumps to the ground between my legs. I stare at her for a long second, barely able to breathe, and then I roll over and throw up.

Waste of a perfectly good cheese sandwich.

Shut up, brain.

And now I'm trapped on one of the most isolated places on the planet, with two corpses for company and no transportation. I guess I'll hike back to the village and try to scare up a radio or a telephone—but first I search through Selkie's bag.

I don't expect to find much, but I'm wrong. There's a journal and a sheaf of notes—it looks like Stoker was having her transport his research in case he was captured, probably because she could destroy it with a prepared spell very quickly.

I glance over at Selkie's body. I expected it to change back to human as soon as she died, but it's been a slow, gradual process, almost like the magic is seeping out of her. I look away again, fast.

The notes are fragmentary, but I piece together what they mean fairly quickly: The object Stoker stole from the McMurdo research facility is called the Shining Trapezohedron, an ancient artifact used to contact other-dimensional beings. Trapezohedron is simply a fancy name for a cube; Stoker's trying to sketch a "deformed trigonal trapezohedron" on a global scale, with each of the murder sites representing a corner of the cube. The center corner—the one that if you stare at a drawing of a cube can appear to either be inward or outward facing—apparently represents both the seventh and eighth points simultaneously, in some sort of non-Euclidean mathematics that I can't even begin to understand.

What I do understand is this: he's taken the trapezohedron to that central point, and he's going to use it to bring the eighth point into focus with our world.

That eighth point was known in ancient times as Mu. Stoker's going to summon a *continent*.

FOURTEEN

I can't figure out how to use the satellite broadcaster to do anything other than what it's already doing, so I just turn it off. Then I trudge down to the village to find a phone.

Turns out I don't have to bother. A seaplane buzzes overhead when I'm halfway there, and by the time I reach the dock it's landed offshore, just about at the limit Stoker mentioned. There's a motor launch at the dock with the keys still in it; I start it up and head out to greet my ride. I've got a pretty good idea who it is.

I kill the motor and let the boat drift up to the plane, bumping gently against a pontoon. The door swings open.

"Hello, Jace," Tanaka says. "Need a lift?"

I stare at him in disbelief. "Tanaka? What are you *doing* here?"

"Doing a favor for a friend. You are very much—what is the saying—a nonperson, right now."

"Persona non grata." I climb into the plane, hoping the tide will push the boat back to its owners and not out to sea. "Yeah, I thought that might happen. Figured Cassius would send *someone* after me—just didn't think it would be you."

"Have you learned anything important?"

"You could say that." I fill him in as he prepares the plane for takeoff. "We have to get to these coordinates," I say, showing him a map I found in Selkie's bag. "This is where he's going, and he's already got a head start."

"I believe we can do so on my remaining fuel—this craft is equipped for extended flights."

"Then let's get going. If we have to, we can stop to refuel in the Marquesas."

I slug down some Urthbone as we get airborne, and my rising headache vanishes. My supply is almost gone—if I don't find a way to get my prescription refilled, Stoker won't have to worry about me as a threat.

"We should radio ahead," I say once we're in the air. "Cassius can probably get someone there sooner than us."

"That is unlikely. This is a Japanese aircraft; I flew out of Tokyo Bay. The favor I am doing is not for Cassius, Jace—it is for you."

That stops me for a second. I'd heard Tanaka went back to Japan after our little talk outside my apartment—I never would have guessed he'd go rogue out of concern for me. "So we're both in the same boat—well, plane—now. Okay, but to misquote Bogey: the problems of two small people don't amount to a hill of beans in this soon-to-be-post-apocalyptic world. Stopping Stoker has to be our first priority—"

He's shaking his head. "You still do not understand. Cassius believes you have defected to Stoker's side. Any communication from you will be viewed as disinformation at best, sabotage at worst. I have heard through my own sources that . . ."

He hesitates, then finishes. ". . . that orders have been given to kill you on sight. For some reason, Cassius now believes you to be as large a threat as Stoker himself."

That stuns me. Not that Cassius could order my death—I think he's ruthless enough to do almost anything, no matter what kind of price he pays personally—but because, somehow, I never thought my actions were irreversible. Some part of me always believed that I could stay cagey forever, that I didn't truly have to commit to one side or the other.

I was wrong. And now I'm stranded in the middle, having

rejected both sides. Tanaka glances at me nervously. He's really not sure if he's made the right choice, either.

It's going to be a long flight.

There's excited chatter from the radio about four hours into our trip. Seems there's some kind of massive seismic disturbance going on in the area and everybody from Tahiti to Pago Pago is worried about a tsunami.

"He's done it," I say. "Or he's in the process of doing it, right now. Can't this crate go any faster?"

"We are still at least an hour away."

Not much I can do about that, so I shut up and sulk. At least Tanaka brought some food with him, which means I'm no longer ready to gnaw on my own leg—though I am ready to bite someone's head off.

The cloud of seabirds circling in the sky is my first clue that we've arrived. I have no idea how they knew what was happening, or where they've come from—there are many islands in this part of the Pacific, but the nearest one is still at least a hundred miles away—but there are thousands of them, wheeling in a dense knot like the forming eye of a hurricane. Directly below is a small, barren island with a single mountain in its center, the vegetation on it a garish explosion of reds and oranges like fall in Vermont. The water surrounding the island is an earthen brown for half a mile in every direction, like a muddy iris surrounding a fiery pupil.

Mu. And not a cow in sight.

We touch down. Unknown objects thump against the pontoons as we skim to a jolting, nerve-racking halt. Tanaka guides us right onto the beach, where we squelch to a halt in thick sludge.

I grab my gear and open the door. The smell that hits me is stomach-curdling, not just ripe but *alien*. The muck the pontoons are mired in has lain at the bottom of the ocean for millennia, no doubt full of organisms as bizarre as something from another planet. Now they've been heaved to the surface, where the change in pressure has made most of them pop like overfilled balloons. What I'm smelling isn't just primeval underwater ooze, it's the exploded guts of a few thousand deepsea creatures; it must have been some of the larger ones we heard hitting the pontoons.

"Be careful." It's the last thing Tanaka says before morphing into were form.

We pick our way over barnacle-encrusted boulders while the seabirds wheel and cry overhead. They're no doubt eager to consume the strange feast that lies before them, but none of them will land. The oranges and reds I saw are coral, looking more like sprawling expanses of some sort of exotic cactus in the harsh sunlight. Strands of seaweed cling to them limply, robbed of their usual swaying grace by gravity.

There's only one artificial structure on the whole island—which is, I realize, only the exposed tip of what must be an immense underwater mountain—and it's about halfway up the slope, set into the rock itself. A blocky gray building untouched by coral or seaweed, as if whatever was keeping the birds from landing was strong enough there to prevent any living thing from ever approaching. Tanaka and I glance at each other, then head for it without a word.

We circled the island once before landing, and I didn't see any sign of Stoker—no other plane, nothing. Either he's traveling by submarine or he's been and gone. Not good.

I spot a large footprint in the remains of a squashed, jellyfish-like thing. Since I doubt Bigfoot wears boots, it's a good bet it's Stoker's.

The slope is hard going. It's not that steep, but every rocky surface is slimy and the coral either breaks off in my hand or cuts me. By the time we reach the plateau the building is set on, my palms are bleeding from a dozen gashes. Tanaka has it easier, his lupine form strong and agile enough to keep his balance while ignoring any minor wounds. He helps me more than once, pulling me up or putting a steadying hand on my back. Every time he touches me, I feel a little jolt of shame—from him, not from me. Guess he still has some issues.

The building is obviously a temple. The statuary guarding the entrance is so monumentally ugly it's kind of awe-inspiring, but only if you don't study it too carefully. I've never seen sculpture that suggests bestiality, cannibalism, and necrophilia at the same time, and I can't say I ever want to again.

The entrance is a square, black maw big enough to taxi a 747 through. I pull out a flashlight and we walk in.

The interior seems empty, except for puddles of foul-smelling water on the floor and more intricate carvings on the walls. It's more like the entrance to a cave, the back wall no more than rough rock. No altar, no pews, nothing at all . . . nothing except for two squat shapes in the very middle of the floor, low enough to the ground that my beam misses them on its first sweep.

We get closer, our footsteps splashing echoes off the distant walls. The first shape is a thick stone disk, around twice the diameter of a manhole cover, a plug that's clearly been removed from the round hole right next to it. The other is a machine, maybe the size of a German shepherd, with treads on top and bottom, two articulated arms ending in clamps, and some kind of camera and spotlight array on top. Muddy boot prints leading right up to and away from the hole tell me the rest of the story.

"Whatever he came here to do, he's done it," I say. I stay a healthy distance from the hole but bend down and examine the device. "Some kind of remote-controlled robot, looks like. Whatever's down there, he must have sent Rover to check it out first."

Tanaka's reverted to human form. "Ghatanothoa," he murmurs. "If the stories are true, Stoker did not descend at all. If he had, he would not have returned."

"You know about this thing?"

He shakes his head. "My superiors told me very little. Only that the being entombed here was supremely dangerous, and to avoid being in its presence at all costs. We should leave."

"Yeah. But we're taking that robot with us—and I think we should drag that plug back into place, too."

He nods. It takes both of us to do it, but Tanaka doesn't shift to were form for the extra muscle. It's as if he doesn't trust himself to become a beast in this place, as if his animal nature might get the better of him; better to be human and struggle than risk losing control and doing something terrible.

I get a whiff of something from the hole just as we slide the plug back into place. I back up, cursing and sneezing, rubbing my nose violently as if I could physically pull the odor out. What I smelled wasn't bad in the sense of something rotten or pungent; it was just *wrong*. Deeply, horribly wrong, like fingernails down a blackboard turned into a scent, like getting an ice-cream headache from eating frozen worms.

We wrestle the robot down the mountain. By the time we get to the bottom we're both muddy, scraped, bruised, and exhausted—me more than Tanaka, of course. The screeching of the birds is like a chorus of the damned overhead. I pause to get my breath back before we load the robot onto the plane.

"Tanaka," I wheeze. "You said something back there, about your superiors. About them knowing about Ghatanothoa. If that's true, why did Cassius keep me in the dark? What possible harm could it do to let me know what I was actually dealing with? Not that I was going to go down that hole anyway, but a little warning would have been nice. . . ."

"He did not tell you because he did not know." Tanaka looks away, and I can feel shame radiating from him; the Urthbone effect seems stronger with him than other thropes, maybe because of the intensity of my first exposure. Or maybe he just feels that strongly about me. "The superiors I was referring to are not the NSA, Jace—it is the Nipponese Shinto Investigative Branch. I'm afraid I misled you. I must confiscate this probe in the name of the Japanese government."

I stare at him. Now I know why he didn't just wolf out

and cart the robot back to the beach himself—he wanted me exhausted, less likely to resist. I go for my gun, but it isn't there.

"I took it from you while we were climbing," he says. "You were distracted." I remember a steadying hand on my back, the little tremor of shame pulsing from it.

"You sonofa—" I stop, unable to think of a good substitute for "bitch" that'll mean something to a thrope.

"I am sorry, Jace. This is too important to let personal relationships dictate our actions."

The depth of his betrayal is beginning to sink in. "The whole 'shoot on sight' order from Cassius—you lied. You just didn't want me making contact."

"Again, I am sorry."

"So what's the plan? Are you going to just leave me here, while you haul your prize back to Tokyo?"

"I see no need to maroon you. You may accompany me back to Japan, once I secure your weapons in a safe place."

How considerate. I'm about to tell him I'd rather risk being stranded on an unholy island filled with nameless terrors and rotting fish than spend another minute with him when I see something on the horizon behind Tanaka. Five somethings, in fact, little specks getting bigger every second. I study them, my eyes narrowed, until I'm sure I'm seeing what I'm seeing—then I give Tanaka a big, evil smile.

"That's okay," I say. "I think my ride's here."

Five fighter jets in tight formation streak overhead like big, angry bees. Bees with the insignia of the USA clearly visible on their wings.

"If I were you," I say, "I wouldn't take off just yet. Not unless you want to come down again in a big hurry."

When I see Cassius, I'm going to give that ancient, scheming, always-one-step-ahead bastard a great big hug.

"You ancient, scheming, always-one-step-ahead bastard," I say, and punch him in the nose.

Okay, so I changed my mind. I had a lot of time to think about it while stuck in the brig aboard the SS *Nosferatu*, the aircraft carrier those fighter jets called home. Tanaka and I were ferried there by a chopper and several large thrope marines armed with what looked like multishot crossbows and aerodynamic meat cleavers. Tanaka didn't put up a fight, and neither did I.

I was in the brig for around six hours, give or take. I spent most of it wondering what you used fighter jets for when you didn't have bombs or guns—maybe they just drop golems on people they don't like.

Two marine guards finally showed up and escorted me to an office, one that looks pretty much like any office anywhere—desk, filing cabinets, computer. Cassius is leaning against the desk, his arms folded, and I'm not really sure what I'm going to do until I do it.

It's a mistake. Feels like punching a frozen side of beef. He raises his eyebrows while I swear and cradle my hand. "Feel better?"

"Oddly, no. Tell me what the hell's going on."

"We had a tracking spell on you. It deactivated as soon as you got to Easter Island and hit Selkie's defenses, but by then we knew where you were going. What we didn't know was how you left Rapa Nui—strangely enough, we had some problems with our satellite surveillance right around then."

I wondered if it was a Japanese satellite. "Too bad. I could have told you where Stoker was going and you could have stopped him before he raised that damn island."

"Not true, actually. Despite appearances, I don't really have the U.S. Navy at my beck and call. Even after we figured out where you'd gone, delicate international negotiations were required before we could act—then we had to get forces into the area. Even with advance warning, we might not have been able to stop him."

"Or maybe you didn't want to."

"That's absurd."

"He brought that mountaintop up to get something. A

weapon. And that's what the NSA has been after all along, hasn't it? Whatever he retrieved from inside the basement of that temple."

"It's not a what, it's a who."

"Yeah, yeah, I know. Elder God by the name of Ghatan-othoa. Except he's not *really* there, is he? Not in a physical sense."

"Not exactly. It's more like a certain aspect of him has manifested, while the rest still exists in another dimension. Possibly more than one; we're really not sure."

"And by 'we' you mean the bright boys and girls at Mc-Murdo Station, right? The ones that were studying the Shining Trapezohedron until Stoker stole it."

He stares at me levelly for a moment before replying. "Yes. That's what they do there."

"So I guess burning six million people alive wasn't enough, huh? After all, you've got almost a million of us still left. What's the plan—let us breed for a few more generations, get the numbers up, then trade us in for what's behind dimensional portal number two? Or maybe you're shopping around, seeing if you can get a better deal from some *other* otherworldly horror—"

"Jace. Please. Do you want an explanation or not?"

I rein myself in. "An explanation. Sure, those are *always* more entertaining than the truth."

He ignores the jab. "Ghatanothoa is not a being you can communicate with, let alone strike a bargain. He is completely, utterly alien, so different from anything we understand that no sentient being from this dimension is capable of even *perceiving* him. We think the legend of Medusa is a dim echo of this creature, of something so hideous that it transforms whatever looks at it."

I remember the smell that came from the hole in the floor, and my reaction. "You're saying this thing can turn people to stone?"

"Worse. Seeing this being changes the viewer into a living mummy. Their outer skin becomes a dry, leathery husk, their muscles and internal organs go completely dormant—

but their brain survives. They can still hear, see, think. They're trapped, aware but in a state of physical suspended animation, one that lengthens their lives indefinitely. The condition seems to be permanent—at least, we haven't been able to reverse it."

That temple was submerged for hundreds of centuries; whoever looked at the big G last did so a *very* long time ago. And if Cassius is to be believed, at least one of those people has been alive and helpless ever since.

"We have a scroll in our possession that will supposedly reverse the mummification, but we haven't been able to get it to work. And extensive testing is . . . problematic."

"Severe shortage in the mummy market?"

"Unfortunately not." He sighs. "You asked me once how I was so sure the Impaler was insane. It's because we know that exposure to certain artifacts used in HPLC *causes* mental instability, even in pires and thropes—but especially in human beings. The scroll is one such artifact, the Shining Trapezohedron another."

That explains Stoker's disconnected episodes on Rapa Nui. I wonder how sane he was before he stole the trapezohedron. "So that's why he used the robot probe. But it doesn't tell us what he took from the temple."

"I swear, Jace, there's no secret superweapon we're chasing. We're trying to stop him, that's all."

"Stop him from what? As near as I can tell, he's accomplished what he set out to do. There aren't going to be any more ritual murders—he's completed the spell. For all I know, he now has superpowers and is going to start blasting us with beams from space."

That sparks a different thought. "Wait. I didn't see a satellite broadcaster on Mu."

"It wasn't in plain sight. We found it a short distance from the temple, behind a boulder. He was probably worried about interference."

So Roger's murder was now on the Web, part of the planet's global memory. People he'd never known would see the footage and shudder, or more likely make bad jokes and scoff at the dismal special effects. Just another random meme in cyberspace. This world's Roger didn't sound much better than mine, but I doubt if he deserved that.

"So. Am I under arrest?"

He shakes his head. "I knew you wouldn't join him, Jace. But I also knew you'd run. You can't stand being under anyone's control—you had to find out the truth for yourself. That's why I was less than honest with you."

Of course. He'd been playing me all along, poking at my insecurities, setting me up as the perfect stalking horse. And it had worked, too—if Tanaka hadn't yanked me off the board unexpectedly, Cassius could have intercepted Stoker long before he raised Mu.

Or maybe I was deluding myself. Stoker managed to slip off Rapa Nui without being caught, and Cassius must have known he was there. Maybe the man really did have a submarine.

"You know, I'm really tired of all this," I say. "I don't know what's true and what's not. I really wouldn't be all that surprised if you pulled off your face and revealed you were really Stoker all along. And at this point, I don't seem to give a damn."

"I understand how upset you are—"

"No. You really don't." I cross my arms. "Gretchen told me you'd been running the NSA since 1935. That means you weren't just around while the whole genocidal birth pact was going on, *you were one of the people in charge.* Weren't you?"

He meets my eyes, looks into them for any trace of forgiveness, and doesn't find it. He looks away. "Yes."

I turn away and head for the door. "If I'm not under arrest, I'd appreciate sleeping somewhere other than the brig."

He doesn't try to stop me as I leave.

FIFTEEN

It's been a long, frustrating, gut-churning couple of days. I've killed my second person and first human being (and first lizard-woman, I guess); I've been knocked out, taken hostage, betrayed, and spent more time on airplanes than I ever have in my life. I grab the first officer I see and harangue him until he takes me to someone with the authority to assign me an empty room, then find the mess hall and demand food. I'm sure all the differences between an aircraft carrier run by supernatural beings and one run by human sailors are fascinating, but I'm kind of fed up with fascinating; in fact, I'd gladly shoot somebody for some old-fashioned boring with a side of mundane. After I eat, I stomp back to my bunk and try to sleep.

I can't. My head feels like it's stuffed with bees. I finally give up and go in search of something to distract me—aircraft carriers are like floating cities from what I've heard. At the very least I'm sure I can find a gym.

I never make it to one, though. I run into Eisfanger first.

He's walking down a corridor with an oversize mug in his hand, deep in thought. I chase him down and tap him on the shoulder. "Damon!"

He stops and looks at me, startled. "Agent Valchek. I'd, uh, I'd heard you were aboard." He looks vaguely guilty, like a friend who's been meaning to write but hasn't.

"They have you examining the robot?"

"Yeah. I was just heading back there, actually."

"Mind if I tag along?"

He hesitates, then shrugs. "Yeah, no, that's fine."

He leads me down several decks to an engineering workshop that's obviously been commandeered. The probe sits on a massive worktable, partially disassembled. Its treads have been cleaned of mud, but a trace of that alien scent still hovers in the air. It's probably a lot worse for thropes.

"We were hoping for data from its cameras—it's got quite a sophisticated video setup, actually—but the memory's been wiped."

I nod. "Whatever he grabbed from Ghatanothoa, he doesn't want us to know about it. I just wonder what could be so dangerous you'd use a god as a guard dog."

There's a cable leading from the probe to a video monitor at the end of the worktable. The screen shows nothing but a shifting, grayish blur. "Is this what you pulled from the memory?" I ask.

Eisfanger gives me a strange look, like I've just told him the punch line to a joke he doesn't get. "I told you, the memory was wiped. That's a live feed from the camera."

"So the camera's broken?"

"What are you talking about? We're right there." He glances at the probe and gives a little wave.

I frown. "I can't see a damn thing."

There's a laptop plugged into the probe as well. Eisfanger hits a few keys and peers at the screen. "Well, assuming there isn't something wrong with your vision . . . I'm just checking on the visual parameters the probe's set for. It's equipped for both infrared and ultraviolet." He taps a few more times, then says, "Huh. Assuming these are the default settings, I'd say that whoever was operating this probe was a thrope or a pire. The wavelengths of light it's utilizing wouldn't be visible to a human being."

The implications of what he's saying hit me like a punch in the gut. "Oh, God *damn* it," I whisper. "Eisfanger, how long was the last murder recording broadcasting before they found the broadcaster and shut it down?"

"I don't know—an hour at the most. Enough time for it

to be downloaded and rebroadcast from dozens of different places. Gretchen says they're having more trouble than usual finding and shutting down the sites—"

Gretchen. Oh, no.

"Get Cassius!" I shout. "Right now! *We have to shut down those sites!*"

We're too late.

Cassius doesn't waste time, but there's not a lot he can do. Stoker's prepared for this; he has hundreds of mirror sites set up all over the Web, bouncing Roger's murder from one end of the digital universe to the other. He's added some kind of mystical twist to the file, too, making it nearly impossible to track. A team of government animists tackles the problem, while this warning is posted worldwide in as many languages as possible:

> WARNING: A video file with the heading "Easter Island Sacrifice" is being disseminated on the Web. **Do not view or open this file.** While harmless to humans, occult footage visible only to hemovores or lycanthropes has been spliced in. Viewing this footage may result in paralysis or coma. If you experience any of the following symptoms, report to a medical shaman immediately:
>
> > Thickening or roughening of the skin
> > Difficulty in movement
> > Stiff or unresponsive muscles
>
> If you have a copy of the file in your possession, **destroy it**.

It doesn't work, of course. You can't put the genie back in the bottle. The Ghatanothoa effect isn't instantaneous, at least not when the victim is only exposed to it subliminally;

the paralysis creeps in slowly, over the course of a few days. But it's just as total . . . and just as permanent.

The navy—on Cassius' orders—took Tanaka into custody when they picked me up. Unlike me, he's still in the brig; I haven't seen him since they took him away.

Until now.

The guard unlocks the door and lets me in. Tanaka's sitting on his bunk, looking forlorn. He glances up when I enter, then back down again.

I sit down next to him. "It's a good thing we grabbed that probe from you. Might have even saved a few lives."

"Are you trying to make me feel guilty?"

"No. I just thought you'd appreciate an update." I fill him in. He doesn't ask any questions, just nods from time to time.

"I see," he says when I'm finished. "So that was his plan. And now, it seems, he has completed it."

"We'll see. Cassius, Eisfanger, and I are taking a chopper to the mainland and a jet to D.C. See if the government animists can find a way to reverse the effects, stop this thing. That's not why I'm here, though."

I pause. "Look, Tanaka. I don't blame you for what you did. You were acting in the best interests of your government."

He nods. "Yes. Following orders. Tell me, Jace—in my position, would you have done the same?"

It's a hard question. "I don't know, Tanaka. Maybe. I do know I sort of envy you; at least you know where your loyalties lie." I get up. "Cassius says you'll be put on a plane back to Japan as soon as the ship hits port. Whatever fallout you have to deal with will come from your people, not ours. It was the best I could do."

He looks up. "Thank you," he says simply.

I leave. I have a flight to catch.

Gretchen was one of the first to succumb.

Mystic computer viruses were nothing new. There were

ways to detect them, protect yourself from them, destroy them. But this wasn't regular animist magic; it was HPLC. The soul-shriveling gaze of a god, hidden and encoded in a stream of data—and Gretchen's job was to study it.

It gets worse. We fly into Washington and are taken straight to the Pentagon. Cassius disappears into high-level meetings while Eisfanger confers with fellow übergeeks and tries to figure out a solution. I spend most of my time drinking coffee, pacing in my hotel room, and beating myself up for how I'd handled the situation.

All of it produces approximately the same result.

Cassius emerges long enough to give me an update, and it isn't good. The number of people paralyzed worldwide is over a million and climbing. New exposures have finally slowed to a trickle, but the damage has been done. And, unbelievably, there's worse news yet.

Cassius and I are grabbing a quick lunch in the hotel restaurant before he has to go back to the Pentagon. He stares at me across the table and says, "Our own HPLC specialists have confirmed it. The Mu site is radiating occult energy, and it's increasing in direct proportion to the number of paralysis cases."

"Sacrifices. They're feeding him, just like the plague spell fed Shub-Niggurath."

"Yes. And if he gets strong enough, he'll manifest fully on this plane. An actual deity." Cassius shakes his head. "He'll be like a bear coming out of hibernation. A *hungry* bear."

I understand. Ghatanothoa will be chowing down on souls, not salmon. "Can you stop him?"

"Maybe," he says softly. "But the cure may be worse than the disease. There's only one weapon we have that's big enough to throw at him."

"No. You can't be serious."

"It's the only option we have, Jace. This is an *Elder God* we're talking about. If we don't stop him, he'll consume the life force of everything on this planet, right down to the bacteria. The one thing that might be able to fight him is an equal."

He gets up from the table, leaving his glass of blood half-finished. "The Department of Defense is already on high alert. If we can't turn this around in the next twenty-four hours, we're going to have summon Shub-Niggurath. He and Ghatanothoa are supposedly ancient enemies; we think that's why Stoker chose him."

"Two alien gods, duking it out for possession of the planet. Yeah, that's the smart choice. You think there'll be anyone left alive after *that*?"

"Maybe not," he says. "But that doesn't mean there won't be survivors."

I stare at his back as he leaves. Cold, ruthless, practical. And grieving.

SIXTEEN

I really don't know what I'm doing on another plane.

I know where I'm going; I just don't know what I'm going to do when I get there. All I know is I have to do *something*, and this is what I came up with.

I look around me. I'm on a C-17 Globemaster, a military aircraft used to haul paratroopers and cargo around. It's a big, noisy, echoing space, the ceiling a good twenty feet above me. The walls are metal, lined with cables and conduits and various pieces of equipment bolted to the superstructure. Seats are flat against the wall facing in, while pallets stacked with wooden crates and webbed with cargo netting sit on rails that run down the middle of the floor. It sort of feels like flying in an industrial Quonset.

Charlie and I are the only passengers. The pilot, co-pilot, and cargomaster are all up front in the cockpit, while we sit back here like two lonely peas in a big empty can. I'm glad he's with me—right now, it feels like he's the only one I can trust. Not that my judgment in that area is particularly reliable, but I stubbornly cling to the notion that not *everyone* is a backstabbing traitor with a secret agenda.

Charlie's dressed in a bright red parka and matching pants. Where we're going, his skin can get cold enough to turn brittle and shatter like glass. The parka has internal heating units to mimic body warmth and keep that from happening.

I was surprised how little arguing it took to get Cassius

to agree to this. I got the feeling that he's desperate enough to try anything, that the clock is running down and we're out of options. One point five million paralyzed worldwide before they finally eliminated all Ghatanothoa footage from the Web. There are still countless copies stored on hard drives of course, but DoD shamans are working on ways to locate and neutralize those.

And I'm about to touch down in Antarctica.

The plane doesn't have rows of windows like a passenger jet, so I can't really see what the place looks like from the air—lots of white, I'd imagine. I'm less concerned with sightseeing at this point than I am with coming up with some sort of plan. You know, a save-the-world-from-being-destroyed-by-other-dimensional-gods sort of plan.

Once we land, we're met by a large vehicle that looks a bit like a trailer on bulldozer treads. The driver is so bundled up I can't tell their sex, let alone if they're a pire, a thrope, or a lem. The sun's up, a hard, bright disk in a blue sky, so they could be any of the above.

The air is bitterly cold, and the snow glare is blinding; the driver lends me a pair of sunglasses. I put them on and we chug our way to the research base.

McMurdo Station is a cluster of small, rectangular buildings around a central Quonset hut. Our driver must be a pire, because all the thropes I see are in half-were form, some of them wearing parkas as well. Even zerkers would throw on some extra clothing in this climate; it can drop to forty below at night, and that's without the windchill. In the summer.

This is definitely a military base. There's no fence, no razor wire, but I see more than a few heavily armed soldiers prowling around; one of them escorts us from the vehicle to a building with a sign on the door that simply reads: Research C.

Inside, it's merely cold as opposed to frigid. Charlie shucks his parka and hangs it up beside the door, but I keep mine on. The guard doesn't come in with us.

We're in a lab, I guess, but it's like no lab I've ever seen. Cracked leather-bound manuscripts are lined up neatly on metal shelves. Clusters of shrunken heads dangle from hooks like grotesque fruit. Yellowing parchments are displayed inside hermetically sealed transparent cylinders. A glass cabinet holds jars that seem to be full of living smoke, curling and writhing in their neatly labeled little prisons. Microscopes and autoclaves stand next to three-legged iron braziers and tiny, intricately carved wooden shrines.

There's only one person in the room, a short, wide figure dressed in garish polyester orange pants and a white lab coat stained with brown and purple splotches. I can't figure out if it's a man or woman at first; despite the obvious breasts, she also has long, shaggy whiskers sprouting from either side of her jawline like sideburns making a break for freedom. Her hair is pulled into two absurd pigtails that are actually shorter than her facial hair.

"Ah," she says. Her voice is marginally more feminine, so I guess she's just an especially hirsute thrope. "You are Agent Valchek. I am Dr. Antoinette Simard."

"Nice to meet you. This is Charlie Al—"

"You should not be here." Her voice is blunt and doesn't sound at all French—more German, I think. "You are wasting your time, and more important, mine."

She's probably right. But I don't like being barked at, so I snap, "Oh? You have something more important to do? Maybe you're working on adding a few *more* alien gods to the mix, turn this into a party. Of course, they'll have to settle for the measly million or so human souls left on the planet."

Her eyes narrow. "I am aware of the seriousness of the situation. All my energies have been focused on the scroll of Undying Release, said to be the only way to reverse the Ghatanothoa paralysis. If we can accomplish that, the trapped souls will no longer feed him; he will withdraw. What I fail to see is how someone with no occult or scientific training thinks she can possibly do what some of the finest minds—"

"Yeah, well, like it or not, that's what I'm here for. So show me the damned thing already."

She glowers at me, then turns on her heel and stalks over

to a table with a tattered piece of parchment under a pane of glass. It's covered in some kind of glyphs or runes, all of which look completely alien. If I was hoping for some kind of picture or symbol that I could point to and say, *Aha! Clearly the answer is to spin around three times and spit north by northwest while speaking Albanian,* I'm out of luck.

I stare at the parchment. I reach out, put the tip of one finger against the glass, trying to will some kind of inspiration to come.

"You have come a long way for nothing," Dr. Simard says. "Now, if you don't mind—"

I'm peering at the frame that holds the glass in place. "How is this held on? Ah, little screws . . ."

"What do you think you're doing? That parchment is *ancient*—you can't just manhandle it like yesterday's newspaper!"

She tries to stop me, and is suddenly five feet farther away than she was a second ago. Charlie smiles at her before he puts her down.

I lift the glass up and set it aside. I reach out and gently put both my hands on the actual scroll itself, knowing that I may just be destroying our only hope.

For a second, nothing happens.

And then the alien scribblings on the page rearrange themselves, flow like ink spilled in water, into somewhat archaic but perfectly readable English. I let out the breath I hadn't even realized I was holding in.

"What did you hope to accomplish by that?" Dr. Simard demands. "All you are doing is damaging an invaluable artifact—"

"Please be quiet," I say. "I'm *reading*."

She shuts up.

Cassius picks up on the first ring—he must be in-between meetings. "Jace?"

"Yeah. I've read the scroll, and I know how to reverse the Ghatanothoa effect."

Stunned silence for all of two seconds. I'd gladly give half a year's pay to be able to see the look on his face right now. "How?"

"Turns out it was mystically encrypted against supernatural creatures—only a human being can read it. Now here's the bad news: the scroll has to be read, out loud, in the presence of the Big G himself. By a human. That'll push him back into his own dimension *and* reverse the effects on all his victims."

"I'll arrange for a volunteer. Get the scroll to Mu as fast as you can—"

"No. *I'm* the volunteer, Cassius. We don't have time to argue about this, and for all we know I'm the only one who'll even be *able* to read the scroll. We can't risk screwing around."

He hesitates. David Cassius, centuries-old vampire used to sacrificing his own troops like pawns on a chessboard, actually hesitates when it comes to putting me in harm's way.

"Yes, you're absolutely right. Get on the plane. I'll see what I can do in terms of support." He hangs up.

I turn to Charlie. "You know, I really should have insisted on something about frequent-flier miles in my contract. . . ."

SEVENTEEN

Twelve more hours in the air. Twelve more hours of being able to do absolutely nothing while the end of the world gets closer. Except, of course, reflect on the fact that *I'm* the one whose shoulders everything rests on.

So we play cards.

Me, Charlie, the cargomaster, and occasionally the pilot or co-pilot. The cargomaster is a cheerful thrope sergeant named Wilma, who efficiently relieves me of several paychecks. The pilot and co-pilot, both pires, are James and Enrico. Charlie does a pretty good job at cleaning them out, one at a time.

It's funny. An imminent apocalypse is rushing straight at us—well, actually, we're rushing at it—but somehow, I have a really good time. I'd happily have these guys over for a few beers and do it all over again; we eat crappy junk food and make bad jokes and get to know each other, all the while locked in a big metal barrel in the sky hurtling toward our doom. It's actually the most normal, social thing I've done since I got to this bizarre world, and I'm thankful for it. I even get in an hour or so of sleep.

Then it's time to jump out of the plane.

There's no runway, and a C-17 can't land on water. Charlie and I strap on parachutes, wave good-bye, and step out into empty air.

I won't make a big thing out of it. I've gone skydiving before, so it wasn't like I was terrified—well, okay, I *was*, but not for the reasons most people would be. I had other things on my mind.

There's somebody waiting for us on the beach.

I don't know how he got here ahead of us—maybe Cassius pulled in some favors from NASA and had a rocket strapped to his ass. However he got there, Dr. Pete waves at us as we drift down from the sky.

I touch down lightly, get out of my harness quickly. Charlie makes landfall with an audible *thump*, but his body language is as graceful as a large jungle cat leaping from a tree.

"Jace," Dr. Pete says. "How are you?"

I give the question careful thought. "Broke, stranded, possibly premenstrual. Let's go kick some ass."

I'm already striding up the beach. Dr. Pete reaches out and snags my arm. "Hold up a sec, okay? I want to take a quick look at you."

"Appreciate the concern, but this isn't the time for a checkup."

"It is, actually." He's studying my face with a professional focus. "Have you had any more hallucinatory episodes? Any unusual smells, tastes, or somatic sensations?"

"I've been taking my Urthbone like a good girl, Doc. Now, if you don't mind, I'd like to get going before my nerve *completely* evaporates—"

"This isn't about your RDT, Jace. It's about your exposure to the scroll."

I sigh. "I only read it once, okay? Then it went into this little mystically shielded poster tube"—I pat the cylinder I have strapped to my thigh—"and I haven't looked at it since."

"HPLC isn't just powerful; it's insidious," he says. "Often, the first exposure is completely harmless—except for a subtle compulsion to reexamine the original artifact, site, or being. Have you had any urges to read the scroll again in the last twelve hours?"

"Well . . . maybe, just a little. But I haven't."

He frowns. "I see. Let me test your reflexes."

He puts me through a series of tests, some mundane, some odd—at one point he asks me if I've had any unusual thoughts concerning fish. "No," I tell him, "but I did have an erotic dream featuring Mayor McCheese once."

"Who hasn't?" he replies, and I'm suddenly glad he's here.

When he's done, he tells me he's coming with me.

"What? You have to be kidding. What could you possibly *do*—"

"I can keep you alive, Jace." He stares at me levelly. "Your blood pressure is low, your heartbeat is elevated. Your reflexes are erratic. You're somewhere around a seven point nine on the Derleth reaction scale. Even if you're not aware of it, reading that scroll once has affected you on a profound physiological and psychological level. Reading it again—out loud—will put your body through tremendous stresses. People exposed to high levels of HPLC have been known to age years in a moment, to go blind and deaf, to drop dead from fear. If I'm there, I may be able to buffer or counteract some of the effects."

I pause. "You have a helluva beachside manner, you know that? Okay, it's your funeral. But do me a favor, will you?"

"What's that?"

"If it looks like I'm about to die, or go irretrievably insane—give me some of the *fun* drugs, okay?"

He smiles, but it's a little forced. "You got it."

And then the three of us begin our climb.

It's eerily quiet—no more spiral of circling birds overhead. The reason is all around us; the ground is littered with white and gray feathered shapes, dead gulls and other seabirds lying sprawled or crumpled on the rocky terrain. I have the overpowering conviction that they simply circled overhead until they fell out of the air, too exhausted or starved to stay aloft, but unable to leave, hypnotized by some subliminal call pulsing from deep underground. The stench from the dead sea life is even worse than before.

We clamber our way upslope. I have better boots this time and thick gloves for gripping mollusk-armored rocks. The black mouth of the temple gets larger and larger, gaping at us like a hungry airplane hangar, until we're standing before it. Dr. Pete, like Tanaka, has chosen to remain in his human form.

We enter. We wrestle the stone plug out of the way and put on helmets with headlamps. Charlie uncoils a thick length of rope, and runs one end back to the entrance, where he ties it around a boulder.

The other goes down the hole, and then so do we.

At the first deep lungful of air I want to turn back. That terrible sense of alienness returns, like the air I'm breathing has had the oxygen replaced by something just similar enough to fool my lungs but not my brain. I begin to hyperventilate, and Dr. Pete notices immediately and calms me down with a few words. His voice sounds strained but under control.

We descend about thirty feet before reaching the floor. It's simply an antechamber, maybe fifteen feet in diameter, crudely carved out of the rock. At the far end, a stone arch outlines the mouth of a tunnel.

Charlie takes point; Dr. Pete brings up the rear. The tunnel slopes downward at a fairly steep angle, and it goes for a long, long way, first curving left, then right, always heading down. My head is starting to pulse with some kind of internal pressure—I can't tell if it's an HPLC effect or just the increasing depth.

Maybe the strangest thing about the tunnel is that it's bone-dry—dusty, even. I can clearly see the treadmarks of the robot probe that preceded us at my feet. I don't know how deep we are, but we're definitely way below the waterline—and before Stoker dragged it topside, the whole mountain was at the bottom of the sea.

The tunnel finally levels and straightens out. I think I see something at the far end, and get everyone to switch off their headlamps for a moment.

There's a faint, bluish glow in the distance, pulsing in time to the throb in the back of my skull. It makes me feel hungry and nauseous at the same time.

We turn our headlamps back on and proceed. The farther down the tunnel we get, the stranger I feel. Everything's contradictory. My body's made of lead; my head's a balloon. I'm exhausted and charged with nervous energy. I feel like I'm heading for the most terrible place in the universe and like I'm going home.

The tunnel seems to go on forever, yet we reach the end of it almost instantly. "Whoa," I say. My own voice sounds weird, like I'm speaking a language I don't understand. "This . . . this is *intense*." The tunnel bends abruptly, the blue glow pulsating just around the corner.

"How . . . how are you doing, Jace?" Dr. Pete manages.

"Holding on. Just barely. Charlie?"

Charlie's tone is almost conversational. "Kind of getting the urge to kill both of you. Think I'm gonna head back."

"Sure, okay, no problem."

"Yeah, yeah, good idea. You do that."

Charlie turns and trudges away. It's just Dr. Pete and me now.

I unseal the tube with hands that don't feel like my own. Ever notice how hands look like spiders? Tiny legs made of bone and skin, scuttling around, crawling over things with their little fingernails going *tic tic tic*—

"Jace. The manuscript."

I'm standing there, clutching the tube with both hands. I force myself to upend the tube and slide the rolled-up parchment out. The pulsing in my head instantly subsides to a bearable level, clearing some of the murk from my thoughts. "I'm okay. Thanks."

"All right. This . . . this is how we're going to do this. We're going to back in there. We have to be close. You're going to read the scroll with your back to the thing, and I'm going to be between you and it. That way, I can see how you're doing and help you if you need it." His voice is ragged but sure. Dr. Pete is a lot tougher than I thought.

"Yeah. Let's do it."

We face back down the corridor, then take our first, un-sure step backward. I've never felt so horribly vulnerable in my life. All I can think of is how incredibly, idiotically ex-posed both of us are. If Ghatanothoa has any kind of nasty, otherworldly guard dogs—hell, if he has a poodle with a bad attitude—we're wide open to attack.

The glow gets brighter as we round the corner. No, that's not right—it gets stronger but *darker*. More illumination but less light, like seeing by X-rays. That's the best description I can give.

We continue our careful, reversed walk. Just around the bend the tunnel empties out into a chamber filled with the pulsing blue nonlight, a chamber I can only see one wall of. I crane my neck upward as I step backward, like a tourist gawking at a skyscraper, and realize just how big this space is; the wall above the arch we just backed through goes up and up and up, raw craggy blue-lit rock like the surface of an-other planet. I have the terrible compulsion to turn around.

Dr. Pete stops. I back into him, almost turn around to apol-ogize, and manage to stop myself in time. "I think we're here," I whisper.

"Yeah. . . ." His own voice sounds far away and dreamy. I wonder if I'm going to wind up looking after him instead of him after me.

I'm not doing that well myself. The room is utterly silent, no sound of water dripping or rock creaking or anything but our own breathing. My own sounds funny, erratic, like my lungs can't quite remember the rhythm.

And, of course, there's a god right behind me.

The sense of its presence is overwhelming, and yet I'm sure it doesn't know we're here. It would be like an elephant noticing a flea . . .

A flea that's about to bite.

I look down at the scroll in my hands. The words on it are now illuminated in little flickering blue flames, which doesn't surprise me at all. I begin to read, my voice hoarse and faltering at first, but growing stronger as I continue. The words themselves don't make any sense—the first few sentences are basic instructions on where and how the scroll should be used, but beyond that it's all *f'tagh* this and *klaatu* that. I just hope I'm pronouncing them right.

About halfway through I feel my heart stop.

Odd kind of feeling. Not painful at all. I keep reading for another full line before I collapse.

Dr. Pete catches me before I hit the ground. He checks the pulse on the side of my neck, then fumbles in his pack for a syringe. I know what's coming; I've seen *Pulp Fiction* five times. Never thought I'd OD on alien god brainwaves, though. . . .

Dr. Pete, thankfully, is a trained doctor instead of a freaked-out junkie hit man. He slips the needle in expertly between my ribs, as opposed to stabbing me in the sternum. I feel the epinephrine kick-start my heart, and my head clears a little as fresh blood surges through it.

I don't bother getting to my feet. I just grab the scroll from where I dropped it, prop myself up on my elbow, and start reading from the last word I spoke.

I get all the way to the end before anything really bad happens.

I utter the last word on the scroll. I stop, feeling like I've just run a marathon, my nerves jittering with the artificial adrenaline Dr. Pete's pumped into my system.

"Jace," he says, "you have to keep going—"

"I'm done. There isn't any more—"

And then there's the noise.

It's the sound of a frustrated deity that's just been told the all-you-can-eat buffet is now closed. It's eerie and terrifying and very, very pissed off. The blue light isn't pulsing anymore; it's just getting steadily brighter.

"Time to go," Dr. Pete says.

Here's the part where we dash out of the tunnel as it falls down around us, narrowly escaping death, emerging into the sunlight as the entire temple collapses for no good reason. That doesn't happen. What does happen is that Dr. Pete transforms into half-were form, slings me over his shoulder, and runs like hell. We make it up to the antechamber in about thirty seconds, and he more or less throws me out of the hole, then leaps after me.

Nothing blows up. Nothing collapses. Nothing happens at all except the endless, ululating howl that follows us, the howl of something ancient and hungry denied. If I ever survive to be an old lady with Alzheimer's, I'm sure that long after every single memory I have has decayed away to nothing, the recollection of that awful, inhuman howl will still echo in my ears.

Charlie's waiting for us outside the temple. "Someone doesn't sound happy," he says. "That's good, right?"

I nod wearily. "We're good."

And then the island begins to sink.

It's hardly noticeable at first. The beach simply and slowly gets smaller. Without a word, the three of us begin to climb.

The howl chases us. It grows fainter, but we can still hear it.

We manage to gain a few hundred feet in altitude before the terrain becomes too steep and slippery to go any farther. We huddle on a rocky shelf and wait.

When the water fills the mouth of the temple, the sound finally stops—on an audible level, anyway. I swear I can still feel it reverberating through the rock itself and into my bones.

The water creeps higher. When it reaches our plateau, Pete and I dog-paddle and let it carry us up, past the steep slope above us, until we can scramble ashore once more. Charlie stays where he is until we haul him up with a rope. Golems don't swim—but fortunately, they don't breathe, either.

This time, we reach the peak.

There's no place left to go.

"Always wanted to ride a lost continent to the bottom of the Pacific Ocean," Charlie says. "Must be my lucky day."

"Too bad we didn't bring an inflatable boat," I say. "We could use you as an anchor."

Dr. Pete's fiddling with the walkie-talkie they gave us. "Hang on," he says. "I've got something—yes, hello? . . . This is, uh, the scroll-reading people?"

The speaker crackles, then replies, "The Valcheck team?"

"Yes! We're—we're on top of a mountain, and it's sinking. I mean, the island we're on, it's not going to be an island much longer—"

"We understand. We're coming to pick you up, just hang on."

I scan the sky, but don't see a thing. "Looks like we may be treading water while waiting for them, Doc. Charlie, how do you feel about scuba diving?"

"The same way an anvil does."

"Don't worry," I say. "We'll tie the rope around you again, and feed it out as long as we can."

"And when you get to the end of your rope?"

"That's where I *live*, Charlie."

"I noticed. I'm not going to drag you under, Jace."

"You won't. I'm going to haul *you* up."

He shakes his head. "That's against the laws of physics."

"So is this whole world. *Screw* the laws of physics."

Dr. Pete interrupts us. "I don't think any of us are going to be visiting Davy Jones's locker. Look." He points—not to the sky, but the ocean.

And there, goggling at us like a nosy sea serpent, is a periscope.

―――――――◆――◆―――――――――

Mu sinks. We're not on it.

The submarine is U.S. Navy. It picks us up and takes us home. We get the good news in transit; the scroll did what it was supposed to. The paralyzed are all, slowly, beginning to move and speak and de-mummify.

But it isn't over.

Both Dr. Pete and I are given a thorough checkup, first by the sub's medics and then by stateside physicians. They seem a little worried by what they find, though they won't tell me squat. It can't be too bad, though, because they let us have visitors after the first day and only hold us for three.

Dr. Pete is descended upon by his family, who fuss over him, bring him huge amounts of food, and engage in a running battle with the nurses as to how many candles they can light.

I get less attention, but one surprise visitor is Alexandra. She's dressed in jeans and a leather jacket but isn't wearing the corpsing fetish; she's actually quite pretty when her face isn't rotting. "Hey," she says.

"Hey yourself."

"I tried to send you some stuff, but it kept bouncing. Government firewall."

"Oh. Sorry about that."

"No prob. Thought I'd bring 'em by personally." She fishes a flash drive out of her pocket and hands it to me. "Three albums' worth—it's all I've got. But I put some other stuff on there I thought you might like."

I smile. "Thanks. I appreciate it."

"Yeah." She pauses. "You know, sometimes I kinda feel like I'm from another world. And it sucks."

"Yeah. Not all the time, though. Helps to have friends."

She smiles back. "I guess. You think maybe we could, like, go for coffee or something when you get out of here? And talk about where you're from? Unless that's, you know, top secret or something."

"I think I can get you clearance." I nod. "Sure. That'd be great."

"Okay, then. Bye." And she practically runs away in that awkward, too self-aware way that teenagers have.

Cassius doesn't come to visit me, but Gretchen does. She's moving a little stiffly but otherwise seems fine. I ask her what the experience was like; she says it felt like being trapped in a meeting that never ended. Her tone is light, but I see something in her eyes that disturbs me: the faintest echo of the scream that chased Dr. Pete and me out of that tunnel, that insane, eternal howl . . .

Or maybe I'm imagining things.

As soon as they discharge me, Cassius asks to see me in his office.

I go in with my head held high. If he's looking for an apology, he's going to need a flashlight, a proctologist, and yoga lessons. I'm not proud of everything I did, but I don't see any other path than the one I chose.

He's sitting on the sofa when I come in, the same one I sat on when I was brought over the dimensional divide all of a month ago.

"Yes, sir?" I ask, stopping in front of him.

"Don't *sir* me, Jace," he says. "Not yet, anyway. Sit down."

I sit down next to him.

"Thank you," he says.

"Not a problem. I mastered sitting a long time ago."

"Not for that. I mean, thank you for risking your life to save a world that isn't your own. One that hasn't treated you very well, either."

"I wouldn't say that. The hospital food's been top-notch."

He winces. "We received a message for you, from Aristotle Stoker. The tech boys have cleared it; there's nothing encoded. You should take a look."

I nod. He pulls a tiny remote from his pocket, hits a button. The monitor on his desk, angled to face us, now shows Stoker's face.

"Hello, Jace." He looks grim. "I don't know how I feel about your survival. Part of me wants you to die for killing Selkie. Another part thinks you're still capable of replacing her.

"I have some bad news for you. It is possible to reverse the Ghatanothoa effect, but it's only been done a handful of times and in every case the revived subject was found to be hopelessly insane. It was assumed this was the result of long years of paralysis, the mind slowly buckling under the sheer horror of total helplessness. As it turns out, this assumption was false.

"Your employers may not have told you this, but exposure to HPLC can cause mental deterioration—and not just in human beings. My research indicates Ghatanothoan paralysis results in some degree of latent mental instability in virtually all exposed subjects, regardless of how long they were immobilized. About ten percent show signs of advanced psychosis. And every single subject showed biochemical changes at the *genetic* level."

He pauses. There's an elevator in my stomach, and it's going down.

"Maybe I didn't accomplish what I set out to do—and maybe I did. Maybe I just wanted the immortals and the indestructible to know what it's like to have a *human* weakness." He shakes his massive head. "They're not so perfect now, are they? Now they can suffer just like we can. Schizophrenia, irrational phobias, multiple personality disorder . . . I've opened up a big can of mental worms, and they're burrowing right into all those supernatural brains.

"Ten percent of one and a half million pires and thropes. That's an awful lot of dangerous crazy people, Jace. I think your schedule is going to be a little full for a while."

The message comes to an end. He doesn't say good-bye.

"I'm sorry," Cassius says. "But as long as he's free, you still haven't fulfilled the terms of your contract. Yes, you saved the world—but we can't send you home just yet. We still need you."

Yeah. He's got a hundred and fifty thousand reasons to keep me around, now. I sigh. "Okay, but I want my own office. I'm tired of being summoned in here like some kind of low-grade demon."

"You may have some demon in you, but it's definitely not low-grade."

"Plus some plants. And someone to do plant things to them, so they don't die."

"I'll see what I can arrange."

"And a title."

His eyebrows go up. "Duchess, maybe?"

"You know what I mean. Something that generates a little respect."

"As opposed to a demeaning nickname?" His voice tells me he knows something I don't.

He's wrong. "Yeah, I know what the other agents call me. The Bloodhound." I shrug. "Considering all that's happened to me in the past month, it doesn't seem to matter much. Hell, I'm just glad they're not calling me lunch."

"If you don't care what people call you, why ask for a title?"

I head for the door. "Because it looks like I'm going to be here awhile—and it'll look good on my résumé."

I stop with my hand on the doorknob. "Oh, and I'm *still* not going to follow a single damn rule I don't agree with."

He sighs. I smile, and leave.

But I'll be back.

Read on for an excerpt from the next book by DD Barant

DEATH BLOWS

Coming soon from St. Martin's Paperbacks

"Okay," I say. "This is new."

The crime scene is a penthouse in a high-rise overlooking the bay. From the heavily smoked windows I deduce the occupant is a pire, from the furnishings an extremely wealthy one.

The body's draped over a treadmill in the middle of the room. The vic's dressed in a head-to-toe red outfit with yellow boots, the kind of thing pires wear during the day to shield themselves from sunlight. No goggles, though, and the face mask doesn't cover the mouth. So far, it doesn't rank that high on my weirdness scale.

All that's left of the body is a skeleton, not unusual for a pire. But this guy's skeleton is *green*—and giving off what seem to be little arcs of electricity, sparks flickering in the empty eye sockets of his skull, glinting off the polished emerald of his teeth. Just to make sure we get the point, there's a lightning bolt emblazoned on the chest of the suit and little lightning designs around the wrists and waist.

And then I recognize him. Of course.

Cassius is standing next to the body, dressed in his usual black business suit. He nods at Charlie and me as we come in, but doesn't say anything. Damon Eisfanger is examining the body without touching it, but looks up and waves when he sees me. "Hey, Jace." Damon's a thrope with both Arctic wolf and pit bull in his lineage, so he's as pale as an albino and square as a linebacker, with ice-blue eyes and short, bristly white hair. He's about as geeky as forensics shamans usually are, which is to say, a lot. "Pretty bizarre, huh? Know why the skeleton's green? I think all the calcium in it has been changed into copper. Good conductor, though gold would have been better."

"Maybe the killer was on a budget. And all the sparks?"

"Lightning. I mean, I've only done some preliminary readings, but this is not house current we're talking about here. This is actual lightning, magically directed. It wants to leave, but there's nowhere for it to go; the treadmill isn't grounded."

"Gretchen was the one who found the body," Cassius says. "She's in the bedroom, composing herself."

"I'll talk to her in a minute," I say. "Okay, Eisfanger— even I recognize that costume, and you're about seventeen levels above me when it comes to geekdom, so go ahead and spit out whatever clever pun you've been holding in for the last twenty minutes before you explode."

Eisfanger looks a little taken aback. "I'm afraid I don't, uh, have anything to say. I mean, I guess I could say something about this being shocking, but that seems really obvious—"

"That's all you got? You've got a dead superhero named 'The Flash' on your hands and you can't come up with a single punchline?"

"A what?" Now he just looks confused.

"The Flash. Guy in a red leotard, runs really really fast. I think he had a TV show, too. Come *on* . . . 'He's been Flash-fried.' 'I'll be back in a Flash, but he won't.' 'My camera doesn't work 'cause the Flash is dead.' You're really disappointing me here."

"A superhero? What is that, a really big sandwich?"

I frown at him. "*Really* disappointing."

The expression on Eisfanger's face has gone from confused to bewildered, and he turns to Cassius to see if he gets the joke. Cassius frowns too, but at me.

"Jace. Neither Damon nor I have any idea what you're talking about."

I stare at them and blink. Something punches me, very softly, in the pit of my stomach. When I first got here—this world, I mean, not this room—that punch would have been a lot more solid. It landed every time I'd been lulled into a sense of normalcy about this world and something abruptly leapt out at me and screamed that I was very, very far from home. You know, like reading the ingredients on a bottle of soda pop and learning it was full of gerbil's blood, or seeing a commercial for a waterbed that lets you literally sleep underwater—handy for those who neither breathe nor prune.

"Comic books," I say. "You don't have—wait. I *know* this world has comic books; Dr. Pete showed me his collection once."

Eisfanger's eyes go wide. Cassius doesn't look surprised, but then, he almost never does.

"*Comic* books?" Eisfanger repeats. He says it with more or less the same intonation you'd use for the phrase, "Eat my own *liver*?"

Cassius sighs. "I was afraid of that. The books Dr. Adams showed you were all pre–nineteen fifty-six, correct?"

"Uh—yeah. Why?"

"Because they've been illegal since then. Did this 'Flash' exist prior to nineteen fifty-six?"

"I'm not sure. I don't think so."

"Then we're dealing with cross-universe contamination." Cassius studies me with cool, calculating eyes. "The killer may be from your world, Jace."

He lets that hang in the air a moment, knowing the impact it'll make on me. "Go talk to Gretchen," he says. "She could use a friend right now. Second bedroom on the left."

I'm thinking furiously as I leave. Does a killer from my world mean a possible way back for me? Why the hell would comic books be illegal? And what was Gretchen doing here in the first place?"

I knock on the door to the bedroom tentatively. "Gretch? It's Jace."

"Come in."

I open the door. Gretchen sits on the edge of a massive

canopy bed, her knees together, a box of tissues in her lap. Gretchen's a pire, apparent age in her mid-thirties, attractive in an intense kind of way. She always wears her blonde hair in a tight little bun, her make-up is immaculate, she speaks in an elegant British accent, and her wit is sharp enough to give a suit of armor paper cuts. I've compared her, more than once, to a predatory Mary Poppins.

Right now, her hair is a straggly mess. Tears have streaked her mascara. Despite that, her voice is strong, her smile firm. "Hello, Jace. I do hope you're going to lend us a hand."

I sit down next to her. "Yeah, of course. What *happened*, Gretch?"

"I—was paying a call on Mr. Aquitaine. He—"

"Aquitaine? Is that—"

"Yes. Saladin Aquitaine. He and I were to go out for dinner. There was no answer when I rang up, so I let myself in. I have a key. I discovered him just as you saw. I called David immediately."

I hadn't even known Gretchen was seeing someone. "So you and he were . . . involved."

"We had an intimate relationship, yes. We've known each other for years, but only recently have we decided to . . . explore further options."

"Friends with benefits?"

"Not exactly." She turns to look at me, and a little of the grief she's feeling forces its way to the surface. It doesn't get far; she shoves it back under with a brittle smile. "I do apologize for not mentioning him, Jace. I've been doing intelligence work for so long I compartmentalize everything. Yes, Saladin and I were lovers, but that's never been anything but casual for decades. About three months ago, I came to a decision, and approached him with an offer. He agreed."

Her face stays calm and composed, but a single tear tracks its way through her ruined eyeliner and down her cheek. "I'm pregnant, Jace."

Pregnant. That's a heavy word at any time, but for pires even more so. The old-school neck-biting method was made illegal long ago, which is good since the current human population is less than one percent of the global total. The way pires procreate on this world is through magic; basically, both parents donate six months of their life for every year their child ages. At some point the spell that made the whole thing possible is cancelled, and all three go back to being immortal—only the parents are now a decade or so older, while the kid is twenty-one.

I have no idea what happens when one of the parents dies before the baby is born.

I put my arm around her. "Gretchen, I'm—I don't know what to say. I'm stuck somewhere between 'I'm sorry' and 'Congratulations.' "

"Stuck. I suppose that's what I am, as well."

"What happens now?"

"I assume the full time-debt for the child. A normal pire pregnancy is eighteen months, the fetus's development slowed to match the mother's aging process; Saladin and I didn't want to wait that long. We used magic to accelerate the process, so I would give birth in nine months instead. But now that he's dead . . . I don't know, Jace. I just don't know." Her voice remains steady, but a second tear has joined the first. If I were to touch it, it would be as cold as a melted snowflake.

"What did he do, Gretch? For a living, I mean."

She plucks a tissue from the box and dabs her face. "He was a geomancer. His specialty was talking to dormant volcanoes, locating kimberlite pipes for diamond speculators. Geologic features operate on a very different time frame, so he would have conversations that would last for years. Sometimes they were fruitful, sometimes not."

I glance around the room. "Looks to me like he hit at least one jackpot."

"Yes, he was quite wealthy. He was a very patient man; I thought he would make a wonderful father."

"Who would do this to him, Gretch? Did he have any enemies?"

"You should speak to Cassius about that." Her tone is abruptly cool, and I think I've offended her before I realize she's simply being professional. Whatever Saladin Aquitaine was into, Cassius knows more about it than Gretchen does—which means this case is getting more complicated by the minute.

"I'll do that. Hang in there, Gretch." I give her shoulder a squeeze and then stand up.

I stride back to the other room, where Eisfanger's taking pictures of the vic. Charlie's in exactly the same position he was when I left, hands clasped in front of him, feet slightly spread. He's very good at being immobile. "Okay, what are we looking at here?" I ask Cassius directly. "There's no local cops, so I assume this is off the books."

"I'll call them as soon as Damon's finished. This is going to be a closed investigation, Jace, and I want you to handle it."

"We'll see. First of all, are we sure this is Saladin Aquitaine?"

Eisfanger lowers his camera. "No fingerprints or DNA, but the remains still have a psychic residue. I'll check it against our animist files."

"Okay. Second, who was Saladin Aquitaine and why would someone kill him?"

"He was a successful geologic surveyor, a geomancer. He made sizeable donations to a number of political parties and organizations. He was fairly active socially. I don't know why anyone would want him dead—which is why I called you."

"You think this is the work of someone mentally unbalanced?"

"Don't you? I admit I don't have your level of expertise, but this hardly looks like the work of either a professional assassin or a burglary gone wrong."

I shrug. "No? I'll tell you what I see. Two shamans, some professional jealousy, and a magical pissing match that got out of hand. The other guy tossed a spell intended to be used on landscape instead of flesh and blood, and this is the result—Mr. Coppertop. Don't tell Gretchen I said that."

As a theory it's full of holes, but I want Cassius to point

them out—one of the best ways to get information is to make your source prove how smart he is.

"Uh, there's one big problem with that," Eisfanger interjects. He's waving a device that looks a bit like a cell phone with dual antennae in slow circles over the corpse's head. "This guy wasn't killed by the lightning—or by having his bones transformed. Those were both done post-mortem."

I frown at him. "Wait. So the whole scene was staged? The treadmill, the costume, the electric skeleton?"

"I don't know about the treadmill—"

"Pires don't exercise, genius. So what *did* kill him?"

"Sharp silver object through the heart. See?" Eisfanger points to a small notch on the underside of one rib. "Chipped a piece off going in—wooden stake wouldn't have done that. I'll take a closer look once I've drained the voltage, but I'm betting I find traces of silver."

Cassius shakes his head. "Someone went to a great deal of trouble to do this. Someone either from, or with access to, knowledge from your world. Anyone who goes to this much trouble to send a message—and I think we can both agree that this is supposed to be a message—tends to want that message understood."

I sigh. "Unless they're speaking their own private language that only the voices in their head understand."

"Oh, I don't know about that," Cassius says. "I think there's at least one person in this room who might be able to translate."

"It's not me, is it?" asks Eisfanger. "I mean, I'm still working on that sandwich thing . . ."